TOPAZ *and* TREACHERY

TOPAZ *and* TREACHERY

a novel by

Lynn Gardner

Covenant Communications, Inc.

Cover images © Photodisc/Getty Images.
Cover design copyrighted 2005 by Covenant Communications, Inc.

Published by Covenant Communications, Inc.
American Fork, Utah

Printed in Canada
First Printing: October 2005

11 10 09 08 07 06 05   10 9 8 7 6 5 4 3 2 1

ISBN 1-59811-017-9

Chapter 1

Everything should have been peaceful in my little world, but for some reason, I awoke with an unsettled feeling. For a welcome change, I wasn't worried about Bart. My husband happened to be at home instead of chasing terrorists across the world. My parents, Jack and Margaret Alexander, had just wrapped up an anti-terrorist conference in Munich and would return soon, so it wasn't worry about them that made me edgy and jumpy.

What could it be? My Greek grandmother would have said I was being prescient. I hoped not, but something was definitely in the air. I stood on the balcony of our cottage under the pines overlooking the blue Pacific Ocean, watching a little black spider spin a silver web that glittered in the sun. A perfectly peaceful morning, it seemed.

Suddenly the noisy roar of the lawnmower shattered the peace and quiet. Bart's patience and mechanical ability had prevailed, and the temperamental equipment finally sprang to life. At the same time, my cell phone rang, and as I hurried to find it, my unease turned to apprehension.

"Alli, is everything okay at the estate?" Mom's words came in a breathless rush.

Chills shivered down my spine. "Why?"

"I thought someone might have tried to break into the estate to steal my stone. Is the new security system up and running yet?"

"Everything's fine. The contractors finished the high-security fence around the property, and Jim's just completing the electronic surveillance system for it. What's going on, Mom? What stone are you worried about?"

"When the conference concluded, some of the old Freedom Fighters from World War II approached us—some who'd worked in the underground with your grandparents. We'd heard rustlings and rumors of this for months but could never pin it down." She took a deep breath. "Alli, it's not rumor anymore. Since I have one of the stones they were speaking of, I feared someone had already tried to get it."

"Rustlings and rumors of what? And what stone? Mom, you're not making sense." It wasn't like my mother to be so harried that she couldn't talk straight. What bad news had sent her spinning into such a state?

"Remember the big, smoky topaz ring my mother gave me when I got married? The one you've always loved that looks like gold leaves are holding the stone in place? Apparently it's one of the stones from a necklace owned by Elizabeth, Empress of Austria-Hungary. Will you run up to the house and check? I'm sure it's still there—I hope it's still there—I haven't worn it for ages. I have no idea what those miserable men might have taken when they broke into the house last time."

"I'm impressed. Where did you get a stone from Empress Elizabeth?" I corrected myself. "Rather, where did Grandmother get a jewel from Empress Elizabeth? While you're telling me, I'll check your jewel box." As we spoke, I left our little cottage and crossed the great expanse of green lawn to the mansion on the hill where my parents lived.

"It's a long story," Mom said, still sounding like she was racing somewhere. "Can I tell you when I get home?"

"That depends on when you're planning to arrive. If it's more than fifteen minutes, tell me now."

"Actually, Allison, I can't even wait until you check the jewel box. Your father needs me. I'll call you back later."

"Mom, you can't hang up without telling me what this is all about. I'm at the house now, opening the door."

"Can't wait, Alli. Will call as soon as I can. Please keep an eye on things, because we're going to see an escalation of events very soon. Love you." And she was gone.

That's not fair, I thought. *Did she do that on purpose just to keep me in suspense, or did she really have to go?*

Hurrying across the white marble foyer, I climbed the circular staircase leading to the bedroom wing. Mom's jewel box lay open, its contents spilling onto her vanity, and I thought at first glance that there *had* been a burglary. But everything seemed to be there, at least the pieces I remembered, and it appeared she'd just been in a hurry when she packed for her trip to Germany. Unless Dad had been helping her. That would explain the disarray.

What crisis had my normally calm and collected mother so addlepated that she couldn't think straight? This was extremely unusual behavior for her.

The smoky topaz ring didn't materialize as I did a quick inspection, so I searched through the necklaces, brooches, and earrings piece by piece. There seemed to be no organization to the collection, though some of them were costly, a couple even rare pieces. She casually mixed the precious jewels with the costume jewelry and wore them in the same casual way.

Mom wasn't impressed by wealth and its ornamentation, though she'd accumulated a fortune years ago as a famous actress before she retired from stage and screen to become an anthropologist.

Not finding the topaz in the jewel box, I searched Mom's drawers. Maybe someone *had* been here before me. Was it possible we'd had an undetected robbery on the estate?

Finally, I discovered it in a small, old-fashioned ring box tucked in the very back of her lingerie drawer. I carried it to the window to get the full sun on the gem. A beautiful, large oval stone, nearly an inch long and over half an inch wide, it had a smoothly polished top with facets around the crown. The rich, smoky-brown gem perched in a unique gold setting allowing the full height of the jewel to be seen and appreciated.

A diamond, ruby, emerald, or even sapphire of this size would be a very valuable stone, but I didn't think smoky topaz appeared high on any jeweler's list of expensive gems. Why would anyone want to steal this?

Then I remembered the perfectly matched diamonds in Marie Antoinette's necklace, which had been separated and sold, and once they began collecting and reassembling the gems for that necklace, the price for individual stones skyrocketed. Did that same case apply here—the reassembly potential made them more valuable? Rather than leave the ring vulnerable in Mom's dresser, I put it in the safe.

Before returning to my cottage, I headed for the Control Center to get an update on Anastasia's agents and discover any problems that might have arisen this beautiful morning. I had a new assignment in our organization, taking care of agents' needs in the field, furnishing whatever information they required at the time, and tracking their progress on anti-terrorist activities.

Anastasia, Interpol's anti-terrorist division, was an elite group of agents recruited and trained by my father to fight terrorism across the world. I'd been one of those agents until I became pregnant and my husband and my father relegated me to the Control Center and out of the field. Fortunately, things were fairly quiet at the moment. I hadn't missed the excitement and adrenaline rush of taking out the bad guys and making the world a safer place for my baby, who would make her appearance in just four short months.

I slipped behind the potted palm in the white marble foyer and pressed the concealed button that opened a small elevator hidden behind the circular stairs. In seconds, it plunged silently three hundred feet through solid rock to a tunnel leading to Anastasia's underground West Coast Control Center and, several feet farther, to the Pacific Ocean.

As the elevator door slid quietly open, tiny lights activated along the tunnel floor. I hurried toward the sound of waves crashing on rocks, then stopping midway in the tunnel, I fingered the depressions in the rock wall, located the indentation that triggered the release, and the door opened soundlessly into the Control Center.

I stopped first at the computer where Anastasia's agents left encrypted messages that the computer decoded. All agents had checked in during the night, and Else, our beautiful Norwegian agent, had left a message. She'd heard rumors of a new faction being formed by old Nazi sympathizers and of an immense treasure they were collecting.

Bart appeared at that moment, still cleaning the grease from his hands on a very dirty towel. "I wondered where you were. Any problems from the field this morning? Anything interesting?" He kissed the back of my neck as he looked over my shoulder at the check-in computer.

"An intriguing message from Else on the neo-Nazis and a treasure. And I had a strange call from Mom just now, which is what brought me here. She sent me to check on her topaz, the one Grandmother gave her when she and Dad were married. She said something about rumors they'd heard being true, and meeting with World War II Freedom Fighters, and now things would begin to escalate. A very puzzling message."

"That's all she said?" Bart slid his arms around me. "How's my Alexandra this morning?"

"Our baby is fine and active." I turned, slipped my arms around his neck, and gazed into those mesmerizing, azure eyes. "Aren't you even interested in all this mystery?"

"All I'm getting is rumor." He kissed my ear. "Give me something concrete to get interested in."

"Okay, you get on the internet and see if Interpol has any new information—if neo-Nazis and treasure have come up in the news lately. I'll investigate Empress Elizabeth of Austria-Hungary and her topaz necklace. Hmm. Maybe I should just call Grandmother." I glanced at the bank of clocks on the wall displaying the time zones of the world. Five o'clock in the evening in Greece. Probably a good time to catch her.

As I dialed, I pictured the beautiful, wooded island of Skiathos, its incredible white sand beaches and turquoise water, and Mama and Papa Karillides' cottage with scarlet bougainvillea cascading over whitewashed walls.

"Mama Karillides, it's Allison," I said in her native tongue. "How are you?"

My grandmother rattled her answer in Greek, and after greeting me with love, she said, "I have been expecting your call. I knew this new development would capture your interest immediately."

"It did. Tell me about Empress Elizabeth and her topaz necklace and how you came to have one of the stones. And why it is suddenly so important."

"Ah, my sweet, curious Allison. Always so many questions, but where does one start on such a long story?"

I suspected Mama Karillides of teasing me, so I played along with her little game. She knew as she provided answers to each question,

I'd only have more for her. "First, tell me how you acquired a topaz ring that had been a part of the Empress's necklace."

"You know Corfu? Of course you do. Elizabeth took refuge from the Austro-Hungarian court on that island and built a beautiful palace that she called the Achilleion, honoring Achilles, the Greek hero she admired. After her assassination in 1898, her daughter inherited the palace but neglected the place sadly, and many of Elizabeth's possessions disappeared, including the necklace. It wasn't seen again until World War II." She paused, and I imagined her recalling the days of that war when she and Papa Karillides were actively involved with the underground Freedom Fighters.

"How and when did it surface in the war?" I asked, prompting her back to the story.

"Field Marshal Kesselring, commander of German forces in Italy, directed his men to loot treasures from all over the country and hide them until they could be transported back to Germany. Those involved thought Kesselring would cheat them out of their share, so several high-ranking German officers were given a jewel from the necklace with a portion of a code etched into the bottom of each stone. When deciphered, the code would reveal the location of Kesselring's cache of treasure, which they'd divide after the war."

"Which explains why the topaz stones would be valuable," I acknowledged, "but how did you get one?"

"We captured a severely wounded German officer left behind by his men. As he lay dying, he took a leather pouch from around his neck and pressed it into my hand. He whispered it was important but died before he revealed why."

"How did you find out about the code etched on the stone? I didn't see anything on Mom's."

"Another of the jewels fell into the hands of the underground in much the same way, but that soldier revealed the secret of the stone before he died." Mama Karillides paused. "We tried to discover how many jewels were originally in the necklace, but apparently a written description of it doesn't exist, only a painting of the Empress wearing it, and the entire necklace isn't visible."

"How many of the stones have been located? More than just the two you mentioned?"

Mama Karillides didn't answer for a minute. "I think we know the location of possibly ten, maybe twelve." Then she added slowly, "But so do those who are now trying to reassemble the necklace and locate the treasure."

That surprised me. "You mean the treasure Kesselring buried hasn't been found?"

"No. Its whereabouts can only be discovered if all the pieces of the necklace are gathered and the etchings on the stones decoded. It will take all the jewels together to locate the treasure."

"Who has the other jewels?"

"Our compatriots in the underground have many. Some have devoted their lives to tracing the stones so they can recover the treasure." Grandmother stopped speaking again. *Why was she having such a hard time telling this?*

"And the problem you're not wanting to talk about is . . ." I asked, knowing there *must* be a problem or she'd have quickly related the story.

She sighed, and I envisioned my petite grandmother settling into her rocking chair on the veranda overlooking the blue Aegean Sea, debating whether to reveal the whole story.

Finally, she continued. "As the old generation prepares to die, they must pass on the secrets they've carried for over half a century so those things will not die with them. A group of neo-Nazis unearthed the secret of the stones and has begun collecting them from the families of the German officers involved. We know they now have at least six. They're tracing the rest to the members of the underground who were associated in any way in that area where Kesselring operated." Her voice saddened, and she stopped speaking.

I suddenly realized the danger she could be in. "Did they find out you had one?"

"Ah, yes, but they are very clever. They sent an old friend from the war to visit, and when we began talking about the atrocities committed during that time, the theft of so many valuable things came up, and then the treasure. Eventually we spoke of the topaz stones, and I said I hadn't seen mine for thirty years. I'd given it away as a gift." Mama Karillides's voice caught, and I heard the fear she tried to cover.

"How did you find out your friend had been sent by the enemy?"

"Another old friend was also approached, but he was killed. His wife overheard the conversation, saw her husband produce the stone, and then left the house to take something to her neighbor. She returned to find her husband dead, the stone missing, and the visitor had vanished."

"Maybe someone else came," I objected. "Maybe it wasn't the friend who visited you."

"Ah, sweet Allison. You are so innocent. We know. There is no doubt. And now we must gather the stones together, those we've held all these years, and safeguard them so they do not fall into the wrong hands. The treasure is immense, and this fanatical group would use it to finance terrible things. That must not happen. Your parents met with our underground—what little remains of our group—and plotted how to bring the stones together right under the noses of those who seek them for power and destruction. We will reassemble the necklace, find the treasure, and return the pieces to their rightful owners or to the museums and cathedrals where they belong."

This sounded like an impossible task. "What if you can't locate all the stones?" I asked. "How will you be able to break the code if it requires the information on every single jewel?"

"We're working on that. Our group grows old, but we have not lost our thinking powers, just our physical agility. We have a plan, dear, and you will play a large part in it."

Chapter 2

"Me?" I asked in amazement. "What on earth could I have to do with any plan?"

"My dear Allison, all of us in the underground—and our families—are well known to those who seek the treasure. But because we've kept your identity and that of your mother a secret all these years, you would be able to move freely anywhere you need to go without suspicion. You have no known connection to us at all."

"Is that the reason I thought I had no relatives, and I didn't even know you were my grandmother until a couple of years ago?" Suddenly, so many things that for so long had seemed a mystery began to make sense.

"Yes, love. All those times you and your mother stayed with us, we used your mother's profession as an anthropologist to cover the visits, so even our closest neighbors had no idea who you really were. I wanted so much to tell you, but we knew one day someone would come for the jewel or for reprisals against the Freedom Fighters, and we couldn't let them know about you." Grandmother paused, and when she spoke again, the sadness had left her voice. "How wonderful it is to finally hear you call me Grandmother."

"And how satisfying to know the woman I've loved more than any other besides my own mother turned out to be my grandmother. And now, Mama Karillides, tell me about the plan that is supposed to involve me."

"How would you and your husband like to take a vacation to Italy and Greece for a couple of weeks?"

"Of course Bart and I would love that, but what does a vacation have to do with the treasure?" I asked, not making the connection.

"Former underground members suspected of having the jewels, and their family and friends, are being watched carefully. There's no opportunity to bring the stones together to reassemble the necklace. We need someone with the special talents you and Bart possess to join a tour group traveling to areas we need covered. We'll reveal your identity to our people, and they'll contact you. You won't have to do anything except mingle with the tour group, pretend to be tourists, go to all the tourist places, and receive the jewels as you're contacted."

"When is this supposed to happen?" I asked.

"Margaret will explain the entire plan when she arrives, but this gives you a little advance notice to pack your bag and make whatever arrangements you need to make to be gone for two weeks. Be ready to leave as soon as Jack and Margaret return and fill in the details." She made it sound delightfully simple.

"I hope we get to see you while we're over there. It's been too long. How is Papa Karillides?"

"Papa is well. Take care, Allison. I'm sure I don't have to tell you to be careful. You know the kind of people you will be dealing with."

"Only too well. Give Papa a hug for me." I hung up and faced my husband's amused expression.

"Did I hear my name used in vain?" he teased.

"I'm not sure it was in vain, but it was certainly used." I slipped my arms around his neck. "Are you ready for a trip? It sounds like one's being planned for us."

Bart pulled me close. "You said Italy and the romantic Greek Islands?"

"Yes. As soon as the folks get home and give us our assignment in detail, we'll be off."

"Any chance we might visit some of those beautiful islands we didn't get to see on our last trip when we were searching for your mother?" Bart asked, pecking little kisses down my neck.

"If I have anything to say about it, Skiathos will definitely be a scheduled stop. Mama and Papa Karillides are getting old, and I want you to meet them before it's too late."

"Did your grandmother have any idea what this will entail?" Bart suddenly became serious. "I will not place you and Alexandra in danger, no matter how important the assignment."

I wiped a smudge of grease off Bart's sun-tanned cheek. "Apparently, all we're supposed to do is join a tour, and as we arrive at certain destinations, someone will locate us and slip us a topaz stone. This will continue until we've received all the jewels from the members of the underground."

"Then what do we do with them?" he asked, releasing me from his arms. Bart's Interpol mind kicked into agent mode, already working out the logistics of the assignment.

"I assume the folks will reveal that when they get here." I don't think he heard me as he started pacing the floor. I knew he'd be analyzing the sketchy plan, searching for weak spots and anticipating problems.

"You know, of course, it will never be as easy as it sounds." He stopped and stared at me. "We probably won't have gathered half the stones before the other side figures out what's going on and you become a target. So," he pointed his finger at me, "you will not be part of this, and you will stay safely out of harm's way at home."

"No way, José!" I faced my concerned husband and pointed my finger right back at him. "You are not going to closet me away from life just because I'm having your baby. Billions of other women have babies, and they don't change their lifestyle one whit. This is a normal occurrence. I'm not fragile, and Alexandra will be born when she's ready, whole and healthy. I have faith that's the way it will be."

"I have faith if I look both ways before I step into the street, I won't be hit by a car. I don't depend on the Lord to prevent that from happening if I'm not cautious."

I wrapped my arms around my husband. "Bart, you can't protect us from life. Things will happen. But I promise I won't do anything rash, and if things get dicey, I will do whatever is necessary to protect myself and our baby. Don't you trust my judgment?"

His arms closed around me, pulling me close. He laid his cheek on my head and sighed. "I couldn't live without you, princess. I want to lock you in a glass tower away from all the bad things of the world. I want Alexandra to grow up in a perfect environment, free from fear and danger. I know it's not realistic, but that's what I want."

I looked up at him and laughed. "Then what are we doing in California? Wildfires, floods, earthquakes, mudslides, raging coastal storms—not to mention traffic and simply falling down the stairs. They're everyday, life-threatening concerns. Enjoying life is all about trusting the Lord to be in charge. So let's leave the worries to Him and just do what we're supposed to be doing. That way, we'll make the world a safer place to raise our baby. Okay?"

Bart leaned down and kissed my nose. "Okay, but maybe He won't mind if I worry along with Him." Then he added sheepishly, "Not that He needs the help."

"Now you know how I feel when you're in some far part of the world and I have no idea what's happening and how much danger you're in. Guess I should think about packing."

Bart laughed and looped his arm through mine as we headed for the door. "Knowing how long it takes you to make up your mind about what to pack, you'd better do more than think about it. I'll finish mowing the lawn and water your mom's roses, then I'll toss a few things into a suitcase myself."

I stopped at the door. "You thought it was bad when everything in my closet fit. Now nothing does. Mmm, Grandmother didn't say if we were going on a tour or a cruise—or both. That will present even more packing problems."

"Maybe we need a quick trip to town. We can't have you running around without anything to wear for the next two weeks. I'll finish the yard work later."

On our way to Santa Barbara, I called Mom's cell phone. "Ready to tell me the rest of the story?" I asked.

"We'll be home tomorrow," Mom said. "Won't that be soon enough? It's a long story."

"Okay, we'll compromise. Tell me if this assignment is a land tour for Italy and cruise for the Greek islands. I have to know because we're shopping for something to wear. And I need to know when we're leaving."

"You've spoken with your grandmother, haven't you?" Mom laughed.

"I couldn't wait for you to tell me, so I went straight to the next best source. What do I need to prepare for?" I asked again. "Grandmother didn't know the details of the plan."

"Briefly, you'll fly to Venice, board a ship and cruise the Greek islands for a week, return to Venice and travel southern Italy by bus.

Two weeks. Barbara's making your reservations. Is that enough information?"

"It'll have to do. Thanks, Mom. See you tomorrow." I disconnected and turned to Bart. "Well, this should actually be the most fun assignment we've ever had! Two weeks vacation—and a cruise for half of it! Probably the longest time we've spent together since we were married!"

"Mmm. A second honeymoon." Bart smiled broadly. "I like that idea."

I leaned over and put my hand on his arm. "Are you sure you don't want me to stay home out of harm's way while you do this alone?"

"Okay," he conceded. "I was being a dork, but I only wanted to protect the love of my life."

"I like being protected. I'll just be with you while you do it." I settled back in my seat, filled with pure joy. "I'm going to enjoy this assignment better than anything I've ever done—besides marrying you, of course."

"Glad you added that exception," Bart said, easing into a parking place at the Paseo del Nuevo. "Now, let's make sure you're the best-dressed woman on that cruise."

Our "couple of hours in town" turned into twice that, plus lunch at Brophy's Beach Restaurant at the Santa Barbara Marina, where the fish and chips were a special treat. After lunch, we strolled the Avenue of Flags, with waves crashing dramatically against the rocks along the breaker as the tide came in, sending salty spray high in the air.

We returned home in the early afternoon to find Bart's parents, Jim and Alma Allan, at the estate. They'd served as caretakers of the estate since I was a little girl. Bart and I had been raised side by side, though he was four years older than me. When we were kids, he'd treated me like the little sister he never had, and I adored him, following him everywhere, pestering the life out of him.

"All those packages remind me of Christmas. What's going on?" Alma said, taking several as Bart handed them from the car.

"We're going on vacation," I told her, swinging my bags in an excited circle. "I can hardly believe it! This must be a first in the annals of Anastasia!"

"How'd you manage that?" Jim asked, following us into our cottage with his arms full. "I thought no one around here ever took vacations. Anastasia has to be the worst bunch of workaholics I've ever seen."

"Our latest assignment, Dad. It's just supposed to look like a vacation. You can bet it won't turn out to be anything of the sort," Bart explained, as if taking a break from their strenuous schedules were a shameful thing.

"If all these are clothes for a vacation, someone's in for a lot of work wrangling them around," Jim said. "Are you taking a valet?"

"Are you offering your services?" I teased. "I'd be happy to have you hassle my luggage for me. The pay isn't much, but the scenery will be spectacular."

"You're on," Jim said, beaming a smile that warmed me all the way through. A gentle and compassionate man, he'd been like a father to me when my own absent father remained undercover for so many years.

Bart and Jim began talking Interpol business, and Alma and I carried my packages upstairs to the bedroom. As I unpacked boxes and bags to show her my acquisitions, she removed the tags and folded the clothes neatly into my suitcase. By the time she'd seen everything, my suitcase was packed.

"You made that so easy," I said, hugging my mother-in-law. "Now I just need to collect my toiletries, and I'm set."

When Jim and Alma went to the Control Center, Bart and I headed to the beach for my daily walk and to discuss Jim's proposals for the his trip. We wandered down the path to the beach at the bottom of the cliffs and had just reached the water when Jim shouted and came running down the trail from the house.

"Uh-oh. This doesn't look like happy news," I said, watching Jim leapfrog over rocks to take a shortcut.

Chapter 3

Bart swung around and ran back to meet him while I trudged a more sedate pace though the sand. I joined them in time to hear Jim say, "So you need to leave right now and make that flight."

"We're not waiting for the folks to get home?" I asked.

"I'll fill you in on the way back," Jim said, heading up the path. "Jack just called. Another of the original Freedom Fighters has been murdered and his topaz stolen. But the really bad news, over and above the loss of a great, old hero, is that word of this treasure has spread through major terrorist organizations, and it's turned into a free-for-all. Every radical group in the world is after it. Organizations need money to fund terrorist activities, and this looks like the pot of gold at the end of the rainbow."

As we reached the top of the cliffs, Alma hurried to meet us. "Barbara's changed your tickets to the four thirty flight. Since David isn't here with the helicopter, I've scheduled the one from Santa Barbara airport for you. You don't have time for the two-hour drive to LAX. Here's a printout of your e-tickets. Instead of flying into Venice and joining the tour once it's already in progress, you'll join them as they disembark their Atlanta flight in Milan, so it appears you're part of the original tour. We can't take a chance you'll stand out in any way from the rest of the group."

I glanced over the papers Alma gave me as we hurried back to the house.

"This is your itinerary," she said, handing me two more sheets. "Fun For Less is the name of the group. James and Carol Tyndall are the directors, and they've been alerted you're joining them."

"Do they know why we're there?" Bart asked as he held open the door to our cottage and waited for me to enter.

"He knows the operation is classified," Jim said, "and that you're Interpol, but that's the extent of the information Jack gave him. If it becomes necessary to tell him more, Jack said the background check they ran turned up nothing that would preclude you from taking him into your confidence, but I can't foresee any reason that would be necessary."

Bart bounded up the stairs and returned ten minutes later with his suitcase, while I gathered the papers, passports, and visas we'd need from Alma and tucked them in my purse. "Are these real or some of Anastasia's emergency stash?" I asked. I could never tell the difference as they were printed on the same special paper and appeared perfectly official.

"They'll get you where you need to go." Alma smiled.

"Is your bag ready, princess?" Bart asked as he snatched his jacket from the coat closet.

"You can take it. I'll stuff my toiletries in my carry-on, in case my luggage doesn't keep up with us."

Before I had a chance to think about grabbing anything else, we were driving along Highway 101 to Santa Barbara's picturesque little airport, with Jim at the wheel. On the way, I left two quick phone messages. One to Nancy, my visiting teaching companion, to tell her I'd been summoned out of town and she'd have to finish our visiting teaching alone. The second message went to Paula to inform her she'd need to find a substitute for the next two Sundays in the nursery unless she wanted to handle our class of two year olds by herself.

Jim dropped us off at the airport, where we were met on the runway by a longtime friend, Tim Harvey. We'd used Tim's helicopter service many times for this type of emergency.

"I'm glad they don't give you advance notice on these jobs," Tim said gleefully as we waved good-bye to Bart's dad and climbed aboard the helicopter. "You're paying for my new BMW convertible."

"Just a Beemer? You can buy a new chopper at the prices you charge!" Bart declared.

Tim started the engine, which precluded any more banter between the two old friends.

When we finally boarded our plane at Los Angeles International Airport, I promptly fell asleep and slept all the way into Hartfield International in Atlanta, where we faced the hassle of changing planes and security checks for the all-night flight to Milan, Italy.

Airborne again, I watched the lights far below as we flew up the Atlantic coast toward Nova Scotia, excitement and anticipation stirring within me as I thought of the two weeks I'd spend with my husband.

As we scanned our travel itinerary, I became more elated. I'd visited many of these places as a child with my mother when she studied the stories, myths, and legends of the ancient cultures of the world, but I had not returned as an adult.

Bart and I passed the long hours quietly discussing how the underground might pass the coded topaz stones to us without being seen and how to keep the gems safe once in our possession. Toward morning, I got as comfortable as possible in the confined space allotted to me, leaned my head on his shoulder and slept.

* * *

Bart woke me as we flew over the Alps at sunrise. What a spectacular sight! Gold and purple streaked the mountains as the sun hit them, and pink-tinged clouds nestled among the craggy peaks. Our next few hours were "hurry up and wait" as we collected luggage, passed slowly through customs in Milan, found our bus, and headed for Verona.

Our first stop should have been to see Leonardo da Vinci's famous painting *The Last Supper*, but apparently the Santa Maria delle Grazzie Cathedral didn't do large group tours on Saturday and Sunday. Since it was Saturday, we missed that stop, which meant whoever had a stone to give us at that location would have to find another opportunity.

As we disembarked from the bus just outside the ancient walled city of Verona, a guide waited for us. Natalia welcomed us to the Gateway to Italy, praising her native city as one of the most beautiful and ancient in all Italy, second only to Venice in wealth and importance.

Verona was charming. We passed through medieval gates, the Portoni della Bra, built in A.D. 265, and found ourselves in what Natalia reported was one of the largest squares in Italy. Bart and I tried to stay on the fringe of the group to be obvious to those with the topaz.

The ancient arena, built in the beginning of the first century A.D., fascinated me much more than did the statues of heroes. As Natalia talked about the gladiator battles fought anciently and about the Shakespearean festivals and opera now performed there, I tried to spot anyone watching our tour, anyone trying to get close enough to give us the topaz. No one seemed to be the slightest bit interested in this dawdling group of American tourists.

We straggled through the ancient streets to the Via Cappello to see Juliet Capulet's family home, where I discovered that Romeo and Juliet were real people whose tragic story had been immortalized by Shakespeare. Vines covered old, pink bricks in the tiny courtyard, and wherever vines didn't conceal them, the bricks were blanketed by little folded love notes stuck to the walls with gum as far up as people could reach.

High to the left of the arched doorway leading into the Capulet home, an ornate stone balcony clung to the wall. People waved from the place where Juliet spoke with her Romeo, and for only three euros, I could wait in line to spend a few seconds on the famous balcony.

"Do you want to go up?" Bart asked. "Since we're supposed to be typical American tourists, we ought to act the part."

"Why not? Make sure you get my picture so it will be worth the wait to climb those stairs." I slipped into the home before another tour group arrived and was surprised to find a tourist shop. I bought a book on Verona to thumb through while I waited for my turn on the narrow stairway.

I stepped out onto the tiny balcony, probably not more than three feet by six feet, waved to Bart as he took my picture, then moved aside for an anxious teenager to take my place. As I sidled down the crowded stairs, an old woman going up stumbled and fell against me. I grabbed her arms, steadied her, and as I looked into her face, she mumbled "Mama Karillides," and pressed something into my hand. Then she continued climbing the stairs.

My heart racing at the brief exchange, I attempted to remain poker-faced, pocketed the item, and hurried to Bart. "Did you get a good picture? Let me see."

He handed me the digital camera, and as I reviewed the picture, I whispered, "I think I may have just received our first topaz. Someone gave me something."

"Okay, everybody," Jim called. "Time to move on." Our group, some sixty-three in number, quickly filled every space we entered, but we were not as quick to exit. Bart and I moved into the middle of the group, and while surrounded by the moseying mob, I opened my purse, slipped the package from my pocket, and put it where I could unwrap it inside my purse unobserved.

"Look," I whispered. "It's just like Mom's ring." Except it wasn't *just* like it. The stones appeared identical, but this jewel, tri-folded in jeweler's paper, wasn't set.

Claustrophobia precluded me from mingling in dense crowds for any length of time, and our tour group now merged with many others wandering the streets enjoying the ancient sites. Saturday shoppers created meandering rivers of humanity flowing through winding cobblestone streets, and diners filled the colorful sidewalk cafés lining the piazzas.

As we entered the Piazza delle Erbe, with its incredible statue of the Lion of St. Mark and the many-tiered fountain of Madonna Verona, I stopped to take a picture of a man in a top hat cranking his portable calliope. The crowd laughed as his brightly colored parrot talked back to him.

A couple of boys tossing a ball high in the air bumped into me, nearly knocking me to the ground. In the confusion, I felt a tug on my purse. I clutched it with both hands as Bart grabbed me to keep me on my feet and at the same time nabbed one of the boys by the shirt collar. The other escaped, disappearing into the crowds.

"Mi scusi, signore. Incidente," he mumbled.

Bart let him go and slipped his arm around my shoulder, pulling me close to him. "Are you okay?"

"I'm fine." We caught up with the group, but as I thought about the encounter and remembered the distinct tug on my purse at the same time the boy collided with me, I knew it had not been an accident.

I glanced up at my husband, who was noticing the passing scenery—a couple of beautiful Italian girls.

"Either those two boys were a couple of little thieves trying to steal my purse, or the opposition is on to us," I said.

Bart's attention immediately turned to me.

"That was no accident," I said emphatically.

"We'll have to remember this is *not* a vacation even though we're supposed to act like it is," he said. "We can't let them snatch the stones after we finally get them." He stopped in front of a store window filled with fruit carved into incredible shapes and, pointing to a watermelon carved into a huge flower, asked, "Is that good to eat or just for show?"

"Mostly for show. It's been carved and then covered with sugar to preserve it, but real marzipan is good to eat. It's ground almonds and sugar molded into beautiful forms." I scanned the square for a public restroom so I could put the topaz in the small nylon pocket attached to an elastic band that circled my waist under my clothes. I usually carried my passport, credit cards, and extra money in it and would stash the stones there until they began to bulge.

"I'll feel better when the topaz is hidden in your waist safe. If someone succeeds in snatching your purse, the jewels will be safe," Bart said, looking for some place where I could make the transfer immediately. He stopped at the next store window, to a deli filled with delicious-looking pastries and Italian gelato. "How about a gelato?"

"Love one," I answered enthusiastically. I examined the list of flavors. Terrible thing, having to choose from all those luscious Italian ice creams. By the time I settled on lemon cream, Bart had nearly finished his chocolate-almond cone, and we had to hurry to catch up with our group. As they meandered back to the bus, we approached the arena, and Carol Tyndall wanted to see the inside.

"I'll go with you," I volunteered, always anxious to explore something new. Or, in this case, something very old. We bought tickets, then raced in to snap pictures of the amphitheater, dating from the first century and second in size and importance only to Rome's famous Coloseum.

We were two of only four people in the entire arena, since it was nearly closing time, and I paid no attention to the young couple that was also taking pictures until they turned their camera on me. Bells went off in my head, and I put my camera to my eye and took their picture, laughed, and waved as if it were a joke, then scooted back into the darkened passageway out of sight. Carol caught up to me, and I took her picture next to the stone lintels. I had to remind myself to act like a tourist, a role I'd rarely had an opportunity to play.

A cold wind whipped by as the sun set behind the battlements at the entrance to the city—as it had done for centuries. I huddled in Bart's arms while we waited on the street for Giorgio to bring the bus. The misty rain didn't dampen the spirits of our group as they chatted and joked and complained with mostly good humor.

With everyone finally loaded onto the bus, no small task, we drove some distance out of town to a hotel and immediately encountered disaster—only one tiny elevator for sixty-three people and at least one hundred twenty-six pieces of luggage. Bart and I headed for the dining room for a bowl of hot soup while the others took turns with the elevator.

We still ended up carrying our heavy luggage up the stairs. "Next time, remind me to pack lighter," I said, stopping out of breath at the top of the last set of stairs.

"But then you couldn't wear a different outfit every day and win the best-dressed tourist award," Bart teased.

When we finally reached our little hotel room, we immediately examined the topaz. It had marks on the bottom of the stone, but they seemed like nothing more than a few scratches. It would take a magnifying glass or microscope to decipher them. Since we had neither, interest in the gem quickly waned. Bed was far more inviting than a cold piece of topaz, and I hurried to snuggle into its warmth. Even Bart slipped out of agent mode and into bed to wrap his arms around me.

"I hope the weather warms up." I shivered. "I didn't dress for cold wind and rain. I came prepared for sunshine and warm weather."

Bart turned out the light and rubbed my arms to warm them, then tickled my ear with kisses. "Mmm. I don't mind the cold if it means I get to keep you warm."

We snuggled together, quietly talking about our day and what tomorrow might bring, and when Bart didn't answer my last question,

I discovered he'd fallen asleep. I lay thinking about the old woman who'd given me the stone. Her face was wrinkled and her body moved slowly, but her eyes snapped with a fire that surprised me. I had no doubt these aging patriots who'd fought so valiantly for their country half a century ago could still manage this latest battle against evil men.

Just as I started drifting into a peaceful, contented sleep, a sound in the hall roused me. I lay quietly, listening. I heard it again. Bart breathed deeply at my side, sound asleep.

The noise, more distinct, seemed immediately outside our door. Curiosity overcame my weary bones. Creeping out of bed, I tiptoed to the door and peeked through the peephole but was surprised to find no one there. I quietly slipped the chain, unlocked the door, and silently opened it.

Chapter 4

A balding man with a cane stopped at the last door on our floor, bent over the lock, then vanished around the corner at the end of the hall. What had he done? The hall was empty, so I left our door ajar and hurried barefoot in my pajamas to see.

At first glance, I saw nothing, but when I bent closer, I could see a slanted cross scratched into the shiny brass doorknob. As I returned to our room, I checked each of the doors. Two others contained the simple slanted cross. I hurried to the far end of the hall. Nine doorknobs, including ours, had crosses scratched on the surface.

Freezing, I hurried back to our room, locked the door, and snuggled next to the warmth of my husband, who barely stirred when I stuck my cold feet against him. I lay awake, recalling every detail about the man: stoop-shouldered with a fringe of graying hair surrounding a large bald spot, a rumpled, baggy, brown suit, and a uniquely carved cane. I hadn't seen his face, but I would certainly recognize him from the back if I ever saw him again.

Why had he scratched the crosses on the doorknobs? What did they signify? Until I knew who occupied each of the rooms, it would remain a mystery.

* * *

Our wake-up call came too early, but we hurried to get ready and vacate our room before the elevator got busy so we wouldn't have to carry luggage down the stairs. We returned upstairs, where I showed Bart the crosses scratched into the doorknobs, and as we watched our group leave their rooms, we tried to determine what the common denominator might be. Why had the old man chosen those particular rooms or couples? No clue. We were a mixed bag. Young and old. No common threads apparent.

As we leisurely enjoyed our breakfast and waited for our driver, Giorgio, to arrive with the bus, I remembered the couple at the amphitheater in Verona who'd taken my picture. We examined it on the digital camera, but neither of us had seen them before, and they seemed just a young tourist couple. Of course, that's what we were supposed to be too. We had a morning full of mysteries even before we reached Venice, a city steeped in mystery and intrigue.

I didn't remember having been to this magical place where streets are canals and taxis are boats and each treasure-filled building is sinking slowly into the water. Our tour guide stopped at St. Mark's Square, expounding on more Venetian history than even *I* needed, so Bart and I slipped away to visit the Doge's Palace, one of the oldest and most costly in Europe. Doges, rulers from 697 until Napoleon abolished the Venetian Empire in 1797, had resided in and ruled from this ornate palace on the Grand Canal.

From its cream-colored, marble façade to the elaborate courtyard filled with statues, the palace was breathtaking. This had been the center of wealth for the Venetian empire—and it showed. I became so caught up in the gold-leafed ceiling panels and masterpieces painted everywhere, I forgot the reason for our trip.

I'd never seen such astonishing, lavish beauty. It flowed continually from the gold-ceilinged stairwells to the carved wooden doors and panels, to paintings, statues, and mosaics. Each room seemed more ornate and opulent, each crystal chandelier more intricate and dazzling, each marble fireplace designed to outdo the ones before.

We wandered through the justice room where judgment was pronounced upon criminals by the doge himself, the ruler of Venice. The criminal was then led across the Bridge of Sighs, a marble bridge with elaborately grilled windows, to the prison. They said the prisoners' sighs were clearly audible as they crossed into the tiny, cold stone dungeons to be imprisoned for their punishment.

"I like being a tourist. Can we do this more often?" I asked, amazed at all the history and beauty surrounding me.

"Be my guest, princess. Any time you want." Bart reminded me of the time. Our stop in Venice was all too brief, but we had to see one last masterpiece before we left the palace—the world's largest oil painting. *Paradise,* seventy-two feet by twenty-two feet, covered one entire wall in a room that felt the size of a football field. Immense masterpieces, framed by massive, intricately carved, gold-leafed frames, covered the entire ceiling of the room.

As I gazed at the paintings in speechless awe, I became aware of a tall, older, distinguished gentleman standing beside me, reading a beautifully illustrated guidebook.

"It leaves you breathless, doesn't it?" he said, smiling at my reaction to the room and the painting. He spoke excellent English with a definite Italian accent.

"Absolutely breathless," I said. "If my life depended on it, I couldn't find words to describe these priceless treasures."

"Then let's hope that doesn't happen."

The change in the tone of his voice tore my attention from the painting. His eyes met mine briefly, but his gaze was intense, as if he tried to read my soul in those few seconds. Then he turned back to his book and started to read aloud to me about the man who had painted *Paradise* and about what it represented. As he read, his pencil followed along, pausing briefly here and there.

"Fascinating," I said when he finished. "Thank you for sharing that. I didn't have time to pick up a book on our way in, and I love the history behind what I'm seeing."

"Then by all means, please accept this as a gift from one generation," he paused dramatically, "to another."

I searched his face for an explanation of his unusual phrasing but read nothing in his expression.

"Are you sure you want to part with it?" I asked. It appeared to be a valuable book filled with page after page of high-quality colored photographs and lengthy explanations and descriptions, not the usual slim, soft-cover tourist publication.

"I would be honored to give it to you. You seem like a person who values and appreciates . . . priceless treasures." Again he paused to give the last phrase emphasis, but this time he didn't look away when our eyes met. There burned in those deep-set, dark eyes the same fire that had raged in the eyes of the old woman on Juliet's stairs. But he said nothing more. He simply handed me the book, tipped his head, and walked briskly away.

"What was that all about?" Bart asked as the man exited quickly through the fifteen-foot doors at the end of the room.

I shook my head. "I don't know. I thought he was going to give me one of the stones, but all he gave me was this wonderful book about Venice." I showed Bart the book. He took it, turned to the pages that told about the painting, and we read it together.

One of the subheadings, "Priceless Treasures," caught my eye.

"That phrase—priceless treasures. He emphasized that when he gave me the book."

We approached the painting to identify each of the figures in the commentary. As my finger traced the sentence about the painter, I noticed tiny underline markings under certain letters.

"There may be a code here," I whispered to Bart. "We need to find a less public place and see if we can decipher it, if indeed it is such a thing."

"What makes you think it's a code? Maybe it's just smears from the printing," Bart said, a doubtful tone in his voice as he squinted at the page. "I don't see what you're seeing."

"There aren't smears in this book, and there's no sloppy printing. It's an expensive publication. I think we've seen enough in here. Let's find a quiet place where I can determine what the marks are."

We found our way out of the rambling palace to the loggia overlooking the courtyard, and while Bart watched those who might be watching us, I sat in a corner and wrote down the underlined letters.

Pigeons in piazza 3:22 P.M. Stay with group.

That was all. A very clever use of the dimensions of the painting and page numbers combined, not to mention it took a whole paragraph under the heading "Priceless Treasures" to underline those thirty-three letters and numbers. And I duly noted the directions given. We'd left our group and come alone to the Doge's Palace without a thought that we might be altering the plans of the topaz-bearers.

"I think I have it," I told Bart, linking my arm through his and heading for the stairs. I glanced at my watch. "It's time to feed the pigeons in St. Mark's Square."

"Is that what it said?" he asked, his tone still tinged with doubt.

I stared at my husband. "Don't you believe me?"

"Princess, I trust you will find a mystery anywhere you turn—and usually solve it too. Of course I believe you. We need a picture or two to show we're tourists. Stand at the foot of these stairs, and I'll get the two statues above you with the winged lion in the middle. I think this is what they call a photo op," he added, winking at me.

I glanced at the statues and nearly laughed out loud. "Bart, catch the faces on the statues. This one looks like a young Paul Newman, and the other resembles an old Charlton Heston!"

Bart looked up from behind the camera. "You're right. Amazing likenesses. Great photo. Get between them."

When he'd snapped a couple of pictures, we hurried from the Doge's Palace around the corner where hordes of people thronged St. Mark's Square. I watched for someone selling bird food, as I assumed that would be the thing to do with pigeons in the piazza. A very touristy thing here. Two old men, several feet apart, sold little sacks of bird seed, and children as well as adults lined up to buy what enticed pigeons to land on heads, shoulders, arms, and wherever they could gain a footing to gobble the goodies.

"You take one, and I'll take the other so we'll have plenty between us," I suggested. I produced the proper euro coin for the little paper sack of pigeon food. When the old man glanced up and saw me, he slipped a bag from his pocket instead of the pile in front of him, and as he handed it to me, he smiled and said softly, "Mama Karillides."

I thanked him, and as he turned his attention to the children in line behind me, he whispered, "Kindinos."

Danger.

My heart quickened, and I hurried away as the children traded their coins for his goods, squealing with delight as they were deluged with greedy birds. Bart and I strolled several feet into the center of the square, away from the press of people. As I opened my sack, I didn't look inside, but felt the contents. Sure enough, as I squeezed, the birdseed shifted to reveal a bulky item in the bottom.

"Bingo!" I smiled at Bart, dumping a little of the food into my hand and holding it up for the pigeons. Dozens of gray birds swooped down on me, landing on my head, shoulders, even the hand that held the food. Bart stuffed his sack into his pocket and snapped my picture as I tossed the food into the air, then poured the rest of it on the marble stones of the piazza to rid myself of my feathered friends.

I held the lump in the bottom of the sack, shook it high so anyone watching would see an apparently empty bag, then stuffed it in my purse and insisted Bart feed his food to the birds while I took his picture. He didn't slip into tourist mode as quickly and easily as I had and needed a little coaxing to get into the act.

Spotting our tour group heading slowly and reluctantly out of the square, we decided we had time for a gelato before leaving one of the most famous piazzas in the world. We sat at a linen-covered table under a warm Italian sun, listening to violins playing just behind us, savoring sweet, smooth gelato. A perfect day.

While I ate my ice cream, I thumbed through the guidebook the man had given me and read aloud to Bart. "Venice is built on one hundred eighteen small islands, separated by two hundred canals, spanned by four hundred bridges." I leaned back in my chair. "Wow! Imagine building a city on little islands. Were they so strapped for land all those centuries ago?"

Bart pulled his chair close to mine, leaned over, and kissed me. "You look beautiful, princess. You're glowing."

"Oh, Bart. This is like a dream come true! A real vacation visiting exotic locations with my husband. No bad guys shooting at us. Sunshine and gelato. Life couldn't be better!"

Bart kissed my ear and then whispered, "Just hang on tight to your purse. Someone right here in this beautiful exciting place you love so much is waiting to take what that old man gave you. And I'm sure he wouldn't care one whit about whether or not he spoiled your day."

I brushed a quick kiss across his lips. "Now who's spoiling my day, reminding me that danger lurks for Anastasia, not only in dark corners, but in sunny squares." I knew he hated to spoil my mood, but it was his job to protect me, and that meant reminding me of the reality of our situation. I sighed. "Our group's probably already reached the meeting spot. The note directed us to stay with the tour, so I guess we'd better catch up with them."

We lingered momentarily at St. Mark's Basilica, rebuilt between A.D. 1063 and 1073, the guidebook said, to provide a resting place for the tomb of St. Mark the Evangelist. The four famous Greek prancing horses on top were masterpieces of 4th–3rd century B.C., brought from Constantinople, carted off to Paris by Napoleon in 1798, and finally returned to Venice in 1815.

As we passed a statue of the bust of a man in ancient Venetian headdress and robe—it winked at me. A man with his head wrapped in a white turban with white makeup covering his face stood in a hollow marble column. At first glance, it was just another marble statue on a pedestal. I laughed and took his picture.

We rounded a corner and encountered a gondolier waiting for his next passenger on the canal. I glanced wistfully at Bart. He shook his head. I knew he would. Even if we'd had time, it wouldn't be wise. Too many narrow, little canals wound through the city. A perfect place for an ambush. Would my life ever be normal, so I could do the ordinary, fun things most people did without thinking twice about them?

We wandered through kiosks and vendors that kept tourists happily supplied with everything from T-shirts to Venetian glass necklaces and ornate masks. Three tall figures in porcelain masks and exotic gold and velvet Carnival costumes moved from the bridge where they were posing for pictures for money. I paid no attention to them since we'd already taken their picture. Suddenly they blocked our way, trapping us between two kiosks. I remembered the old man's warning: *danger.*

One reached for my purse while the other two brandished long, curved, wicked-looking knives. My heart beat wildly as I stared into the black eyes glaring at me from behind the masks. All I could think of was the safety of my baby.

Bart moved quickly, shoving me between two of them and knocking the third one into the street with a swift kick. I managed to stay on my feet by grabbing the corner of the kiosk nearest me, rattling the beads hanging from it, and raced toward the dock. I glanced back in time to see a tall jester's hat flying through the air and my husband jumping a display of flowers to follow me.

As we slipped breathlessly into the center of the group, I whispered, "So much for a perfect day."

"Welcome back to the real world." He slid his arm around my waist and pulled me close. "Guess it's time to send you home and finish this myself."

Before I could object, the tender arrived, and the Tyndalls directed everyone to hurry aboard. As we waited to step down into the water taxi, I heard someone say, "They tried to snatch Laura's purse."

I turned to the person behind me. "Who tried to take Laura's purse?"

"Did you see those three tall people in the elaborate costumes posing for pictures as we disembarked from the tender?"

I nodded, not mentioning I'd just had a personal encounter with them.

"They tried to grab her purse as she left St. Mark's Square."

"Which one is Laura?" I asked.

"The little blonde with the tall man just getting into the tender. Somebody else said that she felt her purse being tugged on in the crowd. She didn't think too much about it since pickpockets and purse-snatchers abound in crowded piazzas. I'm Charlotte, by the way."

I looked into the friendly eyes of the pleasant woman standing behind me. "Hi. I'm Allison. This is my husband, Bart."

Charlotte pointed to a young woman chatting with someone behind her. "This is my daughter, Sara." Sara turned around. She was a classic beauty: tall, slender, porcelain skin, green eyes, long brown hair, and a beautiful, shy smile.

"Someone not only tried to tried to grab Sara's purse, but a gondolier also grabbed her ankle when she was posing for a picture at the canal. Nearly scared her to death," Charlotte added.

Someone spoke up behind Sara. "The Italians are well known for pinching women, and heaven only knows there are pickpockets and thieves everywhere. I've quit carrying a purse. If I can't stuff it in my pocket or my fanny pack, I figure I don't need it."

A fellow traveler agreed. I glanced at Bart. "Sorry, Charlie. This is normal travel in the world today."

We boarded the tender, and I sadly watched Venice's Grand Canal disappear behind us. I'd love to have spent several days there, wandering narrow alleyways, gliding through canals on romantic gondolas, exploring museums, discovering the archeological and historical treasures Venetians were trying desperately to save from the encroachment of the sea.

"A penny for your thoughts, princess? You're as gloomy as that gray cloud moving across the sun."

I leaned against my husband as he put his arm around me. "Just thinking about those beautiful buildings and paintings and statues in danger of being swallowed by the water lapping endlessly at their doors. And wondering if I'll ever get back here—or if they'll be gone before I do."

"Of course you'll come back. All you have to do is say the word. Don't I make all your wishes come true?" Bart kissed my nose. "My whole reason for existing is to make you happy. I'm at your beck and call to grant your every desire."

I laughed. "Don't I wish! You're seldom near enough to be at my beck and call."

The sun emerged from behind the long, dark cloud and glistened off blue water as we passed twelfth-century churches with gleaming, gold domes and red-brick bridges curving over canals. Goods were being unloaded at the door of a warehouse from a barge. A funeral gondola, embellished with shiny black lacquer and red trim, passed us filled with flowers, and through red-velvet-draped windows, I saw an ornate casket. Even Venetian hearses were gondolas. What an unusual, fascinating lifestyle.

The next few hours seemed one long baggage and customs drill until we boarded the bus that delivered us to our cruise ship, the *European Vision*. We'd barely located our cabin, where our luggage waited for us outside our door, when the mandatory lifeboat drill began.

We collected life jackets and filed out to find our muster station. The ship's personnel tried to make it fun, but the process lasted forever and my legs were very tired before we were finally dismissed. As we gazed over the railing at the dock below, I spotted a baggy, brown suit disappearing around a stack of containers waiting to be loaded.

"Did you see that?" I grabbed Bart's arm and pointed, but the dock was empty.

"See what?" he said, leaning over the edge to peer down at the place now devoid of people or movement.

"I saw him. I know that was him—the man who scratched the crosses in the doorknobs in Verona. The man in the baggy, brown suit."

Though we watched for another ten minutes, he seemed to have vanished into thin air. We returned to our cabin, nerves slightly on edge, but when I collapsed on my bed, it felt so good, I wasn't sure I wanted to leave. I totally relaxed and put the baggy brown suit out of my mind. "I'd happily go to bed right now and sleep the rest of the cruise."

"I was about to suggest we grab sweaters and go on deck, get a drink, and watch the ship leave the harbor," Bart said. "We can probably watch the sun set, too." He turned on the little TV in our room. "Or you can watch it from this shipboard camera. Of course, it only shows you what's straight ahead, and we're not sailing into the sunset." As he flipped the channels, I saw the preview of tomorrow's tour: Dubrovnik, Croatia.

"Stay on that channel. Wow. I certainly don't want to sleep through that stop." We watched the film of the last tour of the ancient walled city while I rested my tired legs, then went on deck to watch beautiful Venice, Queen of the Adriatic, pass silently by as our ship sailed into the Adriatic Sea.

Bart brought our hot chocolate to the highest balcony on the end of the ship, and we toasted our good fortune at this plum of an assignment while we watched the last tip of land disappear behind us and the sun sink into a glassy, gray sea. Clouds streaked with silver soon gave way to stars overhead.

Live music emanated from the Flamenco Lounge, and as we passed through on our way to our cabin, I heard excited voices around the corner speaking Italian. I clutched Bart's arm. "Wait. Let me hear what they're saying."

We paused, hidden by a partition that separated the bar from the video games section for young people. When the second man spoke, I fervently wished I hadn't stopped. Cold chills ran down my spine. I grabbed Bart's hand and pulled him through the lounge to the other side of the ship so we wouldn't be seen by the man who'd made the dramatic, deadly announcement.

Chapter 5

Instead of returning to our stateroom, we slipped out to the balcony on the opposite side of the ship from where we'd watched the sun set. In the stairwell, where we couldn't be seen from any direction, we huddled to discuss the startling announcement.

"Okay, I caught the part about their agents discovering receivers of the stones would be on this ship," Bart said. "What else did he say? Something about nine, but I couldn't hear the rest."

"They tortured an old man into telling them how the stones were being gathered. I think we missed a couple of crucial statements, but apparently the gist is they discovered the jewels were being passed by the underground to people on a tour. They have agents watching all American tour groups that hit Italy this week. The man assigned to this group did his homework and narrowed our tour to nine possible couples who could be receivers."

"Thus the scratches on the nine doors," Bart mused.

"Yes, I'm sure now that's what the crosses meant."

"Anything else?" Bart asked.

"Unfortunately, yes." I shuddered. "He told them when they identified the couple receiving the jewels, they should intercept the pass, retrieve the stones, then eliminate them. If they couldn't catch anyone receiving the jewels, they should begin eliminating the couples so there wouldn't be so many to keep track of."

Bart stared at me in disbelief. "He actually ordered the extermination of eighteen people if his agents couldn't figure out which of the eighteen were the receivers?"

"That's what the man said before he stormed out." The wind and the splash of the ship's wake below us were the only sounds in our universe as we tried to absorb and understand the disastrous consequences of the man's statement.

"Did he give a timetable?" Bart asked, pacing the six-foot-square landing.

"I didn't hear one."

"So we don't know if it means the agent has until this cruise is over, or until the whole tour is over, to discover who the receivers are."

I nodded. "Either way, there's a time crunch for them, which won't work to our advantage." As I thought about his statement, I was puzzled. "Why would he want to eliminate the receivers—or possible receivers? You'd think they'd want to keep them alive and catch them in the act of receiving the gemstones. Then he'd be able to get his hands on the jewels. Otherwise, what's the point?"

"Could you have misinterpreted a word? Are you sure they said eliminate? Is there another word that sounds the same but means something different? It doesn't make sense they would kill people just because they can't figure out who will be receiving the topaz."

"I totally agree, Bart, but I'm sure that's what I heard. I hope I'm wrong." I winced. What kind of monsters were we dealing with?

Bart leaned against the railing, staring into the black depths below. He shook his head and muttered about the absence of human decency in this newest bunch of neo-Nazis, exactly like the old ones under Hitler. Suddenly, he glanced at his watch, straightened up, and then looked at me like he just realized I was still there.

"Okay, Sherlock. What have you deduced?" I asked, recognizing the signs when he emerged from agent mode to reenter the present moment.

"I deduce, my dear Watson, it's nearly our dinner hour and if we don't hurry, we'll miss our seating. I'm famished and weak with hunger." His sudden mood shifts always amazed me. I stared at him. What had he thought of that allowed him to put this aside so abruptly and think of dinner?

"Then by all means, let's go. We don't have to dress for dinner tonight. I only need quick refreshing so I won't frighten our table companions, and I'll be ready." We took the stairs down to our deck instead of bothering with crowded elevators.

"I wonder who we'll dine with," I said as I brushed my hair.

"Does it matter?" Bart asked, splashing water over his face and deciding a fresh shirt would also be a good idea.

"Not really. I think we're assigned the same table and same companions each night of the cruise. Seems like it would be a better idea to rotate each evening to get acquainted with everyone in the group."

As it turned out, we were delighted with our dinner companions. The charming Charlotte and her lovely daughter, Sara; Vivian and Wayne, a quiet, accomplished couple from a small town in Utah; the celebrity guest on our cruise, pianist Marvin Goldstein, and his wife, LaNae, along with their associates, Marc and Marcia.

It was a lively evening with Marc and Marvin teasing Sara just to watch her blush. We discovered Sara's father was Greek, so that created a bond between us.

It took us two hours to eat five delicious courses, and then I was more than ready to escape to our cabin and bed. No late-night entertainment for me. "Sorry I'm not a party person," I told Bart on the way to our cabin. "If you want to see the Flamenco dancers with the group, please do. I'm exhausted and will be boring company for you tonight, as I'm sure I'll be fast asleep as soon as I hit the pillow."

"What makes you think I'm less tired than you?" Bart protested.

I laughed. "Because you're not pregnant for one thing. Normally I'd love to see the late show, but my energy is non-existent tonight."

As I followed my husband from the stairway to our hall, Bart whirled around, pulled me against the wall by the stairs and wrapped me in his arms. I hardly noticed the animated voices of men in the hall.

When he finally released me, I sagged against the wall. "I love you too, but what on earth was that all about?"

"Didn't you recognize that voice?" Bart said, peering at the retreating figures.

"I barely heard the voices. You completely swept me off my feet." I joined him at the corner but couldn't tell if I'd ever seen the men before, and we were too far away to hear what they were saying. "To whom do I owe the pleasure of that last embrace?"

"If I'm not mistaken, that was the man we heard giving instructions outside the lounge earlier." Bart took my hand and pulled me toward our room. "Let's see if we can tell what they've been up to in our part of the ship."

As we silently searched our cabin, Bart pointed in triumph to a tiny bug someone had planted to monitor our conversations. What had we said when we first entered our room earlier? Had we inadvertently revealed anything to alert these people that we were not just casual members of a tour group? Or had those two only now placed the listening device?

Bart winked at me as he grabbed his jacket off the bed. "Do you have the energy to go back up on deck? It's stuffy in here, and I'm feeling a little queasy. I need some fresh air."

"Sure. Let me get my coat." I grabbed my sweater and purse from the bed, and we hurried to an upper deck in the stern of the ship where the miniature golf greens were deserted and the area void of passengers.

"I assume the other eight couples also had their cabins bugged." I leaned against the railing and watched lights shimmering in the distance across the black water. "Bart, I'm worried about them. These innocent people could get hurt. Shouldn't we tell them instead of letting their conversations be monitored?"

Bart had apparently been pondering that very thing. "At this point, I don't want to tell anyone. We're the only ones receiving the topaz, and we definitely don't resemble anyone else on this tour, so there shouldn't be any mix-up in delivering the jewels to the wrong people. But we do need to get into the other cabins and disable the bugs."

"By damaging the listening devices so they won't transmit, we'll make those listening think they simply bought a bunch of defective devices, and they won't suspect a thing. Is that your idea?"

"Smart girl. Now figure out how I'm going to get in all those cabins without arousing anyone's suspicions."

"Go directly to the captain. No intermediaries."

"Mmm." Bart was quiet for a minute. "What if the captain's in on this?"

"What do you suppose the chances are he's involved?" I asked. "Think about it. Do you think he'd want his integrity compromised?

He'd lose his ship if it was discovered he'd been a party to passengers' rooms being bugged."

"You're probably right. These guys had to have bribed their way into our room, so the only way we'd get in to the other cabins would be to up the ante. We don't want to reveal we're on to them, and they'd find out fast if our steward, or whoever gave them the key, blabbed. I wish we had some idea who they were besides neo-Nazis. I like to know the face of my enemy."

"Right. Time to call the folks and get something more than the sketchy information in your dad's briefing." I pulled my compact transmitter from my purse and called the Control Center via satellite connection where communications were safely encoded, transmitted, and decoded without fear of anyone eavesdropping on our conversations. Bart's mom answered immediately.

"Good morning in California, Alma. I need you to do a quick background check on the captain of our ship, Marco Fortezze, with the *European Vision,* Festival Cruise Lines. Can you run him through Interpol's files on the computer?"

"Will do. How's the trip so far?"

"Too soon to tell. We've received two stones and had to miss another when our tour in that city was canceled. Did my folks get home yet?"

"Not yet. They planned on arriving here yesterday, but when you'd already left, they made another stop before returning to California. In answer to your question about Marco Fortezze, he has no file with Interpol."

"Good news, because we need to take him into our confidence. Thanks, Alma. Later." I hung up and shivered. "Ready to speak to the captain?" I snuggled up to Bart. The night wind blowing off the water went right through my sweater.

Bart put his arms around me. "While I do that, why don't you go back to our room and fix the bug?"

"Yes, sir, boss." I glanced up at my husband. "Are you sending me back to get warm?"

He laughed and kissed me. "Apparently I wasn't subtle enough, but I can't have you freezing."

"I'll acquiesce this time, just because my teeth are chattering, but next time, you won't send me away without a fight."

Bart linked my arm through his and we started back. "Send you away? I just sent you to do a job. As lead agent, I expect you to follow my orders to a tee."

"Oh, I promise I will," I replied facetiously.

Bart regarded me with a knowing smile. "As long as you agree with my decisions—is that what you're saying?"

I tried to appear properly shocked. "Would I ever disobey a command from my lead agent?"

"Mmm. I recall you have a long history of independent thinking where instructions from your father and your husband are concerned."

"Now that I think about it, I was taught we're all equal. So how can I disobey a command from my superior if we're all equal?"

Bart shook his head. "I can't keep up with your imaginative train of thought."

We paused at the doors leading into the interior of the ship, waiting for several passengers to file through onto the deck. "I'll go play with the bug," I said, happy to get back into the enclosed warmth of the lobby. "When will I see you again?"

Bart leaned against the brass stair railing. "If I can get them all inoperative while everyone's at the show tonight, I will. Otherwise I'll have to wait for another opportunity to get into their rooms. Don't wait up for me. I'll try to be quiet when I come in."

I paused at the top of the stairs. "What are they going to think when the listening devices quit transmitting one at a time?"

"They won't actually quit working. They'll just be so full of static that nothing will be discernible on the other end. But give me thirty minutes with the captain and to get to the first cabin. Then we can do a simultaneous disabling, after which I should be able to do one at least every two to four minutes, so this shouldn't take long or give them any hint about sabotage."

"That makes me feel better. These creeps think they know who we are, but we don't have any idea who they are, or even how many we're dealing with. It'd be nice to have the whole story on this caper. There's bound to be so many other things involved besides what your dad told us."

"Your mind is like a steel trap. Nothing escapes it." Bart laughed, turned, and made for the captain's bridge.

I'd certainly get my exercise on this trip. It may not be an hour's walk on the beach each day, but traversing the flights of stairs several times a day would be even better. My doctor would be very happy. And I was very tired. I couldn't wait to disable that bug and climb into bed.

Luggage still stacked outside cabin doors left room for only one person at a time to walk down the narrow corridor leading to our cabin. Adding to the obstacle course were steward carts parked in the passageway piled high with fresh towels and soap, little bottles of shampoo, and other passenger necessities.

Our steward stood beside his cart near our door. "Good evening, ma'am. Did you have a nice day?" His nametag said Raphael, and his English was excellent.

"I did, thank you, Raphael."

"Can I get you anything?" he asked as I keyed the door to our room.

I opened the door and turned with a smile. "Just some peace and quiet. Good night."

He nodded and smiled, and I shut the door behind me. The light was on, bedcovers turned down, and a chocolate lay on my pillow. Had that pleasant, good-looking young man been a party to the planting of the listening device? He had our room key, got paid to wait on us hand and foot, kept our room spotless, and supplied all our needs. Who else had keys? Who else had opportunity?

My mind entertained these questions while my fingers busily installed the tiny piece of electronic equipment that would introduce static to the device, rendering it all but useless. The padded journal case in which my ceramic gun was concealed contained an assortment of tiny James Bond–style devices for various nefarious activities such as this. The case would have done Q proud.

When I'd completed my task, I finished unpacking my suitcase. As I slid it under my bed, I had a sudden thought. That bug on the lamp was fairly obvious. Only an unsuspecting tourist wouldn't find it. Any agent worth his salt would spot it immediately. Since these weren't amateurs we were dealing with, they should have been more circumspect in placing the listening device. Did that mean the one Bart found was a decoy? Were there more he didn't find?

I thought of the suitcases in the hall, accessible to anyone. Opening my journal, I retrieved the bug detector. With a steward having access to our room at all hours, it may be necessary to sweep the room each time we entered it. I turned up the frequency on the electronic detector and swept the room again. Surprisingly, there were no other devices—at least none I located. I'd fully expected to find something, especially on the suitcase, but I was wrong. That should have made me happy. It didn't.

Chapter 6

Puzzled, I plopped down on the bed. Who were these people? How could we combat them if we didn't know who and what we were dealing with? Did they have advanced surveillance technology that Interpol hadn't yet discovered—or was I overestimating them?

Once again I went over the room and its contents with the debugger, sweeping more slowly, making sure I covered every single area: walls, lamps, beds, and suitcases. I checked the bathroom, the closets, even the clothes. There simply wasn't another device anywhere, at least that I found. Now what?

I paced the tiny space between the beds and door. There had to be something constructive I could accomplish instead of wasting valuable time waiting for Bart's return. But what? As I paced, feeling more helpless and frustrated with each passing minute, a numbing weariness crept over me. Stumbling to my bed, I curled up on the end, determined not to sleep before Bart returned. We had much to discuss, and as tired as I was, if I slept, I might not hear him come in.

Unfortunately, my body didn't cooperate. It apparently needed much more rest than my frantic mind—and took it. I awoke in a darkened cabin, my blanket tucked snugly around me. Bart breathed heavily in his bed. Bright red numerals on the clock read four A.M. What time had he come in? What had he accomplished? What, if anything, had he discovered?

If he'd only been in bed a short time, I didn't want to disturb him, but how could I go back to sleep with all these questions ping-ponging in my head? I tried to turn them off, to blank my mind. It didn't work. I snuggled down, pulled the covers back over my shoulders, and went over everything we knew so far, which seemed frightfully little for an operation of this magnitude. One fear kept nagging at me. How could we protect the innocent people on our tour who had no idea of the danger they were in?

* * *

Bart's shower woke me. I peeked at the clock, then sat up and looked again. I couldn't believe I'd actually gone back to sleep for three more hours. We were due to disembark for Dubrovnik at eight thirty, and I needed breakfast. I jumped up, kissed Bart good morning as he exited the shower, and took his place in the tiny, steamy bathroom.

We hurried through the crowded buffet line and found a table someone had just deserted in a corner away from other tables, and I plied Bart with questions.

"Were you able to get into everyone's room last night?" I whispered.

Bart nodded, his mouth full of scrambled eggs.

"No problem with the captain?"

Bart shook his head. "He has a good friend in Interpol I happen to know, so he was extremely cooperative."

"That was a stroke of good fortune—or a major blessing. Did you find the bugs?"

Again he nodded.

"Did you find more than one in any room?"

He stopped with a bagel halfway to his mouth. "Why?"

I waved a forked strawberry at him. "Don't you think it's strange they were so easy to find? I mean, this shouldn't be a bunch of amateurs, but considering the placement of the devices, they appear to be. I checked our room again—twice—and didn't find anything else." I popped the strawberry in my mouth and waited for Bart to comment. He speared a piece of pineapple and seemed to consider the idea as he ate it.

"You're right," he said. "They *were* easy to find—for us. But if they figured they were dealing with tourists who wouldn't expect to have their rooms bugged, they wouldn't have to be sophisticated in hiding them."

I savored another strawberry. "Were they all in the same place?"

Bart nodded as he spread cream cheese on the other half of his bagel. "On the lamp between the beds."

"Not very imaginative." I saw Jim and Carol, our tour guides, threading through the tables toward the exit and swallowed my last bite of mango as Bart drained his glass of orange juice and stood.

"No dawdling over breakfast this morning or we'll miss the tender to Dubrovnik." Bart pulled my chair out. "Unless you'd rather stay onboard. The weather isn't sunny and warm like the tour we saw on TV last night. It's raining and cool."

"If I hadn't seen the old city on that video, I'd be tempted to spend a leisurely day onboard, but I can't pass the chance to go exploring—and we do have more topaz to find. So break out the umbrellas, and let's go for it."

My first glimpse of Croatia came through a rain-streaked window as we sailed past a modern bridge spanning a wide river. But I felt we'd stepped back in time a thousand years when we finally entered the ancient walled city of Dubrovnik. I easily imagined soldiers with shouldered muskets patrolling the high battlements and imagined families on the wharf waving as ships slipped out of the little, protected harbor with sails billowing when the wind caught and filled them.

The huge, round Tower Minceta, the highest point in the fortifications, dominated the enclosed section of the old city while the newer portion of the city spread upward, filling hillsides with white stucco, red tile–roofed homes nestled in towering, green holm oak trees. Today, the high walls were lined with tourists taking pictures of the colorful town above and below them, instead of soldiers with muskets.

Our tour followed another group under the stone arch of the Pile Gate, where a stream of colorful umbrellas flowed down the wet street in front of us like bright balloons bobbing merrily down a brook.

Oblivious to the light rain misting his dark curly hair, a young minstrel in a brown velvet shirt strummed a shiny, red guitar and smiled at passing tourists as they tossed coins into the velvet cap at his feet. I dug into my pocket and threw a coin in appreciation for his merry music, which brightened a decidedly gray, drizzly day.

I was so caught up watching him, I didn't notice his backdrop—the huge fountain that resembled a Romanesque baptistery with a rounded stone top. Someone behind me was reading about Big Onofrio's Fountain and the aqueduct built in 1438, pointing out the sixteen elaborately carved stone masks from which poured forth the waters of the fountain.

I looped my arm through Bart's. "I need one of those books about the city. I wonder where we can get one."

"Probably in here." He pointed to the twelfth-century Franciscan monastery into which our group attempted to enter as another group tried to exit.

I stopped to listen as the woman who'd been reading about the fountain explained the carved stone figures above the portal. "St. Jerome symbolizes spiritual unity with the rest of Dalmatia."

"I wouldn't have even noticed the carvings over the door if she hadn't been reading about them," I whispered to Bart.

She continued, "St. John the Baptist symbolizes Christian constancy in the face of the Turkish penetration. The Pieta symbolizes the Franciscan's compassion for the poorest members of the community, and the Father figure on top is the Creator, symbolizing opposition to the humanist worldviews of the time."

"I need that book," I repeated. "How can we appreciate what we're seeing if we don't know what it is?"

"Good point," Bart agreed. "That'll be the first thing on our agenda—if we ever get inside."

It was no small task entering the ancient stone building given the incredible number of people who also wanted to see it. We moved shoulder to shoulder through a narrow marble corridor where pictures of the ancient city hung next to fading frescoes from centuries earlier.

"It's so packed, no one could find us if they tried," I whispered. "And my claustrophobia is kicking in big time. I've got to get out of here."

"Before you get your book?" Bart asked, pulling me in front of him and shielding me from the elbowing masses trying to move in the confined space. Suddenly an empty doorway appeared, and we slipped inside the apothecary.

"May I help you?" the young woman behind the counter asked. Startling blue eyes matched her blue pharmacist smock.

"Only if you have something to cure claustrophobia," I said. "Or if you have a book about Dubrovnik."

She shook her head. "No, I'm sorry, but you can get a book in the gift shop at the end of the corridor, across from the cloisters."

I examined the room, so totally different from drugstores in America. Instead of packaged medicines in boxes, clear bottles and jars filled with what I assumed were medicinal herbs lined the shelves.

"Are these the medicines you dispense?" I asked, not seeing anything that even resembled an aspirin.

She smiled. "Sometimes. Or under the counter and in the supply room, we have many of the brands you'd find in your country. We just try to keep it looking as it did centuries ago. This is the third longest continually functioning apothecary in the world."

"Now's your chance to get into the gift shop," Bart said from the doorway. "The other tour just left, and we can move in the corridor."

I started for the door and then stopped with one more question for the friendly, dark-haired girl. "Is it always this crowded?"

"When the cruise ships dock, it is always busy. At least, now that the war with Yugoslavia is over. No tourists came during the fighting in 1991 and 1992. Notice the bullet holes in the wall at the end of the corridor. If you look over the city, you can see where we have replaced roof tiles and portions of the walls and repaired damage from the shells that rained down on us. It was devastating."

Bart grabbed my hand. "You have a window. You have to come now."

I flung a quick thank you over my shoulder and glanced down the corridor. Bart was right. Another tour group poured through the entrance heading our way. We hurried to the gift shop and bought the tourist version of the history of Dubrovnik before the shop filled again. Then we ducked out into the peaceful area of the cloisters, a lovely, quiet, green court surrounded by pillars and columns and statues—a beautiful place for Franciscan monks to meditate and pray.

"We'd better keep moving, or we're not going to get to see the rest of the city," Bart said, guiding me back to the rain-washed street. "Plus, we need to be out where our carrier can find us if we're going to collect another stone here."

Nestled cozily under one umbrella, we strolled along the narrow street made from blocks of marble, peeking up alleyways that seemed to rise straight up the mountainside. Three- and four-story buildings lined the pedestrian-only street, all fashioned from the same golden stone that lent a marvelous uniformity to the thousand-year-old city. At the end of the street rose a tall, slender clock tower with a huge bell at the top. Consulting my book, I discovered it was the Passing Bell— a bell that tolled at the passing of each soul from this life to the next.

The street opened into a square, and in the center stood a tall statue of a young Crusader Knight, sword drawn and shield on his arm.

"What is a Crusader Knight doing here?" I asked, trying to keep my book dry under the umbrella while I found the picture of the column and read about Roland, the legendary medieval knight.

"Holding up the flagpole," Bart said, pointing to the tall, ceremonial flagpole ascending high into the air from a platform atop Roland's column.

"Tradition says Roland defended Dubrovnik from the raids of the Saracen pirates, but the column is also a symbol of loyalty to Sigismund, whose protection was crucial in the strife against Venice."

"And who is Sigismund?" Bart asked, though his tone made it apparent he wasn't keenly interested in the answer. I glanced up to see him scanning the crowd, more interested in who was present today than who had figured prominently in history centuries ago.

"King of Hungary, Croatia, and Bohemia, and later Emperor of Germany," I read. "It seems everyone was warring all the time. Little guys needed protection and chose their protectors from bigger ones who weren't quite as power hungry as others, hoping they'd retain their sovereign identity and not be swallowed up by the conqueror and disappear."

"Not much has changed in all those thousands of years, has it?" Bart commented wryly as he guided me through the square toward the church currently undergoing a good cleaning of its ancient stones.

The square filled quickly with tourists. Over four hundred people from our cruise alone were in town. That didn't include any of the other ships docked here. I assumed Croatians wouldn't enjoy being out in the rain, and they'd already seen these beautiful places, but I glanced around the square, hoping to find someone with an interest in jewels.

The hair on the back of my neck stood up, and I scanned the crowd again. I glimpsed a familiar figure disappearing into the church. "Bart, did you see him? Did you see the little man in the brown suit with the bald spot on the back of his head?"

My husband whirled around. "Are you sure you saw that particular guy? There are so many people here."

I nodded. "It's difficult to tell with the hordes of humanity milling about, but he's definitely a figure you don't easily forget. And I had the unmistakable impression we were being watched just before I saw him." We stood for a few minutes, ostensibly photographing the square, but never saw him again. I didn't like the idea that he was following us.

With others in our group, we filed through the beautiful Baroque church of St. Blasius, which gleamed with golden statues and golf leaf everywhere. I read portions of the guidebook aloud to Bart while we walked through the chapel. "Blasius is the patron saint of Dubrovnik, and the magnificent altars are built of colored marble. We should climb on the walls and call the Control Center. We ought to be able to find a quiet corner up there where we won't be overheard."

Bart turned to me with a puzzled expression. "Let me see that book." I handed it to him, open to the page where I'd been reading. He scanned the text. "It doesn't say anything about climbing on the walls and the Control Center."

"Of course not, silly."

"But you said it all in the same breath and the same tone."

"Simply thinking aloud while I was reading," I explained. "We don't know enough about our adversary. In fact, we really don't know anything. Who and what are we up against? Who heads this group? What are the motives, besides the treasure? How do they operate?"

Bart guided me toward the door without answering. We ran out into the rainy street, not bothering with the umbrella, crossed Luza Square, and entered the atrium of the Rector's Palace. He pointed up the stairs to the second floor, and as we approached the staircase, I was amazed to see two giant concrete hands protruding from the wall, gripping the handrailing that ran up the stairs.

"Innovative," Bart commented.

"Imaginative," I countered as we hurried up the ancient stone stairs and through one of the beautifully preserved rooms to the balcony overlooking the square. "And what are we doing up here?" I asked, enjoying the rain-swept view of the plaza below, bedecked with brightly colored umbrellas bobbing from one historic attraction to another.

"As we climbed the stairs to the church, I spotted this empty balcony. It's about the only unoccupied spot in town. You can call the Control Center and ask Jack what they discovered at their conference and what the underground told them. You're right. We need a lot more information than we now have."

I fished my compact from my purse and pretended to powder my nose while I contacted the Control Center half a world away.

Mom answered the phone on the first ring. "Hi, hon. I've been expecting your call. Where are you?"

"Dubrovnik, Croatia. A delightful, ancient, walled city glistening in the rain. It's time to unload all that information you didn't have time to tell me before. Who are we dealing with, besides some neo-Nazis? Who's their leader? Do they have anything to do with the ones we eradicated in Idaho? Details, please."

"How's your World War II history?" she asked. "Do you remember anything about Field Marshall Kesselring?"

"Grandmother told me a little. You tell me more." I snuggled against Bart, both for warmth and to enable him to hear the conversation.

"I'll make it short. Kesselring had a soft spot for historical treasures. He destroyed many valuable buildings in Florence but might have done worse had he been so inclined. He stripped the city of her treasures, adding to his already immense collection of priceless paintings. But he was in the middle of a war, so he had a vault built in one of the mines outside Florence where he stored his plunder. Your grandmother told you about the code he etched into Empress Elizabeth's topaz necklace?"

"Yes, but that's about all. She said you had the rest of the story."

"Kesselring's men didn't trust him to share, so he promised them they'd meet at the conclusion of the hostilities to divvy up the spoil. He gave each of them a topaz etched with a portion of the code and told them when they brought together all the stones, they might decipher it and discover the location of the mine, known only to him and the engineer who oversaw it."

"What about the men who built it?" I interrupted. "Didn't they know its location?"

"No. They were transported by train at night and blindfolded so they had no idea where they were. When the tunnels were completed, the soldiers who built them were sent to the front lines in the battle against the Allies. Their entire unit perished, so whatever knowledge they had died with them."

"Was that deliberate or an accident of war?" Bart asked.

"At this point, it's anybody's guess," Mom said. "Kesselring revealed the location of the treasure to his son, who was prevented from going near it because he was continually watched by the remaining German generals. Kesselring's son in turn passed the information on to his son, who recently died. On his deathbed, he called his son, Kesselring's great-grandson, to his side and gave him a small, brown velvet bag and a yellowed piece of paper. The attending doctor didn't see the contents, but he felt it contained topaz stones and a map revealing the location of the treasure."

"If he didn't actually see what was given, how can he be sure it was the topaz and a map?" Bart asked over my shoulder.

Mom laughed. "That's actually up for interpretation too. The doctor said he heard the dying man tell his son, 'It only belongs to the world if they know you have it.'"

"Well, if I were keyed in on the treasure, I guess I'd look at it that way too," I said. "Tell us about the great-grandson."

"Inherited his father and grandfather's love of art," Mom reported. "And the family art business as well as the art collection, which includes some priceless masterpieces."

"And political persuasions, as well?" Bart asked.

"Unfortunately, that may be the case. He's been seen with people on Interpol's 'keep-an-eye-on' list. Their activities are questionable, and they're in contact with members of the old SS now spawning new hate groups and terrorist cells."

"How about Kesselring's old generals?" Bart asked. "Have any of them survived?"

"We're researching that now," Mom said. "I'll let you know what we find. I assumed someone was keeping track of all of that and that those names and their status would be immediately available, but I can't put my finger on it right now."

"Do you have your finger on the name of this group exterminating the Freedom Fighters to collect the gemstones from Empress Elizabeth's necklace?" I asked.

"They call themselves Cell Seven, or simply The Sevens."

I gasped and turned to face Bart.

Chapter 7

Surprise flashed in his eyes. His jaw tightened and he clenched his fists. He'd heard of them too. At the moment, all I remembered about them was from an Interpol brief that filled me with repulsion and disgust at their inhumane tactics. I shuddered.

"Do you know where they're from?" I asked, when she didn't volunteer further information. "And do we know who their leader is?"

"No," Mom said tentatively. "David's working on that, and I expect he'll have information for us shortly."

Bart leaned over my shoulder. "What's their agenda?"

"Motivation appears to be the treasure, pure and simple, apparently to achieve their terrorist agenda, whatever that is. After all, this is no small treasure we're talking about." Mom paused. "This is billions worth of artifacts in today's dollars."

"Wow," I exclaimed. "I had no idea how extensive it was." From the expression on his face, apparently Bart didn't either.

"So you can see," Mom concluded, "there's a lot at stake."

"Including a lot of lives," Bart murmured grimly.

"As soon as I have any more information, I'll let you know."

"Wait, Mom. Before you hang up, I've read about this group in an Interpol brief just in the last few weeks. Run it through the computer and see if they've discovered anything more than they had then. It wasn't on the regular terrorist updates, so you might not have noticed it."

"Will do, hon. Be careful. This is a nasty group you're dealing with." Mom said a quick good-bye, and we disconnected.

The Rector's Palace and the antiquities of Dubrovnic no longer held any interest for us. We hurried into the streets, through the market at Gundulic Square where, even in the rain, people manned little stalls selling fruits and vegetables and tourist attractions under the statue of Ivan Gundulic, Dubrovnik's most famous poet.

My mind raced as Bart hurried us through the wet streets, past the shoemaker's shop with a tiny, glossy black child's chair sitting outside, past a jewelry store filled with exquisite coral jewelry at which I barely glanced. If this group was as ruthless as I remembered from the brief, we were in deep trouble.

The world of terrorism had changed drastically in the last few years. We used to deal with professionals who knew how to handle explosives, knew where to place them for greatest effect without huge numbers of civilian casualties. Now they didn't care about human life, sending suicide bombers to public places and buses to slaughter the highest number of innocent bystanders possible. But amateurs could be far more dangerous than professionals, and radicals just upped the ante considerably. Frightening. No, terrifying.

Bart paused under the stone arch of the Pile Gate and glanced back at the old city, giving me time to catch my breath. A young boy pointed at the water gushing under the wooden drawbridge that was suspended by huge iron chains. I glanced over the stone railing at the moat below filled with rocks and boulders. Water dashed against them in a white froth, then boiled and churned down the ravine to the bay. No one would survive a fall into that. I shivered at the thought. Everything had taken on sinister overtones now that we had some idea of our adversaries.

"I expected our contacts to find us before now," I noted as Bart resumed his rush to leave the city.

"Yeah," was his only reply.

"Maybe we're not going to get a stone here."

Bart silently pressed toward the exit and the bus, dragging me along with his arm looped through mine so I couldn't fall behind.

"They don't have much longer to find us, and we have certainly been obvious, appearing in all the tourist places," I said, breathless from our race through the city. "And we diligently stayed with our company today."

Still no response as we left the old city and approached the bus stop. Our group began gathering near the bus. Laura and Mark emerged from a little bakery, and Sara and Charlotte crossed the street with a gelato that appealed to me, even in the chilly rain. The rest of the gang filtered from various locations, slowly filling the bus. Bart was strangely silent, so I let him do his thing while I talked to Sara and Charlotte.

Suddenly it dawned on me what silenced Bart. I sat beside him, put my hands on his face and turned it directly into mine. "Forget it, Charlie. You are *not* sending me home. I'm going to finish this gig right by your side every step of the way."

He took my hands from his face, held them in his and shook his head. "Not now that we know who we're dealing with. I won't subject you and Alexandra to those crazed fanatics. They're too dangerous, too unpredictable."

Jed and Dorothy, a retired couple of golf enthusiasts boarded the bus and stopped to compare notes on what we'd seen. That stopped Bart's intense insistence—for the moment. I knew it wouldn't be the end of the conversation, but it was the end of the subject as far as I was concerned.

When the bus reached the ship, my single-minded husband bee-lined for the gangplank. I didn't want to board yet. I pulled him aside and said quietly, "Wait. Let's give them one last opportunity to deliver the stone, if there's one here."

"I want you back on the ship, princess. It's safer there than out here in the open."

"For heaven's sake, Bart, we've already had this conversation. You can't shield me from life. I have to live it, and you and I have a job to do."

Bart put his hands on his hips and leaned forward, his nose almost touching mine. "But you don't have to put Alexandra in constant danger. *I* can stay here—they have pictures of both of us. If someone's going to pass a jewel, they can give it to me."

"And someone might blow up the ship while I'm on it. We're in a dangerous business, love of my life. We didn't come into it blindly. Come on. I want to check out those beautiful linens and scarves."

At the foot of the gangplank, half a dozen kiosks were positioned perfectly to catch passengers coming or going or to give those who hadn't gone ashore an opportunity to purchase souvenirs from

Dubrovnik. It also gave those who hadn't found exactly what they wanted in town one last chance to shop.

Bart hovered over me like a bodyguard, acting more paranoid than I'd ever seen him. I finally ignored him and struck up a conversation with a friendly Croatian who was tall, dark, good-looking, and spoke excellent English. He stood beside his small covered kiosk watching our tour group get off the bus and wander toward the ship. He asked if we were from America, and when I said yes, he became excited.

"Would you send me a postcard from America?"

"Of course."

"Where are you from?" he asked, pulling a pencil and small notebook from his pocket and writing as he spoke.

"California," Bart responded, surprising me by getting involved in this exchange.

"Ahh, I yearn to go there someday. It is everyone's dream to see California. A land of promise." He handed me the little piece of paper he tore from the notebook "Here is my address. I am Milo." I glanced at the paper as I took it. "I would be so happy to receive your card." He turned to the kiosk. "Stepan, would you like to say hello to these nice people from America?"

A small boy with a shock of black hair falling over his dark eyes peeked around the corner, and when I smiled at him and bent down, he came slowly, shyly toward me, hands stuffed in his pockets, stopping short of arm's reach.

"Hello, Stepan. I'm Allison. How old are you?"

He glanced up at his father who said something to his son that I didn't understand, then nodded his head. Stepan pulled his left hand from his pocket and held up three fingers.

"Three years old! What a big boy."

Stepan said something to his father, who smiled and translated for us. "He wants to know how old you are."

I laughed, held up all ten fingers, flashed them twice, and then held up one hand. "Can he count that high?" I asked.

"Not yet, but soon," Milo said with pride in his young son. "Stepan, will you shake hands with the pretty lady?"

Stepan pulled his right hand from the pocket of his little jeans and took a step forward, looking up at his father, who nodded again.

He held out a little fist, and when I stuck my hand forward to shake his, he thrust something in my hand, then turned and ran back behind the counter of the kiosk. I glanced quickly up at Milo.

"May your journey be successful, granddaughter of Mama Karillides," Milo said softly. "My father said she is a noble lady."

His eyes held mine as I stood. I didn't examine the lump Stepan had given me, slipping the item into my pocket and hoping no one had seen the exchange. I started to answer, but other tourists approached the kiosk at that moment, so I flashed the piece of paper with Milo's address and told him I'd send a postcard when we returned home. Bart took my elbow, and we moved away from the cluster of people gathering around the vendors as the last buses dropped off travelers from the tour.

"Did I just see a successful drop?" he whispered as we walked toward the gangplank.

"I hope so. I haven't dared to look at what Stepan palmed me, just in case anyone was watching from the ship. It's hard, but it's wrapped so I can't tell what the shape is."

As we headed up the gangplank, some of our other cruise members joined us. Two couples were talking about being stalked. Diane and Richard said they became suspicious in the Rector's Palace when they saw the same man they'd seen in the church just before that watching them. He didn't appear to be with a group, nor did he seem interested in the sights. He just leaned against a wall and watched people.

Ann and Marilyn joined the conversation as we reached the top. They'd had a creepy feeling as they left the church but thought it was someone checking them out to snatch their purses. They were accustomed to being targeted since they traveled without male companions, so they just held tighter to their purses and went on with the tour.

Sara and Charlotte arrived in time to hear Marilyn's comment. Charlotte laughed, "Well, we *know* we were being watched. A good-looking young man followed us everywhere we went."

"But Sara is so beautiful, she'll be watched wherever she goes, by every man who has blood coursing through his veins," I said, putting my arm around Sara. They all laughed as Sara blushed bright red.

"I'm sure we were followed," Diane said. "Bruce insisted I'd been reading too many mysteries and that he wasn't following us at all, but each place we went, we saw this funny little man. When we went into a store, he was waiting when we came out. We went into the church and found him standing in the rain at the exit. He even followed us into the Bishop's Palace."

Bruce chimed in. "So did all the rest of these people on the tour."

I glanced at Bart, then turned to Diane, a cute little blonde with a sense of humor and a ready laugh. "Describe him."

"He wore a baggy, brown suit which looked like he'd slept in it. He was bald with a fringe of graying hair around the back of his head, and he carried a carved cane."

"I'm an enthusiast of spy novels too," Bart said. "I imagine any spy worth his salt knows you have to be invisible if you're following people. Since he sounds like a pretty noticeable character, I'd be surprised if it was more than just coincidence, unless he was a spotter for pickpockets. The baggy, brown suit would certainly call attention to him, as that isn't a fashion item these days, even for older Europeans. I think his unique hairstyle and the cane would be something people would readily notice. Don't you think a professional would probably wear a hat and use an umbrella instead of a unique walking stick or cane? At least, according to most of the books I've read."

Diane laughed. "You're right. I think I let my imagination get a little carried away."

My husband linked his arm through mine as a signal we should leave, and we excused ourselves. As soon as we were out of earshot of the group, I exclaimed, "Bart, that's the man! That's the one I saw in the hall who marked the crosses on the doors in the hotel. He's the one I saw on the dock in Venice and just now in the square."

Bart nodded. "I recognized your description of him."

We went directly to our little veranda which we now considered our private balcony on the very back of the ship—feeling a reasonable amount of security there.

"Okay, let's see what little Stepan gave you," Bart said, checking to make sure no one approached from the balcony below.

We settled in the plastic patio chairs, and I produced an object from my pocket smaller than a ping-pong ball, wrapped completely in masking tape. With trembling fingers, I peeled off layer after layer, until white tissue paper appeared. Sure enough, it was a smoky topaz, identical to the one Grandmother gave Mom, which I'd locked in the safe on the estate, and a triplet to the ones we'd received in Verona and Venice. I dropped it in the zipper pocket of my purse.

"Let's get that topaz in your waist safe with the others," Bart said, pulling me to my feet. "Wish we had some place to deposit these so you didn't have to carry them around with you."

"You think the ship's safe wouldn't be a good place?" I asked, suddenly shivering with cold. "Oh, I'm freezing. I just got a chill."

Bart hustled me back inside the Flamenco Lounge. "How about a cup of hot chocolate to warm you up from the inside? Then we'll go back to our cabin and you can put your feet up, snuggle under a blanket, and maybe even have a bit of a nap while I do some internet research."

"Sounds wonderful." We descended to deck eleven and the Chez Claude Grill where we made hot chocolate and took it back to our cabin. "What are you looking for on the internet?"

"Thought I'd see what I can find out about the Kesselring family, past and present. And if I'm lucky, I'll contact Interpol's research division for a couple of items I'm curious about."

I blew on my chocolate to cool it while Bart keyed our door. "If you're lucky?"

He opened the door and stepped aside for me to enter. "The Business Center's usually pretty busy, and I don't know how long I can commandeer a computer or if I can even get one right now. Also, I don't know how much info Interpol will release to an unprotected site."

"Mmm. Hadn't thought of that. You could take the compact up by the miniature golf and contact someone. That's usually a pretty quiet area."

Bart laughed. "I don't think I want to be seen talking into a gold compact, thank you. I'll take my chances with the computers. You relax, and when I get back, we'll grab a bite to eat." He tossed the TV remote control on my bed and stepped back into the hall. I shut the door behind him and leaned against it, thinking about Milo and Stepan as I savored the last of my hot chocolate. Interesting method of delivering the topaz. Who would suspect a three year old of carrying the valuable stone in his little jeans pocket?

I didn't relish the idea of carrying priceless pieces of a multi-billion-dollar puzzle with me any longer than necessary, especially now that we knew the nature of our adversaries. If they were so blatantly watching the tour, what would prevent them from accosting any of us? I opened the padded journal concealing my gun and little spy tools.

Pressing the three hidden clasps simultaneously, I opened the back cover of the journal, where the tools nestled in depressions made especially for them. I removed a couple and fit the three jewels in their places. I transferred the little tools to my makeup bag with tweezers, eyebrow pencil, mascara, and lipstick. They seemed right at home. Well, maybe that was a stretch, but at least they didn't look out of place. And I could lie down without lumps under me.

Then I tucked the journal under my pillow, slipped off my shoes, and snuggled under the blanket; *just for a few minutes,* I promised myself. Just to get thoroughly warm and rest my tired legs. We'd walked a lot this morning, probably enough to make my exercise-happy doctor pleased with my diligence.

I turned off the lights, closed my eyes, and was surrendering to warm oblivion when I heard a sound at our door.

Chapter 8

Had Bart forgotten something? Maybe the computer stations were filled and he couldn't get on the internet. I raised my head off the pillow and peered over the covers, but the sound ceased. Raphael had probably brought his cart down the hall to man his station dispensing passenger needs, which he located right outside our door.

Sinking back into my pillow, I pulled the covers over my head to block out any other noise and concentrated on the gentle movement of the ship as we left Dubrovnik for Bari, Italy. I'd let it rock me to sleep.

Somewhere between being serenaded by a marvelous Italian tenor resembling Andrea Bocceli in a romantic gondola ride in Venice and the frightening repeat attack of the tall carnival trio in their long velvet and gold costumes, I awoke to noises near my head. Bart must be trying to be quiet, but he wasn't succeeding. All the little rustlings were maddening, and I was about to throw off the covers and give up when I opened my eyes and realized it was still dark in the room. Bart hadn't turned on the light. No wonder he was making so much noise. He couldn't see his hand in front of his face.

Then I froze. Whoever was in the room had a flashlight. He also wore a distinctive, overpowering cologne, a scent both heavy and smothering. And making my nose twitch. I tried to stifle the sneeze, but it came anyway. One, then two, three, four in a row.

I sat up and reached for the light on the nightstand. Now thoroughly awake, I decided I must have been dreaming. No one had intruded on my nap. I was alone in our cabin.

Wrong! I wasn't alone! At least, until he opened the door and fled down the hall. Too surprised to scream, I untangled myself from the blanket, jumped out of bed, and ran after him in my stocking feet. As he rounded the corner to the stairs, I caught a glimpse of a slender figure with dark hair in a navy turtleneck shirt, khaki pants, and athletic shoes.

Realizing it was useless to attempt to catch him, I turned back to my cabin as Raphael emerged from the room next to ours.

"Raphael, how would someone get into my room without a key?"

Raphael looked puzzled. "Signora, you must have a key to open the door."

I stood directly in front of him and stared straight up into his dark eyes. "And who has a key to my room besides me, my husband, and you?"

He seemed disconcerted. Or was it uneasy? Or guilty, maybe? "I don't understand your question," he stammered.

"Then I'll tell you clearly what I'm getting at. Someone came through that locked door, was searching my room with a flashlight, and woke me up. When I sneezed, he ran away. I want to know how he got into my room. Did you let him in? Did he pay you to open the door, or did he have his own key?"

The speechless young man stood with his mouth agape.

"I'm waiting for an answer, Raphael. Explain, please, how someone opened that locked door when my key is right here and my husband has his key in his wallet. I assume you have yours?"

Raphael reached into his pocket and produced a card key that looked much like mine. "This is the master key for the cabins under my care. I never leave it on the cart. It is always in my pocket. I do not know how anyone entered your cabin without a key. Maybe the door was ajar? Did you shut it tight?"

He was grasping at straws, looking everywhere but in my angry eyes.

"Yes, I shut it tight. Do we need to take this to the captain? I don't want to be murdered in my sleep, nor do I want to find a stranger in my room—ever again! You are so lucky my husband isn't here right now."

"And if your husband was here, what would he do?" Bart's voice echoed down the hall. I whirled to see him striding toward us, a scowl across his handsome face.

"He would probably take this young man, string him up by his thumbs, pull his toenails out, and stick needles in him all over until he confessed how someone entered my room without a key."

Bart stopped short two feet from me. "Someone was in your room? When you were in there?" He glanced from me to Raphael and back again. "Are you okay? What happened?"

"Noises next to the bed woke me. I thought you'd come back and were trying to find something in the dark. Then I smelled this heavy, nauseous cologne and sneezed. It frightened him away. I started to chase him down the hall but he had a long head start by the time I got untangled from the blanket."

Bart turned his attention to Raphael. "And where were you all this time?"

"In the room next to yours, sir."

"So how did someone gain access to our room without a key?" Bart stepped to my side and put his arm around my waist. "I think that was the question the lady asked, wasn't it?"

"Yes, sir, but I don't know, sir," Raphael stammered. "I did not let him in, and he didn't use my key."

Bart didn't relent. "Then where would he get a key?" he pressed.

Beads of perspiration appeared on Raphael's forehead. "I don't know, sir. No one is allowed access to passenger rooms except the housekeepers and the steward."

"Now we're getting somewhere. Do the housekeepers have individual keys to rooms, or do they have a master key like yours, which opens all the rooms they clean?"

Bart's interrogation was interrupted by passengers returning to their rooms at the end of the hall. We pressed against the wall to let them pass through the narrow corridor. As Bart resumed questioning, Raphael's cell phone rang.

"Excuse me, please." He turned away to answer, but the caller's excited voice was clearly audible, and even with Raphael's back to us, we overheard the whole conversation.

"Raphael, someone has been breaking into passengers' rooms. I have three rooms already with very irate people who discovered their belongings have been disturbed. Watch your rooms carefully. They accused me of going through their things. You know I would never do that, but my innocence is hard to prove."

"Ricardo, do you know who did it?" Raphael dropped his voice slightly. "I also have had at least one room entered while a woman slept. She was badly frightened."

"No, I don't, but I intend to find out. I can't afford to lose my tips. More than that, I can't afford to lose my job."

"Me too. Later, Ricardo." Raphael turned to face us, his expression one of intense relief.

"Mr. Allan, I'll try to find out who was in your room and how they got in. My friend on the other end of the ship just had the same problem. We'll watch carefully and tell the other stewards. You must understand, we had nothing to do with this, and we'll lose our jobs if this continues."

We had to believe him. The phone call couldn't have been staged. While Bart continued talking to Raphael, I returned to our cabin and attempted to determine why the man had been there.

The noises had been near my head, so he had to have been searching for something on the nightstand between the beds. I hadn't left anything on top. I opened the drawer to see what I might have left inside.

Then I had a thought. We'd dismantled the listening device. Maybe they'd tried to replace it. I felt up the lamp under the shade and retrieved the tiny metal object no bigger than a watch battery. Raphael had his back to the open door, so he hadn't seen me.

"Oh," I cried out, then hurried into the hall. As Bart and Raphael turned to discover my problem, I held out the shiny little circle. "I think I just broke something off the lamp when I tried to turn it on. I'm sorry, Raphael. Maybe you can fix it." I dropped it into his outstretched hand and winked at Bart, who immediately took up the charade.

"May I see that?" he asked. Raphael surrendered it to my husband, who examined it, then pronounced with an authoritative air, "This isn't part of the lamp. This is a listening device. A bug. Someone planted a bug in our cabin to listen to our conversations."

I looked at it closely. "Are you sure?"

"Yeah, I just watched a documentary on spies the other night. This is a new breed of bugs." He turned to Raphael. "Does the ship make a practice of spying on their passengers?"

Raphael looked stunned. "Of course not, sir."

"Then how do you explain this?"

He reached the obvious conclusion. "That man in your cabin must have placed it there."

"Why would anyone want to bug our cabin?" I asked innocently.

Then another thought occurred to Raphael. "Will you show me where you found this?" he asked, his voice filled with excitement and discovery.

We crowded into the little cabin, and I ran my fingers up the stem of the lamp. "Right here." Raphael crouched to see, then called his friend on his cell phone.

"Ricardo, check the cabins that have been broken into. On the bedside lamp up near the bulb, feel for a listening device—it's like a tiny, round battery. I think the person who startled my passenger just placed it there." He looked at Bart, then at me while he waited for Ricardo's answer.

"You're right! I just found one in the first cabin. Let me check the other two." In a matter of minutes, he reported, "All three of the rooms had one. Now what do we do? Who put them there?"

Raphael glanced at Bart, a question in his eyes.

"Why don't you check all the rooms?" Bart said quietly. "This is illegal, and if someone finds out their room was bugged, they'll sue the ship's line for breach of privacy. You could all lose your jobs. Have all the stewards check the lamps in all their rooms, and if they find any more of these, have them bring them to you. Tell them to write the room numbers where each bug is found. That's important. When they bring you the bugs, you can give them to me, and I'll dispose of them. The captain won't need to know and your jobs should be safe."

Raphael nodded and passed Bart's instructions on to Ricardo. "Do you want me to check all of my rooms now?" he asked Bart when he hung up.

"Yes. If only a few rooms have them, we'll see if we can determine who's planting them by who received them. Do you know which passengers are together on a tour?"

"Yes, sir."

"Good," Bart said. We'll need to have that information. We're going to grab a bite of lunch, but we'll be back here in thirty minutes. Will you be here?"

"Yes, sir. I'll be waiting for you right here." Raphael appeared tremendously relieved as he headed into the room next door.

I slipped into my shoes, scooped my purse off the bed, and turned to leave when I remembered I no longer carried the topaz in my waist safe. I snatched the journal from under my pillow, stuffed it inside my leather bag, and hurried with Bart along the narrow passage to the stairs. He stopped at the foot of the empty staircase, held my hands against his chest, and gazed down at me with deep concern.

"Okay, princess, I want the whole story, from the time I left you alone in our room to take a nap until I came down the hall." He started to say something else, but I knew what was coming and interrupted before he continued.

"I know what you're going to say. You can't leave me alone for a minute without me finding trouble. As usual, I didn't find it. It found me. I thought you'd come back for something and didn't want to wake me and were fumbling in the dark. You weren't being very quiet, and I was going to tell you to turn on the light when I opened my eyes and realized someone had a flashlight next to my bed. Then I smelled his aftershave. It was horrible—heavy, smothering. And it made me sneeze. That frightened him away. I don't know whether he didn't realize I was there or if he did and the sneeze startled him. He ran. I got tangled in the blanket and couldn't get out the door fast enough to catch him."

"That's it? You don't remember anything else?" Bart asked, trying to jog my memory.

"Yes, he had dark hair, wore a navy turtleneck, khakis, athletic shoes, was young, slender, and you promised me lunch."

Bart laughed and pulled me up the stairs. "I did, and I'll feed you right now. Big lunch or a sandwich?"

"Considering it's nearly three o'clock, probably something light just to tide me over until dinner. I wish we didn't eat so late at night. I'm not used to dinner at seven in the evening." I scanned the faces that passed us on the stairs, watching for someone who fit the description of the intruder in my cabin. Did he know who I was? Would he recognize me? What was he doing in there?

"Let's go through the buffet in La Brasserie," Bart suggested. "I'm thinking a bowl of hot soup would be a good thing to take the chill off this drizzly day."

I glanced up at my husband. His tone sounded so distracted, I wondered where his mind really was. He, too, scanned the faces of each person we encountered.

Fortunately, the cafeteria wasn't filled to capacity at this hour, and we found a table in a corner away from listening ears so we might converse freely.

"What do you think?" I asked, buttering my French roll. "Were they simply replacing the bug or looking for something?"

Elbows on the table, Bart leaned his chin on his fists and gazed over the top of his steaming minestrone. "Those are only the first of a multitude of questions this poses. Who was actually in the cabin? Petty thieves looking for jewelry or cash? Our adversaries seeking something more substantial?"

He broke off a chunk of his French roll, dipped it in the broth of his soup, and then looked quickly up at me. "You do have them with you, don't you? I just realized that I didn't feel your waist safe when I put my arm around you."

"Three of them were getting a bit bulky, especially when I leaned back against a chair. We'll need another hiding place as we collect more."

Bart started up out of his chair. "Did you leave them in the room?"

"No, silly. I wasn't born yesterday. I stashed them in my journal. I have the journal and the 'pretties' right here in my purse." I held up the bag I cradled in my lap so no one could walk by my chair, snatch it, and run.

Visibly relieved, Bart resumed dipping his French roll in his soup broth. "If it turns out passengers in our particular tour are the ones who had their rooms bugged, we can pretty well determine it was Cell Seven and they're after the stones." He scooped the soggy bread with his spoon and smiled as he savored the mouthful.

"And if there's a bug in every room?" I asked, spreading some avocado on my bread. "What will that tell us, besides someone with a lot of money and much at stake is behind this?"

"We need more information." Bart frowned. "We need better communication with the Control Center than we have right now. This is as bad as being out in the jungle. Ship-to-shore phones aren't safe to use for security purposes. The computers are constantly busy with people checking their e-mail. And—"

"And we can go up to our balcony to call the Control Center as soon as you finish your soup." As I sliced a pineapple ring into bite-sized pieces, I had a thought. "I hope they've planned for someone along our way to take the stones we've gathered. I'm getting more and more uncomfortable with the idea of carrying these all over Italy and Greece. Didn't Mom say they were bringing Anastasia into this? Someone ought to be free enough to meet us at one of our stops and take the jewels for safe-keeping."

"Good thinking, princess. I didn't relish the idea of babysitting a handful of topaz *before* I found out the identity of our adversary. Now that we know who's after them, it's mandatory we unload them a couple of times in the next two weeks."

I shuddered thinking of the cruelty and inhumane actions of Cell Seven that I'd read about in the bulletin. If I'd known before we came who we'd be fighting, would I have been so anxious to embark upon this adventure?

"Are we going up or down first?" I asked.

Bart looked up from his last spoonful of minestrone. "Up or down?"

"Down to see what Raphael discovered, or up to the balcony to call the Control Center?"

"Mmm." He nodded. "We'd better go down so Raphael won't have to wait on us and can get back to his duties." Bart tossed his napkin on the table and stretched.

"You don't suppose he's involved in any way, do you?" I pushed back my chair and stood. "If he's the one who furnished the key to the intruder in my room, we can't tip our hand by working with him on this."

As Bart pushed the door open, we were hit by a rush of cold, moist air. I drew my sweater closer around me, and we hurried to the stairs and warmth of the inner ship. Inside the ship, the atmosphere always seemed cheerful and sunny because of the constant bright lights.

"I had the feeling he was as surprised to find that someone had been in your room as he was at the discovery of the listening device,"

Bart said slowly. "I don't think he's involved in any way, but he doesn't need to know about Anastasia. I'm hoping he's going to be an ally. By the way, I didn't tell you, but I thought that little act of yours—breaking the lamp—was brilliant. Good job, Watson."

"Thank you kindly, Holmes. You handled the rest with equal brilliance."

Raphael waited beside his cart outside our room, and when he saw us enter the corridor from the stairs, he hurried to meet us. "I found one in each of these rooms." He thrust a little piece of paper at Bart.

Bart glanced at the notations, then asked "And what about Ricardo? How many did he find?"

"He brought me four, and Demetrius found two in his cabins. The cabin numbers are all there. That makes nine altogether."

"And do any of these people have a common denominator? Are they all on the same tour or something?" Bart asked, though I knew he already suspected the answer.

"Yes," Raphael reported with excitement. "These people are on the same Fun for Less cruise you're on."

"Mmm," Bart said, sounding thoughtful. "I'll have to see which of the people on our tour have these cabins and see if I can find out why just these people were singled out. Thanks so much for your help, Raphael. I've always enjoyed reading a good mystery, and now we have one we can solve. As soon as I figure this out, I'll probably need your cooperation again."

"I will be most happy to be of any assistance, sir. I love my job and don't want to lose it over this." Raphael sounded sincerely grateful, as well as innocent.

As we turned to go back up on deck, I stopped. "What if, when the people who planted these don't hear anything, they come back to do it again? Should the stewards check each day for them?" I looked from Bart to Raphael. "And what if they were just getting started? What if these were the first ones and there will be more in other cabins? Maybe the steward should start checking every room, every day."

"I will tell them." Raphael nodded enthusiastically. "Then I will report to you each evening what we've discovered. Thank you for suggesting these things so we don't have to go to ship's security. I'm afraid they would use this as an excuse to fire us and replace us with their friends. These jobs are very sought after, and everyone envies us."

"You're doing a good job, Raphael. Thank you," Bart said. "I appreciate your help. And tell the other stewards too."

Remembering these young men expected, and needed, the tips from the passengers, I suggested, "I think this will be a good scenario for the book I'm writing. It should be worth about $100 to each one of you if you keep this from the other passengers and just among us and the other stewards. And if you hear anything from the house-keeping staff that sounds like it fits in, please let me know about that too. I write mysteries, and I'm always searching for material for my books." I didn't look at Bart when I made the offer, but Raphael was so excited, I thought he'd bust his buttons.

We left the steward calling Ricardo on his cell phone to report the reward money and further instructions. I think he was thoroughly enjoying his new role.

"Aren't you being a little free with Anastasia's money?" Bart laughed as we walked up the stairs for the umpteenth time today.

"I just thought of it before you did. That's your modus operandi. Besides, it won't hurt to perpetuate the rumor that I'm writing a mystery and enlisting the assistance of various people to do it. Just makes it all the more believable when we're asking for this help."

I was happy to sit in a deserted corner of the Flamenco Lounge instead of on our balcony to make the phone call to the Control Center. Today's weather wasn't conducive to being comfortable outside, and while Bart watched line-dancing lessons, I powdered my nose with the gold compact and talked with Mom.

"Has David discovered anything new?" I asked.

"He said he'd have his report to me later today. Did you connect with the Dubrovnik contact?"

I laughed. "Do you know who the contact was?"

"No, I don't know who any of them are or their plans for transfer-ring the stones. Why?" Mom asked.

"A darling little three year old handed me the topaz."

"You're kidding," Mom exclaimed. "That certainly was innova-tive. Who were your other contacts?"

"An old woman on the stairs at Juliet's house in Verona and an old man in St. Mark's Square selling bird seed. That one involved two people—one who gave me a book with the meeting time and place, and the old man who gave me the stone. And speaking of receiving the jewels, is anyone going to come and gather them up or are we supposed to cart these invaluable puzzle pieces all over Italy and Greece for the next two weeks?"

"I'll see who's available. Maybe Else can meet you and relieve you of them. Let me check your itinerary." Mom was silent for a minute, and I watched the instructor showing a middle-aged woman in shorts and sandals a tricky little step, over and over.

I leaned over to Bart. "She wouldn't have a problem with that if she had decent shoes on. Or boots. Those dances were made for boots!"

"Want to try when you get off the phone?" he challenged me with a smile.

"Are you intimating I can't?" I asked. "I'm not so big and clumsy yet that I couldn't do it. But in another two months, I won't guarantee anything."

Mom came back on the phone. "Someone will meet you just before you board the ship after your stop at Corfu. I think your tour goes to the Achilles Palace and to Kanoni." Mom stopped. "Remember Kanoni, Alli?"

"How could I forget?" I laughed. "I found my missing mother in a canoe at midnight at the monastery on Mouse Island. I was *so* glad it was you who came at me out of the darkness and not the guys who were after you. Wow, what a night that was. We barely made it to the airplane and got airborne before they arrived with guns blazing. You've led a pretty incredible life, Mom."

"You haven't done so badly yourself, hon. Anyway, your next stop is the island of Corfu, where you should receive another jewel. Someone in Anastasia will be at the ship as you board to relieve you of the stones. Then I won't worry quite so much about you. And speaking of that, how are you feeling? Any motion sickness on the ship or anything? Are you getting enough rest? And exercise? You're not eating too much rich food, are you?"

"Enough already. You sound just like a prospective grandmother. I'm fine. We're enjoying this little vacation. So far. Might even do some line dancing. Too cold for swimming, though. Will you call me as soon as David gets the information we asked for? On second thought, I'll call you just before we go to bed."

"I'll contact David and inform him we need the info as soon as possible. Oh, wait a minute. Something's coming on the check-in computer. Hang on, just in case it's for you."

Once again, Mom's end of the conversation ceased. The line-dancing lessons were finished, and a band began setting up. Country western. Big black cowboy hats. Guitars. A big bass. How did they get all that gear onboard? I had a hard enough time with just my small amount of luggage.

Mom came back online, her voice just a whisper. "Alli, there's been terrorist activity at Bari. A huge explosion. Dozens of people killed and hundreds wounded. One of our local agents is in danger and has to get out tonight. Your ship is scheduled to dock about eight thirty to take on passengers. We're arranging to get her onboard as part of the crew. Watch for her. She'll need your help."

"Who is she? What does she look like?" No answer. "Mom, how will I know her?"

My mother was silent for a long moment. "Bart will know her. I have to go, hon. Need to see what else I can discover about this catastrophe." She hung up.

I stared at the silent compact. *Bart would know her?*

Chapter 9

"Bad news, princess?" Bart asked, leaning forward. The band started playing, and our quiet alcove wasn't quiet anymore. The music was good, just too loud for conversation. We stepped outside the Flamenco Lounge to the empty Teen Club, where we'd first overheard the dire news the opposition knew about the stones being given to Americans on tour.

I leaned against the partition separating the lounge from the club and explained, "Mom said there's been terrorist-caused explosions in Bari, many casualties and injuries, and one of the local agents has to escape tonight. The ship's scheduled to pick up passengers, and they're getting her onboard as a member of the crew. We're supposed to watch for her and help her. When I asked how we'd know her, she said *you'd* know her. Do you have any idea who Mom's talking about?"

Bart groaned and rolled his eyes. "It has to be Gabriella, the resident Interpol agent in Bari. I worked with her years ago. In fact, remember Emile, the Frenchman with me in the Tibetan prison, who taught me the gospel? Gabriella's his sister. Unfortunately, unlike Emile, she's not interested in what benefits mankind, only what benefits Gabi."

"She's not a member of the Church?"

Bart shook his head. "No. In fact, she views anyone with deep religious convictions as weak and gullible. She's an avowed atheist. Gabi blames Emile's death on his compassionate nature. He was captured while helping an injured agent instead of just turning and running to save his own neck. Emile died in prison from his beatings.

The monks reached me before I died, spirited me into Nepal, and nursed me back to health."

I nodded. Just thinking of Bart's ordeal, which left deep scars crisscrossing his back from whippings by the Red Chinese, made me shudder.

"She's probably never forgiven me for surviving when her brother didn't." Bart pulled one of the chairs from the table and straddled it, leaning his arms on the back with a sigh. "But there's something about her that's beguiling. She makes you want to do whatever you can to help make up for her hard life, even though she's no spring chicken anymore. Both her parents were killed, and Emile was all the family she had left."

"So how are *we* supposed to help her?"

Bart shrugged. "Guess we'll just have to wait and see what she needs."

"Is she married?" I wanted to know everything about this third party who'd be joining us, which probably meant I wouldn't have my husband's full attention anymore. I thoroughly enjoyed working with him without the usual distractions.

"Not the last time I heard, but it's been over three years since I've had any contact with her, so anything's possible. She is a very attractive woman, so if she isn't married, I'd have to think it would be by her own choice."

"Mmm." A very attractive woman who needed our help. That sounded to me like a dark cloud on my sunny horizon.

Bart stood and put the chair in place at the table. "Mmm? What does that mean?"

I laughed. "I'll let you know after I meet the mysterious, beautiful Gabriella." I glanced at my watch. "Now I think we'd better get ready for Marvin Goldstein's five thirty concert. Since we'll be going directly from there to dinner, I need to dress now."

The concert was wonderful. Marvin's ability to improvise at the keyboard amazed me, plus he had a unique sense of humor.

Each course of our dinner tasted better than the last. I had a delectable onion tart with goat cheese for an appetizer, then a savory bowl of cream of onion soup, green salad drizzled with tart lemon dressing, frog legs surrounded by tender vegetables and rice, assorted cheeses served with nuts, and for dessert, a caramelized pear Napoleon.

"If I keep eating like this, you'll have to roll me off the ship when we get back to Italy," I laughed. "I won't even be able to waddle down the gang plank."

Charlotte and Sara assured me I wouldn't be the only one, but Vivian didn't think we'd have a problem, because during the day on our tours, we'd be walking it off. I truly hoped so.

Bart kept close watch on the time, and the minute I finished dessert, he signaled we needed to leave. We excused ourselves while everyone else lingered over dessert and conversation, and headed for the deck to watch passengers boarding from Bari.

Fortunately, we'd sailed out of the storm. The weather was warm with stars twinkling overhead and only a slight breeze from offshore. I leaned over the railing, watching the few passengers assembled on the dock under the lights preparing to board ship. I didn't see anyone who fit the description of Gabriella.

As passengers were finally invited to board, a taxi drove up to the dock. The driver got out, pulled a wheelchair from the trunk, and helped an old woman who walked with a pronounced limp into the chair. She wore a crocheted shawl, a long dark dress, and a wide-brimmed, felt slouch hat, and she clutched a tapestry valise tightly against her like it contained every last valuable she owned in the world.

Everyone boarded but the old woman, who appeared to be watching for someone to come. Finally, at the last moment, the crew member at the foot of the gangplank wheeled her chair aboard the ship. The ship moved slowly from the dock and out to sea.

We hurried to the lobby where passengers gathered, to see if we'd missed Gabriella. I watched the old woman slouched in the wheelchair. Something about her intrigued me. As if she sensed she was being watched, she tilted her head to peer out from under the brim of her chocolate brown hat and stared back at me.

When she saw Bart standing beside me, her back straightened, and she went rigid. She wheeled slowly in a circle, examining the people in the lobby before she left the half dozen passengers waiting for room assignments and wheeled toward us. I knew before she stopped in front of Bart that this had to be Gabriella.

"Would you be so kind as to wait in that line for me and get my room key?" she croaked in an old woman's throaty voice.

I glanced up at Bart, but I didn't move to do her bidding.

She repeated her request, although, actually, this time it was more of a demand. "You." She pointed a finger up at me and then waved to the short line of people being given keys. "Stand over there and get my room key for me."

"Oh, I'm sorry. Are you speaking to me?" I feigned surprise. "But, of course, I'd be happy to help you." I grabbed hold of the wheelchair and whirled her back toward the purser, who, by this time, had finished with the other passengers and turned to find his last arrival. We were the only ones remaining in the lobby.

The woman flung the hat off, swung the tapestry valise around at me, jumped out of the chair, and whipped the brown dress off over her head. Gabriella stood, laughing, dressed in a long, form-fitting, red-sequined dress. She pulled the pins from her bun, and straight black hair tumbled down her back. Then she turned to Bart and slinked across the floor toward him.

"Why, Bartholomew Allan. Don't tell me you don't recognize me. I'll never forget what we've meant to each other." She put both hands on his chest and slowly moved them up to pull his head down to kiss her.

Bart seemed stunned at Gabriella's brazen approach, frozen with inaction. Then he stepped away from her touch just as I tossed the valise at her, catching her right behind her knees. They buckled, and she clutched at Bart to keep from falling. Score one for me. I'd prevented her from kissing my husband. For the time being.

"Hello, Gabriella. I'm Allison. *Mrs.* Bartholomew Allan." I grabbed her hand from Bart's sleeve and shook it vigorously. "I'm so happy to meet you. I hear you've just had a narrow escape from Bari. I understand clearly why Mom said your life was in danger. You'll have to remain vigilant on the ship, because you may not have left the danger behind."

Bart barely refrained from laughing out loud, and the purser had to turn his head to hide his glee, while Gabriella's expression turned suddenly from one filled with venom to sweet innocence.

"Allison? Allison Alexander? You're Jack and Margaret's *little girl?*" She examined me up and down and amended her question into a statement with special emphasis. "Their *daughter.*"

I nodded, scooping the tapestry valise off the floor and tossing it to her with a little more gusto than was probably necessary. I slipped my arm through Bart's when she staggered a couple of steps backward to maintain her balance. "Yes, except my name is now Allison Allan. Bart and I have been *happily married* for nearly two years."

Gabriella regrouped. She slipped off her worn brown shoes, zipped open the valise, retrieved a pair of red stiletto heels, slipped them on her feet, then stuffed her dowdy costume into the bag and tossed it in the wheelchair. She whirled to the purser, who tried to compose himself, and demanded her cabin key. "My friends will see me to my cabin," she snapped. Then she stopped and looked at him. "On second thought, they seem quite busy. Would *you* show me to my cabin?" Gabriella linked her arm through his, turned and winked at us, and said she'd see us later.

"Not if I can help it," I muttered.

Bart gathered me in his arms and whirled me around laughing. "Princess, I can't believe you! You're jealous."

"Believe it, buster. And the next time she heads for you with the intent of kissing you, she'll get more than a valise. Much more. I don't care if she is twice my age."

"You're wonderful." Bart put me down and kissed me. "I love it when your green eyes blaze like that."

"Just don't invite it," I warned, then pulled away and studied Bart. "When Mom said she was coming onboard as a crew member, I certainly didn't have an outfit like that in mind for her job. Does she have a specialty? Other than trying to steal women's husbands?"

Bart laughed. "She's an entertainer. A singer. I'm sure we can catch her act in one of the lounges later when they get her settled in and on the schedule."

"I'd be most happy to have her take her act on the road. And I'd be delighted to find a little boat to send her in. Tonight."

Bart laughed again, obviously enjoying this. It was then I saw the blood on Bart's sleeve. I looked at my hands. I had a smear on my right hand.

"Are you bleeding anywhere?" I asked, knowing he wasn't, knowing this wasn't his blood or mine.

He checked his hands. "Any on my face?" he asked, puzzled.

"It had to come from Gabriella. We'd better find her, fast." I hadn't thought about asking for her cabin number. At the time, I thought if she needed us, she'd find us. And hoped she wouldn't!

Bart strode across the lobby to the desk. "A woman in a wheel-chair boarded at Bari. The purser took her to a cabin. Can you give me the number of her room?"

While Bart went through all the red tape to get Gabriella's cabin number, I kept watch for the purser to return. Why did everything have to be so complicated? *Just give us her room number, for heaven's sake. Or page the purser.* I stopped pacing the lobby long enough to suggest if they didn't want to give us her room number, they call the purser, Edward, on his cell phone and summon him here so we could talk to him personally.

That worked. Ten minutes later, he hurried off the elevator. Edward was skeptical of our story until I pointed out a red smear on the sleeve of his white jacket where she had clutched his arm. "I think you'll find that is not lipstick," I said quietly. "We need to get to Gabriella quickly to see how seriously injured she is. She came onboard after those terrorist explosions at Bari. She may have been hurt, and in the confusion, she may not have even been aware she was bleeding."

That was a stretch, even for me to believe, but it started him moving in the right direction. We followed him to the elevator and explained she was a friend of Bart's before we were married and that Gabriella hadn't been aware of the marriage.

He flashed a knowing smile. "I could tell."

The elevator stopped on the deck below ours, and we hurried along the corridor, dodging newly boarded passengers transferring luggage into their rooms from the hall where it had been deposited by ship's personnel. We stopped outside a door with no luggage. Apparently Gabriella came aboard only with the tapestry valise she carried, logical if this was a rushed trip out of town.

The purser knocked. No answer. He called to her. No answer.

"I think you'd better use your key," Bart said.

Edward hesitated. Then, knocking again, he said, "Gabriella, this is the purser. We're coming in." When there was no answer, he keyed the door and pushed it open. Gabriella lay in a heap on the floor near the bathroom, a towel wrapped around her arm. The white towel was no longer white.

Edward knelt at her side and felt for a pulse. "It's weak, but it's there. We'd better get her to the medical center." As he reached for his cell phone to call for a gurney to transport her, I wondered at the wisdom of that. What if she didn't want anyone to know she was injured? Or even onboard? She had waited until there was no one left in the lobby but us and the purser to doff her disguise.

"Edward, could you hold that phone call for one minute?" Bart asked and turned to me. "Are you thinking what I'm thinking?" As he spoke, he removed the towel and pushed up the completely blood-soaked, red-sequined sleeve. He wiped away fresh blood oozing from a nasty hole, then pressed the towel tightly against the wound to stem the bleeding. "Gun shot."

I nodded. "We ought to keep her here until we talk to her and find out what kind of trouble she was in."

Bart said quietly, "Edward, will you ask the medical personnel to come here to examine her? If she can be treated in her room, that may be the best way to handle this."

"Sorry," Edward said. "We need to take her to the medical center so they can treat this right. Why would you even think about . . ."

"Because she's a special project of the captain," Bart interrupted. "It's confidential, but you can understand it's important that others don't know who she really is. She's posing as an entertainer. If you talk to Captain Fortezze, he'll verify that." Bart sat back on his heels, still holding the towel compressed tightly against Gabriella's wound. "How about it? Will you ask the medics to come here? Call the captain to confirm and get his permission if you want. Just hurry."

Edward relented and called the medical center, requesting the doctor come unobtrusively to cabin 8209. An injury of special circumstance needed to be treated in strict confidence. While we waited, I pulled the blanket from the bed and covered Gabriella, straightening her legs, hoping to make her more comfortable. As I did so, she moaned, moved, opened her eyes, and looked at the three of us hovering above her.

When she apparently remembered where she was, she flashed a weak smile. "I guess that's one way to get your attention."

"All you had to do was ask," Bart said. "But you prefer the dramatic. What happened?"

Gabriella glanced at Edward.

"We told him who you are. He'll keep your secret that you're a special friend of the captain. Who shot you?"

I bit my tongue, wanting to ask if it was a jealous wife, then decided this wasn't the time or place for those unworthy sentiments, but Gabriella must have read my mind. She shot a knowing glance at me, then with a smile of satisfaction said, "A jealous wife."

"Why do I believe you?" I asked, knowing it probably wasn't true this time, but wondering how many other times she'd been in danger from that quarter.

A rap at the door interrupted the exchange, and Edward jumped to his feet to admit the doctor. I thought she had the wrong room until I saw her medical bag. The young Eastern Indian woman didn't appear any older than me. She knelt quickly at Gabriella's side, pulled her stethoscope from her bag, and proceeded to do her thing.

Midway through, Gabriella asked if anyone cared if she got off the floor. It wasn't the most comfortable place in the world, and it would be much easier for the doctor to take care of her. By this time, Dr. Chandra had determined the bullet wound was her only problem, besides possible loss of blood, and she could be moved.

I slipped the red stiletto heels from her feet and hurried to turn down the bed while Bart and Edward carefully lifted her from the floor. Dr. Chandra suggested we remove the dress before putting her into bed, so I unzipped the form-fitting gown, wondering if I was going to have to peel it off of her, but there was no need.

"Keep your eyes front and center, guys," I said, letting it drop to the floor. Bart and Edward lowered her gently into bed, and I tossed the sheet over her.

"You needn't be so careful, Allison," Gabriella purred. "Bart's more than familiar with the subject matter already, and I'm sure Mr. Hanson is no stranger to the female form."

Edward laughed, Bart blushed, and I turned away, silently fuming at her audacity and lack of modesty. Dr. Chandra shooed us away from the bed and sat on the edge to examine Gabriella's wounded arm. "I can clean this here, with their help, but I suspect you are going to need a blood transfusion. How long have you been bleeding?"

"A few hours."

"You were fortunate. The small-caliber bullet just missed all the vital tendons and veins, so you have a flesh wound." Dr. Chandra glanced up from the wound at Gabriella. "And I'm sure you have a good reason for not seeking medical help until now?" she said, a trace of sarcasm in her voice.

"As a matter of fact, I was chasing a couple of terrorists who planned to blow up a music festival. I got too close. They shot me. I played dead. They left to finish the job, I followed and hit one of them, but the other escaped."

Dr. Chandra treated her story as just that. A story. She brushed the apparently preposterous explanation aside with one more question. "Do you happen to know your blood type?"

"A-positive," Gabriella said.

The doctor looked around at us. "Do any of you share that type with the patient?"

Bart and Edward glanced at each other and shook their heads.

I hesitated before answering. "I do."

Chapter 10

"Any reason why you couldn't, or shouldn't, give a pint of your blood to this woman?" Dr. Chandra asked, without looking up from her work.

"She's pregnant," Bart offered before I could answer.

"We'll have to find someone else," Dr. Chandra stated. "How secret does this have to be? With the captain's permission, of course, do I have to keep it out of the ship's log, or can I just slightly delay the entry until your special circumstances are past? That will determine how quickly I can find a donor with her blood type."

"How about a little sugar water instead?" Gabriella asked. "My blood needs to be thinned a little every once in a while just to cool it down."

Edward laughed. Bart looked at me and winked. I wasn't quite sure what that meant, but then, my sense of humor was slightly off at the moment, so I wasn't enjoying this as much as the rest of them. Knowing how hard it was to find people both able—and willing—to share their blood, I wasn't sure the odds were in Gabriella's favor.

"I'm only five months pregnant, and I'm in good health," I offered. "I'm sure there would be no problem in sharing a pint. I'll just drink lots of fluids for the next couple of days and replenish it."

Gabriella's eyes widened. Dr. Chandra turned and stared up at me over the rim of her granny glasses.

"If she needs it, and I have it, why shouldn't you use mine?" I insisted. "You may not find anyone else in the necessary time frame."

"Thanks, but we never ask a pregnant woman to give blood, under any circumstances. I'll take this sample back to the lab and see what the blood count is. Maybe we can take care of it as she suggested." Dr. Chandra showed her first signs of actually having a sense of humor. She stared Gabriella directly in the eyes and said, "I'm sure she could use some cooling off." Then Dr. Chandra turned again to me. "You look tired. Why don't you go to bed?"

I hesitated, not knowing what to do. I was definitely ready for bed. In fact, as I thought about it, I was exhausted, but I didn't want to leave my husband here with Gabriella, even if she needed him. Even if she was weak and injured. I just wasn't that magnanimous.

Not that I didn't trust Bart, but there were five blank years in my knowledge of his life when he'd been undercover. Since I still didn't know all the details of where he'd been, who he'd worked with, and how intimately involved with them he'd been, my insecurity reared its ugly head.

Gabriella's insinuations didn't help. Had there been something between them, or was it a figment of her imagination? Or wishful thinking on her part? Or was her siren persona just a façade?

My husband gallantly rescued me from my dilemma. "Let's follow the good doctor's orders and get you to bed. Gabriella's in good hands with Edward and Dr. Chandra, and since her injury isn't life threatening, they shouldn't have to hold her hand all night." Bart leaned over and kissed Gabriella's forehead. "Good night, Gabi. Sweet dreams. And don't get out of bed and wander the ship until you get your strength back. You probably shouldn't be seen until you go on stage."

As we left the room, Bart put his arm around my shoulder. "How about a cup of hot chocolate to relax you and get you ready for a good night's sleep?"

I looked up at my husband. "There's only one thing that would ensure a good night's sleep."

"Name it, princess. You know I'll do anything you ask."

"Tell me about your relationship with Gabriella."

Bart didn't respond immediately, and I quickly filled the awkward silence. "Does that mean there's something you have to think about before you can tell me? Do you have to form your thoughts carefully?" I stopped at the foot of the stairs and stared into Bart's blue eyes. "Or do I really want to know?"

Bart leaned down, tilted my chin up, and gently kissed me. "I told you, you're the only one I've ever loved. No one, not Gabriella or anyone else, has ever tempted me to forget you for a single minute."

"She said . . ."

"That I knew her body? I dragged her out of the water after she attempted suicide. When I came to tell her Emile was dead, she said she had nothing left to live for. I thought she was just being dramatic, but when I went back to her house the next morning to tell her good-bye, I saw her swimming out into the ocean beyond the reef. I grabbed a boat and went after her. If she hadn't been such a fighter, she probably would have just sunk beneath the waves and drowned. But she just kept swimming, hand over hand, one stroke after another. She was so exhausted by the time I reached her, she didn't even resist when I hauled her into the boat."

He laughed. "That came later when I took her to her house and tried to convince her she really did have reason to live. We talked for hours—actually *argued* for hours—and all the while she was shivering in the briefest bikini I'd ever seen, but she refused to get dressed."

"She wanted physical comfort. You didn't take the hint?" I asked.

Bart seemed surprised. "I thought she just wanted to show off her great body. She was always flaunting it, teasing with it. She was proud she looked so young, and she worked hard to stay as youthful-looking as possible."

We resumed our stroll up the stairs while Bart recited the rest of the story. He'd delayed his departure to teach her the gospel and bring some closure for Emile's death and some peace to her troubled soul. She vowed she couldn't believe in a God who would be so cruel and knew Emile had been brainwashed into believing that nonsense.

"She said I was as big a fool as her brother, but if I ever came to my senses, she'd be interested in instructing me in her life philosophy."

"Which is?" I asked as we reached the Chez Claude Grill and the hot chocolate dispenser.

"Take what you want when you see it, and don't worry about anybody else."

"Does she really believe that, or is it part of her façade?" I asked, thinking even Gabriella must have more compassion than that in order to be an Interpol agent.

"I think it's part of the act. It's her protection against the world."

"What's her motivation in Interpol if she feels that way?"

Bart sipped his chocolate as we strolled to the railing to watch the steam rising from the swimming pools and the few brave souls laughing and enjoying the water. "I think she picked up Emile's torch when he died. I think she does it for him, for his memory."

The bed felt wonderful, and I fell asleep immediately.

* * *

I awoke at six A.M., totally refreshed. Bart still slept soundly, so I quietly dressed and slipped out of the room to see how Gabriella had fared during the night.

When I tapped on her door, she opened it immediately and looked surprised to see me.

"I thought I'd better see how you're feeling this morning," I explained. "I'm amazed you're out of bed."

"It takes more than a little bullet hole to keep me down. Besides, I needed a shower more than I needed to lie in that hard bed another minute."

"Did Dr. Chandra get you a transfusion, or did she just fill you full of 'sugar water'?"

"Neither. I promised I'd drink lots of water and get lots of rest, and she let me off the hook. In addition to the fact that I hadn't actually lost as much blood as it appeared. My blood count turned out just fine. Come in." Gabriella pointed to the bed. "Sit down."

I sat on one corner at the foot of the bed, and she took the other corner. "Thanks," she said softly, "for offering your blood."

Not sure what to say, I murmured, "You'd have done the same for me."

"No," she said simply. "I wouldn't have. I don't know you. And even if I did, why would I go through the pain and bother?"

I tried to hide the shocked expression I knew must have spread across my face at her candor, but apparently I failed.

Gabriella smiled. "You don't like me." She held up her hands when I opened my mouth to object. "I don't blame you. I wouldn't like me either if I were in your shoes. I'm a threat to married women with attractive husbands. Especially when I've known them as well as I've known Bart." She paused, waiting for my reaction, but I only smiled sweetly and waited for the rest of her act. I would not rise to the bait.

She changed the subject. "What are you and Bart working on?"

"Working on? Just relaxing," I replied innocently. "This is a well-earned vacation. And since my travel will be curtailed shortly, we decided now was a perfect time to take a second honeymoon."

"I've never known Anastasia to take vacations." Gabriella frowned and regarded me like she didn't believe me. "They work harder and longer hours than any other Interpol agency in the world."

I laughed. "Have you ever known anyone in Anastasia who was expecting a baby? I'm a first, except for Mom when she and Dad were the only members of the group. So Bart and I are blazing new trails, setting new traditions for the organization. And speaking of Bart, I left him sleeping, but he'll be frantic when he wakes and finds me gone. I'd better get back. I just wanted to make sure you're okay. We were planning to go ashore at Corfu, and I didn't want to leave if you needed . . ."

I was going to say "my blood," but that sounded so ghoulish. Then I thought of saying "if you needed anything," but I didn't want to leave that open ended, as I wasn't about to offer "anything."

Gabriella laughed. "Thanks. I don't need anything. Go and enjoy your day. Maybe I'll see you when you get back. I'm supposed to do a short show at five in the Vivaldi Lounge, then they've slipped me into the 'Welcome to Las Vegas' act the crew does later tonight in La Gondola Theater. You'll have to come and see me perform. Bart's seen my act. I'm sure he'd enjoy seeing it again."

"I'm sure he would," I said, going to the door. "We'll see you at five. Get some rest."

I met Bart at the stairs.

"I thought you'd probably gone to check on Gabriella," Bart said, bending to kiss me good morning. "How was she?"

"She's . . . Gabriella. What can I say?" When I reported our conversation, Bart laughed.

"Yes, she's different from anyone you've probably ever met, princess. I don't know whether to believe her or not when she says she wouldn't give her blood if it were needed. She's certainly not predictable."

"I am."

Bart seemed puzzled, then he grabbed my hand and pulled me up the stairs. "Yes, you are predictable. You're hungry. And so am I. La Brassiere cafeteria should be open by the time we get up two more flights of stairs."

I had a hard time deciding which of the fruits, breads, cheeses, eggs, sausage, cold cuts, and pastries I wanted to expend my calorie count on for breakfast. After I finally chose the French toast with strawberries, we hurried through breakfast to disembark and catch our bus for the tour of Corfu.

This particular tour was of special interest to me, as our first stop took us to the Achilles Palace of Empress Elizabeth of Austria.

Only part of our group came on the bus. I had to admire several of the older souls. They struggled to get on and off the bus with the aid of canes, walking painfully up the hills and over uneven cobblestone streets, but they weren't home sitting in their rocking chairs. They were still living life as fully as they could and were out there trying instead of giving up. Then I had a sobering thought. What if some of these good people were included in the nine couples Cell Seven had identified as possible receivers? They'd have no way to defend themselves against terrorists.

My somber thoughts were interrupted when our guide, Ellie, boarded the bus and began her historical sketch of Corfu. Her deep, rich voice reminded me of Melina Mercouri, the Greek actress of the fifties. Since our first stop would be Achilles Palace, she acquainted us with Elizabeth, Empress of Austria and Queen of Hungary, Europe's darling "Queen Sissy." Elizabeth was called the "sad empress" because she never smiled—her teeth were bad. Ellie conjectured she might have been anorexic, as she was extremely slender—and very beautiful.

But Elizabeth was restless and depressed, living in the royal court with its strict protocol. After the death of her first child, she took a long trip around the Mediterranean, stopped in Corfu, and fell in love with the beauty of the island and its friendly people. She had a palace built on top of a hill, and because she admired Achilles, she named it after him.

As Ellie recited her history, Bart slipped his arm around my shoulders and pulled me close to his side. I knew immediately what he was thinking. *I* was carrying *our* first child. What would I do if something happened to her? And if something dreadful happened on this trip, Bart would never forgive himself for not insisting I go home and take care of myself and Alexandra.

I slid my hand in his and smiled up at him. "We're okay," I whispered. I now identified even more with Elizabeth.

As Ellie quoted from a book about the Empress, I opened my journal to take notes and scribbled Elizabeth's words: "It's the Dying Achilles to whom I have dedicated my palace, because he is the image of the Greek soul and the beauty of the heart and its people. I love him also because he, like Hermes, was swift in running, and he was strong and proud and stubborn as a Greek mountain, and like a cloud he defied all kings, all customs, all laws..."

"Ah, there's the key," I whispered to Bart. "She identified with Achilles as a free spirit—probably envied his freedom. I'm glad I wasn't born into royalty. Being on display each minute and having to do everything perfectly would be dreadful."

"I think you'd be very good at it, princess. You've had lots of practice," Bart said.

"Being your pretend princess isn't the same thing, silly."

We arrived at palace gates adorned with Greek key designs and golden griffins and filed slowly inside while listening to Ellie explain the significance of the treasures surrounding us. I especially liked the blue and white Della Robbia porcelain plaques of Mary and the Christ Child in Elizabeth's private chapel. A poignant mural of the Savior being taken bound before Pontius Pilate covered the entire domed ceiling in the small room.

"This is the famous *Stella del Mare* or *The Sea Star*," Ellie said, pointing above the altar at the huge icon of the Madonna draped in blue with her baby in the clouds.

"Our Elizabeth seems a very religious empress," I whispered to Bart. "But she also loved all things Greek. Look outside." We slipped through the group to the window to get a better view of the statues I'd glimpsed. "I'm ready to go outside. It's way too warm in here and too crowded. I'll have to appreciate the beauty of this from the pages of the book I'm going to buy at that little kiosk where the bus parked."

"Lead on, princess. I've had enough marble—and crowds—to last me all day."

We slipped ahead of the tour and peeked into all the rooms to see if there was a picture of Elizabeth wearing the topaz necklace. But the tour wasn't allowed upstairs, and there was no portrait of her wearing the necklace downstairs. Disappointing.

Gleaming white marble statues of mythical gods and goddesses and carefully shaped shrubbery filled the gardens. We leaned against the wrought-iron fence that enclosed the top of the hill and gazed out over lushly wooded hillsides sloping down to the azure waters of the sea.

"What an idyllic spot," I sighed. "No wonder this was her favorite place, her refuge from the world." I turned around and surveyed the two statues of Achilles erected in this part of her garden, one the victorious Achilles, tall and proud, gazing across the water, the other the dying Achilles, clearly in agony, clutching the spear thrust through his heel.

"I wonder what her Achilles' heel was," I mused aloud. "If she identified with him in so many other ways and admired him so much, did she identify a weakness in herself as well?"

Bart wrapped his arms around me from behind and kissed my ear. "You're my Achilles' heel, my weakness. I can't live without you."

I turned in his arms and stared up into solemn blue eyes. "You won't ever have to. I'll always be right here by your side. Or in your arms. I do prefer that."

Someone cleared her throat loudly, and I looked around to see Charlotte and Sara pointing a camera at us. "You're caught forever on film." Charlotte laughed.

We joined them to explore the rest of the garden, and Bart took pictures of me in front of the statue of the muse Melpomena, the goddess of tragedy for whom I was named. My first name, Melanie, represented the darkest part of Mom's life, when she lived in fear of being caught by an assassin, and the name Allison represented the light that came when I was born.

Sara stood beside a statue, imitating the pose with arms outstretched, and I was struck by how much her profile resembled that of the statue. She was a classic Greek beauty. I bought a book on

Corfu at the tourist kiosk just before we boarded the bus and glanced through it while we waited for everyone to find their way back.

"I'm disappointed we didn't find a picture of the topaz necklace here." When Bart didn't answer, I glanced at him. His eyes were closed, but I was sure he wasn't sleeping. I leaned toward him and said softly, "Penny for your thoughts."

Without opening his eyes, he said, "You don't want to know."

"Of course, I do. Especially when you tell me I don't. Then I really must know what you're pondering so deeply."

"Life."

"What aspect? Whose? And why now?"

Bart opened one eye and peered at me. "Don't you ever get tired of asking questions?"

"Not nearly as tired as you do of avoiding them."

Jed and Dorothy offered us candy they'd purchased at the kiosk, and our conversation ended, but I couldn't help wondering what he was thinking about. Gabriella? At first I'd been surprised when he didn't talk to her about the explosions. But since that was her case, and she hadn't volunteered any information or made an opportunity to discuss it, I assumed we wouldn't get involved. Plus we had our hands full with our own case.

Ellie resumed her history lesson, and I put Gabriella out of my mind—a pleasant thing to do. Scenery flew by the bus window— palm, fig, and olive trees and stark, white stucco houses brilliant in the sun. White statues against dark green foliage flashed by the windows so quickly, I couldn't identify them. We passed ruins being excavated but nothing unusual or exciting enough to bring me out of my "zoning" mode.

Suddenly, the bus pulled into a parking lot and stopped. I realized I hadn't been listening to Ellie's narration and had no idea where we were. One glance out the window brought me upright in my seat.

"Bart, it's Kanoni!"

My husband sat up, and we both tuned in to Ellie's narration about these two tiny little pieces of land that had figured so promi- nently in our lives two years ago.

"The monastery dominating the tiny island of Pontikonissi is dedicated to Panaghia of Vlacherena and was built in the seventeenth century. On the little, tree-covered island behind it, the thirteenth-century Byzantine church was dedicated to 'The Almighty.' This will be a stop for pictures only, so you have ten minutes to see one of the most photographed spots on Corfu." Ellie stopped her narration, and our group gathered cameras and bags to exit the bus.

I jumped to my feet. "Let's hurry so we'll have time to go down to the church." We were out of the bus before most were on their feet and headed down the hill toward the red-tile roofed, white church that stood out dramatically against the deep blue of the bay.

"She just said this was the monastery. Wasn't the convent here two years ago? And the monastery was over there on Mouse Island, or am I getting my memories mixed up?"

When Bart didn't answer, I glanced back at my husband, who was lagging a couple of steps behind. I followed his gaze up the hill over-looking the bay where danger in the form of a killer had lurked when we were here before.

"Look out!" I screamed.

Chapter 11

A man whose small cart was piled high with sticks struggled to pull it up the hill, failed, and was chasing it as it plummeted down the road toward the spot where we stood. Bart grabbed my hand and jerked me off the road just as the cart flew by us, hit the rocks at the shoreline, and shattered into hundreds of pieces. Sticks flew everywhere.

The old man stopped and stared at what was left of his cart. You couldn't tell the splinters of the cart from its load. Even the wooden wheels were in pieces.

I sagged against Bart. It took a minute for me to find my voice. "Whew. My deepest gratitude, Sir Galahad, for saving my life once again."

Bart's arms went around me, and he held me tightly against him. He didn't speak, just held me. Finally, he took a deep breath, released me, and stared into my eyes. "How can one person attract so much trouble? Serious trouble," he said slowly. "Why is it you're constantly in danger?"

"To keep you on your toes? To give you lifetime employment?" I stepped away and took a deep breath. "We may have to think twice about coming here again. This beautiful little place seems to have it in for us."

Those members of our group who had come for a closer look at the picturesque church approached, exclaimed about our narrow escape. We walked together down the rest of the hill and out on the long, cement causeway that also served as a dock for both private and excursion boats.

Laura and Mark asked us to take their picture at a point on the causeway where the church and bell tower made a perfect backdrop. Then we gave them our camera, and they took our picture.

There was no doubt it had been an accident—a total coincidence we happened to be in that spot at that particular moment. But still, my knees were a little weak, and I clung to Bart's arm as we neared the church. I had to smile when I thought that Mama Karillides would have said the gods had it in for us.

Memories flooded back. This was the place where I'd first seen the deep, ugly scars crisscrossing Bart's back, where I'd first heard his story of the Tibetan prison, where I'd donned scuba tanks and crossed the expanse of water between the islands in the dark, hopeful I'd meet my mother who'd been fleeing an assassin, and fly with her to safety.

"Brings back a lot of memories, doesn't it?" Bart said as we hurried around the perimeter of the little church and gazed across the lagoon at Mouse Island.

"And lots of emotions. Our first adventure together. Thank heaven for your immaculate timing, swooping down with the airplane to pick us up, or we wouldn't be here having this conversation." I looked up at Bart. "My knight in shining armor. Always riding to the rescue just at the right moment."

As he encircled me with his arms, he whispered softly, "You'd better hope my timing is always so meticulous if I'm going to spend the rest of my life snatching you from the brink of sudden destruction."

I reached up and kissed him. "Thanks for always being there." We clung to each other for a moment more. "Guess we'd better hurry," I sighed. "Everyone else is nearly back to the bus already."

"If we run, we can get there before they get loaded. I'll race you," Bart challenged and took off running.

I knew I didn't have a prayer of catching him but ran after him anyway. I'd almost reached the bus when a boy on a bicycle raced up and paced me. Was this my contact? Another topaz? But with everyone on the bus watching?

As he pedaled beside me, he gave me the pitch. I was a rich American tourist. He was a poor, Greek island boy with a sick mother, who needed expensive medicine. Would I please help him?

I looked at his racing bike, stopped and turned to face him. "You must be running a pretty convincing scam to afford an expensive bike like that. Better pick up an old relic somewhere so you'll appear poor. And trade your high-dollar athletic shoes for some with holes in them. Americans aren't all as rich or gullible as those you watch on TV."

Bart waited for me at the door to the bus. I boarded without comment. I would not come to this place again. It had held such wonderful memories for me, even though that had been a desperate, dangerous time, but now I only wanted to get as far away as possible. I wasn't even sure why I felt such sudden gloom. As I surveyed the lagoon one final time, a cloud moved overhead, and the water turned from deep blue to seasick green. An omen? Grandmother would agree.

"Penny for your thoughts, princess," Bart said quietly when we were back on the road again.

"They aren't worth a penny."

"What did the kid want?"

"Money for his sick mother."

"Why the gloomy face?"

I stared at Bart. "To tell you the truth, I don't know. I was so excited to come back here. Whenever I've thought of this place, it's been good. Getting to know you better after all those years you'd been gone, finding Mom and getting her out of here just in the nick of time. I remember it as a beautiful, romantic place."

When I didn't continue, Bart prompted me. "And now?"

"That little accident couldn't have given me this dark feeling. It's almost a foreboding. Well, maybe not that, but . . . I don't know." I shrugged. "Just a doom and gloom, dismal feeling all of a sudden."

"Did that kid have anything to do with it?"

"No. Wherever we go, someone has a hand out. He's just another in a string of many." I thought about it for a minute. "Maybe my expectations were too high. Maybe I hoped we'd create another wonderful memory here. At the least, I expected to retrieve another topaz."

Bart didn't reply, and I tried to tune in to Ellie's narration on more of Corfu's history to take my mind off my unexpectedly dour mood.

Then my husband leaned over and said quietly, "I think your running days are over for a few months. It appears Alexandra is slowing you down a bit." I glanced up to see two azure blue eyes full of laughter.

I pictured how I must have looked, running back to the bus. Or was I waddling? "You're probably right. Was it that funny?"

"Let's just say you were not the epitome of grace, even though you are still the epitome of beauty."

I laughed. "Thank you, kind sir, for those contradictory compliments. I'll try to remember to not let anyone see me running and will attempt to act a little more dignified from now on."

Ellie announced we were now in the historic district of the old city of Corfu and pointed out the French architecture of the two-block-long buildings on one side of the square. They reminded me of New Orleans, which, of course, was reminiscent of Paris. "Guess I don't need to go to Paris if this is a copy of those famous buildings she mentioned," I whispered.

She led us to the Palace of St. Michael and St. George, the English addition to the city, to see the Museum of Ancient Art. The tour took far too long, had nothing to do with the Greek city of Corfu as far as I was concerned, and was a huge waste of time. I was anxious to get into the old city or even climb the battlements of the castle just across the park.

Finally, Ellie led our group like a gaggle of geese into the old part of town to a Greek Orthodox Church where a service was in session. She just took us right in, sat us down, and gave her spiel while the worshipers kept worshiping. I was so amazed, I don't remember a thing she told us about the church.

I wondered, rather impatiently, how we'd receive another stone if we spent all our time in private tours of museums and churches. As she dismissed us, Ellie warned that no map of the ancient city would get us where we needed to go because only the old residents knew their way around the narrow, winding streets. I was so fascinated by the first street, I didn't care if we found our way back. Given an hour on our own for shopping and sightseeing, Bart and I wandered the narrow streets lined with fascinating shops, turning up one alley and then another. My mood lifted, the sun came out, and my wonderful husband bought me a stunning silver necklace and matching bracelet with the Greek key design, something I'd wanted for a long time.

We met a couple of shopkeepers, who were the ultimate saleswomen. I'd stopped to admire the vivid blue-and-purple swirl fabric in a pair of wraparound pants, and before I knew it, I was in the shop trying them on. One woman, delighted when I spoke her language, treated me like a long-lost sister, but when I started to bargain the price with her, she said, "What are you? Italian?"

Bart laughed and paid her the full price. She patted and hugged me, blessed me and my baby, then slipped a pair of tiny hoop earrings into the bag. "For your bambino," she said. When we left, I was laughing so hard I could hardly breathe.

"Glad you feel better, princess," Bart said. "Guess what you needed was just a good dose of shopping to take your mind off . . ." He stopped and looked at me. "What? What had you so gloomy?"

I shook my head. "Chalk it up to hormones, I guess. I don't know. I have no idea what came over me. Maybe I'm like Empress Elizabeth. I just need more freedom and less restriction."

"Freedom from what?" Bart asked, a frown creasing his forehead. "Me?"

"No, silly." I grabbed his hand and squeezed it. "Freedom from stuffy museums and confining busses and crowds of people packed into hot rooms."

Bart looked relieved. "I'm with you there. If we didn't have to stick with our tour and be available to pick up the stones, I'd skip the tours, and we'd do our own thing. But if we're not with the tour, our contacts won't know where to find us."

"Speaking of finding us, for some reason, I felt we'd get our next jewel at that magical place I remembered as Kanoni. Maybe part of my disappointment came because we didn't receive the topaz." I glanced at my watch. "We're to be onboard ship at three thirty, which means we only have thirty minutes before we head for the bus."

"Then we need to move," Bart said with a broad smile. "There's still half a city you haven't seen and dozens of shops at which you haven't spent a dime."

"How can we help improve the local economy if our money stays in our pockets?" I laughed.

We turned a corner and found another street so narrow that merchandise hanging above the stores on one side of the street mingled with merchandise from the other. The selection of goods was unending, everything from cheap tourist trinkets to valuable pieces of silver, incredible carvings, expensive paintings, clothing of every kind, and even blue, glass, flying dinosaur wind chimes.

"Oh, look. I wish I had someone to buy those for. I've never seen anything like them."

"How about the bishop's kids?" Bart suggested. "Isn't one of them into dinosaurs?"

"Probably. Aren't all kids at some point in their lives?" I looked around to find the shopkeeper, but no one seemed to be minding the store. Just a toothless, wrinkled old woman sitting on a little stool across the narrow alley watching people go by. I approached her and asked in Greek if she knew where the owner of the shop was. She shook her head, tilted it to peer up at me, squinting in the bright afternoon sun. Then she slowly held out her hand.

I pulled ten euros from my pocket, bent over and pressed it into her palm. "Here you go, Grandmother," I whispered to her in Greek. "Go home to your family with dignity tonight." I turned quickly and headed for the next shop. "So much for blue glass dinosaurs," I said. When Bart made no comment, I turned to find him buying a new navy leather wallet.

"How do you like this?" he asked, holding it for me to admire.

"Smart."

"Your enthusiasm is overwhelming." He looked at me. "I think you're tired."

"Don't tell me that or I will be." I checked the time. "But our fun is over for another day. It's time to find the bus."

In less than five minutes, we arrived in the crowded square. Several of our group had found a gelato shop and were enjoying a creamy cone to cool them off. Others had discovered the McDonald's on the corner and were sipping drinks under the golden arches with Venetian lanterns hanging along the walls. Definitely an international spot.

I whirled to Bart. "I know what we missed!"

Bart laughed. "Lunch."

"How did that happen? I'm suddenly starving." But we didn't have time to discuss whether we'd settle for gelato or a drink. Carol and Jim signaled for everyone to board the bus. No lunch today. As I turned toward the crowded street where the bus parked, a tiny, bent lady with a shawl over her head and a basket of violets on her arm approached me.

"Flowers?" she asked in a voice as small as she was.

Bart pulled out his wallet, anticipating my purchase, when someone bumped into him from behind, apologized, and hurried away. He paid for two small bouquets that she held up, then as he gazed into her faded blue eyes, he changed his mind, gave her thirty euros, and emptied the basket into my arms. He returned the empty basket and stooped over to kiss her wrinkled cheek. "Tell her to take the rest of the day off," he said. "And tell her the flowers are beautiful, perfect for my beautiful wife."

I relayed his message in Greek, she bowed over and over, saying thank you again and again, then reached into her pocket under her apron and pressed something into Bart's hand. Before he could examine it, she scurried away and disappeared into the crowd of people milling near the outdoor café.

Bart tucked his wallet in his back pocket, took my arm and guided me toward the bus. "I think we just made contact," he said, sounding surprised.

I looked up at him.

A grin spread across his face as he stuck his hand in his pocket. "Yup. I think this little packet she slipped me is another topaz."

When we boarded the bus, I walked down the aisle, passing out bouquets of violets to all the ladies while Bart settled in his seat to unwrap the object the woman had given him. Was it a topaz? She hadn't said anything. All the others had spoken Grandmother's name or mentioned her. And they had given the stones to me. Why was this different?

I sat down beside Bart. "Well? Was it a topaz?"

"I have good news and bad news," Bart said with a strange expression on his face. "The good news is, it's a topaz."

"And the bad news?"

Chapter 12

"My wallet was stolen." Bart sounded dumbfounded. And angry.

"With your credit cards and money? And room key? And ID?" I groaned, thinking of the red tape and effort it would take to cancel the credit cards, get replacements, get a new ATM card and new ID. Agghh.

"No," he said, shaking his head. "No. Not my old wallet. I had it in my hand when that guy bumped into me. I was paying for the flowers. He must not have seen me take it out. He only saw the bulge in my other pocket and went for it. He stole my new wallet." Now he was plain mad.

"Oh, Bart, I'm sorry. But at least you didn't lose all the important stuff in your old one. Can you imagine having to replace it all?" Then I stopped. "Do you realize you were just incredibly, and immediately, blessed for performing a good deed for that little old lady?"

Bart stared at me blankly.

"If you'd only bought one bunch of violets, you'd have paid with the change in your pocket. When you decided to buy more, you pulled out your wallet to get bigger denominations. Your wallet would still have been in your back pocket if you hadn't made such a wonderful, generous gesture. Thank you for the violets, and thank you for helping that old woman. And the Lord thanked you too by protecting all your valuables in your wallet."

Before Bart could answer, Ellie turned on her microphone, pointing out the old Venetian part of the city, and told how the Venetians had been invited to protect the island of Corfu from pirates and had stayed for four hundred years. I wondered if they'd worn out their welcome in that time. The bus rounded a hill and suddenly, unexpectedly, we were at the ship.

"Mom said someone from Anastasia would meet us to collect the jewels." I glanced up and down the dock as we exited the bus. "Can you see anyone? She said Else might be here."

"If Else were here, you couldn't miss her." Bart laughed. "She's too stunning to miss, even in a crowd."

Else was probably the only beautiful woman in the world who didn't elicit emotions of jealousy in me when coupled in the same thought with Bart. As genuinely good as she was lovely to look at, Else was more like my sister than anyone else on earth. And she was a paradox: she could be a deadly assassin, was the most accurate marksman in Anastasia, had been a bodyguard for the royal family, was even related to them, but remained a sweet, sincere, humble person until she went into action against the bad guys. Then they were in for serious grief.

But Else wasn't waiting on the dock. Nor was anyone else from Anastasia. I turned to Bart. "Do we hang around until the last minute before boarding? Maybe they got hung up somewhere and will meet us when we disembark at Santorini tomorrow. I really don't want to keep carrying these pretty little treasures around everywhere I go."

Bart ran his finger down the side of my face. "I'll stay and give them the stones if you want to go back to the cabin and put your feet up for a while. You're looking a little saggy."

"I'm feeling more than a little saggy, but I can handle another thirty minutes." It was then that I saw Gabriella leave the ship and head straight for us. "Uh-oh. Here comes trouble."

"Hi, you honeymooners. Did you have a good day ashore?" Gabriella hooked her arm through Bart's and turned luminous dark eyes on him, flashing a warm smile, then quickly linked arms with me. Probably to keep me from punching her out.

"We had a marvelous day," I cooed. "And you? How are you feeling?"

Gabriella held out the bandaged arm covered by her sweater and waved it around. "Almost as good as new." Then she winced. "If I don't use it too much. Oh, I have a message for you from that delightful Chinese agent, David Chen. He is one beautiful man."

I glanced up at Bart. The frown on his face wasn't meant for Gabriella, but she saw it anyway. "Is something wrong?" she asked, more interested than ever.

"Depends on the message," Bart said quietly. "I don't want work interfering with our first vacation in years. What did he say?"

She shrugged. "That he was still seeking the information you requested and hoped to see you in Santorini with what you needed." Gabriella looked at me, then turned to Bart. "Anastasia doesn't send an agent halfway around the world with that kind of message. What's going down here? You aren't keeping anything from your little Gabi, are you, handsome?"

"Why would we do that?" Bart asked.

"That's what I'd like to know, sweetie." Gabriella fingered the zipper on Bart's jacket as she gazed up into his eyes. "We're all employed by the same company. We shouldn't keep secrets when we could be helping each other."

"If you promise not to leak a word, I'll tell you what it was all about," I said through gritted teeth. It took all my self-control to keep from scratching her flirting eyes out.

Gabriella whirled from Bart and faced me, black eyes glowing in anticipation.

"Well?" I prompted. "Will you promise not to mention this to anyone, and especially not to David when you see him the next time?"

"Of course," she gushed. "I won't say a thing."

"David's on his way to an assignment and we promised to pick up something special for a friend of his. He's such a private person that he didn't want anyone to know and doesn't want to be teased for finally getting hooked."

"And what special thing did you find for him?"

Gabriella wasn't going to let me off easy. Did she suspect I was making this up? I was, but she didn't need to know that. I pulled the little sack from my purse containing the bracelet and beautiful silver necklace Bart bought me, unwrapped the tissue paper, and held out the bracelet to Gabriella where it sparkled in the sun.

"Mmm. Luscious, but why Corfu? And why didn't he get it himself?"

I was getting in deeper and deeper all the time. One fabrication led to another. If I kept this up, I'd have trouble getting my temple recommend renewed.

"He didn't say as much, but I gathered, reading between the lines, he met her on one of the Greek islands. He wanted to give her a gift to remind her of their first meeting but didn't have time to shop himself as he's working on something for Dad. He trusts my taste and asked me to get something I thought would be perfect for the occasion while we were here. I fell in love with this as soon as I saw it." That was definitely the truth. "Bart even bought the matching necklace for me, I liked it so much."

Gabriella still seemed dubious. "I still can't understand why he wouldn't pick it out himself."

"I don't think he's ever bought a present for a woman before, except maybe for his mother. Wouldn't you rather have someone who's used to shopping for women pick out your special present? Or would you rather have a perfect novice finding you a really special gift?"

She laughed. "You're right. I want an expert with a huge bankroll buying my presents! None of that nickel-and-dime stuff."

Three thirty and boarding time. The ship would leave the dock at four o'clock. We'd lost our opportunity to be free from the responsibility of the jewels. Hopefully David would try to contact us again tomorrow, and we could divest ourselves of these precious puzzle pieces and the pressure and stress they caused me carrying them around. We boarded the ship together.

"You've just time to change and come and see my act before dinner. I promise to perform just for you." Gabriella stepped close to Bart, ran her fingernail down the front of his shirt, and gazed up into his blue eyes to make sure he knew she was talking to him.

"We'll be there, Gabi, if Allison isn't too tired. I'm taking very good care of her and Alexandra these days." Bart reached for my hand and pulled me to him, then raised my fingers to his lips and kissed them as he ignored Gabriella and looked only at me. I adored him more than ever at that moment.

Gabriella whirled and stared at me, then back at Bart. "Alexandra?"

"Our baby," I explained. "She's a girl, and we've named her Alexandra."

Gabriella rolled her eyes, reached out to pat my rounded tummy, and then thought better of it as her eyes met mine. She gave a little two-finger salute and sashayed away from us, her perfect figure reminding me that mine was fast becoming more like a snowman than anything else.

I turned to Bart. "Thank you. That was the sweetest thing you could have ever done."

"It's the truth. I am taking very good care of you and our baby. And speaking of the truth, you rolled out the story of David's girlfriend like an old pro. I didn't know you were such an accomplished prevaricator."

We headed back to our cabin. "No, just a good storyteller. There is a difference, you know."

Bart laughed. "You'll have to brief me on the finer details. I'm not familiar with them."

"The difference is I don't think we should let your friend Gabriella in on this topaz caper, so I was protecting the confidentiality of the case. I gather you agree as you didn't explain either."

Bart nodded. "I'm sure she's busy enough with whatever she's doing. Funny, when agents from different units get together, we usually discuss our work to see if anyone has info that might shed a new light on the case. She hasn't said anything about hers, and I have no desire to share this."

"I have no desire to share either," I said pointedly, glaring at Bart. "The case or anything else."

He laughed. "Not to worry, princess."

I had to admit, Gabriella was quite an entertainer. She had a full, sultry voice, and with my eyes closed, it was easy to imagine Patti LuPone on stage singing the songs from *Evita* instead of Gabriella. She teased the men in the audience and even made Marc blush when she sat on his lap and played with his ear while crooning a love song. Marsha laughed. I wouldn't have been laughing if she'd been sitting on Bart's lap. Why did I have to become such a green-eyed monster where beautiful women and my husband were concerned?

Since she was a crew member, we were spared having her join us for dinner, which didn't break my heart in the least. The less I saw of the beautiful Gabriella, the happier I became.

Dinner was a French menu again. Sara and I conferred over the list for ten minutes, trying to decide which, from the many choices available, we'd have. I chose jellied consommé filled with layers of roasted vegetables and feta cheese, cold rhubarb soup, salad with hearts of palm and yogurt pepper dressing, and prime rib with luscious yams, which Bart didn't like, so I enjoyed a double portion.

The Goldsteins had been invited to a special dinner, and Marc and Marsha were at another table tonight, which afforded us the opportunity to get acquainted with Vivian and Blaine. Adept at getting people to talk about themselves, Bart steered the conversation so they didn't have time to ask questions about us and what we did.

Charlotte's coworkers had sent a little gnome with her to photograph in various historic spots. As we waited for dessert, she showed us the digital pictures of where she'd placed the colorful creature. What a fun idea. I pulled our camera from my purse to see how our pictures had turned out and started at the beginning of the clip to review them all, from Verona till today.

There, with Carol in the ancient arena in Verona, holding their camera up to take my picture, was the smiling young couple who'd followed our tour through the Museum of Oriental Art today. I handed the camera to Bart. "I knew I'd seen them before. Just couldn't remember where."

"Seen who?" Vivian asked. I handed her the camera. "I saw them yesterday too at Dubrovnik." She returned the camera. "They must be on our ship."

That explanation was simple enough. I really didn't need to find sinister motivation behind everything, though it was certainly easy to suspect strangers who took your picture.

We'd just finished dessert when our cute waitress arrived with a tray full of scrumptious-looking chocolate mousse. "Here's a treat from your friends at another table. They asked the chef to prepare something special for you."

As she distributed crystal cups of mousse, I passed. "I'm sorry. I couldn't possibly eat another bite. Too bad they didn't send it before I ate the strawberry mille-feuille. Don't suppose we could save it for tomorrow?"

She shook her head. "I can't even take it back to the kitchen. We have no place to keep leftovers."

"What a shame," Charlotte said. "In that case, I'll just have to sample one bite to see if it's as good as it looks."

Sara pushed hers away. "I'm through. I can't believe I'm too full for chocolate, but I am."

Blaine and Vivian agreed. Bart leaned back in his chair and eyed his. "Maybe in a minute," he said.

"Who did you say sent this?" I asked as she emptied her tray.

"I don't know. Your maître d' just told me to deliver it to you from friends at another table."

Sara laughed. "It was probably from Marc and Marsha, apologizing for abandoning us for other company tonight."

"Apology accepted." I slid it to the center of the table. "I just can't eat it."

Charlotte nibbled tiny spoonfuls, and Bart finally had one taste before pushing his chair back. "If I stay here, I'll eat the whole thing, then be miserable all night." He held out his hand to me. "Are you ready?"

"For a long walk around the decks to work off my dinner? Definitely." I stood. "See you all tomorrow."

We left the dining room, noting a few of the other tables in our tour were also sampling the chocolate mousse.

"Wish I could have eaten it," I told Bart as we climbed the stairs in the brass-trimmed atrium. "It looked so good."

"It was," Bart said. "Are you sure you want to climb all these stairs? The elevators aren't busy."

"Seven decks of stairs is what it's going to take to work off enough dinner so I can sleep tonight. You can take the elevator if you want."

"What I want," he paused for effect, "is to know what information David had for us. Why couldn't he stick around to deliver it? Margaret said he was researching the remaining generals who worked with Kesselring and hoped to have a line on who heads up Cell Seven. Is he actually going to show up in Santorini tomorrow, or was that just to put Gabriella off?"

"Guess maybe we'd better call the Control Center and find out. If he's still in the area, we need to be sure to make contact with him. I definitely want to get these stones in Anastasia's hands for safe-keeping, and I'm anxious to see why he came instead of Else."

We went directly to the balcony off the Flamenco Lounge only to find it already occupied by two couples with colorful cocktails, who were having a rousing good time.

"Back to the golf course," I said, leading the way up another flight of stairs to the thirteenth deck level. Apparently passengers felt golf was a sun sport, since the area nearly always appeared deserted in the evening. When the sun set, the location became a perfect spot to make confidential phone calls and not be worried about someone overhearing the conversation.

I called the Control Center on the gold compact and waited to hear Mom's perky voice. There was no answer. I glanced at my watch. "Nine o'clock here, it should be noon in California. Wonder where everyone is?"

"Call your mom's cell phone," Bart suggested.

"Good idea." But Mom's cell phone wasn't on.

"Try my mother," Bart said, pacing the deck beside me.

"No answer there either."

"Try the big house."

I speed-dialed Mom and Dad's mansion on the estate. It rang over and over, but not even the answering machine came on. Then I tried Bart's parents' home. No answer. No answering machine.

"What's with this?" I asked. "Since when do they turn off their answering machines?"

"Do you have David's cell entered in that?" Bart asked. "We should have called him first since he's in the area."

David's cell reported no service.

"Try Else," Bart said quietly, the tension audible in his voice. He quit pacing and stood at my elbow.

"No answer there either." I tried each of the other members of Anastasia. Not one had their cell phone turned on, or they were in an area where there was no service.

"It would be far too big a stretch to believe this is coincidence," I said. "Where are they? Normally, if Mom isn't manning the phones and computers at the Control Center, your mom is, or they have Mai Li come. Especially when we have a job like this under way." I looked up into Bart's worried face. "What's going on? They can't all be incommunicado at the same time."

"Did you try Oz and Mai Li at their home?"

"I did. I've tried everyone's cell and their home. No one answers either phone. No one has an answering machine connected. It's as if everyone just unplugged and walked away."

Chapter 13

Bart paced again. "What was the last thing your mother said when you talked with her yesterday?"

"David was working on getting the information on the generals and Cell Seven, and Else would probably meet us to pick up the stones."

"Did she say what Else was doing in this part of the world?" Bart stopped and stared at me.

I thought about it, then shook my head. "No. Just that it would be a good idea for someone to relieve us of the topaz we'd collected thus far and get them out of the reach of the terrorists."

"Else had been working on a French angle. She wasn't anywhere near here. David was in Norway following another case. Why bring them here? Now?"

I joined Bart pacing back and forth along the little greens then to the railing to peer out into the darkness and back again. "Oz and Mai Li were in Thailand, investigating terrorists smuggling arms with manufacturing products from that area. Then they were making a short visit to her parents and family in Chang Mai. Her parents wouldn't have a phone, but I can't imagine Oz and Mai Li turning off their cells."

Bart nodded. "The odds of everyone having their phones off at the same time is as great as me winning the lottery—without buying a ticket."

We leaned on the railing, letting the sea breeze wash gently over us. Another ship passed ours a couple of miles away, its lights moving slowly through the black night. Bart put his arms around my shoulders and pulled me close. "Cold?" he asked.

"A little. How about if I try one more time to connect with someone, and then we go to our cabin?"

Bart nodded, and I ran through the list again with the same results as the first time. "It can't be the compact. I'm getting a live signal. It's eerie. Where are they?"

Bart didn't answer, but simply wrapped his arm around my shoulder, and we headed downstairs to our cabin. I brushed my teeth and washed my face, and when I came out of the bathroom, Bart was lying on the bed with his arms around his stomach.

"Problem?" I asked.

"Stomach cramps. Probably from stuffing myself at dinner."

"Maybe it was something you ate. Do you have anything in your toiletry bag for an upset stomach?"

"Yeah. I'll get up in a minute and find it. Go ahead and get ready for bed."

Happy to do that, I snuggled into my pajamas and propped the pillows up on the bed to read my scriptures for a few minutes and write in my journal while Bart disappeared into the bathroom. It wasn't until I heard retching that I began to worry. An upset stomach was almost a given for occasional travelers to foreign countries, but Bart, accustomed to traveling and eating different foods, hadn't encountered problems for years. His stomach must be cast iron. What made him suddenly very sick?

What did he have for dinner that I didn't have? He'd ordered the same appetizer, but a different soup and salad. We'd both had the prime rib, but he hadn't eaten his yams. I had. We both ate the mille-feuille. Then I remembered the chocolate mousse. The "gift" from friends.

I called Sara and Charlotte's room. Sara answered. Yes, her mother was throwing up in the bathroom. I called Vivian and Blaine's room. No answer. They must have gone to the show. Dorothy answered when I called their room. Jed was sick. Yes, he'd eaten the chocolate mousse. She'd been too full and hadn't even tasted it.

That was enough of a sampling for me to determine the culprit was the chocolate mousse. But who'd ordered it, and who had doctored it? And what exactly was in it? Then I heard Raphael outside our door with his cart.

I slipped on my robe and slippers and opened the door. "Raphael, I need a favor."

"Yes, ma'am."

"Is it possible for you to find out who ordered a special chocolate mousse dessert tonight, who prepared it, and which tables received it?"

He looked puzzled.

"As we finished dessert, our waitress brought a tray full of chocolate mousse. She said a friend had ordered it especially for us. When I told her I was too full, and asked if we could save it for tomorrow, she said there was no place for leftovers and they would have to throw it away if we didn't eat it tonight. I didn't touch mine, and three other people at our table left theirs. My husband had a spoonful, and another woman tasted hers. They are both deathly ill. I called others in our group. Whoever ate the mousse is very sick."

Raphael nodded, finally understanding what I wanted.

"And before you do, can you run to the medical center and get something for my husband? It sounds like we're going to need something far more powerful for food poisoning than we have with us."

"I will go right now." He ran down the corridor.

I went back to the phone, called Sara and Dorothy and told them to go to the medical center to get medicine for Charlotte and Jed. Something to combat food poisoning. Pepto-Bismol wouldn't touch this baby.

When I hung up, I began some serious worrying. Bart, my big, strapping, healthy husband, was violently ill. He'd only had a spoonful. How much had Charlotte eaten? She'd taken a few tiny bites on the tip of her spoon before we left the table. If she'd quit then, she probably hadn't ingested any more than Bart's one spoonful. How much had Jed eaten? And who else was sick?

If one spoonful did this to my husband, what would happen to someone who ate the whole bowl? I could only hope it had been designed to make one very sick and was not a fatal dose. I racked my brain, but no poisons that reacted like this came to mind. I was still pacing the floor when Raphael knocked on the door with the medicine.

"I will go quickly while they are still cleaning up the meal and see what I can find out for you."

"Thanks, Raphael. I appreciate it so much. If you can find some of the mousse, please bring it to me so we can have it analyzed. We need to know what it was so we can find an antidote for whatever made them so sick." I shut the door, read the instructions on the packet of medicine Raphael brought, and handed it to Bart in the bathroom. I hated to have anyone see me sick, so after asking if there was anything I could do, and getting a quick shake of Bart's sweat-covered head, I quickly shut the door and left him alone.

Then I started praying. I couldn't think of anything else to do. I needed my husband to get better, and he only had until morning to do that. Then we had to go find another jewel, as well as find out who was behind this poisoning and why.

It was a long night. Bart didn't spend a lot of time in his bed until nearly morning. Our saving grace was that we weren't scheduled to arrive in Santorini until noon, so when Bart finally vacated the bathroom permanently, he could sleep in.

* * *

About eight o'clock I showered, dressed, and slipped out of our cabin, leaving Bart sleeping soundly. I expected to find Raphael at his usual post outside our door with his cart, but he wasn't there. Had he discovered who ordered the mousse and who had received the doctored dessert?

Unable to find Raphael to answer my questions, I went to the medical center. Dr. Chandra should be able to tell me who'd asked for medicine last night. At first, she wasn't excited about releasing any information at all, but I finally convinced her we were actually with a private security firm working with our tour, and we were trying to prevent just this sort of thing from happening.

She showed me the list of passengers who requested treatment or medication for stomach problems last night. Ten in all, and all ten were members of our tour group. Two had even had their stomachs pumped. They must have eaten the whole bowl of chocolate mousse.

Cell Seven was behind this. I had no doubt at all.

I explained the unusual circumstances to the petite, dark-eyed doctor but told her only a portion of the story.

"You understand that this is highly confidential information? You must not repeat a word of what I am going to tell you to anyone."

She nodded, perched on the corner of the desk, and waited for the rest of the explanation.

Then, before I launched into the story, I hurried to add, "Not even Gabriella. She's in a different department in our company, working on a different case. She doesn't have a need to know anything about our case. I must ask you to promise not to speak to anyone about any of this, except the captain. My husband has been working with him, and he's cooperating with us."

Dr. Chandra silently nodded again, and when I finally felt satisfied that she understood the importance of confidentiality, I continued.

"Someone fed poison to several members of a tour group. We're with a security agency that investigates this sort of thing, and I need your help to find out who did it so I can determine why the poison was administered, and why to this group particularly. Apparently someone wants them out of commission."

"Even to the point of poisoning their food?" Dr. Chandra sounded incredulous.

I couldn't think of a delicate way of stating the problem without scaring her to death. I nodded. "I need your help. Can you go to the kitchen and talk to whoever oversees the food preparation, and make sure personal requests are handled by someone beyond suspicion?"

"You suspect someone in the kitchens did this?" She appeared even more incredulous.

"I suspect someone in the kitchen was bribed to lace the chocolate mousse with whatever substance made everyone sick. I want to make sure it doesn't happen again. Someone might die. We don't want that. If the people in the kitchen know we're looking for this kind of thing—that someone is actively investigating, it will either prevent it from happening again or take a lot more bribe money before they'll hazard a chance a second time."

Dr. Chandra stood. "I'll see what I can do."

"Thank you. I'll check back with you later." As I was about to leave, I heard a sound from the examining table enclosed in the white privacy curtain.

I glanced back at Dr. Chandra. "Someone else is sick?"

She nodded. "We're putting him ashore at Santorini in the morning so he can get extensive medical care that we can't give him here."

"Stomach problems?" I asked.

"No, a head injury." She turned away and went back to work. I'd been dismissed, but as I left, I peeked through a gap in the curtain. The patient's head was wrapped in gauze—mummy fashion—and the patient was strapped to the bed. Must be a pretty severe head wound.

On my way up from deck seven, I stopped on deck eight to check on Gabriella. I wanted to keep tabs on this lady. What was she running from? What happened in Bari that made her flee the city in the middle of the night? And why wasn't she discussing her case? This little quirk alone was mystifying.

As I raised my hand to knock on her door, I heard Gabriella's animated voice inside. It took her a minute to open it, and when she did, she didn't invite me in. She blocked my view of the interior of the room, leaning against the door with her hip.

"Good morning, Gabriella. How are you feeling this morning?" I tried to sound cheerful, enthusiastic, and filled with energy.

"Good. And you?" Her silk, flowered dressing gown wasn't belted and though she clutched it with one hand to hold it in place, her curves were still obvious.

"Wonderful. Today we tour Santorini. I'm *so* excited. This is one of the Greek islands I've always wanted to explore. Do you get to go ashore on these excursions, or do you have other duties as a member of the crew?"

"I usually get to sleep in during the day because I'm doing shows all night." Her tone was cold, and her voice filled with annoyance. "And speaking of shows, you didn't catch mine last night."

"Bart and I . . . got a little . . . busy in our room last night and forgot the time." I stammered the explanation filled with innuendo and even, I hoped, managed a little blush. "We'll see you another time. And since I'm apparently keeping you from an important tête-à-tête, I'll leave. Sorry I disturbed you. Next time I'm concerned about your well-being, I'll just call on the telephone."

Gabriella flashed a saccharin smile. "Next time, don't bother at all. Unless, of course, you just want to send Bart. You do let him off his leash occasionally, I assume."

"If Bart wanted to come to you, you'd have seen him in the last three or four years. I'll let you get back to your morning constitutional." I turned and walked down the hall until I heard her door slam shut, then stopped, retrieved a convenient little tool from my journal's spy kit, and hurried back to Gabriella's door. Making sure I was alone in the hall, I stuck the device over the peephole. It reversed the glass, enabling me to see inside her cabin much as Gabriella might see out into the hall when she peeked through her peephole.

A tall man with dark hair curling at his neckline emerged from the bathroom, slipped Gabriella's dressing gown from her shoulders, and bent toward her lips. She slid her arms around his neck and gazed seductively into his face, red lips slightly parted, anticipating his kiss.

The man had his back to me so I couldn't see his face. *Just give me two minutes with this little gizmo and I'll know what you're up to, Gabi, and I'll bet it's no good.*

Unfortunately I didn't get my two minutes. I heard voices at the door behind me, and pocketing my viewing device, I escaped, hopefully unseen, into the stairwell. I didn't want to be spotted lurking around Gabriella's closed door.

I felt a slow burn all the way up the stairs. Gabriella flaunting her voluptuous figure at me made me angry. Or was it jealousy I felt? It had been weeks since I'd had a discernible waistline, and I felt positively frumpy compared to her. Then I had to check my emotions. Maybe *she* was jealous of *me*. After all, I was the one carrying Bart's child. *It's all in the perspective,* I thought with a smile.

My empty stomach complained loudly, but I had one more errand before I indulged in breakfast. I hurried to the miniature golf course, bypassing delicious aromas emanating from the breakfast buffet on deck eleven, and even passed the Flamenco Lounge with our no-longer-private balcony on deck twelve. I had serious business to attend to and needed no interruptions in the middle of a conversation.

I must make the connection today, I thought as I hurried along the length of the ship. If not, we might have to consider something as drastic as jumping ship at the next port to find out what on earth was going on with Anastasia.

Chapter 14

The entire stern of the ship was deserted this beautiful clear morning. Apparently too early for golfers. I leaned against the railing in the sun and called Mom at the Control Center. This time, after several rings, Alma answered.

"Allison, it's so good to hear from you." Alma's sleepy voice revealed I'd awakened her.

"I'm sorry, Alma. I know it's midnight there, but we couldn't reach anyone yesterday when you would have been up. What's happening? Where is everyone?"

"In Europe. Didn't you know?"

"Europe?" I couldn't believe my ears. Had Alma been dreaming? "What are they doing in Europe, and how would I know they were there?"

"I thought Margaret called you."

"No, we haven't heard from anyone. Else was supposed to meet us yesterday to take the jewels we'd collected thus far, but David showed up instead, and we missed him. He left a cryptic message with Gabriella."

"Gabriella Cardin?" Bart's mother sounded puzzled and surprised. "What's she doing with you?"

"Heaven forbid she should be *with* us! She boarded the ship when we stopped at Bari, apparently fleeing some situation there. She had a gunshot wound in her arm. Can you find out why she had to get out and what she was involved with and what kind of help we were supposed to give her? She hasn't indicated she needs any yet."

"I'll do a little digging and see what comes up."

"Alma, why are all of Anastasia's people suddenly gathered over here, and why did none of them have their phones turned on last night? We couldn't reach anyone. Even your phone was off and your answering machine disconnected. What's going on?"

"Haven't you seen the news, dear?"

"No. We were in Corfu most of yesterday, then had dinner and never turned on the news."

"Cell Seven made headlines all over the world with a huge explosion outside of Florence. I think they intended to destroy some of the priceless treasures there, but apparently their bomb went off prematurely, and they ended up bringing a mountainside down on themselves instead."

"And why did that bring Anastasia to Italy?"

"Because they announced it beforehand, telling the world what they intended to do, and they listed the rest of their targets in the next four weeks if their demands aren't met."

My stomach did a funny little flip-flop, which had nothing to do with the fact I was starving to death. "And what are they demanding?"

"Kesselring's treasure, of course."

"But no one knows where it is!"

"You and I know that, and maybe they do too, but they're demanding it anyway, probably hoping their demands will speed the discovery of its location. Their list contains some of the greatest historical treasures of Europe, and from the size of the explosion yesterday, they have the means to carry out their threats."

"Alma, this is insane."

"They *are* insane. That's one reason they're so dangerous. And now that they've gone public with their demands and their agenda, every crazy radical in the world is clamoring to join them."

"All this happened in the last twenty-four hours?" Unbelievable. How had we missed these horrifying developments? Why hadn't Mom reported this when I had her on the phone? Then I remembered our conversation and how distracted she'd been. The news of an explosion had come in, and she told me about Gabriella. Were the two explosions connected?

"Where are Mom and Dad now? And the rest of Anastasia, for that matter?"

"Margaret and Jack are in Florence, where they'll stay based. Else's in Paris, Dominic's in Athens, Oz and Mai Li were sent to Rome, and David should be in London by now. Rip Skylar is covering Berlin."

"What are they doing?"

"Working with local authorities to prevent Cell Seven from destroying the targets they've announced."

"And what can we do?" I suddenly felt claustrophobic being confined to the ship, even up here where I had absolutely no confinement at all.

"Just keep gathering the jewels. The sooner we get them all, the sooner we can solve the puzzle they contain."

"But, Alma, we'll be on this ship for another four days. We don't reach Athens until Friday. Can we get off there and do something more constructive?" Bart would be climbing the walls until we docked in Venice on Sunday. And I didn't mean the ship's fake climbing wall. Bart would be impossible to live with if he couldn't do something physical to help.

"Alli, you're not listening to me. The greatest help you and Bart can be is to gather up the topaz stones and bring the necklace back together. You're in place. The underground's gone to great effort making arrangements to meet you in public places where tourists congregate without exposing either themselves or you to the factions who want the stones. They know the schedule of the tour, where you'll be each day. That's where they'll be safest contacting you. We can't change plans now without endangering the Freedom Fighters or their families who have planned just where and how to meet you."

That she was right didn't help me feel any better. And how on earth would I break this news to my husband?

"Alli, are you still there?"

"Yes. I was just thinking how hard it's going to be on your son, being tied to the tour instead of out chasing the bad guys."

"I know, dear, but I'm sure you'll think of something to keep him entertained." I could hear the smile in her soft voice. Then it changed to a more serious tone. "Besides, I expect things will just keep escalating. That should make your action-hungry husband happy. Be careful, dear. Everyone who wasn't already after the stones will be trying to get their hands on them now."

"Thanks, Alma. Please keep in touch and let me know what's going on. I feel terribly isolated from the rest of the world right now."

"That's the whole reason for going on vacation, dear. By the way, how is the cruise? And how are you feeling?

"I'm great, and the cruise is wonderful, like a second honeymoon, especially since there are no volcanoes to slide into. Today we dock at Santorini for the whole afternoon. This is the one island I've always wanted to see up close."

"How's Bart handling the inactivity?"

I laughed. Only Bart's mother would know to ask that kind of question.

"Rather well, at least, until I break this news to him. In fact, I left him sleeping in to make this call." I didn't bother to tell her the rest of the story. When she finally did hear about it, there wouldn't be anything to worry and fret over.

"Well, just relax and enjoy the quiet moments you have together. You and I both know it won't last. Good night, dear."

I left the railing and sat on one of the pilings that decorated the edge of the miniature golf course, pondering this new information. But I couldn't think past my rumbling stomach and Alma's admonition to enjoy the quiet time because it wouldn't last. Yes, I knew that so very well. Finally, I gave up and went down to breakfast. Because the dining room was crowded, I took my tray on deck to one of the patio tables in the Chez Claude Grill. I needed time and quiet for serious contemplation.

My thoughts kept returning to the innocent people who would be hurt or killed if we weren't able to get the topaz stones together and decipher the instructions to Kesselring's hidden treasure. It was frightening, so frightening that it took my appetite away.

I decided I'd better see if my husband exhibited any signs of life this morning. If it had been me retching all night, I'd probably have stayed in bed all day. Bart couldn't do that. Even if all he did was just move to the deck and lounge in the sun in a deck chair, he'd have to leave our little cabin. And maybe Raphael had some news for me.

Raphael's cart was outside our door, but he was nowhere in sight. I opened our door quietly, hoping if Bart was still asleep I wouldn't wake him, but he stirred at the creaking door, opened his eyes, and stretched.

"Are you still in the land of the living?" I asked, sitting on the side of his bed and stroking his day-old stubble.

"No. I turned myself inside out last night and gave up the ghost. Living didn't seem to be a viable option."

I noticed he made no attempt to sit up. "Dare I ask how you feel this morning?"

"I don't know. Do you? Do I look that bad?"

I cocked my head to one side and pretended to examine him closely. "Mmm. You've looked better, but you still beat any other male on this planet."

"You're slightly prejudiced. What have you been up to while I've been sleeping off the effects of the toxic mousse?"

"I've been busy as a bee. Last night I enlisted Raphael's help to find out who prepared your deadly dish, and who ordered it. I haven't seen Raphael, but I ended up asking Dr. Chandra about it myself to see who ingested it, or, at least, who came for medication. Apparently the special dessert was served only to our group, and ten sampled enough to experience the effects."

"You've been a busy lady."

"That's not all. I caught our gorgeous Gabriella in a liaison with a mysterious, dark-haired stranger before nine o'clock this morning. On second thought, maybe it was a carryover from the night before. At any rate, there's no longer any pretense of concern or care between us. She doesn't like me because I have you, and I don't like her because she wants you. So we can now just ignore each other."

Bart tried to laugh but held his rib cage instead. "Oh, that hurts. Remind me not to laugh for a couple of days, will you?"

"I promise not to crack any funny jokes. Ready for the rest of my morning report?"

"You mean there's more?"

"Oh, much, much more. When I left Gabriella and her guest, I called the Control Center. Your mom answered. Guess where everyone is?"

"Getting away from it all on a cruise in the Mediterranean?"

"You're closer than you think. They're all in Europe. Cell Seven introduced themselves to the world yesterday with an explosion that was supposed to destroy a valuable target in Florence. It went off prematurely and dissolved a mountain instead. Then they announced that they wanted all the stones from the topaz necklace immediately or they would destroy a series of world treasures. Mom and Dad are in Florence, and they've sent all of Anastasia's agents to various capitals to see if they can prevent any more explosions."

Bart reached for the remote control to the TV and flipped on the set. CNN Europe was just announcing a second explosion credited to the mysterious Cell Seven, this time in Istanbul. Pictures of St. Sofia Basilica in the background and smoking rubble in the foreground filled the screen. We watched, hypnotized by the images of cars and buses and homes, and, unfortunately, people, who had been caught in the blast.

I shook my head, not believing what the announcer was saying. "A second miss? They can't be that clumsy, can they?"

"Good point, princess. Maybe that's just what they want the world to think."

"That's the impression we had of them, remember? You said they were a bunch of amateurs and radicals, and the two were a deadly combination."

Bart nodded absently. "Anything else happen while I was in Never Never Land?"

"Not yet. Although your mom's last words to me were to enjoy the quiet while we can. It won't last. If you can muster the strength to get up and dressed, we dock in Santorini at noon and have eight hours on that incredible volcanic crescent. Do you feel like going?"

"I'll tell you better after my shower." Bart raised himself carefully off the pillow. He sat on the edge of the bed for a minute, cradled his head in his hands, and didn't move. "Whatever they put in the mousse sure packed a wallop. I'll never be able to look at another one of those in my whole life."

"I don't think we'll ever know what they gave you without being able to analyze the mousse, and unless Raphael was able to get some last night, I'm sure the evidence has long since been relegated to the dishwasher. They have to get those dishes off the tables and into the dishwasher, and then they reset the tables for the last dinner seating. But I'll check with Raphael and see if he's discovered anything." I opened the door. Not only was Raphael missing in action, but even his cart was gone. "Guess he's working another hall."

Bart stood unsteadily, holding himself up with one hand on the wall all the way to the bathroom. I plumped my pillows and leaned back to watch the report on CNN. When the reporters had exhausted all they knew about the explosions, they turned to a different subject—breaking news in the art world.

I sat up abruptly as the news anchor introduced the subject of the report and a headline filled the television screen. "Discovery Rocks Art World!"

Chapter 15

"What other treasures remain to be uncovered?" the CNN reporter asked as a picture of a famous painting by Cezanne splashed across the small screen. "This painting has been lost since World War II and was feared destroyed in the Allied bombing of occupying German forces in early 1945. It surfaced yesterday at Christie's, but sources have not revealed how nor where it was discovered. Cezanne's oil painting is being offered by its anonymous owner for two million dollars, but ripples in the art world say the bidding could be vigorous, and if the price reaches new heights for the artist's work, they're wondering if that might offer an enticement for collectors to pull out other treasures that haven't been seen for over sixty years."

I became more intrigued when I saw the next item on Christie's list of offerings. A small, amber rose, perfectly formed, exquisitely detailed. Again, an anonymous owner, and like Cezanne's painting, its location for the past half century was mysteriously unknown.

I stared at the TV screen. Could that delicate Amber Rose be one of the artifacts from the long lost Amber Room? My head spun with possibilities. Simply a coincidence Field Marshall Kesselring's grandson had just died, revealing the possible location of his ill-gotten treasure to his son? Had the newest heir, Kesselring's great-grandson, begun selling off the treasures already? Items he didn't want? Things that didn't suit his taste?

Or could he be in financial trouble, with immediate need for cash? So immediate he couldn't postpone the sale of these items for a reasonable amount of time after the death of his great-grandfather? Or did someone else, some organization he belonged to, need the money immediately?

Okay, Alli. Start over. You're getting carried away on this tangent. Begin again. Why were these treasures surfacing now? Were they part of some private collection and the owner needed funds? Had some individual discovered them in an attic or basement? Was this all perfectly innocent and had nothing to do with our topaz puzzle?

No matter how hard I tried to conjure up another scenario, my mind kept returning to Kesselring's stash. Then my imagination went wild. Where were my parents, and for that matter the rest of Anastasia, yesterday, that they had no cell phone coverage? In high-level meetings with local officials trying to figure out how to prevent Cell Seven from blowing them to smithereens?

No. Either Mom or Dad would have left their cell phone on and excused themselves to answer it. They simply didn't cut off all communication—especially not in the middle of a crisis. And this appeared to be a crisis with worldwide implications.

So, if they didn't turn them off to prevent interruptions, where were they that they couldn't receive my phone call? My satellite phone call at that. A mine? Cave? Crypt? Catacombs? There were plenty of those in Italy. Those should be the only places our phones didn't reach.

But why hadn't Mom called me about the explosions? That impacted our activities, our case, all we were doing. It was totally out of character for her to not keep us abreast of any new development.

Bart emerged from the shower with a little color back in his cheeks, and while he dressed, I recapped the TV broadcast and my thoughts.

"And what conclusions have you reached from all of this?" he said, stretching out on his bed with his hands behind his head.

"No conclusions. Well, maybe a couple." I sat on the edge of my bed. "It's beyond coincidence that everyone had no service on their cell phones yesterday, or they were simply all turned off at the same time. Doesn't play, right?"

Bart nodded.

"So where were they?"

"You tell me, Dr. Watson."

"In a cave. Someone discovered a stash of treasure, not necessarily Kesselring's," I offered quickly, "but something hidden before or during the war. It's happened before, and things will continue turning up as people remodel homes or tear down old ones to build new ones. As development spreads out into countryside. As kids explore caves. As old mines are re-opened to tap into new resources."

"Sounds reasonable," he nodded. "And . . ."

"And when I talked to Mom last, she told me about an explosion in Bari and said we were to find Gabriella. If there was a second explosion right after that and they mobilized with the news from Cell Seven, she might have thought—in her haste to get on their way—she had told me about the other explosion. That would explain why she didn't call."

"I'll buy that. What else?"

"Why did David come especially to pick up the jewels and not stay to get them?"

"Good question, princess. Why?"

"Mom said Else, or someone, would meet us at the dock just as we were boarding before leaving from Corfu. They have our itinerary. They know the tour schedules. They know where we'll be so the underground can meet us. They knew our tour would return to the ship at three thirty to board. Unless something drastic happened, we wouldn't be at the dock before then because we'd be with the tour."

"And all this leads you to . . ."

"The next question. What was Gabriella doing on the dock talking to David? Did she tell him something that caused him to leave before he accomplished what he came to do? Or did he give her a message for us that she never relayed?"

That got his attention. Bart sat up. "Like what?"

"That's as far as I've thought this through. And the more I think about it, the more questions I discover. Like why hasn't Gabriella asked us to help her? Mom said we needed to help her do something. She just didn't say what. Gabriella doesn't strike me as the modest type. If she was involved in preventing the bombing of the music festival as she suggested, why hasn't she shared the details? We love to congratulate each other on our successes. Why not her with this one? Or was it not a success?"

"Mmm. Good point," he murmured. "Keep talking."

"Why are these art pieces surfacing right now, just as the Sevens are making their big play?"

"Coincidence?"

I stood and paced the short distance between the door and the beds. "Like you said, as much chance of that as you winning the lottery without buying a ticket."

"Didn't Mother tell you anything?" Bart asked, pulling me beside him on the bed to keep me from pacing back and forth in front of him.

"No, and I didn't think to ask any of these questions. I didn't know enough when we talked to even know what questions to ask. She may have thought we knew more than we did, but then, I woke her. It was midnight there. I'm sure she didn't have her wits about her."

"Then we may have to disturb her sleep again." Bart rose to his feet and stood still for a minute.

"Do you feel up to a trip to the top?" I jumped up and took his arm. I wasn't sure Bart had the strength to do all those decks to the top after his strenuous night.

"We'll compromise just this once. We'll take the elevator up and do the stairs on the way back."

"You may even want to stop for a few minutes and have a bite of breakfast, just to replenish all you lost last night." I grabbed my purse and headed for the door.

"Only if you promise I won't have to face any of that mud."

"Mousse," I corrected.

"I prefer to think of it as mud. A vile, muddy witch's concoction. No food should ever do those things to your body."

I whirled around and stared at Bart. A witch's concoction? A witch who would have access to the kitchens? A witch who would and could ask favors of the kitchen help? A witch who would know what kind of potions would make one very sick, but not kill, and who had access to them. A witch who could entice men to do anything she wanted. A witch with an agenda. But what was that agenda?

"Yes?" Bart said, grabbing his jacket from the closet.

"Yes, what?" I asked innocently.

"You just had an interesting thought," Bart said, closing the door behind him. "You're not going to share?"

I was saved from answering that question at the moment. A good-looking young steward with a worried expression on his face rushed down the corridor, peering in all the open doors, speaking to the housekeepers and other crew members he happened to find, then hurrying on toward us.

He nodded as he passed us, then abruptly called out. "Excuse me. Are you in cabin 9018?"

We turned around. "Yes," Bart said.

"You're Mr. and Mrs. Allan?"

"Yes."

"Have you seen Raphael this morning?"

"No, I haven't seen him at all." I retraced my steps to face him. "Maybe he's in one of the rooms here."

"He is not answering his phone."

I was close enough to see his nametag. "You're Ricardo, Raphael's friend."

He nodded. "We were helping you. Looking for bugs."

Bart joined our conversation. "We appreciate your help. Did you find more?"

Ricardo shook his head and held up both hands. "No. That is not why I came. Raphael went to the kitchen last night to find out about the food poisoning. He was supposed to meet me later but never showed up. I thought Emanuella had detained him so I did not question it then. But he does not have his cell phone now, and no one has seen him."

"Have you talked to Emanuella this morning?" I asked, thinking of Gabriella's tête-à-tête in her room. Maybe Emanuella and Raphael were also an item.

"She did not see him last night. No one saw him last night. Or this morning. It is as if he is just disappeared overboard."

I didn't like Ricardo's choice of words. And I didn't like the horrible feeling that descended over me, thinking I may have sent Raphael on a task resulting in his no longer being with us. Had he asked too many questions? Had he discovered who ordered the mousse? And who spiked it?

"Could he have received an assignment to some other part of the ship?" Bart asked.

"No, but even if he had, he would have told me."

"Do you always have your cell phones on?" I asked.

"Of course. We need to be in contact with our supervisor at all times in case any of our passengers need something. The supervisors immediately call us, and we take care of those needs. You are never to be without your phone, and it is never to be turned off."

I began to understand why Ricardo was so worried about his friend. I was worried too about my part in Raphael's disappearance.

"Have you spoken to your supervisor about Raphael?" Bart asked.

"Oh, no, sir. I would not want to get him in trouble."

"He may be in big trouble right now," I said, glancing up at Bart to see if his thoughts were running along the same lines as mine. They apparently were.

"Ricardo, how many people knew you were checking for the listening devices?" Bart asked.

"All the stewards. We were all looking for them."

"And how many knew Raphael was trying to find out about the poisoned mousse?" I asked.

"Only me. He did not tell anyone else—at least, I think he did not tell anyone else," Ricardo corrected. "He said it was important to find out who ordered it, who doctored it, and who was supposed to receive it."

"That was the assignment I gave him," I acknowledged, more sure than ever I had caused harm to the innocent young man. "Ricardo, can you meet us here in one hour? While we see if we can find out anything, you keep searching."

Ricardo clutched his hands in front of him and nodded vigorously. "I will meet you here in one hour." Then he scurried around the corner and disappeared.

I turned to my husband, feeling like an executioner. "Oh, Bart, what have I done? What if I've sent him to his death? We aren't dealing with nice people here."

"Too true." Bart guided me along the corridor toward the elevators. "What did you have in mind when you asked Ricardo to come back in an hour?"

"Last night, I sent Raphael first to the medical center to get medicine for you, then asked him to find out what he could discover in the kitchen. He brought you the medication, then said he was on his way to investigate. That would have been around ten o'clock."

Our conversation halted while we played sardines on the crowded elevator to deck eleven. I knew there was a good reason I always took the stairs instead of elevators. I couldn't stand being in such close proximity to so many people in such a small space. I wanted to run screaming from there when the doors slid open. Freedom was everything to a claustrophobe.

As fresh air flushed through the open door, a sobering thought pounded in my head and repeated with each beat of my heart. I may have not just taken Raphael's freedom from him with this assignment. I may have taken his life.

Chapter 16

"You were saying?" Bart reminded me as we picked up our trays. We were the only ones in the brunch line for a change.

"Yes, I was saying . . . What was I saying? I forgot."

"Why you wanted to meet Ricardo in an hour."

"I thought that would give him time to cover all his possibilities in case he actually did locate Raphael." I studied the selection of brunch possibilities. Someone mentioned the croissants were to die for, so I picked one of those, in spite of the number of calories I knew it contained, then filled the rest of my plate with fresh fruit. *That should strike some sort of balance,* I rationalized.

"And what if he doesn't find him?" Bart asked quietly, choosing the pasta, no meat sauce, and some vegetables. He appeared to be carefully introducing food back into his body. Nothing to cause possible upset.

"When we finish this oddly timed meal," I whispered as someone came behind us with their tray, "we'll check with Dr. Chandra to see if he came back to talk to her. If he didn't, then he must have gone straight to the kitchen."

As we settled at a quiet corner table away from everyone, Bart continued his questions. "And who do we talk to in the kitchen to find out who Raphael might have questioned?"

"I have an idea, but I think I'll just do a little snooping around and then let you know what I find." I crunched into my croissant and tried to appear charming with flakes all over my mouth.

Bart leaned across the table and stared at me. "You mean you're not going to tell me?"

I nodded enthusiastically, trying to finish the bite that stuck to the roof of my mouth and crumbled all down the front of me.

"Is that, 'yes, you're going to tell me,' or 'yes, you're not going to tell me'?"

I took a long drink of ice water. Bart wasn't going to like my answer, either way. "Yes, I'm going to tell you—after I've done some checking."

"Allison," Bart started, his tone low and ominous. He didn't have to say any more. I knew when he called me by my given name he was displeased, but I'd known he would be before I said anything.

I held up both hands "Stop right there. If I told you what I suspect, I wouldn't like your answer because I know what you'd say about my theory. If I don't tell you what I suspect, you'll be temporarily upset while I run and ask a couple of questions. If I find I'm wrong, then I'll apologize for what I've been thinking. If I'm right . . ." I let the sentence drop. "Finish your lunch. I'll be back before you're through. And don't follow me. Just relax and enjoy your pasta."

I dropped my napkin in my chair and hurried out the door, knowing Bart's weak legs wouldn't allow him to catch me before I was down the stairs and out of sight. I went directly to the kitchen and stood in the doorway, watching the hurrying and scurrying that always took place during meal preparation. A rotund gentleman dressed in baker's white inquired politely if I needed help, reminding me passengers weren't allowed in the kitchens.

"I have a message for . . ." I put my hand up to my mouth. "Oh, dear. I've forgotten his name. Gabriella asked me to tell her friend something, and now I can't tell you who I'm looking for."

"Gabriella?"

"You know. Long black hair, drop-dead gorgeous. Sings in the lounge in the evening and is in the show at night. She came in last night and requested a special order. Wanted chocolate mousse delivered to some tables after the first seating finished their dinner. Remember her?"

He nodded his head so vigorously his hat nearly fell off. "Oui! Oo la la. Who could forget that one?"

"Then you probably know who I'm supposed to give the message to. I think he would have helped her with the mousse."

"Oui. It is Andre."

"He's tall, has dark hair that sort of curls at the back of his neck?" I pulled at my own dark hair to demonstrate.

He nodded. "Andre. He said some special guests were aboard and this mousse would be a treat they'd never forget."

"You're right there. They'll never forget it." I turned to go. "Thanks. You've been very helpful."

I hurried back up to La Brassiere cafeteria to find Bart scowling over his pasta. He stood so quickly when I reached the table, he had to lean over and grip the sides to keep from falling.

"Still a little weak?" I asked sympathetically.

He nodded and plopped down into his chair. "Where were you? What were you doing?"

"Proving a theory. Tell me what you know about Gabriella's politics."

Bart looked surprised. "Politics?"

I nodded. "Where do her allegiances lie? She's French. Is she as anti-American as many of her countrymen? Is she neutral so she can be objective in her Interpol investigations? Does she have a separate agenda from her Interpol work? Who are her friends? Has she had any marks on her record lately?"

Bart looked dumbfounded.

"Before you accuse me of simply being a jealous wife, I'll tell you what I just discovered in the kitchen. Gabriella came last night and asked that a special dessert be prepared for some guests. Her accomplice in this undertaking was a tall, dark-haired man with curls at his neckline named Andre—the man in her cabin this morning. The chef remembered her distinctly. 'Oui. Oo la la. Who could forget that one?' It definitely wasn't a case of mistaken identity. As he said, you don't forget Gabriella."

Bart couldn't find his tongue. Or his voice.

"So you were poisoned by your little friend. Or maybe it was meant for me. Women don't refuse chocolate desserts as often as men. Maybe she was planning on me eating the whole thing, on putting me out of commission so she'd have you all to herself. But excuse me if I don't think along those lines right now. I'll also depart from the jealous wife role. I don't think she wanted you. Except I'd married you, which made you an obvious target for her attention. I think little miss Gabriella is up to her false eyelashes in something bigger than husband stealing."

I stopped and waited for my astonished spouse to respond. When he didn't, I continued. "Why did she come aboard at Bari? Was she really running from danger? What kind of danger required a ship out of town instead of slipping quietly over the mountains in a car? Or lying low in a safe house?"

Bart was recovering slowly from the shock of my revelations. His eyes didn't have that glazed look anymore, and he seemed to actually be following my train of thought.

"You're with me on this?" I asked, just to make sure.

He nodded.

"Okay, she notifies Interpol she has to get out of town, stages an explosion to lend credence to her story, and gets herself wounded to elicit sympathy. Possibly even shoots herself in the arm since it was a low-caliber bullet and it conveniently missed all the vital spots. But how does Mom get involved? There's no way Anastasia would be notified of this unless Gabriella made the right calls, pulled the right strings to make it happen. We have nothing going in Bari. She shouldn't know about our topaz case unless someone at Interpol Headquarters in Lyon told her, but that's a pretty far stretch. My folks have a policy to let only the director know what they're doing unless they need help from another agency. How did she find out we were going to be on this ship?"

No answer. Bart just shook his head slowly.

"Another coincidence?"

He continued to shake his head.

I leaned forward. "Right. No coincidence. Gabriella knew we were going to be on this ship. She knows about the topaz collection. She's either going to try to stop us before we make contact to collect the stones, or she's going to try to intercept during the pass, or she's going to let us collect them and try to take them from us."

"And Raphael?"

That question took the wind out of my sails. "I hope she just took him out of commission temporarily, not permanently. He either found out about her or was getting too close." I prayed it was just temporary and we'd find him before she disposed of him for good.

"Where do you think he is?"

"That's where Ricardo comes in. If he hasn't found Raphael by now, I think he needs to search Gabriella's cabin. She might have drugged Raphael if she didn't just toss him overboard already. Or she may have stashed him somewhere onboard, in costuming or some other place she has easy access to without anyone being suspicious of her presence there."

"La Gondola Theater?" Bart guessed.

I nodded. "That would be my first guess if he isn't in her cabin." I toyed with the honeydew melon on my plate. "I don't really know what she would do to him. How cold-blooded is she? I can easily visualize her enticing him to her cabin, distracting him from his investigation. He'd be wide-eyed with wonder at the attention from this incredibly beautiful woman, even if she's three times his age. But then what? Does she simply slip him something to put him out of commission until she can dispose of him? That would be the smart thing to do, just in case she gets caught. There's no body. It's only a case of seducing a fellow crew member who now has a terrific hangover."

"And maybe an impaired memory of what happened to him if she slipped him Rohypnol," Bart said.

"Exactly. The date-rape drug." I glanced at Bart's abandoned plate. "Are you through with your lunch?"

Bart nodded absently. I wondered if he'd even tasted it. We hurried back to our cabin, again taking the elevator since Bart still had shaky legs. Ricardo paced the hall outside our door and hurried to meet us when he saw us coming.

"Have you found him?" he asked anxiously before I had a chance to ask him.

"No. But can you get us into cabin 8209? He just might be in there." I hoped and prayed we'd find him there.

Ricardo didn't even ask why we thought he might be in a passenger's cabin; he just turned and headed down the corridor immediately. We followed him one deck below to Gabriella's cabin.

"What are you going to say if Gabriella opens the door?" I asked my husband quietly so Ricardo couldn't hear.

"Didn't you have something in mind?" Bart asked.

"Nope. I'd probably scratch her eyes out first and ask questions later. I'll let you handle this. Your emotions are a little less involved, I think." I glanced at Bart. "I hope. Unless you'd like to punch her out for poisoning you."

Bart laughed. "I'll think of something."

As it turned out, the cabin was empty. No Gabriella. No Andre. No Raphael. But I did find a cell phone under the bed.

"Ricardo, call Raphael."

Ricardo punched into his cell phone the number for Raphael. The phone in my hand rang. We exchanged worried looks and quickly abandoned Gabriella's cabin before she returned and discovered us there.

"Now what do we do?" Ricardo asked as we went back to his floor.

"Search the theater areas where any costumes or trunks might be stored," Bart instructed. "Do people take their costumes to their rooms or are they left in an open area, a closet or similar location? This woman is an entertainer with access to those places."

"Think of any other place she might have stuffed Raphael after she drugged him, if that's what happened," I added, still holding out hope that Gabriella was smart enough not to commit murder.

"Yes, I will do this," Ricardo said, his enthusiasm laced with relief.

I glanced at my watch, then at my husband. "We're supposed to catch the tender to Santorini in a few minutes. We have go to ashore."

"I can take care of the search, Mrs. Allan. You go ahead. I will see you tonight when you return, and I will tell you what I find. Or what I do not find."

We hurried back to our cabin to gather our things for the trip ashore. I'd looked forward to this stop since I'd first seen it on the itinerary, but now I wasn't sure I wanted to leave Ricardo to search alone. I felt responsible for Raphael.

"It's okay, princess. He can do this without us, and we have a stone to collect, remember? No one else can do that for us."

I stared into sympathetic blue eyes. "You were reading my mind."

"It's pretty obvious what you were thinking, but you have to remember this is our job. They won't pass the stones to anyone else.

We have to be there to get them, and the sooner we have all the jewels, the sooner we can get that treasure back to wherever it belongs."

"Funny. That's just what your mom said this morning when I complained about having to stay on the ship and not being free to help Anastasia elsewhere."

Bart leaned down and kissed me. "Then I guess you'd better get on that little boat which will take us ashore to one of the most picturesque spots in Greece and make yourself available to the passer from Santorini."

We stood at the railing of the ship, watching the snow-topped islands grow larger as we neared. The different colored layers of sediment were clearly visible on these rough, craggy, barren rocks that rose straight up out of the deep blue water with no shoreline. It wasn't until we were in the bay that I realized that it wasn't snow outlining the top of the crescent-shaped island. Houses, white-washed and gleaming in the sun, clung to the rocky cliffs.

We were fortunate to find a seat atop the tender instead of down inside, so we enjoyed the cool breeze as we headed for shore. It was a hot, sunny day, and I certainly didn't need the jacket I'd thrown around my shoulders. A big, modern tour bus waited for us at the little dock with a local guide prepared to inform us about her island.

We wound up a steep, narrow road filled with hairpin curves and switchbacks, which our driver navigated as if he were driving a little sports car. Thank heaven for good brakes! At one point, I glanced out my window and looked straight down the mountain to the slender crescent of beach where our tender had dropped us. We were on the edge of the world. Little white sticks dotting the deep turquoise water in the bay far below were actually tiny boats dwarfed by the huge white ferry moored at the dock.

Our guide pointed out the dry, rocky soil that received moisture only from condensation at night or rain in the winter. None in summer. Tomato vines were short with tiny, red tomatoes that looked like cherries from the bus window. Grape vines were so small they resembled squash plants crawling across the rock-strewn ground, no more than twelve to eighteen inches high. And squash hung in little, orange clumps from anemic-looking vines. How did they make anything grow in this barren soil?

Our destination was Profitis Ilias Monastery—built in the early 1700s at the top of the hill on the highest point on the island. Rocky, terraced fields and white houses dotted the landscape below us, and the bus stopped long enough for everyone to take pictures of the scene spreading below us. The view from the top proved the entire island was simply a caldera shell remaining from a volcano. The rest of it had exploded and blown into the sea.

While the passengers unloaded from the bus—not a speedy activity—Bart and I walked a short distance away and called Alma to see if she had discovered anything about Gabriella. I wondered if she'd stayed up to do the research or had gone back to sleep when we'd hung up.

Alma's voice was wide awake when she answered. Apparently my wonderful, ambitious mother-in-law had immediately gotten busy to find the answers to my questions.

Chapter 17

"Alli, I'm glad you called back, but I still need more time to answer the rest of your questions. In fact, I may need the rest of the day to delve into everything deep enough to get the real answers."

"That's okay. I can call again. What did you find out about Gabriella?"

Alma hesitated for minute. "She's Emile's sister, isn't she? Bart's friend from Tibet."

I glanced up at Bart, standing near enough to hear the expression in his mother's voice. "Yes, she is, but she wasn't like Emile in any way. I suspect she's gotten even further afield now."

"I'm afraid that's true. Her last evaluation report from her boss in Interpol raised a few questions about decisions she'd made under fire. She wasn't placed on probation, but there was a notation in her file that said all evaluations in the future needed to be measured against past performance." Alma paused. "That's Interpol language for 'watch everything she does because there's something a little different about her actions and decisions now.'"

Bart nodded and spoke into my elegant gold compact. "Had they noted anything specific or just the general warning to be aware of changes in her behavior?"

"Good morning, son. It's good to hear your voice. You sound relaxed."

I had to smile at that comment. Bart was so relaxed, he could hardly stand up for any length of time, but it wasn't because of a restful cruise.

"Oh, I'm very relaxed, Mom." He winked at me. "Everyone should take a cruise once in a while. Back to Gabriella. What did the file say?"

"Nothing specific, just the general warning she'd strayed a bit from standard procedure and they wanted her supervisors to keep an eye on her. That kind of notation is usually placed in the file because supervisors can change frequently, so when someone new moves into that slot, they have to be able to know what is going on with the agents newly under their supervision."

"Thanks, Mom. Anything else for us this morning?" Bart said, taking my arm and walking me several more feet down the road. People were returning to the bus, and he didn't want to be close enough for anyone to hear our strange conversation—one that included a third person not present. He pulled out the camera and snapped some pictures to appear busy.

"Yes. I spoke with Margaret. She reported on their activities yesterday when you weren't able to get ahold of anyone. I'm sure you've guessed where they were."

"I figured they must be in a cave where there was no cell phone coverage and the satellite couldn't reach," I answered.

"Smart girl. They had a lucky break after the big explosion yesterday outside of Florence. One of the bombers was injured and left for dead by his fellow terrorists. Local authorities captured him, and as he was dying, he revealed the location of their headquarters. A sort of deathbed confession to clear his conscience, I guess. Jack called in our agents, and they raided the cave with the police. Would have been last night your time, probably when you were trying to reach them."

An incredible piece of good fortune! "What did they find?" Bart and I both asked at the same time.

"Of course, everything hasn't been sifted through and evaluated yet. That's going on right now, but Margaret said they discovered the identity of at least two of the terrorists, which led to a couple of surprising conclusions." Alma paused. I waited for her to continue, but she didn't—at least, not fast enough to satisfy my piqued curiosity.

"Alma, you're as bad as Mom! Finish the story. What did they find?" The group began boarding the bus. We didn't have much time left for this conversation.

"Sorry, dear. I was searching for my notes so I'd be able to get it all straight. Two of the terrorists they identified used to work with Osama bin Laden, but they didn't escape with him when he fled into hiding in Afghanistan like most of bin Laden's men. They started their own cell and began recruiting teenage Muslim girls from Iraq, Syria, and Iran."

"Abu Iyad and Omar Abdel," Bart whispered. I nodded.

"Mom, we have to go," Bart said. "The bus is waiting for us. We'll call you back at our next stop to get the rest of the story."

I hated to end this conversation just when we were finally discovering something that might help us. We were the last ones on the bus and had to wait to discuss our findings while everyone exclaimed over the unusual scenery.

In the spring, this terrain might be beautiful and green, but in October, after the hot summer, it looked barren and scorched, though the terracing of the hillsides and the gleaming white houses trimmed in bright blue made it picturesque. As the bus wound down the hill and across the island, we passed men on donkeys riding toward small, whitewashed villages. Each little town had a church with a tall steeple or bell tower and blue tile trim or a blue dome.

"You know how they find their recruits, don't you, princess?" Bart asked quietly, pointing out a windmill.

I nodded. "Young women who have been disgraced and cast out because they were seen talking to a man other than a family member; young women who were seduced or used by a family member and disgraced, unless they were killed; or young married women who haven't been able to bear children and were divorced by their husbands. They have no place to go. No one will marry them. They're paid to join the terrorists as suicide bombers, and they're redeemed from disgrace by becoming martyrs and by giving their lives to Allah."

Bart shook his head with a sigh. "It's tragic they think they have no other choice."

"Yes, but it's really tragic they believe that by blowing themselves to bits—along with as many infidels as possible—they're doing Allah's will and will be rewarded. It's just incredible to me that people, any people, actually believe they're doing God's will by slaughtering innocent bystanders that way."

We arrived in Pyrgos, the village, our guide said, which most vividly maintained the characteristics of the old, medieval settlements of Santorini. We unloaded from the bus again and planned to spend an hour there. I immediately ran into the little tourist shop by our bus stop and bought a book on Santorini, including history and maps and information about the volcano that totally dominates everything about the island.

I liked being with our small group, away from the other tours from the ship. This was a very nice group of people, and fortunately, we were the only tour bus in Pyrgos at the moment, so we had the village all to ourselves.

Our guide gave us the mandatory historical sketch, then pointed out the path that would lead us up through the village built on the hillside to the ruins of the ancient fort and wall that had surrounded the city for protection.

Bart and I glanced at each other and headed straight up the tiered walkway, through white stucco arches, past cats sunning themselves on ancient walls and donkeys sheltered in cubbyholes between homes. We needed to make another phone call.

As we reached one beautiful, blue-domed church, a donkey brayed at us. He'd been tethered in a courtyard next door to the church with the sign, "Take your picture with me and leave the money in the box." A little box sat near the donkey, and those coming behind us took advantage of the Kodak moment and tossed their contribution in the box. The enterprising owner had discovered a lazy man's solution to earning a living, as long as tourists remained honest and paid for the use of his cute donkey instead of stealing his earnings.

We hurried to reach the top of the hill before anyone joined us there, and called Alma in the Control Center again.

"You're not getting much sleep tonight, are you?" I said when she answered the phone. "I'm sorry we have to keep waking you."

"It seems everyone on your side of the world is wide awake and needs something, so I woke Jim, and we're both busy fielding calls. We'll catch a catnap later when you go to bed. Where were we when you had to break off?"

"You were telling us about Iyad and Abdel's terrorist cell and what they found in the cave," I reminded her.

"Oh, yes. Jack faxed photographs of maps they found showing the targets they planned to destroy. Oh, Alli, it will be tragic if they succeed."

"Then I guess we'll just have to make sure they don't," I vowed.

Bart interrupted. "How many targets, and what are they?"

"It appears Athens may be the next target. The ancient Acropolis is circled, so Else and Dominic went there. If possible, they'll try to meet you when your tour arrives on the hill Friday morning. Oz and Mai Li are in Rome. The circle on that map was too big to pinpoint one specific building or even an area, but since the Vatican was in the center of the large swirl of red ink, we're assuming that's the target."

"That would be a fairly safe assumption, since it's the center of the Catholic Church and, to many, the symbol of Christianity throughout the world," Bart said. He'd have been pacing the rough stones outside the fort if he held the compact, but since he was loath to be seen holding a gold compact near his face, he had to stand still and stay by my side. I was perfectly content to lean against the rough stone wall and gaze out over the crater arc of the island at the deep blue sea beyond.

"The House of Parliament and Westminster Abbey were circled in London. David was there working with M-5 to control that."

"What else did they find, Mom?" Bart asked. "Any identifying symbols or logos or paperwork that identified this as Cell Seven?"

Mmm. Good question, I thought. Most terrorists devised some symbol or mark they left as their calling card.

"There's a black spider on enough papers that Jack felt this must be their symbol. They thought at first it was just somebody doodling, but I think they've pretty much decided Cell Seven's symbol is a black widow spider."

A little shudder ran through me. I'd seen a black spider spinning a web on our balcony the morning this all began. I'd felt unsettled, worried, and then the phone rang and Mom set all of this in motion asking me to check on her topaz. If I were as superstitious as my grandmother, I'd have known for sure that had been an omen. A bad omen.

"Gotta go. Our tour caught up with us. We'll try to check in again at the next opportunity. We need to know everything you can tell us."

Bart turned his back on Charlotte, Sara, Mark, and Laura, who arrived at the fort just ahead of Bruce and Diane. "We need to be with the tour and look like tourists, but how are we supposed to have enough privacy to keep up with these new developments?" he muttered, leaning over the wall as if to examine something below.

I handed him the camera. "Here, take my picture, Mr. Tourist."

We wandered back along the immaculate walkways, long sloping steps between whitewashed homes where beautiful crimson bougainvillea draped over doorways and where hanging baskets and flowering vines bloomed everywhere. Then back on the bus, past Fira, the capital of Santorini, and on to Oia, one of the most photographed spots in the Greek islands.

It was a fairy tale location, a white-frosting village topping chocolate-brown rocks rising straight up from the blue sea. We were at the end of the tourist season. In fact, our guide told us, today was really the last day of the season, so though prices on this island and especially in this beautiful village were usually very expensive, we'd probably find some good sales since people weren't anxious to store their merchandise until next season.

"But what about the people who live here?" I asked. "Don't they buy from the shops?"

She laughed. "No one lives here. This quaint, picturesque village is a tourist mecca. All these private homes have been turned into bed and breakfasts, inns and hotels, and leased as private rentals. The villagers, first of all, can't afford to live in their homes, and second, they don't want to be trapped in them when the next earthquake or volcanic eruption occurs. The last one is all too vivid in their memory. Since 1925, there have been at least four major eruptions."

We left the guide answering questions from some in the group and wandered the narrow streets between picture-postcard white- or cream-colored houses trimmed in blue or red. The view between the homes was breathtaking—we could see across the bay where the island curved into its crescent stone arc, or far out to sea across the glassy smooth water, marred only by the silent wake of an occasional ship.

"Let's head for the tip of the island," Bart said, taking my hand and hurrying me along. "If we make it to that stone lookout point our guide told us about, we may have a few minutes alone to call Mom again."

I'd stopped to watch a dog barking and jumping up at a cat that stretched lazily atop a sunny wall, ignoring him. Or was she taunting him? She settled down on the wall, her tail swinging slowly back and forth and one paw hanging over the edge of the white ledge as if to say, "See, I'm not concerned about you in the least."

We slowed only long enough for me to take a picture of a donkey with a sign across his head which read "Taxi," and to photograph an amazing statue of part woman, part lion, part bird which perched precariously on someone's balcony overlooking the bay. A mythical sphinx in Greek lore. When we had the fort in sight, I pulled out the compact and called Alma again.

"I'm sorry this has to be so disjointed," I apologized. "I'm sure we're interrupting you, but we only have a few minutes alone at a time on a tour like this."

"It's quite all right, dear. Jim and I decided we'd just have to adjust to your schedules while this is going on. We'll be sleeping when it's day here and night there. That way we'll be awake and alert enough to give whatever help you need."

"Good thinking, Mom," Bart said. "Otherwise you probably wouldn't get any rest until this is over."

"Something else, dear. Margaret called again. The underground members around Florence will bring the stones they've collected thus far to her. Someone will meet you to get those you have in Rhodes before you board ship to sail to Athens. They'll photograph the inscriptions etched into the stones and have someone start working on the code immediately. They hope to make headway before you finish gathering the rest of the jewels from Greece and southern Italy."

"I'll be delighted to get rid of them," I said, thinking what a relief it would be not to be responsible for such a crucial part of the treasure hunt. "Who's meeting us in Rhodes?"

"Margaret will be in touch. She said she'd try to contact you tonight after you go to your cabin."

"Thanks, Alma. What other news do you have for us? Anything more on Gabriella? Or other possible sites Cell Seven is targeting?"

"I assume you saw the news report on the explosion in Istanbul. And on the one in Egypt?"

"Not Egypt. Where was it and what happened?" Bart moved closer so he wouldn't miss any of his mother's newest revelations.

"It's unbelievable, but it was another near miss. They were apparently targeting the great pyramids, but someone ran their truck off the road just half a mile before they reached their destination. This time there were no survivors, but Cell Seven claimed responsibility. The hole it left proved they had enough explosives with them to badly damage the pyramids or the Sphinx, or even destroy them."

"Was there any other communication from Seven—other than taking credit for the explosion?" Bart asked, standing in front of me to block me from view as a group entered the arch leading to the ancient fortress where we stood.

"Not that we know of yet. But there was an interesting development—"

Total frustration swept over me as not only a group of our people arrived on the scene, but also some other tourists as well. The small square filled quickly with people, and there was nowhere to go to get away from them.

"Oh, Alma, we've got to hang up," I whispered and quickly disconnected.

Chapter 18

Charlotte and Sara joined us to wander up the hillside toward a beautiful villa with a large, white windmill that reminded me of a sentinel on the edge of the cliff. Below, we could see the doorways of homes carved into the hillside—homes made from hardened lava flow.

While Bart photographed it, I read about the little chapel of Agios Nikolas perched at the foot of the hill on a rock near the sliver of Armeni Beach. The narrow dirt path leading down from the homes on the steep hillside looked little used. No wonder. The book said the chapel was locked and was only used during festivals once or twice a year.

I kept watching for someone to approach us with a topaz—but there were so few natives about that they would have been quite obvious. We climbed narrow, little stairways, ducked through picturesque arches, wandered through zigzagging alleys, and finally found ourselves back at the main square where we'd assemble to return to the bus.

As we entered the square, I was amazed to see a beautiful white church with the blue dome and triple bell tower, which I had completely missed when we came through the square the first time. It sat off to one side, and apparently we had been in such a hurry to get out to the point to call Alma, we hadn't stopped to explore the square.

"Let's peek inside." I pointed to the church. "We have a few minutes before we leave."

Bart humored me, and we walked quietly into the church, which had a plain, white façade with eight arched windows and a rectangular door. Nothing fancy like some others we'd seen. But inside, one whole wall was filled with golden carvings, altars, candelabra, and icons. The afternoon sun streamed through western windows illuminating it in a blinding blaze of sunlight. Marvelous murals of prophets, apostles, and the Lord Jesus Christ covered the walls in rich, deep colors.

Sitting in elaborately carved, dark wooden seats, a priest in black cossack and tall mitre spoke softly to a tiny, wrinkled woman in a black dress that was almost more severe than the priest's frock, since around his neck hung a large, ornate gold cross with a ruby in the center, and she had nothing to adorn hers. Her hard life was etched in the deep lines of her once-beautiful face. What character shone there.

As ours eyes met, I smiled and dipped my head in silent greeting. She glanced away without acknowledging my presence. Bart and I stayed several minutes, identifying the stories portrayed in the murals and marveling with Charlotte and Sara at the costly and extravagant display of gold.

Then as we headed quietly for the door, I saw the old woman rise, bid good-bye to the priest, and walk quickly to the door, arriving a few steps ahead of us. She stopped, turned, and looked at me, then took my hand. With her other, she reached out and touched my face in a tender gesture.

"You look so much like Mama Karillides did at your age," she whispered in Greek. As she squeezed my hand, she transferred something to me. "Be watchful. Someone will try to take this from you."

She glanced around the room, but the priest had vanished, and the only other souls in the place were Charlotte and Sara. She turned quickly and hurried out the door.

"Bingo," I whispered to Bart and transferred the little package to my pocket. Sara was leaving with us, and Charlotte followed close behind, so I hoped they hadn't seen the exchange. "I'm going to find a restroom before we get on the bus again. You haven't seen one close, have you?" I asked.

"Sure," Sara volunteered. "I'll show you where it is. This is the main town square, and all the tourists come here, so they prepared for us."

Had I simply looked around the square, I'd have seen it next to the church. Tourist facilities like this were unusual and highly appreciated when we found them. I transferred the little lump to my journal, hiding it with the other four in the slots my spy tools usually occupied, then hurried to join Bart resting on the wall that bordered the square and overlooked the houses spilling down the rocky cliffs.

From this vantage point, storage areas were visible on the flat roofs where occupants stored rain in the rainy season for their household use. Now, our guide told us, water was brought in from outside to meet the demands of the locals and the increased demands of the five hundred thousand tourists who visited the island each year.

Our bus pulled into the capital city of Fira, or Thira on Greek maps, as the sun began to set across the bay, streaking the sky with shades of purple, gold, and pink. We were fortunate to catch one of Santorini's famous sunsets.

Lori, our Canadian guide, pointed the way down Gold Street, named for the beautiful and costly jewelry sold there. She told us we could return to the ship anchored in the harbor at the bottom of the cliff in one of three ways: walk a couple of miles to the tram and ride down, walk the winding staircase, or ride the donkeys to the bottom of the hill.

When someone asked where to find the donkeys, as that had been touted as an adventure everyone should have on a trip to Santorini, she said simply, "Follow your nose."

"Want to ride the tram or walk?" Bart asked as we window-shopped along famed Gold Street.

Puzzled, I glanced up at my distracted husband. "What about the donkeys? They were the third option." The lights of the tram on the hillside seemed a long way from where we stood.

"You shouldn't be riding donkeys, should you?" Bart stopped and stared at a shop with giant, green glass beetles and bugs all over the wall and in the windows.

I laughed. "No, thank you. I don't think we need any of those, and why shouldn't I ride a donkey?"

"I just thought . . ." Bart stammered.

"No, it won't hurt me. Let's do it. We've been on trams before. That stairway is a very long walk down, and the tram looks like it's on another mountain."

Several in our group were also riding the donkeys, and we became aware of why our guide had directed us to simply follow our noses. As we turned one corner, it was apparent they were close, and in one more turn, there they were, smelly, dirty, sweaty, and cute.

We each paid three euros, mounted our donkeys, then had to fight to contain them while the little old donkey keeper filled the rest of the donkeys in his string. When he was finally ready and commenced leading them down the steep winding stairway, the donkeys obstinately decided they wanted to go back up top. He jerked on the rope bridles, struck their flanks with a switch, and cursed them at the top of his lungs.

My donkey kept trying to brush me off on the wall. He went directly under each over-hanging branch so it slapped me in the face, and at the switchbacks, he loped across the small landing to hit the wall on the opposite side, trying to crush my leg against the columns on the stairs.

Night fell as we descended the long stairs—pitch black night—and there were only occasional dim lights on the steep, winding stairs. As we descended, it became obvious this was the only trail to the bay at the bottom of the hill. Had we walked, we would have shared it with the donkeys that didn't care if pedestrians were present on the stairs or not. They had the right of way and took it.

People scrambled out of the way of the donkeys' headlong rush to the bottom. That danger was bad enough, but in the dark, on the trail where donkeys ran back and forth all day, how would you miss stepping in their droppings? I was so glad we'd decided to ride instead of walk!

I wasn't even unhappy when the little old man stopped the donkey before we reached the bottom of the hill and indicated it was the end of the trail. I dismounted and prepared to give him a little tip when suddenly the donkeys took off running back up the hill without him, and he had to race after them to prevent the donkeys from stampeding over pedestrians descending the hill in the dark. So much for his tip.

We queued up on the dock, waiting for our turn at a tender to return to the ship. I was hot, sticky, smelly, and tired. My clothes reeked of donkey. I couldn't wait to get back on the ship and shower.

And there was no place to sit, so we all just stood in the line, which grew bigger and longer as people descended from the top to catch the last few tenders.

The time certainly didn't fly, but neither did it drag, as we talked with members of our tour about their experiences on the island and what they liked best.

Sara liked the donkey ride. "What will be your best memories of Santorini, Allison?"

I thought for a minute before I answered. "I came to Santorini with extremely high expectations, higher than for any other place on the whole tour. After all, this is the place every travel poster shows. This is the jewel of the Greek Isles, according to the tourist bureau." I stopped and took a deep breath. "It met—and exceeded—all those expectations. I loved the ambiance, the delightful white and blue villages, the churches, the whole fairy-tale quality of the place. I loved the sun. And I especially loved Oia. I would come back here just to relax and wander those picturesque, narrow, winding streets for a month if I could."

"How about the donkey ride?" Charlotte asked.

"I'd take it again if I could handle the bridle myself and make the trip in the daytime," I laughed. "Otherwise, next time I think I'll take the tram."

It finally came our turn for the tender. We barely made the cutoff, being the last two to board. It was so crowded that we stood near the chain that spanned the exit and entrance to the little boat. People laughed and talked loudly, sharing tales of their excursion on the island. It was decidedly different from being with our own small tour group. This was a mixture of all those from the ship who had gone ashore today.

Some who'd been drinking in the little beer garden near the dock began singing, and others joined in their happy songs. The tender wallowed in the black water with her heavy load and rolled a bit more than usual when it hit the wakes of other tenders transporting passengers back to the ship. A couple of inebriated men thought it would be fun to make their fellow travelers seasick. They stood and tried to rock the boat.

Unexpectedly, one of them appeared to stumble, fell against me, and staggered for the chain across the entrance to the boat with me hooked in one arm. Bart reacted instantly, grabbing my hand and pulling me back toward him. At that, the second drunk tackled Bart, and both of them sprawled toward us. The drunk nearest me reeled again, throwing one arm around my waist, and fell toward the gap in the railing. I grabbed the chain with one hand to keep from going overboard, and looped my purse over my head with the other. I mustn't lose my purse, no matter what happened.

We went down, and as we sprawled across the deck, the drunk lying across my legs grabbed at my arm and then at my purse as if to pull himself up, but our eyes met. There was no drunkenness there. This man was sober. And he was after my purse. *I should have left the jewels in my waist safe,* I thought, as I scrambled to get out from under the man pinning me down.

Bart struggled with the bigger man who contended with him. Normally, it wouldn't have been a problem. Bart could easily handle the drunk, no matter the size disadvantage, but I feared my husband was still weakened from the poison and was in no condition for this kind of physical exertion.

Two passengers finally reacted and helped me to my feet. Bart shook off the fellow tugging at his clothes and rolled toward me, but the man kept pulling him back. Just as it seemed the two strapping passengers were going to prevail and separate these two trouble makers from us, my attacker jumped to his feet, picked me up, and tossed me overboard.

I hit icy black water and sank deep.

You're a good swimmer, Alli. Don't panic. You'll come up for air any second. You can swim to shore, and Bart will bring the tender back to find you. I relaxed and let my limp body begin its normal ascent back to the surface.

Without warning, something came at me out of the blackness, pushing me back down into the deep water. I panicked. I needed air.

Chapter 19

I tried to free myself from the entangling arms, tried to fight off the strangle hold someone had on me. I kicked and scratched, but there was no force behind my struggle. The water nullified every blow I tried to administer, every swing I took.

I was running out of air. I needed to surface. Now. Suddenly, my hands connected with his head. I stopped trying to push my attacker away and grabbed at his head with both hands, pulling it close, feeling for the eyes. I couldn't find them, but I found an ear and bit down hard. I just kept biting, harder and harder, taking my fury and desperation out on this man with every ounce of strength I could muster. All at once, my attacker headed for the top, dragging me with him.

I needed air desperately, but I didn't want to be anywhere near this man when we surfaced. As he struggled to push me away, I let him and propelled myself backward out of his reach.

We exploded out of the water at the same time, and I breathed deeply of that wonderful life-giving substance my lungs cried out for, gasping in great gulps of air. Bart called to me, too far away to reach me before my attacker did. I didn't dare answer, or I'd reveal my location to the man cursing me only ten feet away. Bart was much farther than that and was behind my attacker. I'd have to go through or around this man bent on killing me.

Moving through the water as quietly as possible, I stopped when the man stopped to listen for me, moving again to circle him when he thrashed about trying to find me. Searchlights flashed across the bay in the wrong direction. Bart's frantic voice sounded closer, but I wasn't in the clear yet. I still needed to get around this deadly obstacle in my path.

As I changed my position, lights from our ship illuminated the water in long silver and blue streaks that reached out toward me. Bart was now silhouetted in the reflections on the water, bobbing up and down, still shouting my name. I slipped underwater and swam toward him, surfacing only long enough to breathe and to determine that I was still heading in the right direction.

Just as I got close enough to call out and let my worried husband know where I was, I heard splashing behind me. The ship's lights, which had guided me to Bart, now directed my attacker to me.

But I was tired. I couldn't fight him off again. I had on too many heavy clothes, my limbs were freezing and exhausted, and my purse weighed me down. I took one more deep breath and swam with all my might underwater, then surfaced and yelled at Bart. He headed for me immediately, and the splashing behind me increased. I rolled on my back and kicked toward the safety my husband offered, pulling my purse around so it rested on my stomach. I almost laughed at the image of a seal swimming on his back opening oysters on his midriff, except my circumstances were not the least bit humorous.

My gun wouldn't be of any help in the water, but I had one weapon my attacker wouldn't expect. Reaching into the outer pocket of my purse, my fingers closed around my ballpoint pen—a weapon just as lethal as a knife when administered properly.

Hoping and praying Bart would reach me before the attacker did, a sudden thought sickened me. Normally a much stronger swimmer than my husband, I was already exhausted. Still weak from last night's food poisoning episode, Bart had been in the water as long as I had. He'd be just as tired, or more so.

This man could overpower both of us, take the topaz, and we'd not only fail in our assignment to keep the treasure from the terrorists, but my baby would lose the opportunity for her turn on earth. That, above all else, must not happen.

I let my purse dangle behind me, slipped my shoes off, and pulled my jacket off. Lighten the load. Decrease the drag. Both men swam closer, and in answer to Bart's frantic call, I yelled, "Here. In front of you. And so is the guy trying to drown me."

The intensity of Bart's splashing increased, as did the man's who was coming for the topaz. I peered intently through the darkness, trying to see him, hoping the lights from the ship would illuminate his face so I could see my attacker—how close he was, who he was. I stopped moving, waiting, knowing he could see my silhouette, knowing he knew exactly where I was even though I didn't have that same advantage.

His splashing stopped abruptly, and I knew he'd gone underwater. I also knew I'd feel his presence before I saw him. I stopped floating on my back, came upright in the water, raised the ballpoint pen over my head, and waited, counting.

Five seconds later, I felt a hand brush against my foot, then two hands grip my ankles. I didn't wait to be dragged under. Drawing my knees up to my chest, pulling the man closer, I stabbed the pen into the water with all the strength I could muster. I hit the target, where, I didn't know, but he let go of me and shot to the surface.

Bart arrived at the same moment a searchlight cut through the water and found us. I waved frantically, never taking my eyes from the murderous expression of the man in front of me. As he lunged forward, I gripped the pen tighter, ready for one last thrust, knowing it was all I'd get before he pulled me under.

My attacker surprised me by grasping at my raised arm instead of attacking from underneath. As we struggled, he forced my head underwater, trying to drown me. Terrified he'd succeed, I prayed for heavenly intervention as my teeth closed on the hand that covered my face, biting again with all my might.

Suddenly Bart entered the fracas, attacking with a force and energy I didn't think he could muster. I burst to the surface for air and found men in the water around us, shoving life preservers toward me.

"Separate them," I choked, gesturing at the churning water. "He's drowning my husband." Three men disappeared underwater, and five men shot to the surface, gasping for air. Many hands reached over the side of the tender and pulled me aboard.

I collapsed to the deck, weak kneed and totally spent. One of the crew bent over me. "That man tried to drown me." I pointed at the man still struggling against the three men who were trying to subdue him and bring him aboard.

Bart was hauled over the side and sank beside me, smothering me in an embrace. "Are you okay, princess?" he whispered.

"Yes," was the only word I uttered before I began shivering uncontrollably. Whether from cold or exhaustion or the sudden realization of just how close I'd come to never seeing another day or a combination of all three, I didn't know. I gratefully accepted the blanket someone threw around my shoulders and just sat numbly on the wet deck saying "Thank you! Thank you!" over and over for our rescue. I'm not even sure whether I said it out loud to those who had pulled us from a watery grave or whether I said it silently to a benevolent Father in Heaven, who had heard and answered my prayers, but I was truly grateful.

I also had the sure knowledge our rescuers had been guided to us at that crucial moment by divine intervention. I did not believe in "nick-of-time" coincidence.

My attacker fought free of the three men who tried to bring him aboard and disappeared into the deep, black water. The crew member hovering above us kept peering at his watch as they searched in vain for the man or his body.

Bart finally suggested they just leave him with life preservers floating in the area and deliver this group of people to the ship. Apparently the man hadn't wanted to be rescued, so Bart suggested they give him his wish. There were still several loads of passengers on Santorini waiting to be tendered back to the ship, and Captain Fortezze had a schedule to keep. They had to be underway at ten thirty, and if this tender delayed much longer, they'd never make the schedule. After consultation with the ship's captain, the tender headed for the ship, much to the relief of the passengers, who'd been kept waiting onboard during the search for us.

We were the first ones off, and I was helped back aboard the ship by Bart on one side and a young crew member on the other who seemed painfully aware of my pregnant figure, which was pronounced by my wet clothes clinging to every curve.

"Ma'am, I think you should go to the medical center and have Dr. Chandra check you to make sure . . ." He stopped, apparently not knowing what to say. "To make sure everything is okay," he stammered.

"Good idea," Bart said, over my objections.

"I'm fine," I insisted. "I just need a hot shower to get warm and then bed." But no one listened to me. Apparently the captain had been notified a pregnant woman had been thrown overboard, and he wasn't taking any chances, because he met us personally at the door to the medical center.

Bart introduced me, and when Captain Fortezze recognized my husband, he nodded knowingly. "I assume this altercation had something to do with your assignment in Interpol." When Bart nodded, the captain turned to me. "Don't you find your husband's occupation a little dangerous?"

Bart and I looked at each other and smiled. "Yes, but it's sort of a family affair," I explained. "My mother and father started the tradition thirty or more years ago, recruited Bart, and now I'm part of the group too, so it seems if one of us isn't in someone's line of fire, the other is."

Dr. Chandra opened the door to admit us, shooed the men to the other end of the medical center, and drew a curtain around the examining table, where I sat dripping all over her floor and everything else.

"I see your patient with the head wound got off the ship." Rather obvious since I was now occupying the spot where the patient had been.

She glanced up, a blank expression on her face.

"The one whose head was all wrapped in bandages," I reminded her.

She shook her head as if clearing her mind. "Of course. I've been so busy tonight, I completely forgot about him. Yes. They took him off the ship to Santorini."

"I'm sorry I'm getting your office wet. I wanted to go change clothes first, but they insisted I come here. I'm sure you'll find I'm okay. I'm really quite healthy and used to swimming in cold water."

Dr. Chandra stuck a thermometer in my mouth, putting an end to my questions, my apology, and my explanation. She took my blood pressure, then listened for the baby with her stethoscope. As she pronounced all seemed well, she tucked her short dark hair behind her ear and bent to enter something in her report. I noticed a discoloration on her earlobe. Interesting. I'd never seen a birthmark in that particular spot before.

When Dr. Chandra glanced up from her paperwork, I asked if I could please go now and get out of my wet, freezing clothes. As she nodded and returned to her report, I slipped off the table and through the curtain. Bart and the captain had stepped into the corridor, where I joined them. We excused ourselves to take the elevator up two decks to our cabin. A hot shower and being warm again were my overriding desires.

As we entered our corridor, Ricardo rushed to meet us. "Have you found Raphael?" he asked, anxiously rubbing his hands together in front of him.

I shook my head, my teeth chattering so violently I couldn't answer.

"No one's seen him?" Bart asked.

"No," Ricardo said, looking even more worried. "I have talked to everyone. He has not been seen or heard from since he headed for the kitchen last night after the first seating for dinner. He is just vanished into thin air."

"Ricardo, I need to shed these wet clothes and shower," I managed to get out.

"I am sorry. I should have been more thoughtful." He nervously fingered the little gold cross he wore in his left earlobe, and the earring came out in his hand. "Oh!" he exclaimed, and bent to retrieve the back clasp that had fallen to the floor.

Bart held open the door to our cabin for me, and Ricardo straightened up as I turned to tell him I'd talk to him as soon as I was warm and dry, and we'd devise a plan to find Raphael. His hand went to his ear to restore the earring to its place, and my eye followed. I'm sure I was not meant to see what I saw. I almost wished I hadn't.

Chapter 20

"Princess, you have no shoes," Bart exclaimed as he tried to help me.

"I kicked them off in the water. They got too heavy." I was shivering so hard I could hardly get my clothes off. "I was afraid I'd never be able to fight off that guy with all my clothes dragging me under. I'm sorry. I lost the beautiful jacket you gave me."

Bart hurried into the tiny bathroom to turn on the hot water.

"Did you see Ricardo's ear?" I called after him. No answer. He couldn't hear over the noise of the running water. I dropped my wet clothes in a heap on the bathroom floor and climbed into the shower, letting the hot water wash over me. It wasn't quite as good as a soak in a hot bathtub, but eventually warmth permeated body and soul.

I waited for Bart to shower as I donned warm pajamas, said grateful prayers for our deliverance, and snuggled into bed. I wanted to tell him about Dr. Chandra and Ricardo. That little discovery on Ricardo's ear might explain a couple of things, but it also added to the mystery. I picked up my scriptures from the nightstand and tried to focus on the verses but had to struggle to keep my eyes open.

* * *

"Princess, wake up. Sweetheart, if you want any breakfast, we're going to have to hurry. We're supposed to go ashore at Rhodes in less than an hour. The ship's already docked."

I climbed out of a deep sleep, up through a fog, and opened my eyes in a bright room. I shut them quickly. Bart tried again. "If you can get by without breakfast, you can sleep another thirty minutes, but if you can't, then you have to get up right now."

"What time is it?" I must have dozed off while he was in the bathroom. I felt the coverlet for my scriptures.

"It's seven fifteen. You were asleep when I finished showering last night. Dead to the world. I knew you were exhausted, so I let you sleep as long as possible, but our tour leaves the ship at eight o'clock, and if you need to eat, we only have forty-five minutes before we disembark."

That grabbed my attention. It took forty-five minutes to get up to breakfast, eat, and get back to our cabin. I jumped out of bed and grabbed the first thing I found in the closet. Bart had emptied my purse and was drying it with my blow dryer. I noticed the padded journal had been disassembled and was being dried too.

"I totally forgot about my bag last night," I said with a mouthful of toothpaste foam. "Thanks!"

"You're welcome. It's a good thing the gun compartment is waterproof, but it's a shame the camera bag wasn't."

I turned to see the array of items laid out on my bed while Bart went over them with the hair dryer. The pages on the journal were quality paper with a high rag content, but this would be its last trip. I'd definitely need a new one.

Today, the topaz jewels were in my waist safe buckled in place. I wouldn't take a chance on someone snatching my purse, no matter how uncomfortable I was with the five jewels nestled in the small of my back. As Bart held the door open for me, a thought flitted through my mind. Take the bra safe. I discounted it, then as I stepped into the corridor, I had the same thought again. I stepped back in, grabbed the little nylon pocket from the closet shelf and stuffed it in my purse.

Meals were supposed to be long and leisurely on cruises. Why did it seem ours never were? I spooned oatmeal and cream into a bowl to eat now and grabbed a couple of French rolls and cheese to stuff in my purse for lunch. This had become a daily routine since we never seemed to stop for lunch on our forays away from the ship. I stuck a banana in my purse to eat later too and a handful of grapes.

As I stared at the grapes on my plate, I suddenly had an idea. Why I would ever need it, I didn't know, but I wrapped five grapes in pieces of paper napkin and tucked them inside the little nylon pocket, then stuck it back in my purse until I could attach it to the front of my bra. They would nestle unseen under my shirt, and as long as someone didn't give me a bear hug, they'd be perfectly okay. Otherwise, things would get a little sticky!

We gulped our breakfast, I ducked into the restroom to stash the grapes, and we rushed to catch our bus to Rhodes. I much preferred it when the ship docked and we simply walked off onto dry land instead of being tendered ashore. After last night, I'd had enough of tenders to last a lifetime.

"What do you know about Rhodes?" I asked Bart as we all followed Jim and Carol to the bus, like a string of ducklings behind mama and papa duck.

"That the Colossus of Rhodes was one of the Seven Wonders of the Ancient World and supposedly straddled the harbor entrance here, acting as a lighthouse until it was destroyed by an earthquake. How's that?" Bart asked with a smug smile.

"Pretty good. Have you been brushing up on your history?"

He laughed. "I cheated. I read the ship's handout on the city."

"That's not cheating. That's why they provide it. I glanced at it too, and before we leave today, I want to explore the Street of the Knights in the old town. It sounded intriguing."

Today we had another Canadian guide, Maria, who said she came here twenty years ago and stayed. I totally understood why. As we traveled, she narrated the history of the area and pointed out items of interest.

We completely bypassed the old city, the part which interested me the most, and drove around the west side of the island to find a modern city with black sand beaches on the Aegean Sea. But we didn't stop; just drove up a hill and wound around a temple of Pythian Apollo on Mount Smith Hill from the second century B.C. We didn't stop there or at the monastery on the top of a high hill with a beautiful blue bay at the base. I didn't care for this part of the tour, seeing things only at a distance.

Our destination was a place called Seven Springs, and we exited the bus, young and old, firm and frail, with a great deal of excitement to see what must be a wondrous place. I envisioned waterfalls and beautifully landscaped ponds and springs and fountains. But after a refreshing climb up a rocky, narrow, treacherous trail that we shared with goats, large and small, we discovered a small pond with little trickles of water bubbling forth from seven different locations.

I couldn't believe this was the famous Seven Springs. Maybe it was a special place for the dry island of Rhodes, but such spots were located all over the United States. Most of the people on our tour came from Utah and Idaho, where springs were commonplace. Even on the estate in California, we had streams that cascaded down from the mountain above us in several places, finally joining together in one waterfall, until late fall when it became more of a trickle.

As we took pictures of this little pond and its trickles of water that masqueraded as a major tourist attraction, someone cried out in alarm. I whirled around and felt the sting of rock fragments shattering near my leg. Bark split from a nearby tree. Another cry went up.

"Someone's shooting at us!" Wayne yelled. He pulled Vivian behind a tree, and everyone who couldn't scramble to a tree hit the dirt.

Bart had been examining an unusual plant on the edge of the clearing, and when the shouting began, he started up the hill behind the little pond on a run. I jumped up and ran to the edge of the clearing to watch him loping up the narrow rocky trail toward something that glistened in the sunlight. Then it disappeared.

All was deathly quiet in the clearing. The birds had stopped singing. Even the little trickles of water seemed to hush their gurgling.

"What happened?" Margie asked, brushing the dirt from her clothes as Ralph helped her to her feet.

"Someone was taking potshots at us from above the pond," he answered.

Jim and Carol hurried to gather their tour together and make sure no one was hurt. Bart returned, reported he'd found empty shell casings and footprints, but whoever had been there shooting at us had hightailed it out. He grabbed my hand, and we started down the hill as quickly as we could navigate the rocky path, followed by everyone on our tour.

Unfortunately, a couple of our elderly people stumbled and fell on the primitive trail and were cut on the jagged rocks that protruded from the hardpan soil. We took a short break while Carol and Diane administered first aid, then we headed for the site that made up well for the unfortunate first stop on our tour.

The buzz on the bus was all about the shooting. Could it have been intentional? Was it only kids playing dangerous pranks? The "why" was as much discussed as the "who" it could have been, but of course, no one had any real clue. Except us. And we didn't join in the conjecture. Fearful the danger for our group had escalated, we were at a loss as to what to do to prevent it.

Jim got on his cell phone immediately, making numerous calls all the way to our next destination. Maria, our guide, apologized over and over and said it had to be some kind of terrible joke some young men had been playing. Everyone agreed it must have been, and their fears and anxieties abated with that assumption. Bart and I remained silent, our anxieties increasing.

Lindos was a picturesque white town sprawled at the foot of a castle perched atop a rocky promontory. As soon as we exited the bus, I bought a book so I'd know what we were seeing. I had a hard time staying close enough to Maria to hear her history of the area, and I loved that part. Bart stayed on high alert, not relaxing for a second, scanning the crowds, peering into alleys, looking for any other danger that might appear unexpectedly.

Our injured were treated at the local hospital, accompanied by Carol and some compassionate members of the tour. Maria, umbrella raised high overhead so we wouldn't lose her, led the portion of the group who wanted to climb to the castle, reminding us it would be more strenuous than most of the tours we'd had thus far. More strenuous I could handle. More dangerous I didn't even want to think about. But it was easy to see how that was foremost on Bart's mind.

The climb, steep but pleasant, wound through the narrow street, up the hill between little shops, around a church, and even through a couple of switchbacks. Hot sun beat down on us when we left the shaded section of shops and town behind, but innovative little old ladies braved it, spreading their beautiful linens beside the stone path to the castle. Lovely hand-embroidered tablecloths, scarves, and doilies covered each bush and rock and hung on lines between the trees.

Huffing and puffing by the time we reached the top, I noticed that even my husband was happy to sit on a rock and wait for the rest of our group to arrive so Maria could describe the castle and environs. We vied for space in the courtyard—a very popular, crowded spot—

with at least three other tours. Surely a place to collect another topaz. Hopefully not a place for another sniper attack.

We peered over the rock wall surrounding the castle at the inviting cobalt blue bay beneath the hill. Its cream-colored sandy beach sported row after row of white beach umbrellas shading people who'd arrived on the ferries and private yachts anchored in the harbor.

I sat on the wall and read the tour book to Bart. "According to Homer, Lindos was built by the Dorians in the twelfth century B.C. Rhodes sent nine ships to the Trojan War, and most probably came from Lindos. The Lindians were first to draw up a naval code of justice, known as the Rhodian Naval Code, which became the basis of Roman naval justice and is the core of modern maritime law."

"Mmm, I'm impressed," Bart said, peering over at the pictures in the book. "What's this?"

"That's the Temple Athena, built in 550 B.C. I think that's what we're going to see when we get on top, if we ever make it up there. It says that in the early 1900s, the Archaeological School of Denmark began excavations on the acropolis and found stone tools from the third millennium B.C. Wow. That could equate to about the time of Abraham."

"Even more impressive," Bart commented.

"But, it says, they also found two marble plaques inscribed by Timochidas, a priest of Athena in 99 B.C. One contains a list of Athena's miracles, with a list of the visitors to the temple."

"Anybody we know on the guest list?" Bart asked absentmindedly, watching the donkeys carrying people up the hill on the path below us.

"The guest register lists Herakles, Helen of Troy and Menelaos, Artaphernes, King of Persia, and Alexander the Great, just to name a few you'll recognize."

Maria finally gathered the stragglers from our tour, and we headed into the castle itself, up very steep, narrow stone steps, past the graceful prow of a trireme, a ship carved in the rock in 170 B.C.

"How many steps did Maria say it was to the top of the castle?" I asked, stopping midway to catch my breath.

"Six hundred," Bart said, "But I don't know if that included these thirty or forty into the castle or if it was just that many to the courtyard."

When we reached the actual castle and climbed over the ruins of stone pillars and blocks into what had once been a Crusader castle, I felt a little thrill of pleasure. I'd loved the stories of the Crusader Knights as a child, and now I walked on the same stones they had trod.

We took a picture of a tabby cat perched like a statue on the remnants of a centuries-old pillar and hoped Bart had dried out the digital camera sufficiently so it still worked. The view from the top was incredible. Below on one side lay the blue bay and sandy beach we'd seen earlier, and on the other, the Bay of Saint Paul, so named for the Apostle Paul when he stopped there to preach the gospel.

I thought we'd come up to see just the castle and temple. However, on the acropolis, the large, flat surface at the top of the massive rock on which it was all built, we found the Knight's Castle, remains of a Roman temple, a Greek stoa dated to the third century B.C. with forty-two doric columns along the façade, and the ruins of the Byzantine church of St. John.

Then we faced more steps, called the "stairs to heaven" because they gave the impression you were mounting into the clouds. We had no clouds today. Just a brilliant blue sky and heady breeze, which thankfully cooled the hot sun baking the ancient ruins.

We climbed the wide staircase leading to the open area of the Propylaea, then up to the fourth and highest level where the small Temple of Lindian Athena was tucked back in the narrow triangular corner of the acropolis. Not as many tourists had come up this far, and only a few of our tour group had made it to the temple. This would be the perfect spot to receive another jewel, but no one approached us, even when we dawdled at the viewpoint above Paul's Bay.

Peeking over the side, I saw a dramatic plunge straight down a high rocky cliff to the sea. I shuddered. Maybe this wasn't a good place to wait for someone to find us, especially if whoever found us happened to be the wrong people.

For the first time today, I had time to think about our narrow escape. I led my husband by the hand to a sheltered rock where the wind didn't whip so vigorously around the ruins and pulled him down beside me at the base of an ancient pillar.

"Everything happened so fast last night, I didn't realize we'd been identified until I ended up in the water. Did you see that coming?"

Bart slid closer and put his arm around me. "No, princess. It came out of left field and caught me completely off guard. I had no idea those goons were anything other than a couple of obnoxious drunks until one tried to throw you overboard. By then, the other one had me pinned down, and I couldn't get to you." His arm tightened around my shoulder, and he turned my face up to his. "I can't tell you how I felt when he tossed you overboard. My whole world disappeared under that black water. I think it was the most terrifying feeling I've ever had." His hand caressed my cheek, and his eyes became moist.

"Terrifying is right." I kissed him. "Thank you for coming after me. Once again, Sir Galahad rides to the rescue."

"Better riding than swimming. I thought I'd drown you trying to save you." He laughed. We needed a lighter moment. That had been far too close, and the memories rushed back, detailed, vivid, and frightening.

"And that brings up the question, how did they spot us?" I asked. "Did Gabriella finger us?"

Bart shook his head. "I don't know, but at this point, I wouldn't trust her to buy me a Coke without having it tested."

I didn't bother to add that I hadn't trusted her since I first saw her, but for entirely different reasons. Then I remembered Ricardo.

"Oh, I didn't get to tell you what I saw last night!" I jumped up and stood in front of Bart. "I was waiting for you to get out of the shower and fell asleep before you came out. Ricardo has a small black spider tattooed on his left earlobe."

Bart frowned. "I didn't see a tattoo on Ricardo."

"The little gold cross he wears in his ear covers it. He fiddled with it while you unlocked our door, and it fell off. Before he put it back on, I saw the spider. I meant to tell you about it as soon as we got inside the door, but you turned on the water, and I was so anxious to get in the shower and get warm, I totally forgot."

Suddenly I spotted two men ascending the stairs two at a time. I grabbed Bart's arm and pulled him around to the other side of the pillar. "We'd better leave. I don't like the appearance of those two gentlemen who just came up the stairs of heaven. They don't look like tourists to me."

Bart peeked around the pillar. "You're right, princess. They look like men with a mission."

Chapter 21

"I don't think they've seen us yet." I pointed to the cordoned-off work area. "If we slip under the scaffolding where they're restoring those columns, we might be able to circle around them."

We stayed behind the pillars until we reached the "Danger, No Entrance" sign, then skirted the blockade and ducked under the scaffold. The pillars being reconstructed hid us until we could squeeze between the walls of the temple and some huge natural rocks that cropped up at the edge. We stopped long enough to make sure we hadn't been seen, then hurried through the castle and down into the courtyard.

Apparently we'd eluded them. Since the tour was unorganized at this time and we were free until it was time to board the bus, we hurried to the bottom of the hill to get lost in the little shops on the narrow cobblestone streets. On our way back to Lindos, I'd planned to purchase a white linen doily embroidered in blue with the Greek key for the center of our little table, but that didn't seem a wise thing to do at the moment. Souvenirs were the last thing on my current agenda.

Bart kept watching over his shoulder to see if we were being followed, but when we reached the shops, there was still no sign of the two men.

"Do you think we were just spooked?" I asked, slipping into a tiny shop with an open door at the other end. "Maybe they really were tourists after all."

"Tourists with no camera and wearing jackets on a hot day?" Bart noted. "Jackets hide guns. Nearly everybody up there wore shorts, and not a single other person had on a jacket."

"You're right. I didn't stop to analyze why I didn't think they were tourists. I guess they just looked like a couple of hoods to me, and since we're usually the target, my danger antennae started tingling."

Bart glanced at his watch. "We have twenty minutes until we're supposed to board the bus. We can probably just stay in these little shops, out of sight, until then. You might even find a prize you'd like to buy."

When I saw a tiny outdoor café with little tables under blue umbrellas in a vine-enclosed arbor, I knew where I wanted to spend my twenty minutes. I pointed, and Bart led the way.

We bought two drinks at the beverage counter, carried them to the table nearly hidden from the street, and I pulled out the rolls and cheese from breakfast. "Voila, instant lunch," I said, spreading our picnic on the napkins in which I'd wrapped them.

"You are too good," Bart laughed, breaking off a chunk of his roll and covering it with slices of Swiss and Gouda cheese. "This lunch would probably have cost us five euros each if we'd had to buy it."

"If we could have found just bread and cheese. They usually don't offer anything quite so simple." I kept an eye on the street in front of the little café, indulged in my simple but delicious lunch, and then tackled the immediate problem of our safety.

"If Gabriella has thugs out searching for us, watching our every move, will we compromise the underground's effort to get the stones to us?"

Bart thought before he answered. "Probably, but they know the odds of getting caught are high. This just makes them higher. Our passers will have to be even more clever than they've been, and we'll have to be more alert." He leaned forward on the table. "I'd almost convinced myself, until last night, this was a real vacation. It's amazing how you can let your guard down when you're with people who don't have a care in the world except which pictures to take, what to eat, and which clothes to put on in the morning."

"Yeah, kind of nice for a change, isn't it?" I reached across the table and slipped my hand in Bart's. "Do you realize this is how other people live? Normal people. I could love getting used to this lifestyle."

A strange expression crossed his face, then quickly disappeared. He concentrated on my hand, rubbing his thumb thoughtfully across my palm, then gazed at me for a minute before he asked softly, "Are you unhappy, princess?"

"Unhappy?" I squeezed his hand. "I've just had six whole days with my husband all to myself, seeing some of the beautiful places of the world and relaxing." I laughed and amended, "Mostly. Until last night, we didn't even have any bad guys in close proximity. And to add to that, our beautiful daughter will make us a threesome in four more months. Unhappy? No way. I'm probably the happiest woman on earth. And the most blessed."

Bart reached over and kissed me, then whispered, "Hold that thought when we get to the square and try to get on the bus without being seen." He kissed me again. "I love you. Whatever else happens on this trip, or ever, always remember I love you more than life itself."

"Guess that prepares me for just about anything, doesn't it?" I laughed. But I didn't feel as lighthearted as I had two minutes ago. My great mood dissolved in the face of reality. Our lives really were in danger, and that wouldn't change once we boarded the ship, because now Gabriella had pointed her long, treacherous finger at us and sent the goon squad chasing us. The only bright spot in this change of circumstance was that maybe now the other eight couples who had been singled out with us as possible receivers might be out of the crosshairs and safe from Cell Seven's terrorist tactics.

We searched the faces of the crowds packing the narrow streets as we headed back to the square at the bottom of the hill, where we were to meet the bus. Ninety-nine percent tourists. Didn't the locals come out at this time of day? Probably not. It was hot and crowded. Smart people were in their homes or shops away from the masses that thronged the small, cramped streets.

The floor of an empty, open courtyard covered with black and white designs beckoned to me through a unique arch, and I looked up to see a beautiful, three-tiered bell tower, not the traditional white stucco of most Greek churches, but multicolored blocks of marble or stone stacked in delicate arches. I grabbed Bart's hand.

"Let's peek in for just a minute." The floor of the courtyard was made entirely of uniformly sized white pebbles that had been stood on end in sand, with black pebbles forming leaf and flower motifs. I flipped through my book until I found the church, called the Church of Our Lady, and the description of the courtyard stones. It was a process called "chochlaki," and it began centuries ago in the Hellenistic period.

We quietly entered the church and were delighted to find the entire floor of the chapel fashioned of chochlaki in zigzag designs. This church was much like the one on Santorini, with murals covering the walls and ceiling and an incredible array of golden altars and candelabra at one end.

We were at the front of the chapel, awestruck at the ostentatious display of gold, when my danger antennae tingled a warning. I heard the door creak open behind us, and without turning around, I grabbed Bart's hand and pulled him through the side door. I had no idea where it led, just that I didn't want to be in the chapel one minute longer, and this was the first avenue of escape.

We wound through a series of halls and small rooms and finally came to a door leading out into a garden, probably the priest's private residence and garden. I didn't think he'd mind if we used it for a shortcut back to the street. As we hurried through the tiny garden, I heard the door slam open behind us and running feet pursuing us.

"Time to disappear again, princess," Bart said, pulling me through one shop, out the back door onto another street, and down the cobble-stones, through the press of the crowd until we found ourselves back in the main square and saw the bus waiting across the street. We headed for it on the run, dodging cats and dogs, kids on bikes, old women with canes, and old men standing under the trees talking, not to mention two busloads of tourists unloading into the square.

"Are you two racing again?" Jed asked as we boarded the bus out of breath.

"Silly, isn't it," I gasped. "He always wins, so I don't know why I let him talk me into it."

"Wish I was young enough to do that without having a heart attack." Dorothy laughed.

We chatted amiably while we watched out the windows for the two men we thought were after us. Our bus was loaded and getting ready to leave, and I'd just decided I'd been paranoid and we weren't being followed, when the two men emerged on the square, and they were not happy campers. They scowled at the crowd as they hurried through, definitely searching for someone. I decided it was definitely us. I wanted to wave at them and stick out my tongue as our bus pulled out on the highway, but checked the impulse.

I totally relaxed and watched the scenery fly by as we rode back to the old city of Rhodes. Crusader castles dotted the hilltops, and donkeys and goats were the animals most visible in the countryside. In the city, it was cats—sleek, healthy cats peering down from walls, sitting on doorsteps, curled up in chairs besides the door, perched on windowsills. Cats everywhere.

When our bus arrived in the old city, we bailed out at the port gate along with half a dozen others of our group. We had exactly forty minutes to see the medieval walled area, so we raced through the streets searching for the Street of the Knights which the book said had once been the main street and was now probably the best-preserved medieval street in Europe.

We came to a corner with streets leading in five different directions and had no idea where to go from there. I ran up to a young man selling brightly colored banners and asked directions. He pointed along a cobblestone street with no shops, just two-story buildings constructed from the same tan stone.

We turned the corner and there it was. Over six centuries old, the buildings lining this fabled street had housed the Order of the Knights of St. John in the individual inns or langues (tongues or languages) of each different nationality. Each "inn" was identified by its coat of arms. The street ascended toward a covered arch with bright, blue sky peeking underneath.

"Ready?" Bart asked.

I looked up, puzzled by his question. "Ready for what?"

"Ready to do something besides just stand here and stare in wonder? Maybe even ready to do some fast exploring? Your time is ticking away."

"Sorry." I laughed. "My mind filled with images of knights on prancing horses riding into battle against Saladin and then Suleiman the Magnificent. Yes, let's go. We've got to find the Palace of the Grand Masters which, I think, should be at the top of this street."

We hurried along, peeking at coats of arms on arched doors set back in the straight, long front of the buildings. I spotted the statue of the

Virgin and Child on the façade of the Langue of France, stuck up high in a little niche in the corner. Wrought-iron lanterns hanging on the buildings on one side of the street were the only ornamentation along the entire façade. No hanging baskets of flowers, no steps out into the streets, nothing to break the beautiful, simple symmetry of golden stone.

A young girl on a scooter rode down the street, a couple of other tourists wandered in front of us, and an old woman clutching a black shawl around her shoulders sat in the sun in a doorway, her feet sticking out across the narrow sidewalk. We had to wait for some scooters to pass before we could step around her in the narrow street.

We reached the courtyard of the Palace of the Grand Masters, and I gazed in absolute awe and admiration at the golden stone battlements stretching heavenward into the cloudless blue sky. I could almost hear the trumpeters calling the knights to battle. My reverie was abruptly shattered by the noisy buzz of scooters echoing up the narrow cobblestone street we'd just climbed.

"Sounds like Rhodes's version of Hell's Angels," I said, turning to see if they were coming into the courtyard. If so, I didn't want to be standing here in the middle of it.

Bart frowned. "Let's go see the garden, princess." He grabbed my hand and pulled me, on a dead run, into the garden just to the right of the magnificent entrance to the palace.

"This says no admittance," I objected.

"We're just going to step behind those two big statues for a minute and see who's making all the noise."

We'd no sooner ducked under the chain across the sidewalk and scrunched behind a huge statue of someone in a toga, holding up a torch, before eight scooters roared from the plaza into the courtyard and turned circles around each other while they examined the tourists gathered there.

"I think you may have made a good decision just then," I whispered. "Two of them are the guys from Lindos. I recognize the red jacket and sunglasses on one and the blue-striped shirt and black jacket on another."

Bart glanced at his watch. "I hope they don't think we went inside the palace and wait for us. We'll miss the ship if they don't leave in the next five minutes. We're fifteen minutes from the dock on foot."

I scanned the garden for a back gate, but the trees and bushes were so thick the garden walls were hidden. "Do you want to take a chance and wait or go exploring right now?"

Bart looked behind us. "Let's find a way out. If they leave, and we exit right behind them, they might double back and see us."

We scurried through the dense bushes, crouching behind trees and statues until we could no longer see the entrance to the Grand Palace. We finally came to a high wall and followed it, hoping it would soon lead us to an exit. When we found a gate, it was locked. Then we hit a corner, and the wall turned in the opposite direction from the ship. We were running now, dodging branches and roots and shrubs that hugged the wall.

I checked my watch. Fifteen minutes until we had to be aboard the ship. If we were as far from it as I thought we were, even if we found a way out of here right away, we still wouldn't make it back to the ship in time.

"There! This has to be it." Bart pointed. A tall, arched, doublewide door, set deep in the wall just had to be one that would get us out of here. He grabbed the big iron circle and pulled. Nothing happened. We searched for locks but found none. He pulled again and I helped. Slowly, the huge door creaked open. Bart peeked out, nodded, and I slipped out. Bart followed, and we tugged it shut again, then found we were on a main street of some kind. Cars whizzed by and scooters vied for their road space, squeezing through tiny little places I'd never dare to try.

I searched for some landmark, something familiar. "I think we have to get around that tower before we can tell where we are."

"Let's do it." Bart grabbed my hand, and we took off again. Thank heaven it was only one long block, and as soon as we rounded the corner, we saw the harbor. Not that we were anywhere near it, but at least we weren't lost anymore.

I leaned against the wall to catch my breath as a couple on two scooters stopped at the stop sign in front of us. Bart waved at them and asked if they'd take us to our ship. One glance at my rounded tummy and flushed face, and they seemed most happy to oblige. I climbed on behind the young woman, and Bart hopped behind the man. In less than five minutes, we were at the ship.

When Bart tried to pay them, they wouldn't take his money. "Bon voyage," they called as they sped away, smiling and waving. We didn't dawdle dockside but quickly scrambled aboard ship, not taking any chances on someone taking a potshot at us.

Only then did we remember we hadn't received the topaz from Rhodes, and someone from Anastasia should have been at the dock waiting to relieve us of those we'd collected.

Bart slapped his forehead. "I can't believe we forgot what we were supposed to be doing."

"We've got to go back," I said, turning around at the top of the gangplank.

We hurried back to the dock and, in order to have an excuse for dawdling in the area, spent a lot of time photographing the ruins being excavated just below the ship. A round tower with battlements on top had been completely restored, and several round foundations were emerging from the rubble, as well as large rectangular and smaller square foundations.

No one resembling a topaz passer was anywhere in sight. A few workmen sorted through the stones, and an occasional scooter went by, but no one seemed the least bit interested in us. Then I noticed the boy.

A young boy on a bicycle turned lazy circles in the parking lot near the edge of the excavations. I caught him watching us while Bart scrutinized every road, car, bus, and vehicle of any description in the vicinity. I focused my camera on the boy to take his picture. He looked much like the kids at home, except his beautiful eyes seemed coal black and his hair was so black it had blue highlights in the sun. Just like the ravens in my trees above our cottage.

"No," he called, waving his hand in front of his face. "You must not take my picture."

"Do you want me to pay you for it?" I asked.

He rode over to where I stood and dismounted. "You are late," he whispered. "I nearly went home without finding you. My grandmother will be worried when I'm gone so long. Take your picture, then pretend to pay me. I have something to give you for your grandmother."

He posed on his bicycle with a big grin while I took his picture, then I dug in my pocket for a coin and thrust it at him. He palmed the coin in exchange for a small round package a little larger than a jawbreaker. He flashed a smile, waved the coin, and called thank you over his shoulder as he sped away.

"Good job, princess. But where's Anastasia? We have about two minutes before they pull up the gangplank."

"Maybe they got tied up somewhere else and couldn't come."

"Possible, but they need these stones so they can begin working on the code. Who knows how long it will take to decipher it? They want them now. Today."

"Since Dominic and Else are in Athens, maybe they decided to pick them up from us tomorrow. They're supposed to meet us at the Acropolis."

Bart took my arm, and we started back to the ship when we heard a car screech to a stop behind us. We both whirled and were poised to run when a blonde emerged from the car and waved to someone onboard ship who'd apparently been watching for her. She threw money in the open cab window and raced up the gangplank.

"That was just about us," I laughed as we approached the foot of the gangplank and prepared to board the ship without being able to pass along the topaz we'd collected.

Suddenly brakes squealed again right behind us and a car skidded to a stop.

Chapter 22

I didn't know whether to throw myself on the ground or run behind the gangplank, but it turned out to be just another taxi screeching to a stop as close as it could get to the embarkation area. The back door flew open, and Gabriella jumped out and ran to us.

"David tried to come for the topaz you've gathered, but he's been spotted by the terrorists, who know what he's here for. He led them away and told me where you'd be waiting for him. I'm to pick them up and meet him later so they can decipher the code. You must be on the ship to collect the rest of the stones, but I don't need to be, so I can miss the sailing."

Something was definitely rotten in Denmark, and it wasn't Danish blue cheese! Without any hesitation, I unsnapped the bra safe from under my shirt and pressed it into her hand.

"Then get away from here fast before they catch you. If you know about this meeting, they will too. Go!" I shoved her toward the taxi, and with a surprised expression, she turned and jumped in the cab and slammed the door. The taxi revved its engine and peeled out as if she thought I'd change my mind and want the stones back.

The only thing I wanted back was an opportunity to punch out her lights for poisoning the mousse and making my husband so sick and for siccing the thugs on us who tried to kill us. It had taken every ounce of self-control to refrain from smacking her right in the face. The one thing that prevented it was knowing it was not Christlike, and would cause the Holy Ghost to leave me. Heaven only knew how much I needed the Spirit to guide me through this escapade. This had been a perfect example of what could happen when you listened to the still, small voice.

Bart and I hadn't even had time to comment on that implausible occurrence, when a third vehicle roared up to the spot barely vacated by Gabriella's taxi. Except this was a Harley Davidson motorcycle, glistening black with gleaming gold trim. Else pulled off a motorcycle helmet and shook out her long blonde hair. Not only was this a scene straight from the movies, but Else was Hollywood chic with her skin-tight black leather from the tip of her high heel boots to the mandarin collar of her designer leather jacket.

"Else! Hello!" I ran and threw my arms around her. "How good to see you!"

"Greetings, my sweet sister. I see what they tell me is true. You are blooming, Alli."

"Yes." I laughed, patting my roundness. "Isn't it wonderful!"

Bart greeted her with a kiss on the cheek. "Did you see Gabriella just now?"

Else gasped. "Gabriella Cardin?"

I nodded. "She just came for the topaz we'd collected. Said David was busy evading terrorists who were after the jewels, so he'd sent her for them."

The cool, nothing-ever-rattled Else nearly fell off her bike. "You didn't give them to her? In the name of Odin, tell me you didn't give them to her!"

I looked up at Bart and laughed. "I gave her my bra safe containing five grapes wrapped in paper napkins. We caught on to her last night, thank heaven. I have the real topaz right here in my waist safe."

Bart stood close behind me to block, as much as possible, the view of our transaction in case someone watched from the ship, while I unzipped the pouch secured to my waist and pulled out the five smoky topaz stones. I handed them to Else and fished in my pocket for the one the boy had just given me.

"Only five?" Else asked. "Aren't there supposed to be six?"

"Voila!" I produced the sixth one from my pocket. "We haven't had possession of this one for even ten minutes."

"Good work, my darlings." Else zipped the six precious puzzle pieces into her leather jacket pocket and smiled. "We'll see you in Athens tomorrow?"

"Right," Bart said. "But we need you to work on a little problem that's come up. Gabriella knows we're collecting the jewels. She obviously knew you were going to meet us here to take the stones to start deciphering the code. How did she know? There's a leak somewhere, and we'd better find and fix it before we end up losing some of the grand old underground—or before we have another episode like last night."

Else raised one elegant eyebrow and glanced from Bart to me and back again.

"Just a little unexpected swim in the bay on the way back to the ship. Nothing serious," I explained.

"Nothing more serious than I nearly lost my wife," Bart shot back.

I slipped my arm around Bart's waist. "We survived, but it seems clear that Gabriella IDed us, so the next few pickups will be extremely dangerous for the underground, as well as for us. She just increased the risk exponentially for all of us. Get the word back quickly, and see if you can find where the cracks have appeared in the system. Let everyone know she's changed allegiance."

"I've never liked the woman, but at least we were working on the same side," Else said, shaking her head and sending shock waves through her long, silky blonde hair.

"We have no proof, but I suspect she's working with Cell Seven." Bart let that sink in for a second, then added, "By the way, if a black spider is the symbol of that group, then one of the stewards is a member."

"You two sure have a way of discovering interesting new problems, don't you?" Else frowned. "Apparently this group is more established than we thought."

I nodded. "I'm afraid so. They've been with us since Verona, the very beginning of our trip, so they received their information from someone as we were still in the planning stages. That's pretty scary."

"We've got to go," Bart said. "They're signaling us to come aboard. Where do you want to meet and what time?"

"You're scheduled to arrive at the Acropolis around nine. To make sure nothing happens—they are having strikes all over Athens—let's say ten o'clock in the museum."

"See you then," Bart said. "Oh, I like your wheels. Where'd you get 'em?"

"Car rental agency." Else laughed. "Faster and more maneuverable than a car. As you know, we need that in this business." She blew kisses, donned her helmet, and was gone with a roar of the mighty engine.

I stared through the cloud of dust she left behind. "I can never believe the things that incredible woman does. She just amazes me."

Bart led me up the gangplank. "You amaze me, princess."

"How, besides the fact you think I attract more trouble than anyone else you know?"

"Your self-control, for one thing. I guess I actually expected you to throw a punch at Gabriella the next time you saw her, like you threatened to do, and instead you coolly passed off the fake topaz, subtly told her the enemy's on to her, and sent her on her way."

"Getting physical isn't ladylike, and Mom always taught me to be a lady." I carded onto the ship, and we headed for our cabin. "Besides, what kind of example would I be setting if someone knew I was a member of the Church and then watched me smack somebody? They'd have no way of knowing she was a traitor, that she'd nearly poisoned my husband and nine other people, and had caused a near-fatal drowning incident."

"You have a point there," Bart admitted as we trudged up the stairs.

"But the overriding reason I didn't just punch out her lights was that little bit of inspiration I received this morning to bring those grapes. I had no idea why I was doing it. It just seemed a good idea at the time. I need that kind of inspiration constantly, and I think our need will get even more dire as we get deeper into this, since she's identified us to Cell Seven. So I'd better mind my Ps and Qs and be worthy to continue getting the Holy Ghost's inspiration."

"Have I told you lately that I think you're wonderful?" Bart asked, keying the door to our cabin.

"No."

He shut the door, kicked off his shoes, and headed for the bathroom. When he came out, I was still standing where he'd left me. He looked puzzled.

"What are you doing? You're not going to crash for a few minutes?" he asked.

"I'm waiting."

"Waiting for what?"

"Waiting for you to tell me you think I'm wonderful."

He wrapped his arms around me and smothered me with kisses until I begged for him to stop, and we fell laughing on the bed. "I think you're wonderful," he whispered, nibbling my ear.

"I think you're pretty wonderful too." I traced his eyebrow and down the side of his suntanned face with my finger. "Thanks for indulging me in all the sightseeing today."

"I just enjoy being with you, princess, whatever you want to do. It's something we've missed out on, so I'm finally finding out the kinds of things you do when I'm not with you."

I sighed. "Most people discover these things while they're dating. We sort of skipped that phase of our relationship while you wandered off to exotic places and played spy for five years. So I sat at home wondering what happened to the man who proposed marriage and then dropped off the face of the earth."

Bart leaned up on one elbow, stared at me, and said with a mock stern tone, "You did not sit at home." He twisted a strand of my hair and tickled my nose with it. "You were busy getting your degree, working as a glamorous translator at the U.N., and getting engaged to be married to someone else. How did you even have time to think of me with all that going on?"

I slid my arms around his neck, pulled him down, and kissed him. "I thought of you all the time because I loved you."

"Even while you were telling someone else you'd marry him?" Bart teased.

"That was just to keep him from asking me each time I saw him. And while we're talking about liaisons, I could mention a few beautiful women who have cropped up from your dark and mostly unknown past."

"None even worth mentioning," he murmured, trying to divert my attention from the subject by kissing me until I was breathless. When I finally pushed him away so I could breathe, he struck the final blow to the conversation. "I loved you so much, I even withstood the temptation of the incomparable Else. If, after nearly five years of not being able to see you, I could still walk away from her inviting arms, you should have no doubt you're the only woman in the world for me."

"Thank you. I'll be eternally grateful for that." I scrunched the pillow under my neck and turned on my side to look at Bart. "And now we'd better get back to work. We need to talk to your mom, or mine, and find out what new developments they had last night and today while we were swimming in the bay and sightseeing. We didn't call, thanks to my exhausted state."

"Mmm," Bart murmured and closed his eyes. "We were just a little busy."

"Are you going to sleep?"

"Only for a minute. Snuggle here with me and rest for a few minutes, then we'll get snazzied up, head topside and call, and then go to dinner."

That sounded wonderful to me, so I totally relaxed and fell asleep immediately. Two hours later we woke, peeked at the clock, and panicked. I flew into the shower while Bart shaved, then he jumped in the second I finished. No fancy hairdo tonight—just a quick blow dry. I slipped into a glitzy dinner dress and was ready when Bart finished dressing.

"You look ravishing, princess," he said, holding the door open for me.

"Thank you," I laughed. "You clean up pretty good yourself." He had to be the most handsome man aboard the entire ship. But as I stepped into the corridor and saw Raphael's cart outside, my delightful mood vanished. Just like Raphael.

"Oh, Bart. What are we going to do about Raphael?"

"Good question. I had hoped Gabriella would let him go if she held him somewhere, but after your little discovery about Ricardo, I'm afraid I'm not optimistic about finding him alive, especially if those black spiders are the symbol of the Sevens. It would be iffy enough if Gabriella worked alone, but with a network of terrorists in place, they won't take chances on having the organization compromised. I'll speak to the captain to find out if anyone's seen him or if he's just missing in action."

I glanced at my watch. "Do we dare take time to make a phone call before dinner, or should we wait until after?"

Bart checked his watch and decided we'd better go to dinner first since we might need a good long conversation to catch up on all that had transpired during the last twenty-four hours.

As soon as I sat down and smelled the warm bread on our table, I discovered I was ravenous. I ate two rolls while I waited for dinner to be served. Conversation over dinner centered first on the gunshots at the Seven Springs today and then on our little swim after the wild donkey ride down the hill from Fira. No matter how often we changed the subject, it came up again and again and again.

"Weren't you just terrified when he threw you overboard?" Sara asked, her beautiful blue eyes wide with wonder.

"Only when he jumped in on top of me, and I thought he was trying to drown me." I laughed, trying to make light of the incident. No one needed to know the attack was premeditated instead of just an obnoxious drunk's out-of-hand antics. "Besides, I learned to swim in the Pacific Ocean, and I'm a strong swimmer, so I wasn't worried about not being able to get to shore if the tender hadn't returned for us."

The minute we could excuse ourselves, we did. Everyone readily accepted my explanation that all the stairs up to the castle at Lindos today, plus racing through old town Rhodes had exhausted me—definitely the truth. They were experiencing the same tired legs and exhaustion.

Our mini-golf course was deserted again, so we settled on the pilings to talk to whoever answered at the Control Center.

When Alma answered, her voice was filled with relief. "Oh, I'm so glad to finally hear from you. We've been worried sick when you didn't call last night or today."

"I'm sorry. We had a little incident last night, and by the time we returned to the ship, we were so exhausted, we didn't even think to call. This morning we overslept and didn't have time. We did connect with Else, and she has the six topaz gems we've collected so far. Any new developments since we talked to you last?"

"Oh, Alli, I don't even know where to start."

Chapter 23

"How about any new explosions?" I prompted.

"Oh, dear, yes." Alma sounded distressed. "They gave us a list of targets they'd destroy if the treasure wasn't turned over to them, and then they proceeded to blow up half a dozen other places, which came as a complete surprise."

"What did they hit?" Bart asked.

"A centuries-old church in northern Italy, a monastery in Greece, some ancient stone formations in the countryside in England, archeologically valuable caves in France, an area in Egypt with newly discovered Egyptian tombs, and an ancient temple in Malaysia. They're going to destroy the world's historical treasures before we can even *collect* the jewels, much less decipher the code and find the treasure."

"Alma, what news do you have on the art treasures being auctioned at Christie's? The painting by Cezanne and the Amber Rose. Any idea where they were found? And when?"

"Oz and Mai Li are working on that. Christie's signed a confidentiality contract, and we're having a hard time getting them to release the owner's name or any other information."

"Any news on the leader of Cell Seven?" Bart asked. "Is it Abu Iyad and Omar Abdel, or are they just recruiters for the terrorist cell?"

"Phone records traced from the cell phone of the captured terrorist at the cave led to a number in Paris that he'd called several times. They're trying to contact the owner of the apartment, but he's on an extended vacation, and the people living there don't have any idea where he is or when he'll be back. They said they're just housesitting, and he told them he'd give them a week's notice before he returned."

"Do you know the name of the owner?" Bart asked, commencing his usual pacing back and forth in front of me, staying close enough to hear his mother's report.

"Merle Vachel, a French man with a history of questionable World War II associations. His dossier says he converted to Islam about ten years ago and has been financing the building of mosques all over Europe since then."

"Contributing to the construction of the buildings or financing terrorist activities using radical Muslims?" Bart asked.

"You'll have to read between the lines until we get more concrete evidence. Interpol is checking into that for us now."

"While they're researching, have them scrutinize Gabriella Cardin's activities," I suggested. "To say I don't think she's on our side anymore would be a *gross* understatement."

"Did something happen?" Alma asked, her voice filled with worry.

"Oh, nothing serious," I laughed. "She *only* laced Bart's dessert with something that nearly killed him, then sicced a couple of goons on us who tried to drown us, and sent a couple of others to catch us in Lindos and Rhodes. Then she raced up to us at the ship and said that David had sent her to collect the topaz so you could start deciphering the code."

"David wasn't in Rhodes. Oh, dear," Alma exclaimed. "You didn't give them to her, did you? Else was supposed to meet you and get them."

"Never fear, Mother, dear. My brilliant wife caught on to the glamorous Gabriella right away. Else has the stones and should be on her way back to wherever she's taking them. But Gabi is on the loose, and she's going to be furious when she unwraps five green grapes instead of five smoky topaz. Vengeance will be uppermost in her mind."

"Oh, my dears, please be so very careful."

"Something else, Mom," Bart said, sitting beside me to talk into the satellite compact. "Margaret said David had been researching the generals who worked with Kesselring to see if any of them were still living. Did he find out anything before this blew up in our faces?"

"I think I saw his report on that, but right this minute I can't tell you anything about it. I'm sure you can guess how wild it has been here with all of this going on. The president has called up the National Guard, those who aren't already mobilized in Iraq, to protect our national monuments. With the widespread bombings all over the world, he feels it's just a matter of time before we're hit."

"He's probably right." Bart sat silently for a minute. "Do you have anything else for us, Mom?" Then he added sardonically, "Any other glad tidings?"

"I'm so sorry to be the bearer of such awful news. I wish I had something good to tell you."

"I wish you did too," I said. "But if there's anything else you think of, make a note, and we'll call tomorrow before we go ashore in Athens. We're meeting Else and Dominic at the Acropolis at ten o'clock. I'm sure we won't have another stone to give them by then, unless we get lucky."

"I'm sorry to sound so rattled this morning," Alma apologized. "I haven't had much sleep in the last forty-eight hours, and I don't think your dad has slept at all. We're doing our best to provide support and keep Anastasia informed on everything they're requesting, but I'm not as quick as I used to be. I'll be so glad when you get back, Alli, and can take over the Control Center. You'll do much better on your own than both Jim and I together."

"Not true, Alma. You're doing great." Then I added, "In fact, since it's night here and things may quiet down a bit, why don't you go grab a quick catnap before things get wild again?"

"Wonderful idea, if the phones will just stop ringing and the computers will stop printing requests for information. Anything else I can do for you?"

I glanced at Bart. He shrugged his shoulders, then shook his head.

"Thanks, but I don't think so. Go get some sleep. That's what we're going to do."

I disconnected and slipped the gold compact in my purse. "Wow," was all I could say.

"Double wow," Bart echoed. We just sat there, immobilized by the immensity of the thing.

"This is terrible." A sense of helplessness swept over me. "Bart, we've got to stop them, but where do we start when we don't even know who their leader is?"

"Or leaders *are*. That may be plural instead of singular," Bart said. He jumped to his feet and paced the deck, fueled by nervous energy. "What do we know? Start from the beginning, and let's review this piece by piece."

"Field Marshal Albert Kesselring, one of the most formidable technicians of war in the twentieth century, confiscated, accumulated, and just flat-out stole precious art, artifacts, and other treasures from the Italians—civilian, military, and church—and hid them in a salt mine near Florence."

"That's one. Next?" he said.

"His heir is the great-grandson who inherited the family art business and art collection and has questionable contacts who appear to be associated with neo-Nazis currently stirring up trouble all over the world."

He held up two fingers. "That's two."

"Long-lost art objects are turning up at art auctions."

"Keep going." Bart nodded.

"The old underground Freedom Fighters from World War II are gathering all the topaz stones from Empress Elizabeth's necklace so the code engraved on them can be deciphered. Then the treasure can be found and returned to its rightful owners. Probably should have listed that as number two."

Bart stopped pacing and leaned over to kiss me. "We're not concerned with order, just the facts, ma'am." He smiled.

"In that case, the next thing that comes to mind is our part in this. We're supposed to meet people who quietly and unobtrusively deliver the jewels to us since they are being watched and can't deliver them openly to anyone. However, I'm not sure that'll work anymore, since Gabriella broadcasted our ID and intentions to the terrorists."

"We've definitely been compromised. That's five. Going for six?"

"Gabriella, I'm convinced, shot herself in the arm, set off an explosion—I wonder if that one was so small that it hasn't been connected to the others." I shook my head. "Anyway, Gabriella came onboard to either take the topaz from us or to stop us from receiving them so Cell Seven, or whoever she's working for, could get to them first."

Bart nodded. "That's still a little nebulous, but I think you're on the right track. Anything else?"

"Yes." I stood and paced with Bart. "Something isn't right. The first explosions were supposed to be in two announced locations, and both were misses. Near misses, but misses nevertheless. Were those failures actually accidents or were they planned that way?"

"Mmm. Good question, princess. And?"

"And why all the unexpected explosions? Are they really connected to the announced targets of Cell Seven?"

Bart stopped pacing and faced me. "And you're thinking what?"

"What if another group—or groups—decided to take advantage of the chaos that has ensued from Cell Seven's announcement? What if some disgruntled citizens or some smaller terrorist cells or even individuals with revenge in mind for something decided to exact their revenge while they have an opportunity to get away with it. After all, someone has already taken the blame. Nobody's going to investigate carefully when the Sevens have claimed responsibility."

"And how did you come up with this scenario?" he asked, hands on his hips and a bemused smile on his face.

"Cell Seven, unless they're a lot larger organization than we've been led to believe *and* unless they have a lot more funding than we think they do *and* unless they have a lot of really dedicated and talented people in charge, couldn't make this all happen on so many fronts in such a short amount of time."

"I'll bite. Why not? Why couldn't they send an individual to each of those locations with the instructions to blow it up whenever they wanted? Or to wipe it out at a designated time? Or why couldn't they have recruited people from each of those areas, trained them, provided the explosives or the funds to procure them, and left them on their own? "

"Oh, all of those are very real possibilities," I admitted, "but tell me what you know of Cell Seven, and then I'll tell you why this just isn't gelling with me."

Bart thought for a minute. "Very little, actually. And on that note, why don't we hit the business center and see if we can get through to the Interpol line. A tidbit of info's hovering at the back of my mind, but I can't retrieve it. I'd like to read that bulletin again."

I agreed, then had another thought. "Do you suppose we ought to locate Ricardo and see if he has any news of Raphael, or should we wait for him to come to us? Since I no longer believe anything about his story, I don't know if I want to talk to him or not, but I do want to find out about Raphael."

Bart shook his head. "I keep forgetting about Raphael. I was going to go to the captain first thing to find out if he knows anything. Why don't I take you back to the cabin, and you can put your feet up for fifteen minutes while I find the captain? I'll come back and tell you what, if anything, I've discovered. Then we can decide if we need to find Ricardo or if we can just go to the business center and get on a computer."

"Sounds good. There should be internet hook ups in each room so we could stay in our cabin and get at this information instead of charging such big bucks to get online. It's sure not convenient."

"Or cheap." Bart wrapped his arm around my shoulder, and we started down the stairs to our cabin, descending four decks' worth of double staircases. By the time we reached our room, I would have been perfectly content to climb into my pajamas, fall into bed, and forget everything else, including Raphael.

Bart left to find the captain, and I sank on my bed with my pillows under my legs instead of under my head, relieving my aching back.

What happened to Raphael? Someone took him out of the scene, but who? And why? He went to the medical center to get medicine for Bart, brought it here, then returned to the medical center to find out who else was sick and to ask about the doctored dessert. I hadn't seen him since. Did he talk to Ricardo before he went to talk to Dr. Chandra? Did Gabriella spot him in the kitchen, or was it her boyfriend?

I'd suspected Gabriella since we found Raphael's phone in her room. Who would have been involved in his disappearance if she wasn't? I sat up on my bed. Oh, my gosh. That was so obvious—why didn't I think of it before?

Chapter 24

It had been right there under my nose the entire time! The patient with the head injury on Dr. Chandra's examining table—that was Raphael! And the birthmark on Dr. Chandra's ear wasn't a birthmark at all. It was a black spider. I didn't recognize it because I hadn't yet seen Ricardo's. And Raphael had been alive when I last saw him in the medical center, so if, as Dr. Chandra said, they took him ashore in Santorini, hopefully he'd still be alive now.

What would they do with him? If they'd administered Rohypnol, he wouldn't remember what had happened, but would they dare take a chance that he would never remember? Or did they care after this was over? If they could keep him out of the way long enough to collect all the topaz and find the treasure, they might not care at all how much he remembered.

But if he had sustained a head injury, they might have taken him ashore and dumped him somewhere. Then we'd never find him. Captain Fortezze needed to ask the authorities on Santorini to search for Raphael. I had to know what happened to the innocent young man I'd involved in this.

Bart didn't return. I thought of going to find him, but knowing we'd probably pass on opposite staircases and never see each other, I decided that wouldn't be wise. Instead, I busied myself with my bedtime routine. I read my scriptures but had a difficult time concentrating. I wrote in my journal and finally prepared for bed, even saying my prayers, and he still hadn't returned.

Had he simply gone to the business center without me? Was he waiting for an opportunity to speak with the captain? Or . . .

My mind conjured up wild, fearful scenarios with Ricardo and Dr. Chandra and even Gabriella's boyfriend, Andre. How many other members of Cell Seven were aboard the ship? Ricardo and Dr. Chandra hadn't looked like terrorists, but, then, neither did the pictures of the beautiful young women who became suicide bombers. They were definitely terrorists. And the handsome young men who posed for pictures with their proud mothers before they blew themselves and dozens of others to smithereens. The face of the terrorist had changed drastically in the last ten years.

That must have been my last conscious thought before I succumbed to the soft, inviting arms of slumber. My next conscious thought was an urge to kill whoever set the alarm for such an ungodly hour. It couldn't possibly be time to get up already. I opened one eye, peeked at the clock, quickly shut it again, and groaned. We were on a cruise! Supposedly a leisurely vacation. Who on earth would set an alarm for six o'clock in the morning?

My first clue came when I heard Bart whistling softly in the bathroom. When the musky aroma of his aftershave tickled my nose, I opened my eyes and gazed up into two smiling blue eyes.

"Good morning, Sleeping Beauty. Today is Friday, and this is Athens. The ship has docked and, though it's still dark outside, we're going to miss breakfast and our bus to the Acropolis if you don't roll that beautiful body out of bed and get a move on."

I stretched, sat up, and slipped my arms around Bart's neck. "I don't suppose staying in bed is an option?"

"Sorry, princess, not today. We've got places to go and people to meet, but as soon as this is over and you're back on the estate, you can sleep in as long as you want."

"Right. Just like your mom and dad are sleeping in. Being in the Control Center is not going to get me any more rest than being in the field—it just won't be as exciting and strenuous, or as fun."

"You may be right, but it will make me a happy man to know you're safe and not being shot at and that no one is trying to drown you or poison you every time you turn a corner. Now, do you want me to bring your breakfast while you get ready, or are you going to hurry and dress so you can eat in the dining room?"

"Mmm. Why don't you spoil me and bring me breakfast in bed?" I stretched and yawned and would have pulled the covers back over my head if my husband hadn't suddenly flipped them right off the bed.

"Tomorrow, I'll spoil you with breakfast in bed, and you can sleep as long as you want. You won't even have to get out of bed at all. Today we meet Else and Dominic, hopefully collect another topaz, and I will actually get a chance to stand on Mars Hill, where the Apostle Paul preached. That will be the highlight of my day. So get your buns moving, m'lady, or we'll miss our bus."

"You're a slave driver, you know that? This is cruel and unusual punishment."

Bart held out his hands, and I gave him mine so he could pull me to my feet. "If you hurry, I'll tell you what I found last night. If you don't, you'll have to find out in the report at the end of our mission."

"Two can play at that game, Captain Hook. If you don't tell me what you found out, I won't tell you what I discovered, or at least decided."

"Truce!" Bart cried. "We'll tell all over breakfast if you can get ready fast enough. Otherwise, we'll go hungry today."

We didn't have to go hungry, but we did have to hurry through the line, eat breakfast so quickly we didn't have time for conversation, and rush to meet our group to disembark together. It was still dark when Jim and Carol led us through a winding passage from the ship around the dock to the customs entry. Our guide wouldn't cross the transportation strike picket line, so we had to wait for another. Hurry up and wait—the motto for these kinds of things, I decided.

Once that was taken care of, we had to walk all the way back around the fence on the other side to the bus. Without the strike, we'd have simply walked off the ship and a hundred feet to the bus. I wondered what other interesting problems we might encounter today with everyone involved in transportation on strike, including the garbage men.

I vowed then and there I'd never go on a tour in which the people who made all the arrangements didn't accompany you. We'd have been totally stuck and missed out on our Athens adventure if Jim and Carol hadn't been there with a backup plan to instigate immediately.

I noted absently as we drove through the city that when some people strike, it's not always apparent to the causal observer. When garbage workers strike, it's immediately evident.

Our bus ride from the Port of Piraeus to the city of Athens afforded us our first opportunity to catch up on the discoveries from last night. Rush hour added to the normally thirty-minute trip, so we had plenty of time to talk. Quietly.

"What took you so long to get back? Couldn't you get to the captain, or did you just go to the business center and get on the internet without me?" I asked.

"Since the captain had special guests at the second seating for dinner, and I couldn't talk to him until he was finished, I went to the business center and waited about fifteen minutes for a computer. Unfortunately, I couldn't access the Interpol sites I really wanted to get into, so I don't have any new information on Cell Seven. Tell me what you discovered that had you so excited."

"Did I tell you about the patient at the medical center when I went to ask Dr. Chandra to discover what she could about the poisonings?"

Bart frowned and shook his head. "I don't remember that, but, then, I wasn't really sharp there for a few hours, so maybe I just missed it."

"Doesn't matter. Someone with a serious problem—their head totally bandaged mummylike with gauze—lay on the examining table. He moaned, so I knew he was alive. Dr. Chandra said he'd suffered a head wound and would be transported to the hospital in Santorini. When you took me to Dr. Chandra to be examined after our dip in the bay, the table was empty. I asked about the patient, and she said he'd been taken to Santorini to the hospital. I saw then what I thought looked like a birthmark on Dr. Chandra's left ear." I glanced at Bart to see if he recognized the significance of any of this yet. No reaction. I continued.

"A few minutes later, we met Ricardo in our corridor and spotted the spider on Ricardo's ear."

"*You* spotted the spider," Bart corrected.

I ignored him. "Then last night as I worried about Raphael, I remembered the timing of my first visit to Dr. Chandra. I went there first thing in the morning, right after Raphael had disappeared. No one saw him after he had headed for the medical center to ask who'd been poisoned by the mousse. I contend that Dr. Chandra is involved somehow in Raphael's disappearance. I don't know whether she bopped him on the head, or Gabriella, or Ricardo did or whether he was drugged or what, but between the three of them, I believe they rendered him unconscious and took him off the ship disguised as a patient on the way to the hospital."

"Which jives with what the captain told me. He said Raphael had an accident—slipped on wet tile in a bathroom and sliced his head open. They took him ashore to the hospital. I had the captain call and find out how he's doing." Bart stopped, his attention drawn to something outside the bus.

"And?" I prompted.

Bart pointed out the window. "That's the original Olympic stadium built in the fifth century B.C. Did you know the first modern games were held right there in 1896? The entire amphitheater, which seats seventy thousand spectators, was rebuilt in the 1800s using the original marble stones."

"I'm impressed," I marveled.

"With the stadium or that I knew such historical trivia?" Bart asked.

"Both. And that Greece actually finished all this for the 2004 Olympic Games. Pretty impressive."

"Actually, you're pretty impressive, princess, that you put together Raphael and the patient on the table. Now have you figured out Gabriella's next move?"

I shook my head. "I just know we won't like it. She'll be furious, first, that she was fooled and received grapes instead of the topaz, and, second, that we're on to her, and, third, that I got the best of her. And since she has an inside track on what we're doing, we can expect her or her goons to show up at any time along our planned route. Too bad we have to stick so close to the announced agenda. That'll make things extremely easy for her to take vengeance."

"True. I hope Else and Dominic have something concrete for us today. I'd sure feel a lot better if I knew more about these people and what they intend."

Our Greek guide recited lots of great history, much of which we were missing because we were talking, but I'd learned most of it from Papa Karillides when I was a child, although I still had problems discerning fact from myth. He'd wound the two so closely together that I didn't remember who were the actual Greek heroes and who had been the mythical ones.

We arrived at the Acropolis, a rocky hill that completely dominated the center of Athens, rising over five hundred feet above sea level. Our guide stopped us at the bottom of the hill to recite the history of the ancient site.

It had been inhabited since 3500 B.C. and had been the most sacred of all places of worship—the temple of the goddess Athena and the religious center of the state from at least the eleventh century B.C. It became a fortress, then the palace of the Mycenaean kings, who erected walls to prevent enemy attacks.

As she dismissed us to discover the Acropolis for ourselves and take pictures, the Greek military in traditional uniforms marched down the hill to military music. They wore short, white, full skirts and white tights, full-sleeved white blouses, and blue and gold vests, with tassels on their berets and at the knees. They'd just concluded the flag-raising ceremony, and we'd missed it, standing at the foot of the hill listening to a history lesson! What a major disappointment.

I ran to the ticket office of the museum to buy a book on the site to identify all the major ruins, and we wandered the hill, taking the mandatory tourist shots of the Temple of Athena Nike built in the fifth century B.C. to commemorate the Greek victories over the Persians. We kept watching for someone wanting to get rid of a topaz, but no one seemed inclined to accommodate us.

I posed in front of the Erechtheion, famous for the six incredible marble statues of beautiful women with baskets on their heads holding up the portico, and Bart posed in front of the Parthenon, built on the highest part of the Acropolis.

The underground museum was just beyond the Parthenon, and while Bart waited outside, I ran in to see if Else and Dominic had arrived. I wasn't interested in remaining inside the museum. With Gabriella on the loose and her heart bent on revenge, I didn't want to be contained anywhere I couldn't see her coming first.

They hadn't yet arrived, so we leaned over the wall and took pictures of the ruins of the semicircular Theater of Dionysus on the slope beneath the hill where from the sixth century, plays by

Sophocles, Euripides, and Aristophanes had been performed. My guidebook said it was also used for public meetings. Had Paul spoken here when his audience was too great for the small area on Mars Hill?

Ten o'clock. No sign of Else or Dominic. "Does that mean trouble?" I asked Bart.

"Maybe just heavy traffic. Let's wander down toward the entrance since they have to come up those stairs. There's no other access up here unless they climb the rocks. Unfortunately, we only have a short time, then we have to get back on the bus. I don't know if they have the rest of today's itinerary and would know where to find us if we have to leave before they arrive."

I glanced at the map in the book. It was true. There was no other entry to the top of the Acropolis but the stairs. "I'll tell you what. I'll wait right here so I can clearly see and be seen, and you can run to that kiosk and get us something to drink."

"Good idea." Bart ran down the stairs and stood in a long line at the only food place on the premises. I sat on one of the massive rocks that were stacked awaiting reconstruction and watched the stairs, the long walk which wound up from the street. There was simply no sign of Else or Dominic.

The butterflies flitting in my stomach had absolutely nothing to do with the fact that I suddenly felt hungry. Unless something dire had happened, Else would not be late. Granted, traffic was unpredictable, but scooters and motorcycles were her preferred method of transportation because of that very fact, so stalled traffic wouldn't be a major consideration.

Bart returned with a fresh-squeezed orange juice for me, extra-large over ice, and an extra-large soda for him, over ice.

"Now what?" I asked.

"Now we sit and wait."

"You wanted to climb Mars Hill," I reminded him. "Since they aren't here yet, maybe you'd better do that now, or you may not have time. I'm afraid we're going to be cutting this awfully close."

"You sure you don't mind staying alone while I go play?" he asked.

"Nope. Here comes some of our group. I'll visit with them while I watch for our tardy friends."

Sara and Charlotte had run out of film and were trying to decide whether to pay ten euros for a roll. "We only paid six euros on Santorini yesterday, so it feels like we're being ripped off," Charlotte complained.

Sara nodded. "But if you want pictures here, you must pay their price. They know they have you, so they can charge whatever they want."

"I saw some nice postcards in the museum ticket office where I bought this book," I said. "The cards were reasonable, and, of course, taken on perfectly cloudless days with beautiful blue sky behind them. You might get postcards instead of spending all that money on film, then grab film at a shop off these expensive premises. Do you know how much Bart paid for this drink?"

Charlotte shook her head. "I don't want to know. Sara, you get us one drink to share, and I'll get postcards." They deserted me as one went up the stairs and the other went down.

At that moment, the hair on the back of my neck stood on end, and my danger antennae began to tingle.

Chapter 25

I slid off the rock and stood behind it, watching the dozens, probably hundreds, of people coming and going up the stairs, one tour group after another emptying into the street from the buses parked two deep and eight wide at the foot of the hill. People of every color, nationality, size, and shape. They all appeared to be nothing more than innocent tourists.

But something wasn't right, and I didn't know what. I scanned the faces of those flowing up the stairs. I turned to see those coming down. Their eyes were on the treacherously steep stone steps. As I turned back, out of the corner of my eye, I saw a sudden movement to my left.

I dodged behind the nearest tree. When I peeked around, two boys were leaping from rock to rock just off the stairs while they waited for their family to catch up to them. Their mama chastened them for running ahead and made them take her hand.

My feeling of unease increased. *Bart, please hurry back.* Mars Hill, below the Acropolis and to the right, was really just a huge mass of rock overlooking the teeming city that spread below. Its partially flat top didn't have much room to sit on or stand on. When Paul preached his famous sermon to the oldest justice court of Athens, they either didn't stay long, or they didn't mind sitting on uncomfortable rocks.

Bart stood atop the hill, known also as Areopagus, with several of our tour group. His light blue shirt stood out against the cream-colored rock. A perfect target. *Bart, please come down from there now.*

I turned to scan the crowds pressing toward the stairs and those heading for Mars Hill. If they all were simply sightseers, why was my skin crawling?

As I glanced back toward the refreshment kiosk, a scuffle caught my eye, one man behind another with his arm around his neck. The aggressor released the man, who slumped to the ground at the foot of a tree as if unconscious, and he melted into the crowd moving up the stairs toward the top of the Acropolis. I followed his progress as he slipped between groups, in and out, hurrying up without looking at the ruins along the way, which most stopped to examine. Finally, he raised his head.

Dominic Vicente, our flamboyant, impetuous Spanish agent. I hurried to intercept him before he reached the second set of stairs.

"Dom," I called and waved, staying in the rocky area off the stairs, trying to avoid the crush of pedestrians climbing up the high stone steps. "Over here."

"Niña bella!" Dominic grabbed me, whirled me around and kissed my cheek before setting me on the ground. "Let me look at you." He held me at arm's length. "Motherhood becomes you, belleza. You are radiant."

"Thank you. Where's Else?"

"She should be along in a minute, after she gets rid of a tail."

"Like you just did?" I asked.

"What do you mean?" Dom's dark eyes glanced first at me, then down the hill to the refreshment kiosk where the man still slumped near the tree. He grinned. "You saw that?"

"Just as you let him go. Who is he?"

"Someone a little too interested in Else. She spotted two of them following her, pointed them out, and led this one to me. He had Cell Seven's spider tattooed on his ear, so I figured he had malicious mischief in mind." Dominic studied me. "You've heard about our discovery at the caves?"

"Only the briefest sketch from Alma. Fill in the details, please. We're dying to hear what's been happening. I feel we've been isolated for a whole week."

"We found maps with targets marked and propaganda with black widow spiders drawn in the corner. At first it appeared to be doodling. Funny how you can miss something so important until it's pointed out. After we figured out it must be the symbol of this cell, we found it everywhere."

"Have you seen it on anyone in a spot besides their ear?" I asked, curious if that happened to be the specified location for the mark or if the ones we'd seen had simply been a convenient place for it.

"So far, each person identified with Cell Seven's had it tattooed on their left ear, but that doesn't necessarily mean it's the only spot they use." Dom pointed. "Here comes Else."

Bart had spotted Dominic beside me and descended from Mars Hill on the run. Else arrived, resplendent in white linen capri pants, matching short sleeve jacket, and luscious turquoise silk shell, only steps ahead of Bart.

"I don't suppose you've acquired another topaz?" Else said, brushing a kiss across my cheek.

I shook my head. "No such luck, at least not yet. I'd hoped we would so you could take it, and I wouldn't have to carry it back to Italy."

"You two are going to have to be very careful. We were followed," Else flashed a smile and smoothed a wrinkle in her jacket, "which is why we're late. We put the competition out of contention for the prize. Now let's get off this hill so we aren't sitting targets." She looped her arm through mine, and we descended the steep steps to the tree-shaded area at the bottom of the hill.

Dominic and Bart followed, with Dom bringing Bart up to date on all they knew about Cell Seven.

"You haven't mentioned if you've discovered the identity of the leader or leaders," I said. "Is it still a mystery, or did you neglect to report that minor detail?"

Else frowned. "Still a mystery. I'm feeling we're close. I'm also feeling it will be no surprise."

"Why is that?" I asked, leaning against a tree and enjoying the shade after baking in the hot sun on the hill.

"We're not finding too many tentacles on this yet," Else said. "We're still working our way up through the ranks to the top, but the group is small so far."

"Why did they announce those specific targets, then without warning hit half a dozen different ones spread across Europe and Asia?" Bart asked.

Dominic squinted in the sun and moved under the shade of the tree. "Puzzling, huh?"

"Alli had a theory," Bart said. "What if, after Cell Seven announced their targets, individuals or small terrorist groups with some kind of agenda just started destroying things, knowing they wouldn't be investigated since Cell Seven had already taken credit for the explosions."

"We have considered that. It makes as much sense as anything else we've come up with."

"I have another question."

Dominic interrupted with a mock shocked expression. "Only one? That would be a first."

They all laughed, but I continued, ignoring the implication. "Do you think Cell Seven really botched the Florence, Istanbul, and Egyptian explosions, or was that grandstanding? There would be no reason to attempt to make us think they're less than they are. Even if we assumed they were a bunch of amateur bunglers, we'd still have to go after them wholeheartedly just to protect all the treasures they've threatened. Something about this just doesn't make sense."

"You're absolutely right, belleza," Dom agreed.

"That's why you have to be more careful than ever," Else cautioned. "This whole thing is bizarre, and that makes it scary. Totally unpredictable behavior is frightening."

"Have you any idea where Gabriella's getting her information and why she changed sides all of a sudden?" I asked. "She seems to know everything we do."

As Else nodded, her silky blonde hair fell across her face. She tucked it behind her ear and asked quietly, "Remember the old man they tortured and took the topaz from?"

"Yes," Bart and I answered simultaneously.

"He told them the jewels would be passed to Americans on an organized tour and gave them the first two contact points, which was all he knew, fortunately. We figured they met all the tours coming to Milan from America on that day and followed them. When we computed the odds of them determining which tour to follow, it amazed us how easy it became. Only two ended up in Verona the first night, and Venice to the ship the second. Every other one stayed in Milan, then did Pisa or somewhere before they boarded a ship."

"And how did they determine which of the two we were on?" I asked.

"I think that's where Gabriella came in," Dominic offered. "Word leaked that the underground had organized a meeting after the anti-terrorist conference Jack and Margaret attended. I think Gabriella connected the two and figured someone from Anastasia would be involved in the pickups. Since she knows all of us, the rest became easy. She sends pictures of us to her people, they watch the crowd and as soon as they come across a familiar face, it's simply a matter of getting her aboard the ship and in contact with you."

"It's a good thing Alli figured out Gabriella had switched sides, or she might have actually ended up with the topaz." Bart put his arm around my shoulder and kissed my forehead. "She sure pulled the wool over my eyes."

Else laughed. "Don't feel badly, Bartholomew. All men are blinded by her beauty and charisma. It takes a woman to see past that."

"If she was dangerous before, she'll be twice that now since I gave her grapes instead of jewels. I'm not looking forward to our next meeting." I felt a little chill run down my spine in spite of the hot day. "Still, I wish I knew what prompted her change of allegiance. That might give us a much-needed clue in this puzzle."

"There's another disturbing development evolving that you're probably not aware of," Else said. "This newest terrorist group may or may not be involved in it, but it seems the sort of thing they'd embrace wholeheartedly. Several thousand neo-Nazis and skinheads marched through Dresden recently, now beautifully restored, protesting its incendiary destruction by Allied forces sixty years ago. They're trying to portray the Germans as victims of World War II. I think it's the beginning of an effort to rally young people to them by rewriting history and distorting the facts of what really happened."

I shuddered just thinking about the consequences of their success. "If they can convince this new generation the Allies were the aggressors and destroyed all those cities simply to conquer Germany, instead of for the real reason of liberating Europe from Nazi Hitler, what's happening with Cell Seven right now will seem trivial."

Dominic shuffled his foot in the dirt at the foot of the tree, kicking at an embedded rock. "Franz Schoenhuer, a former Nazi SS officer from Munich actually said, 'Here in Dresden, genocide took place in 1945, just like it did in Hiroshima. We're not afraid to call them war crimes.'"

"And what does he call what the SS did to all those people?" I declared hotly. "A celebration of life?"

"To his credit," Else countered, "Chancellor Gerhard Schroeder is criticizing extremists for trying to minimize the Third Reich's responsibility for the war and the Holocaust. He promised he'll oppose in every way the attempts to rewrite history. So at least the government's aware of what's going on, and they've placed new restrictions on public protests by neo-Nazi groups. Unfortunately, in the last two years, the number of hard-core Nazis and their sympathizers has increased substantially."

"They've even been making inroads into politics," Dom added glumly. "They're arguing that Dresden was bombed out of existence because it would be in Soviet control after the war and Britain and America were just ensuring nothing would be left for the Soviets." Dominic straightened and his eyes hardened. "What they're glossing over is the Nazi stronghold in Dresden and Saxony, which had to be destroyed to end the reign of terror by the Nazis. They also ignore the fact that for days before the bombing, Dresden was drenched in leaflets telling people to evacuate because the city was going to be destroyed."

"Mmm. Neo-Nazis going into politics, successfully." I shook my head. "That's unnerving."

Mark and Laura and Bruce and Diane walked by and called, "Jim and Carol said to pass the word it's time to head for the bus."

"Thanks." I waved at them, then glanced around for Sara and Charlotte, who'd been nearby. "I'll ponder this some more, but I just had a thought that's really terrifying. How much more damage could terrorists do if they were not *fighting* governments, but were in control of the legislature and parliament? Think about that and see where it leads you."

"Watch your backs, kiddies," Else said, turning to walk with us to the bus. "The playground is becoming more dangerous by the minute."

"There's certainly motivation there," Bart said. "Cell Seven is a collection of neo-Nazis with close ties to the old SS. If they got their hands on this treasure, they'd have money to attain the power they want. There's no telling the damage they'd do in the free world."

Dominic looped his arm through mine. "You be especially careful, mi belleza. If Gabriella has fire in her eye, you don't want to be anywhere in the vicinity."

"Dom, dear, I'll be more than happy to stay out of her line of fire if you'll tell me how I can do that and still collect the topaz you need to decipher the code."

Dominic glanced up at Bart. "Can't you send her home?"

I whirled on Dom. "Don't you even suggest such a thing. None of you are ducking under cover, so why should I? I have an assignment and I intend to complete it, just as all of you would do."

Else laughed. "I think you touched a nerve, Dom. You'd better do some of your famous fancy footwork and get out of the bull ring quick."

Bart put his arm around my shoulder. "Nice try, Dom, but I met with the same 'bull-headed' posture when I attempted to send her out of danger."

"Oh, you are so *punny!* Why don't you all just get out your red capes and wave them at me."

"Alli, dear, we're just worried about you," Else said softly. "Your assignment to collect the topaz had placed you like sitting ducks *before* Gabriella came on the scene. Now that danger has increased because she has a personal vendetta, not just a professional interest in the jewels. You must be more than careful, for the sake of you and your baby."

"And me," Bart declared. "Don't forget you must be careful for my sake, as well."

"The proud papa." Dom laughed. "I envy you, my friend."

"Then go find the leader of this cell, and let's put an end to it fast," Bart said, "so I can get my wife and child back to California and breathe easy again."

We'd arrived at the bus just in time to end this intolerable conversation. I kissed Else and Dom good-bye, and she promised to meet us again in a couple of days to retrieve the additional jewels.

Some of our group were still missing, so instead of waiting on the hot bus, I pointed to a street vendor who'd spread his papyrus paintings on a grassy area. "I'd like one of those for a souvenir. Come with me to see them." I grabbed Bart's hand and dragged him toward the pictures.

Many were copies of famous Greek paintings or frescoes or scenes of Greek gods and goddesses from mythology. I loved the bright coloring and gold and black accents in three and was having a terrible time making up my mind which to get when the vendor abruptly began gathering up his papyrus. Glancing around, I saw a policeman approaching rapidly.

I grabbed the closest one, thrust a five-euro coin in the man's hand, and he was gone before the policeman reached him.

"Hope that's the one you really wanted," Bart laughed.

"I hope it is too. They were all so beautiful, I couldn't decide. Don't you think that will be great on the hall wall between the bedrooms?" I held it up for him to see.

He nodded. "I'm sure you'll make it look wonderful, princess."

Sara came to admire it and showed me a lovely Greek bracelet she'd purchased in the tourist shop behind the buses. "Did you accidentally run into your friends, or did you arrange to meet them?"

"We arranged it. We don't get to see them often, so while we were in the area, I thought it would be fun to visit for a few minutes. Wish we'd had time for lunch. Oh! Why didn't I think to introduce you to Dominic? He used to be a matador. You'd adore him."

"He's very handsome. I thought he belonged to that beautiful blonde, or I'd have asked for an introduction." Sara nodded her head at the group of little shops behind the buses. "Speaking of good-looking guys, check out that one. He's been watching you ever since your friends joined you. I must say, he gives me the creeps, for all his good looks. He has such a brooding, evil air about him."

I turned slowly and scanned the stores. Leaning against the window of a photo shop, a man in dark sunglasses dressed in a black turtleneck and gray jacket turned his head away when I looked toward him. Sara was right. Though he was well dressed and clean-shaven with a neat haircut, there was something about him that gave me chills. And I had only gotten a quick glimpse.

"Bart, do you recognize the man over there?" But as I spoke, the man pulled his ball cap lower over his eyes and entered the shop.

"Did you see him?" I asked, hoping the man hadn't disappeared before Bart saw his face.

When Bart didn't answer, I glanced up at my husband. His forehead creased in a frown, his eyes narrowed, and the smile vanished from his face.

"Do you know him?" I asked, though the answer became obvious at his reaction.

Without a word, Bart took my arm and escorted me onto the hot bus.

Chapter 26

"So who was he?" I asked when we'd settled into our seats.

"Remember the assassination attempt on the U.S. ambassador to an African nation six months ago? A reporter covering the ambassador's visit to a hospital photographed the guy as he raised the gun to shoot. The reporter shouted at him and saved the ambassador's life. The picture splashed all over the news for a week or so."

"Mmm, yes, but I must not have had a good look at his face. I didn't recognize him." I sat back in my seat. "So what's he doing here?"

Bart didn't answer. I glanced at my silent husband, who'd tilted his seat back and closed his eyes.

"Are you trying to avoid answering my questions?" I asked, leaning against his shoulder.

He replied without opening his eyes. "I'm trying to get a little shut-eye since bedtime came extremely late last night, and I was up very early this morning."

True, but I knew my husband didn't need as much sleep as most, and he hated being the bearer of bad news. Especially if it concerned me. I pondered the situation. A notorious hit man in town the same time our ship visited Athens. Coincidence?

Of course, I'd been on that hill watching for Else and Dom and probably in plain sight of the man the whole time. He could easily have picked me off with a silencer and been halfway across the city before Bart returned from Mars Hill. No wonder my skin had been crawling and my danger antennae quivering! But maybe we weren't his targets. Maybe he was just visiting, playing tourist too. I assumed paid assassins had some kind of normalcy to their otherwise bizarre employment.

Our guide resumed her narrative of Athens as the bus wound through the city, stopping briefly at the Tomb of the Unknown Soldier. We hoped to see the ceremonial changing of the guard, but heavy traffic held up the arrival of the fresh guards, and we were back on the bus before the ceremony got underway. We did take pictures with those Greek guards already there who were as unflappable as the Swiss guards at the Vatican or the English guards at Buckingham Palace.

Browsing at the famed Plaka turned into a non-event. Our guide pointed in the wrong direction when the bus stopped to let us off, and we wandered streets with expensive shops in a beautiful newer part of Athens instead of the oldest quarter of the city. So we never found the narrow lanes with all the souvenir and handicraft shops or the Greek taverns where we'd planned to grab a bite of lunch or the Monastiraki, famous for the flea market and artisan shops.

Hot, tired, and disappointed, I was more than happy to return to the ship. Bart seemed uncharacteristically quiet, so I refrained from plying him with questions. When he was ready to share his thoughts, I'd be an eager listener.

Unfortunately, because of the transportation strike, we had to repeat the long, winding trek back to our ship instead of hopping off the bus at the ship's door, or gangplank, as the case may be. As we exited the bus, I mentioned to Bart how disappointed I'd been in not getting to see the Plaka, but more especially, in not receiving a topaz. "I really expected they'd meet us at the Acropolis, the tourist center of the city, the most obvious location for a pass. I wonder why they didn't."

"Maybe they spotted the man by the bus and changed their plans."

With that thought, I scanned the faces of those in the area. I noticed my husband seemed more alert, more wary, more worried. My skin prickled as I turned in a circle to see who might be hovering on the perimeter of the crowd that pressed toward the customs area.

Seated at a table near the entrance, a man in a black turtleneck and sunglasses was partially hidden behind a newspaper. I grabbed Bart's arm, positive I'd seen that same man at the bus. The assassin. But when he turned the page on his newspaper, it wasn't our man. I shuddered, a deep sense of relief rushing through me.

As we neared the customs entry, a scruffy looking fellow in a well-worn, wrinkled sport jacket and black beret approached. "Postcards of

Athens and Greece? Good deal, lady. Ten for five euros. Better than you get with your camera. Shots from airplane. Good pictures."

Before I opened my mouth to say no thanks, Bart dug into his pocket and produced a five-euro coin. The man grinned, handed a packet of postcards to Bart, and thanked him. "And for the little mother, a bonus." He gave me a small, brown paper sack. "Extra postcards so you will remember your trip to Greece with pleasure." He winked, then whispered, "Mama Karillides will be pleased to have a great-grandchild. Stay safe."

Aboard the ship, we collapsed on our beds in our room, trying to decide whether to have a leisurely lunch in the Marco Polo Restaurant or the buffet in La Brassiere. I opened the sack and dumped out the lump in the bottom, unwrapped it, and held it up to the bedside light. "These postcards are sure nice. I'm glad he stopped us. Here's a lovely shot of the stadium we'd never have gotten." I handed the postcard to Bart, along with the topaz.

He stared at me strangely, as if I'd just lost my marbles. I pointed to the small lamp on the nightstand. From my pillow, I could look up at the underside of the light where another little silver bug clearly clung to the stem. He rolled off his bed and knelt beside the table, ran his hand up the light and found it. I pulled my journal from my purse and gave Bart the debugger from the spy kit hidden there. He rendered the device inoperable and dropped back on his bed.

"You're welcome," I said.

"Mmm. Thanks," he murmured absentmindedly. "I'm hungry. Did you decide what you want to do for lunch?"

"Your choice."

He sat up. "We have the whole rest of the afternoon open. How about a leisurely lunch where someone serves our meal instead of us standing in line with a tray? I'm ready to be waited on."

"Sounds good to me." I stood, dropped the gleaming smoky topaz in my waist safe, zipped it shut, and smoothed my shirt to cover it. "Lead on, Lochinvar. Whither thou goest, I will go."

"Is that like mixing metaphors, when you mix characters? You've mixed Ruth and Naomi from the Bible with Arthurian tales from Jolly Old." He held the door open for me.

I pulled a face at him. "I know whence I speak, silly. You wouldn't have given it a second thought if I'd separated the two with two minutes' time and space. And speaking of time and space, when we finish lunch, we need to reach Mom. I'm worried about Mama Karillides. My grandmother may be in more danger than ever now that everyone knows I'm her granddaughter and we're the ones collecting the topaz."

"What are you thinking?" Bart asked as we descended the stairs to the Marco Polo Restaurant.

"They might get to her to get to us. We have a stash of topaz stones they want. It would be simple for them to land on Skiathos, take my grandparents hostage, and barter their return for the jewels."

"Do you want to call now? We can eat lunch later."

I hesitated. I didn't want anything to happen to my grandparents, though I felt quite sure Mom would have thought of their safety and hopefully gotten them off the island to safe hiding. Then again . . .

"Yes. Gabriella knows Else picked up the stones yesterday, so she may stand down until we have a couple more before she tries to get to *us* again. However, grabbing my grandparents and holding them for ransom can be done anytime to obtain the jewels we've already turned over to be decoded."

We reversed our trek from descending the stairs and headed up. About deck ten, my legs gave out. "I surrender. I need to take the elevator. I can't make it to thirteen today."

"No problem. My knees are feeling today's exercise too."

Golfers crowded the mini-golf course this afternoon, but we found a quiet corner by the railing and watched the ship leave Athens's Port of Piraeus as I called Mom's cell phone. I reached her voicemail, left a message, hung up, and tried again. I shouldn't have any trouble calling her back later since we'd be on the ship for the next thirty-six hours, but I wanted to connect right now. I had such a feeling of urgency that I planned to sit right there until I heard Mom's voice and discussed my fears.

Fortunately, the second attempt succeeded. "Hello, Alli. I'm glad you called back. I couldn't get to my phone before voicemail came on. Where are you?"

"Just leaving Athens. Mom, I'm worried about Mama and Papa Karillides. Are they still on Skiathos?"

"Yes, why?"

"Thanks to Gabriella, everyone, including Cell Seven, knows that I'm their granddaughter and I'm collecting the topaz. I'm worried the terrorists may try to kidnap them and hold them hostage for the jewels."

"Allison! I hadn't thought of that. You're right. They could be in grave danger."

"Mom, listen. I'm sure they'll oppose any plan to move them to safety, but what if you had them flown to California to help Alma and Jim in the Control Center. They may not know much about computers, but they're living libraries with knowledge of the things Alma's having a hard time researching. Convince them they'd be of vital assistance there."

"Wonderful idea, hon."

"An added incentive might be to stay for a few months and be there when the baby's born. I'd like that."

"I'll get it in motion immediately. Speaking of the baby, how're you doing?"

"Fine. What progress are you making? Have you discovered the identity of Cell Seven's head yet? Have you found out—?"

"Whoa." Mom laughed. "One question at a time. Progress? We discovered Mr. Vachel has not only been funding the construction of mosques all over France, but he's also been financing the training of terrorists in Iran. And he has close connections to Abu Iyad and Omar Abdel, the suicide bomber recruiters who seem to be fairly high up in Cell Seven."

"That's progress. What else have you discovered?" I slid to the deck with my back to the railing and pulled Bart down beside me, resting the compact on my knee so I appeared to toy with a shiny object while talking to my husband.

"David found the names of the generals who'd worked closely with Kesselring, most long since gone. Two died shortly after the war. Three moved to South America, and their families dissociated themselves from the Nazi regime. Two more were tried at Nuremberg and died in prison. That leaves only three who walked away from the war without serious disruptions in their lives and settled down as gentleman farmers or businessmen."

"And they are?" I asked, anxious to know if any were involved in Cell Seven.

"We've discounted one of the three, who's old and dying and has no family to speak of, at least none we can locate. He seems to be spending his last days alone, writing his memoirs."

"Can you get a hold of his memoirs?" Bart asked. "They'd be fascinating reading."

"We'll see what we can do. It doesn't seem to be of great urgency at the moment, given the problems confronting us with Cell Seven."

It was apparent Bart didn't agree with Mom, but he might be right. The memoirs might contain clues for us, and heaven only knew, we needed all the help we could get right now.

"And the other two generals?" I asked, anxious to finally acquire the information we'd been seeking since this whole thing started.

"General Erhard and Kesselring were good friends, remained close after the war, and their families stayed in close contact. We've lost one branch of the family—a daughter married and moved away, then remarried a couple of times, and no one seems to know her current name or location. Alma's working on that, so hopefully we'll locate information on her soon."

I glanced up at Bart and shook my head. Alma, already overwhelmed with all the other demands on her time and resources, wouldn't get to it soon enough. "What about the second one?" I asked.

"This is the most interesting of all. Kesselring's daughter, Jane, married General Burkhardt's son, Eber, and they've been working in the family business all these years with Kesselring's son and his wife. So you have the two couples running the art business together in what seems to be a well-oiled business relationship—at any rate, no problems have received publicity in the last forty years."

"And what about the next generation of Burkhardts?" Bart asked. "Where are Jane and Eber's children, and what are they doing?"

"Funny you should ask," Mom said, her voice growing quiet. "We finally found information on General Burkhardt's two grandsons, but nothing on his daughter, their mother. Here's the genealogy. As I told you, General Burkhardt's son, Eber, married Jane Kesselring. Eber and Jane produced one daughter who had two sons. Both boys, now close to fifty, were educated in America's best universities. One returned to Germany, became active in politics, is a member of the National Democrats, a far-right political party supported by neo-Nazis, and he's a popular candidate running for a seat in federal parliament."

"Not good news," I said, remembering our conversation with Else and Dom just a couple of hours ago. "What about the other?"

"He stayed in America and is a tenured professor at one of the Ivy League colleges."

"I'm guessing his politics are pretty far left for America, then," Bart said.

"Correct," Mom confirmed.

"So one returned to Germany to raise up another generation of neo-Nazis, and one stayed in America to reinvent World War II history and recruit rich, young Americans to his ideology." Bart summarized it succinctly.

"That's about the size of it," Mom said.

"You said there was a daughter, didn't you?" I needed to write this down. I pulled out my journal and scribbled the information Mom finally had for us. "Do you have a name for her? A location? Anything?"

"Lionel's pursuing that. He's in Paris, her last known location. Right now we have no information on her except a first name. Hopefully, he'll have something very soon."

"That brings us to Kesselring's great-grandson, Kesselring IV," Bart said. "Did his inheriting the art collection and gallery have any effect on the two Burkhardt grandsons and their families? Any fallout from that quarter?"

"It may be too soon to tell," Mom said. "No lawsuits have been filed against the estate, so no one is contesting the will of Kesselring III—at least, not yet."

"Mom, have any more long-lost art treasures surfaced in the last couple of days? We've been a little too busy to watch the news."

"Only the Cezanne and the Amber Rose. And we've hit a dead end on that so far. Anything else I can do for you while we're connected?" Mom asked.

"Nothing I can think of at the moment." I glanced at Bart who shook his head. "The only thing on my mind is my rumbling stomach. It's long past lunchtime, and I'm starving."

"Then by all means, go eat." Mom laughed. "That's the trouble with this business. We never get regular meals."

"Oh, I do have one more question. You're in Florence?"

"Yes," Mom said. "We're up a little alley close to Piazza San Croce."

"We're supposed to be there Sunday or Monday—I forget which. I hope we can meet. I'm sure every group tours the Church of the Cross since many of the historical luminaries are buried there. Maybe we can sneak away and meet you for a gelato in the Piazza San Croce."

"We'll work toward that end. Relax and enjoy your day at sea, you two. Things will only get more crazy the closer we get to collecting the rest of the jewels, breaking the code, and tracking down the treasure. Sky just arrived to start the deciphering process, so we're hopeful our resident expert won't take long to crack the code and end this insane business."

"Insane is right," Bart said. "It'll be a race to see who gets to the treasure first."

"We'd better cross the finish line first, or the world's in a lot of trouble," Mom said quietly. "Bye, kids. Be extremely watchful. Love you."

As ravenous as I felt, I just sat staring across the deck. Mom couldn't be more right. So much hung on our getting the topaz from the Freedom Fighters who'd put their lives on the line sixty years ago and who were doing so again. Rip Schyler, David Chen, and whomever else they brought in, had to immediately decipher the code Kesselring etched into the stones. Then we had to find the location. Nothing cranked up the tension like having a deadline that threatened destruction of the world's archeological and historical treasures.

"If you don't feed me soon, princess, I won't have the strength to raise a fork to my mouth."

"Then by all means, let's get you to the dining room." We rode the elevator down seven decks to the Marco Polo Restaurant, where we were seated at tables with white linen tablecloths and crystal glasses, a definite step up from the cafeteria.

After a leisurely lunch, we spent a lazy afternoon relaxing, our first opportunity to do so in a week's cruise. Three hours later, we woke from our nap, then had to race to prepare for the gala. Bart finished getting ready first, so he went ahead to save us seats for Marvin Goldstein's five thirty performance in the Vivaldi Lounge. I did my hair and donned my fanciest party dress for the gala. Men were so lucky, just jumping into a suit to get dressed for nearly anything.

Finally ready, I slipped out of our cabin and headed for the performance. As I rounded the corner, I ran smack into Ricardo.

Chapter 27

"Ricardo! Excuse me. I didn't mean to run you down."

"No, Mrs. Allan. It is my fault. I should have been more careful. Did you have a nice time ashore today?"

"We did, thank you. I'm on my way to meet my husband, and I'm late. I'll see you later."

I tried to hurry off, but Ricardo called after me. "Mrs. Allan?"

I turned and kept walking backward. "Yes?"

"Did you hear about Raphael?"

That stopped me. "I understand he had a head injury and was taken ashore in Santorini. Have you heard how he is?"

Ricardo stared down and shuffled one foot on the carpet. "He is dead. The hospital called the ship a little while ago. He slipped into a coma, and then they discovered he was bleeding internally. He did not wake up."

"I'm so sorry to hear that, Ricardo. I know you were good friends. I'm sure you'll miss him very much."

Ricardo glanced up, a strange look on his face. He didn't speak, just nodded his head, turned, and hurried along the corridor.

I stared after him. What lay behind his expression? Real sorrow? The knowledge he'd been involved in the death of his friend? Or had he? Had it been Gabriella all along who'd gotten Raphael out of the way? Or Dr. Chandra? When Raphael went to her to discover who had been treated for food poisoning, had she simply dispatched him right there? Or sent him to Gabriella to get taken care of? Maybe Ricardo hadn't had anything to do with it at all.

Still, I thought as I descended the three decks to the Vivaldi Piano Bar, he wore the mark of the spider, Cell Seven's deadly black widow tattoo. He couldn't be too innocent if he belonged to that fanatical terrorist group.

I slipped in beside Bart as Marvin asked for our favorite songs. I volunteered "Granada," "O Sole Mio," "Maleguena," and "Torna a Surriento," four of my favorites. When others added six more to the list, he perched the little scrap of paper on the piano and played a marvelous impromptu medley incorporating each of the songs into his delightful act, amazing us all.

Dinner was another epicurean adventure, and to complete the gala, they offered a buffet spectacular: ice carvings, fancy molded butter, marzipan, and more incredible, beautifully prepared food—not just a taste delight, but a feast for the eyes as well.

We skipped the festivities after dinner. I felt too weary to participate in anything but bedtime rituals. Even with our nap that afternoon, bed had not felt quite this good for a long time. Bart massaged my tired legs and feet, and after I reciprocated, we crashed.

* * *

What a wonderful feeling not to have to get out of bed until I absolutely couldn't lie there a minute longer! Bart brought breakfast, as promised, and we ate in our cabin, then headed on deck to find a quiet corner to discuss what we'd learned the day before from Else and Dom and from our conversation with Mom.

"Did you bring your journal?" Bart asked. "This is getting complicated, and we need to keep track of what we've learned."

I produced my journal, a little worse for the plunge in the bay the other night, but still usable. We spent the next couple of hours recording all we knew. Computers were so much faster, but they were a luxury we didn't have access to at the moment since the business center was packed as usual.

The rest of the day, we wandered the ship, enjoyed the sun on the pool deck, and watched an Argentine tango lesson in the Flamenco Lounge. Judy and George came up to find a quiet corner while she wrote in her journal as I caught up on mine. Charlotte occupied our balcony, reading Irving Stone's *The Agony and the Ecstasy*, the story of Michelangelo, and everyone in our group enjoyed our final day on ship simply relaxing.

I knew once we hit the streets again, there would be no relaxing. We'd be prime targets for Gabriella and her Cell Seven terrorists and anyone else who wanted to take a potshot at us. How would we prevent it, as we had to be in plain sight for the topaz passers to find us? Catch-22.

On our last night on the ship, even dinner exceeded the excellent meals we'd been served previously. I skipped the salad and ordered two appetizers that sounded so delicious. The first, a mango fruit cup with yogurt dressing, and the second, a layered feta concoction that tasted sensational. My crab soup, pink, cold, and delightful, contained avocado and some sweet fruit I couldn't identify. I chose sweet and sour pork for my main course—an excellent decision. When the dessert we'd ordered appeared, Bart and I glanced at each other and pushed it away. It looked exactly like the chocolate mousse Gabriella had delivered to our table. We excused ourselves and left the dining room.

"I don't know about you, but when I saw that chocolate mousse, I nearly lost my cookies," Bart said, holding his stomach. "Just thinking about it gave me stomach cramps all over again."

I stared at him in alarm. "Did someone doctor your meal?"

He shook his head. "No, but I have to tell you, when my eyes saw that, my stomach immediately contracted into knots and communicated to my mouth if one bite of it entered that orifice, my entire system would object strenuously by shutting down."

I laughed out loud at the visual image his words created. "Your message came through loud and clear."

We climbed several flights of stairs to the swim deck to walk off our dinner, but when the cool night breeze evolved into a cold wind, a return to our cabin became mandatory. We still had to organize luggage tonight and leave it outside in the corridor to be off-loaded first thing in the morning when we reached Venice. That required careful packing of the bags we carried with us in order to keep our toiletries and a change of clothing, plus our nightclothes.

As Bart placed our suitcases in the corridor, a feeling of unease washed over me. "What if they put a bomb in there tonight?" I said as he shut the door on everything we'd brought with us, leaving it vulnerable to all who passed by.

"We'll just have to make an opportunity to scan it with the bug detector the minute we retrieve it at the dock in Venice. We certainly don't need to take a bomb onboard the bus."

* * *

Morning came early. We hurried to finish breakfast and be ready to leave at eight o'clock, when the ship docked. I wanted to watch the sun rise on Venice, so we took our carry-ons and went up to the sun deck, where I shivered in the frigid morning breeze.

We watched, fascinated, as our huge ship followed a tiny pilot boat through the winding channel—very slowly so as not to create a wake. Beautiful, centuries-old buildings stood at sea level on all the little islands scattered in the Gulf of Venice, and waves of any size would encroach on the low-lying buildings.

As with the homes in Venice proper, many families had vacated the ground floors, now underwater, and lived in the upper stories of their homes and buildings. Many young people simply moved away to find work, since tourism remained one of only a few methods of earning a living left to them in Venice.

The drill of picking up our passports (a horrible mess with everyone trying to do it at once), carding off the ship, locating luggage in a huge warehouse with thousands of other passengers' luggage, and finally, connecting with our driver, Giorgio, and our bus, consumed what felt like hours. What a fiasco.

But, finally, we were on the road to Florence, the Cradle of the Renaissance. Excitement bubbled inside me. I'd been here as a child and remembered incredibly beautiful statues, fountains, and buildings. I couldn't wait to experience it again, this time with my husband. That would make it even more special.

Jim regaled us with his fascinating life story, making the hours on the bus fly, and in no time, we arrived in the fabled city. Giorgio drove as close as possible to the city center, where he left us on foot for the remainder of the day, following our guide Patricia through the ancient, historical streets.

Bart tried to appear interested as he listened to Patricia point out the Piazza San Marco, where Michelangelo had studied as a youth.

When he looked longingly at the dozens of scooters parked in front of the building that still housed the art school, I knew my action-craving husband would give anything at this point to escape on one of them.

Patricia led us a few blocks to Accademia Gallery, home to some of Michelangelo's most famous sculptures. While we waited for Jim and Carol to get tour tickets, Bart watched the streets, and I bought a book at the kiosk on the sidewalk just outside the door. They slipped my purchase into a beautiful, big, heavy plastic bag with a colorful picture of the Duoma on one side. Even shopping bags in Florence were works of art. I folded it, tucked it inside my purse, and opened the book. To prevent Bart's nervousness from rubbing off on me, I read to him what we'd shortly be viewing inside.

When we entered the Gallery, everyone made a mad dash to see *David,* Michelangelo's masterpiece. As Bart studied the enormous statue, I read to him from my book: "Commissioned by the Republic of Florence as the symbol of Florentine freedom and placed in front of the Palazzo Vecchio in 1504, where it stood for centuries exposed to the weather and elements."

"Don't I remember several other artists had already rejected the huge block of marble because it had a lot of veins running through it, which would make it particularly unstable to carve?" Bart asked.

"You did pay attention in art class, after all. Yes. And Michelangelo not only overcame all those problems, he used 85% of that original slab of marble in the finished statue. Amazing, isn't it?" I marveled.

"What amazes me is he studied the anatomy of cadavers to get everything just right. Each muscle and tendon, every vein you see in marble, he had to learn from dead bodies." Bart's face expressed his bemusement. "Have you ever wondered where they all came from?"

"To tell you the truth, I've never given it a single thought." We gazed in awe at the amazing statue, considered the most perfectly proportioned statue ever chiseled from a block of marble, Michelangelo's monument glorifying Renaissance man.

"Keep moving," Bart whispered. "And stay close to me." He guided me away from the central gallery, where *David* attracted the biggest crowds, to a smaller gallery with Michelangelo's famous "Prisoners" statues. At first glance, they looked like unfinished creations, but the genius with the chisel and unfailing eye had fashioned figures of men emerging from their rock prisons. St. Matthew's muscles bulged as he struggled to escape from the rock in which he'd been encased.

"Who or what are we avoiding?" I whispered as I read the description posted on the wall.

"See the guy with the black T-shirt and with the big camera around his neck?"

I slowly turned to stare down the long, narrow gallery. "The one blocking the exit we have to use to leave here?"

"Exactly. Anything seem strange about his camera?"

"Mmm. Give me a minute to check it out." I crossed to the other side of the aisle to examine Michelangelo's *Palestrina Pieta* but didn't give it the perusal it deserved. I walked back and forth, pretending to study each work, and each time I crossed the aisle, I looked at the man's camera, which had a long lens protruding from the front. Bart was right. Something about it appeared different. I finally got close enough to see it clearly when the man jostled it as he turned to leave. Two tubes were visible, running along the bottom of the lens from the camera.

"Okay, eagle eye. So you're being more vigilant and observant than I am. What do you think he plans to do with the pea shooter attached to the bottom of his camera?"

Bart took my arm and hurried me after the man. "Care to venture a guess what he has in mind?"

"No. I don't even want to think about it. You don't really think they'd just shoot us right here in front of *David,* do you?"

The man left the gallery with us close on his heels. "Do you think this is wise, to stalk our stalker?" I asked, not quite ready to step out into the street in plain view of those who might have a reason to end our existence.

"*We're* not going out. *I* am," Bart stated in a voice that warned me not to argue. "You're going to stay right here while I find out who he is and what he's up to."

With that, Bart slipped through the glass door and stood out of sight behind the kiosk where I'd bought my book on Florence. I opened the door slightly to watch the man's progress down the sidewalk, but when he stepped into the street, the kiosk hid him from view.

Suddenly Bart darted into the street. I couldn't see where he headed or why. My heart leapt into my throat. What was he doing? Fury flashed through me at being left behind, replaced quickly by terror that something would happen—could be happening—to my husband this very moment.

Chapter 28

Sorry, Charlie, I'm not going to let you get shot if I can help it. As I pushed the door open with one shoulder, I unzipped my purse, stuffed the book in it, flipped the catch on the journal with my index finger and grasped my gun, leaving it hidden inside my purse but ready for action. Slipping behind the kiosk, I peered out. Bart knelt between two cars, examining something on the ground.

He looked up as the man with the camera ran up the alley and disappeared. I hurried to his side. "What happened?"

"Allison. What are you doing here?" Bart stood and grabbed my arms. I thought for a minute he would shake me as I stared up into angry, blue eyes.

"I couldn't let you face whatever happened out here alone," I explained.

"You mean, you couldn't stand not knowing what was going on." He took a deep breath and relaxed the tiniest bit.

I smiled up at him. "That too. What happened?"

"Our friend with the camera saw this guy hiding behind this car," Bart motioned to the black Mercedes next to us, "and pointed his camera. Zap. This guy falls to the ground between the cars. The guy with the camera looks around, sees me watching, touches his finger to his cap, and disappears."

Only two people were in the vicinity, both hurrying to their destinations and intent on their conversation. Apparently they hadn't noticed a thing. I glanced at the body sprawled on his stomach at our feet.

"I don't suppose he has a black widow spider tattooed on his left earlobe," I said, not wanting to touch the man to turn him over and check. I truly didn't like dead bodies. In fact, I had a definite aversion to them.

Bart knelt, turned the man's head, and nodded. He stood, and we quickly walked along the sidewalk to wait for our group outside the Accademia Gallery. I pretended to browse the tourist memorabilia while Bart watched the street. No one had yet discovered the body lying almost hidden under the Mercedes. Apparently no one saw our participation in the silent but deadly tableau.

If the man with the camera had shot the man with the spider tattoo, did that mean Spiderman had been lying in wait for us and Cameraman was on our side? There evolved an endless spectrum of possibilities from that scenario.

Patricia emerged from the Gallery speaking in animated tones about the ceiling in the foyer, which appeared to be carved but was actually flat paint and how that popular technique revolutionized the decor in homes through the centuries. I was sorry I had missed it.

We followed her down Via de Servi, and just before we reached the famed Duomo, she pointed out the neighborhood where Collodi, the author of *Pinocchio,* lived when he wrote the children's classic. *David* may be the serious art symbol of Florence, but Pinocchio held the distinction of being the fun mascot. Every shop window had Pinocchio items for sale, from keychains to Christmas tree ornaments, plates, clothing, books, and even full-sized wooden statues.

When Patricia finally stopped at the corner of the Piazza di Duomo to recite the history of the white, green, and pink marble masterpiece rising into the heavens before us, I pulled Bart against the building. I could read for myself all I needed to know about the huge, famous cathedral.

"Tell me what you think just transpired back there?" I whispered, leaning close to him so no one else would hear.

"What do you think happened?" Bart asked.

"I don't trust my own judgment right now. Give me your eyewitness opinion of what occurred."

"You're asking if the guy with the camera did us a favor?"

I nodded.

"Absolutely."

"You think the other guy lay in wait for us?"

Bart nodded solemnly.

"That means the one with the camera is on our side."

"It would appear that way."

I glanced at my husband. His blue eyes were laughing at me. "You are maddening sometimes, you know it?"

"And you're not?" The twinkle faded from his eyes, and he became serious.

"No, don't even go there," I warned. "I know you told me to stay put, but I'm not going to hide behind a door while you're lying in the street bleeding to death. Forget it, Charlie. We're partners, and partners stay together. Partners protect each other's back. I can't do that if I'm cowering behind a door."

Bart held up both hands in mock surrender. "Okay. It doesn't do me any good to try to protect you, because you'll do what you want anyway. But, please, be careful. This just proves again Cell Seven is actively seeking to stop us."

"And that the underground knows it and may be actively trying to protect us against them. Hold that thought for a minute. We need to catch up with the group." We hurried to join our tour at the white and green marble octagonal baptistery where Patricia told about the famous sculpted doors. We listened as she pointed out the south door with scenes from the life of St. John the Baptist created in A.D. 1330 by Pisano.

The north door's bronze scenes from the New Testament by Ghiberti from 1424 were incredible, but the east door had to be one of the great masterpieces of early Renaissance art—the *Door of Paradise* sculpted in bronze with Old Testament stories by Ghiberti. Like everyone else, we tried to identify which panels told which Bible stories.

When Patricia plunged into her recitation of the history of the Duomo, or Cathedral of Santa Maria del Fiore, Bart decided he'd been patient long enough.

"Isn't this the church we saw on the History Channel special about the Medicis? Cosimo de Medici ordered the cathedral built, including a dome, before the technology to span it with a dome was available. So they built the cathedral and left the hole in the top for years until Brunelleschi figured out how to design and build the dome?"

"Good memory. This is the place. I take it you're finished touring and ready to go catch some bad guys."

Bart nodded emphatically. "Right on, Watson."

"Okay, Sherlock, find out where and what time everyone is assembling to get back on the bus. Then we can take off and find the folks. That should give you enough action to keep you happy for a while. Didn't Mom say the Florence topaz would be taken care of now that they were here?"

Bart nodded. "We shouldn't have to worry about staying with the group today and being a sitting target."

We caught up with Jim and Carol, reported we were meeting my folks, who were in Florence, and would spend the rest of the afternoon with them. Where could we connect with the tour tonight?

I opened my book to the map of Florence, and Jim traced the approximate route on which Patricia would take the tour, then told us to meet them at the Loggia della Signoria on the River Arno near Ponte Vecchio at seven o'clock. If we weren't there, we'd have to find our own way to our hotel because Giorgio couldn't wait with the bus where he'd be parked. I scribbled the name and address of our hotel in Pisa, just in case we didn't make the appointed time and place.

"Now, lead me to your folks," Bart said, taking off with long strides across the piazza and pulling me behind him.

"Stop," I cried, jerking on Bart's jacket. "I have to check the map. Actually, I have to call Mom first and find out just which alley off Piazza San Croce they're in." I located the Duomo on the map in the center of town, and found the Piazza Signoria. From there it was simply a left turn and along the street to Piazza San Croce.

"Okay, I know where we are and how to find the piazza, but give me one more minute to call Mom."

"I hope Jack's there. I need to talk to him," Bart said, pacing while I dug the compact out of my purse and called Mom's cell phone. While it rang, we walked toward the piazza. But her phone rang and rang with no answer, and finally her voicemail came on. I tried the same tactic as the day before—left a message and immediately called back. Still no answer. I left another message and tried again.

"Where is she?" I asked. "Why isn't she answering her phone?"

"Call your dad." Bart's crisp command erased all doubt as to his current mood.

The voice on the other end of Dad's phone was not my father. "David! Why are you on Dad's phone? Why aren't you in London? Where's Mom? She's not answering her phone."

"Hello to you too, Allison." David's calm, soothing voice quieted my initial panic at not reaching my parents.

"Hi. Sorry. I panicked when I couldn't get hold of Mom. We're in Florence and wanted to meet them. What's going on?"

"Your arrival is very timely. Where are you now?" I detected a slight bit of tension in David's quiet voice. Not a good thing. David Chen was as self-possessed as Else, another cool, calm, usually unflappable agent who'd been with Anastasia since before I took my training.

"We're approaching Piazza della Signoria."

"Meet me at the Neptune Fountain. I'll be there in five minutes." I thought he'd hang up without saying good-bye, but he only paused before adding, "And make sure you're not followed."

"Yes, David. Will you be wearing a red rose or a white carnation?"

He laughed. "You can identify me by the black umbrella I'll be carrying." That time he did hang up.

"What's the red rose or white carnation bit?" Bart asked, gazing skyward and holding out his hand.

I held mine out and felt sprinkles coming from a big, dark cloud that threatened to open up and pour on us at any minute. I glanced around and pulled Bart into a little tourist shop filled with postcards, plates, ashtrays, flags, Pinocchio souvenirs, and replicas of *David* along one wall and a case of pastries and gelato along the other. A rack of umbrellas stood next to the door, and Bart plucked out a couple without even checking the color or design.

While he paid for them at one counter, I chose a dozen Italian pastries and two bottles of water and paid for my purchases at the other counter. We hurried outside just as huge raindrops splattered the streets. I placed the sack of pastries in my beautiful shopping bag with the picture of the Duomo and dropped my purse inside too, to keep it dry. A fortuitous purchase.

"You didn't answer my question," Bart reminded me as we dodged puddles already forming on the stones under our feet.

"David is unduly serious, as you well know, and rarely jokes or makes light of anything. So we have a little game between us. I try to make him smile, and if I actually make him laugh, he buys dinner."

"Interesting," Bart commented.

As we entered the piazza, the one I remembered from my childhood, Bart pulled me out of the stream of people we'd been following, and we ducked under a green awning overhanging the street.

"Now's the time to make sure we're not followed," he said quietly. "Where's the Neptune Fountain?"

I pointed across the square at the entrance to a narrow street. "Between Palazzo Vecchio and that lower building to the left. Neptune is the huge, white marble figure in the center surrounded by tritons and sea horses and nereids."

Bart stared blankly at me. "Nereids?"

"Sea nymphs, fifty beautiful daughters of Nereus and Doris who reside in the Mediterranean Sea and help sailors in distress. They usually ride dolphins." I checked my book to name the others. "In front of the Palazzo Vecchio is the copy of Michelangelo's *David,* and on the other side of the entry to the palace is Bandinelli's *Hercules and Cacus.* I remember these statues from my trip with Mom when I was just a little girl. I couldn't believe this wonderful open-air art gallery where you don't have to go inside a museum to enjoy the art."

"Also where the pigeons can enjoy them," Bart said, appearing unimpressed with my knowledge of the art and artifacts of the famous city, so I closed my book and dropped it in my bag with the pastries and my purse. Back to the art of war.

No one appeared interested in anything but getting out of the rain, and finally Bart seemed satisfied we were not being watched or followed. Across the square, where the horse-drawn carriages sat abandoned in the rain, I watched David emerge from the narrow street behind the Neptune Fountain.

"There's David."

Bart nodded. "Let's go."

We dashed into the rain and splashed across the square toward David, who examined what appeared to be a map under his umbrella. As he glanced around the square, he saw us, put his finger on the paper, turned slowly around, and then did a perfect interpretation of someone who's just discovered where he was and how to get where he needed to go.

He headed back in the same direction from which he'd just come, and we lagged far enough behind that we didn't appear to be following him. When he turned a corner a few blocks down the street, Bart stopped at the entrance to the street.

"Watch where he goes while I see if we're being followed." I faced the direction David had taken. Bart turned around and looked behind us. We hurried after David only after Bart was satisfied we were alone.

David took us on a circuitous route through one alley after another, and I was getting wetter by the minute while these two grown men appeared to be having a great time playing spy games.

"I have a super sense of direction, and I can tell you we've been going in circles. There better be something pretty important going on to keep up this little game of cat and mouse."

Bart didn't answer. Not that I expected an answer. If there was a good reason, Bart wanted that information as much as I did. I just appreciated creature comforts more than my husband, and at the moment, I felt as uncomfortable as I wanted to get.

At last, David stepped into an alcove with topiary trees and a blue awning that appeared to be the entrance to an expensive eatery. He shook out his umbrella, and we followed suit. Without a word, he entered the posh foyer to the fancy restaurant. How did he know I'd been starving? I'd be delighted with real food and could save the Italian pastries for later.

But dinner had not been our objective. David made an abrupt left turn at what looked like elaborately carved paneling just before we reached the inner door and the dining room. He stopped at a small still-life painting, moved it aside, and punched in a combination of numbers on an electronic pad. The panel slid open, and David moved quickly inside.

We followed him silently along a narrow hall with deep-pile red carpet and paintings of every size and subject hanging on dark, wood-paneled walls. At the end of the gallery, a portrait of a majestic man on horseback with a flowing red cape covered the entire wall.

As David pressed the gold nameplate on the ornate mahogany frame, the painting swung backward out of the frame. He stepped through the opening, and we followed. He then repeated the ritual he'd performed at the first door, punching in a combination of numbers on an electronic pallet before he led us into another hall and up two flights of stairs to the third floor.

"Is this elaborate setup to keep the bad guys out or the good guys in?" I asked.

David turned and actually smiled. "It will be good to have you here, Allison. We need someone to lighten the heavy mood that's descended on Anastasia."

My heart quickened, and my throat constricted. I immediately remembered Mom's endlessly ringing phone and David's answering Dad's. I opened my mouth to speak, but nothing came out.

Bart voiced the question for me. "And what brought on the heavy mood?"

"You will see in one minute." David stopped at a nondescript door, keyed it, and stood back to let us enter first.

I stopped in the doorway and stared.

Chapter 29

Mom lay white and still on a canopied bed in one corner of the huge, elegant room, a bandage around her head and on one arm, and an IV in the other. I ran to her side, fear gripping my heart and soul. She appeared to be sleeping. I hoped she was sleeping. I whirled back to David.

"What happened?" My voice came out in a whisper.

"She met with members of the underground last night, and someone tossed a bomb into the room." He raised his hand at my reaction. "Just a little bomb, but damaging enough to put nearly every one of them out of commission, probably for the duration of this treasure hunt. Before we dug them out, she'd bled a lot from her numerous shrapnel wounds, so she's re-hydrating with the IV. They also gave her a sedative. She felt she should be chasing down whoever did this to her mother's friends."

"What happened to her mother's friends?" Bart asked, sinking into one of the office chairs at the bank of computers lining one wall. They seemed totally out of place in this Renaissance room with cardinal red draperies hanging from fifteen-foot windows, crystal chandeliers, and ornate furniture which could be six centuries old.

"They sustained injuries on a par with Margaret's," David said, closing the door behind him. "Except they're mostly in their eighties, so some of them may not survive the trauma."

"Where did this happen?" I asked. "Certainly not here."

"No. Jack and Margaret traveled outside Florence to a little village where some former Freedom Fighters live. They'd called the meeting to give your folks information that might reveal the location of the treasure."

"Dad was there too?" Could I take more bad news? The question emerged in a frightened whisper. "How is he?"

"He's fine," David assured me quickly. "He'd returned to the car for his laptop. The hoodlums came in from behind the village. They took out the old man sitting guard at the kitchen door and tossed a small homemade bomb in through the back door."

"Who is 'they'?" Bart asked.

"A bunch of punk skinheads with Nazi armbands. Jack hit a couple of them. Unfortunately, they can't tell us anything now, so we don't know if they're connected to Cell Seven or if they were working on their own."

"Did anyone see how many there were?" Bart asked. "Any idea of the strength or numbers of their group?"

"To tell the truth, this is a tiny little village. There shouldn't have been anything of this kind going down." David's calm demeanor cracked, and he pounded his fist in his hand. "This should never have happened. The village should have been a safe place to meet. Just a coffee klatch between a bunch of old women." He turned and stared out the rain-streaked window.

"Is it safe to stand in the window?" Bart asked.

"They're mirrored. We can see out, but no one can see in," David answered without turning around.

"What happens now?" I asked. "We can't just sit here grieving. We've got jewels to gather, a code to decipher, and a treasure to find. What's the plan? Where's Dad? Where is everyone?" I looked at all the computers with their dizzying, multicolored screensavers swirling in endless patterns. "Do you have people for all these computers?"

David nodded. "We do. Jack just took everyone to dinner. They've been working nonstop since we brought Margaret back here last night—without even a coffee break."

"Where are they?" I identified with the foodless routine of spy work and hour after hour of not eating. How long had it been since I'd consumed anything?

"Downstairs, in a private dining room off the main restaurant. Want to join them?"

"Absolutely," I said, "unless you'd bring me something up here, in which case I'll stay with Mom."

"I'll take you downstairs, then I'll stay with her while you eat." David headed for the door.

I turned back to check on Mom. Thoughts of how close she came to not being here terrified me. Few were ever prepared to lose their mother, but I couldn't imagine having this baby without her help and advice. Mothers should be there for their only child's firstborn.

I hesitated, and Bart must have read my mind. He stood and pulled me into his arms. "It's okay to leave her, princess. She'll be here when we get back, and you need some nourishment. You're feeding two, remember, and breakfast was hours ago. She'd be the first to send you to the dining room, wouldn't she?"

I clung to Bart and nodded against his shirt. She would. I sighed and let go. "I'm okay. It shocked me to see her like this, and then it hit me how blessed I am to have her still alive." I looked up into Bart's understanding blue eyes. "I'm blessed to have you too."

David moved quietly to the door and held it open. The movement in the room brought us out of the moment, and I blushed and turned to the door.

"Sorry, David. Traumatic moment there."

As I moved past him, he reached out and touched my cheek. "I understand, Allison. We were all deeply affected by your mother's injuries, and knowing how close the two of you are, I can only imagine how you feel."

"Thank you. Since Anastasia is such a close-knit family, I know this had to have been hard on everyone, especially with the stress and pressure increasing hourly. And Dad will only be tied in knots, which leaves everyone else the same way. I'm sure it was a frightfully long, hard night last night."

David almost smiled. "You have a talent for the understatement, Allison." He guided us along the same corridor we'd just traversed to the fancy foyer where he turned left into the dining area.

A waiter in a yellow dress shirt, hunter green vest, and black tie met us at the door. When he recognized David, he escorted us behind a lattice partition covered with ivy and silk gardenias, through a short hallway that led toward the kitchens. We stopped at a door halfway down the hall.

David ushered us in, then turned to the waiter. "Antonio, they'll want to order as soon as it's convenient for you."

"Yes, sir. I'll be right back with the menus."

Dad jumped to his feet the minute he saw us and crushed me in his arms. His greeting, always enthusiastic, bordered on intense today.

"Too close for comfort, huh, Dad," I murmured.

He took a deep breath. "Much too close, bunny. Much too close."

Dr. Rip Schylar, Anastasia's grandfather figure and senior member in age, stood and embraced me as soon as Dad let go. "Allison, you're absolutely radiant. Congratulations, you two." Sky's résumé included a doctorate in criminology, one in abnormal behavior, and other degrees in various subjects ranging from psychology to cryptography. Our resident scholar.

Sky greeted Bart while I turned to see who else had gathered to solve the riddle of the topaz code and stop Cell Seven. Lionel came around the end of the table and whirled me off my feet. "Cherie, you look wonderful. It is good to see you."

"How come everyone is so glad to see my wife, but no one has said it's good to see me," Bart said, greeting Lion with a mock cuff to the head.

"Because she is prettier than you are, and she spoils us with treats. Do you ever get us treats?" Lion asked. Lionel Brandt, our fun, flirtatious Frenchman, had an untamable mane of golden curly hair, a double reason for his nickname of Lion.

Dominic rose, kissed my cheek, and pulled out the empty chair between Else and Dad. I sank gratefully onto the plush velvet seat and glanced around the table as everyone took their seats and resumed eating.

"Bunny, there are some people here you may not know. Next to Dominic is Rachel, on loan from Interpol, an expert in ciphers. She's working with David and Sky to decipher the code etched on the topaz."

Rachel smiled and nodded. She reminded me of an elf—petite, up-turned nose and short, dark hair. Gamine seemed a perfect descriptive term for her, pert and lively with sparkling dark eyes.

"Next to her is Steven," Dad continued, "also from Interpol, with degrees in history and art. We hope this walking encyclopedia will have at the tip of his tongue all the information we need, when we need it."

Steven glanced up from his plate, saluted with two fingers, and promptly turned his attention back to his dinner. He had collar-length, ash blond, curly hair, which looked permed, not natural, but the pin-striped suit, purple shirt, and tie told more about him than would probably have been revealed in an hour's conversation with him.

Steven was obviously a young man on his way to the top. Everyone else in the room dressed in working-casual, except Else, the epitome of good taste and fashion, who always looked like she had just stepped from the pages of a glamour magazine.

"And last, but not least in our list of new additions is Henry, who would easily win Geek of the Decade if they gave such an award. He can get into any computer, slip through any firewall, crack any password code, and strip you of all your secrets in seconds."

Henry peered over his glasses and grinned. "Minutes, actually, not seconds, but I'm good."

"I'm delighted to meet you all. Welcome to the team," I said, looking at each of them and nodding. I turned to Dad. "It appears we're all here but Oz and Mai Li."

"They're on their way," Dad assured me as the waiter returned with our menus.

Else leaned over and whispered, "The lamb is delicious, but I think you'd enjoy the chicken Marsala more."

I glanced at the menu, the chicken sounded great, so I ordered it and handed the menu back. "Okay, where are we? Did you learn anything last night from the underground?" I looked at Dad.

He shook his head. "We were just getting to that part. I'd gone to the car for the laptop to take notes and call up the maps we'd loaded to pinpoint the locations they were talking about, when disaster struck." He stopped. I imagined he relived the explosion all over again.

"Were you with them the whole time up to that point?" I asked.

Dad nodded. "We were all together until I went for the computer. Why?"

"I wondered if they would have told Mom something you didn't hear just before the bomb went off. You know, someone conjecturing or thinking out loud, or simply not waiting for you to get back and beginning to tell what you wanted to know."

"I guess that's possible," Dad said, a thoughtful expression on his face. "I didn't ask her. To tell you the truth, by the time we'd dug them out of the rubble, the furthest thing from my mind was the information we'd gone there to get."

I leaned over and kissed his cheek and squeezed his hand. "Normal reaction, Dad. Each one of us would have felt the same way." I glanced at Bart, knowing how he would have reacted had it been me in that house and felt a wrenching as I thought about trying to dig him out of the rubble.

I scanned the faces around the table. The look that flitted across Steven's face surprised me. Instead of the compassion evident in everyone else's eyes, Steven's expression seemed haughty and filled with disdain. He quickly concentrated on buttering his roll. Ambitious. Cold. Unsympathetic. All revealed in a fraction of a second. Steven and I would not share much common ground, it seemed.

"Any breakthrough on the code yet?" I directed my question to Sky, whose gaze riveted on Steven, and from his slight frown, I assumed he'd seen the expression that flashed across Steven's face. Good. The psychologist in Sky would have figured out this arrogant young man immediately, important if we were going to work closely together.

Sky turned his attention to me and smiled when he saw I'd been watching him. "You'll be happy to know this isn't as tough as the German machine cipher used during the war, but it isn't a piece of cake either. However, Rachel is as clever with codes as you are with languages, so we'll have it broken before the day is out."

Dad glanced up from his lunch. "Is that a promise?"

Rachel flushed a little at the praise, but replied with a confident tone I liked. "Yes, sir, I think we can deliver on that. Our little operation here won't compare to the famous Operation Enigma, when they broke that 'unbreakable' code, but we're not too shabby at our work, either."

"Excellent," Dad said. His voice conveyed immense relief.

Our lunch appeared far sooner than I'd expected, which delighted me. I dug in with gusto and had just savored my first bite of tender, tasty chicken when Dad dropped a bombshell.

Chapter 30

"I want you and Bart to go out to that village this afternoon and talk to as many of those women as are in a condition to speak." He pointed at me. "I think you can glean more information from them than anyone else besides your mother or your grandmother."

That rendered me temporarily speechless.

"We have a driver to take you there and bring you back in time to join your tour before they leave for Pisa," he continued. "He's with the local office, so he knows the back alleys and shortcuts."

Recovering from this surprise, I found my voice. "Good, since Giorgio won't be able to wait for us if we're late. Of course, if we're left behind, your driver will have to deliver us to Pisa so we can collect the stone from there." Then I had a thought. "You did get the topaz from Florence?"

"We have that one," Sky said. "When we set up shop here, they brought it in."

I gazed around the table. "Is it common knowledge you're here?"

Dad looked a little uncomfortable. "Yes, unfortunately, most of the old Freedom Fighters are familiar with this place since it belongs to one of them, and whenever the underground gets together, which is far more frequent than I would have thought, they meet here."

"Does that bother you, Mrs. Allan?" Steven asked, the slightest edge audible in his voice.

"Only because I've spent a fair amount of time with older people, and I know how easy it is for them to talk about everything in the same breath—rumor, hearsay, and secrets. It's crossed their lips before they're aware of it. If anyone wanted to know, and knew the right questions to ask, I can imagine it might be quite easy to acquire the information they needed in less than an hour's conversation."

He started to say something else, and from the expression on his face, I knew I wasn't going to like it. In fact, I decided I didn't like him. I didn't like his know-it-all, condescending attitude, and it was apparent he resented my place in the group.

From his slight accent, I'd determined his native tongue to be French, so before he spoke, I said quickly and quietly in French, "You don't have to like me, but we do have to work together. Truce?"

His eyebrows shot up in surprise. He glanced around the table, and when no one seemed to understand what I'd said, he nodded, a smirk crossing his face. "Truce," he answered in French.

My impression of Steven might have been wrong, but I'd have bet he was so self-absorbed he hadn't taken the opportunity to find out that Sky, Else, Lionel, David, and Dom all spoke French fluently. Even Bart spoke the language, having learned it during his six-month ordeal in prison with Emile. I didn't know about Rachel and Henry, but most people working in Europe, especially for Interpol, spoke a smattering of French and German, plus Italian or Spanish, besides their own language.

I focused my attention on Dad. "When do we leave?"

Dad looked at Bart. "Any problem in going right away?"

Bart would throw his napkin on his plate and run for the door given the word. He just laughed. "Only that if I take my wife from her lunch before she's finished, she'll never forgive me."

"You're so right, Charlie Brown," I said, waving my fork at him. "I probably wouldn't even have had breakfast regularly if we hadn't been on that cruise ship for a week. My meals are too few and far between, so relax and finish your lunch while I enjoy mine. I'm sure it will be the last food I see the rest of the day, unless some of those dear old ladies take pity and feed me."

Everyone relaxed as we bantered and finished the meal, and the slight tension produced by my interchange with Steven dissolved. We headed back up to the third floor.

Mom still slept soundly. "You're sure she's going to be okay?" I asked Dad as he bent to kiss her bruised cheek.

He brushed a lock of black hair, slightly tinged with gray, from her forehead. "I think so, bunny. I hope so."

"There's still time to become a forever family, Dad," I whispered. "Then you don't have to experience this agony every time something happens to one of you."

He straightened and put his hands on my shoulders, a tender look on his face. "Don't give up on us, sweetheart. Who knows what might happen when this is all over?"

I hugged him, then turned and joined Bart, deep in a discussion with Sky and David about the code. Rachel added to their conversation from her computer as they explained to Bart just where they were in the process.

Henry's total focus centered on his computer screen, and I'd bet he wasn't hearing anything going on in the room. Steven, however, listened intently, not even pretending to be doing anything else, although his eyes never left Else. No surprise there. He wasn't in her league, however, by a long shot.

Then I had a thought. "Steven, I've been curious about the Amber Rose that just surfaced for sale at Christie's. Do you suppose it was part of the Amber Room treasures? And have any of the other items from there come to light recently? Has anyone ever found the panels that lined the room? I'm out of the loop there, so I don't know what's happened in that area. I've always been intrigued by the story. I'm sure you know everything there is to know about it."

Before he could answer, Bart turned from the group and took my hand. "Ready when you are, princess."

"David can take you to your driver," Dad said as he settled behind the large mahogany desk in the center of the room. "I'm sure you'll think of all the right questions to ask to get whatever information they might have. But be careful." His expression grew serious. "I don't need anything happening to either of you."

I turned to Steven as Bart steered me toward the door. "I hope we have time to talk later. I'm anxious to learn what you know about the Amber Room."

Rain puddled in the streets, but the downpour had stopped. David flagged a little, dark green foreign car parked down the narrow street, mostly on the sidewalk, forcing pedestrians to go around it. The lights flashed on immediately, and a couple of scooters had to dodge it as it pulled on to the street.

David opened the back door, and I slid in with Bart right behind me. David introduced Enzio, a middle-aged man with steel gray hair and piercing black eyes, then slammed the door, and Enzio slipped the car seamlessly into the stream of pedestrians, scooters, and cars that flowed along the narrow, wet street.

"So, you're the granddaughter of Mama Karillides," he said over his shoulder, never taking his eyes from the road.

"I am. Do you know her?"

"Everyone in the underground knew Alessia Karillides, although when the war started, she was just a young girl, not yet married."

"Alessia!" I exclaimed. "I didn't know that was her name." I turned to Bart, delighted at this new discovery. "Alessia is derived from Alexandra. We're naming our daughter after my grandmother!"

Bart laughed and kissed my nose. "Your eyes sparkle when you're excited."

I turned back to Enzio. "Tell me what you know about her. I didn't even know she was my grandmother until a couple of years ago, after Bart and I were married. Because of the topaz, they kept it a secret from me. Everyone thought Mom and I just came to visit them for Mom's work."

Enzio nodded. "Even my mother didn't know Alessia had a daughter, much less a granddaughter."

"Were they together in the underground during the war?" I asked, hoping to learn about the delightful lady I'd known only as Mama Karillides.

"Yes," Enzio said, edging his way through the busy streets. "They grew up together in a little town, and when the war started, they delivered messages between villages. Two teenage girls weren't suspect when they rode bicycles with baskets full of produce or bread from village to village."

Bart put his arm around my shoulder, and I nestled against him, happy to discover more about my amazing grandmother. I hoped Mom had convinced my grandparents to stay in California so I could learn firsthand how they'd met and could hear the adventures they'd experienced fighting invaders to their country.

Enzio pulled into a major street I recognized as the one on which we'd driven into town a few hours earlier and continued his narrative.

"As the real war, the shooting war, came closer, their parents made them stay off the streets, but that didn't stop them from getting into trouble, or making trouble for the enemy. They helped hide Allied soldiers, they slipped through the woods to pour salt into the water of the German camps, to feed castor oil to the pigs and beef that were to be slaughtered to feed them. Every kind of mischief that could be devised to torment the enemy, these two girls helped carry out."

"Sounds like you came by it naturally, princess," Bart whispered. "It must be in the genes."

We were speeding on the four-lane highway now, and before Enzio had told me half as much as I wanted to know about my grandmother, we exited into an area of rolling, tree-covered hillsides. Walled castles and steepled churches topped the highest hills like a cluster of candles on a birthday cake.

"Where's your mother now?" I asked as we wound around one of those high green hills and drove deep into the beautiful countryside.

"We're going to see her."

I caught my breath. "Was she there last night?"

He nodded silently.

"Oh, Enzio, was she hurt?"

Again, he nodded.

When he didn't elaborate, I had to ask. "How badly?"

"She's not good. We'll see how she feels today. She is a strong woman, but at eighty years of age . . ." He let the sentence fall away and remained quiet.

I pictured Mom, white as death, lying so still and quiet on the pillow. The thought of my normally animated, vivacious mother being struck down by a skin-headed kid, some punk tossing a bomb into a kitchen where a bunch of little old ladies were drinking coffee, made me furious. This group of thoughtlessly cruel, totally misguided idiots had to be stopped immediately. There was absolutely no excuse for attacking a bunch of defenseless old women.

We entered a small village, not more than a dozen houses, all creamy white stucco, some with red brick repairs showing. The gardens were still green and beautiful, the orchards lush and heavy with fruit. At the end of the village, just beyond a tiny church with a tall steeple, Enzio stopped the car and turned off the key.

At first glance, it appeared to be like all the houses in the village. Until you looked closer. The whole back section of one wall was gone. Enzio pointed at that area of the house. "That used to be her kitchen."

"This is your mother's house?" I asked, aghast.

He nodded, opened the door, and stepped out, ignoring the light rain that fell. Bart opened his door and stood in the mud, flexing his cramped knees, which had been scrunched too close to the front seat, then held out his hand to help me. I wasn't sure I wanted to do this anymore. Reality can at times be too difficult to face. This might well have been one of those times.

Enzio led us silently under the bougainvillea-covered arch to the front door.

"Do you want us to wait here while you go in?" I asked, not sure what local protocol decreed when visiting an injured person whose house had just been bombed and whose kitchen had been blown out of existence.

"No, there is no need for that. If she is able, she will have a refreshment waiting for you. If she is not, I will do it." He waved his hand at me as I started to refuse their proffered hospitality. "No, you will only offend my mother if she isn't able to offer you something." At that, I deferred and followed him into the house, which still reeked of explosives.

Enzio's mother, her sun-browned face alight to see her son, reclined in an overstuffed chair that had seen better days. One bandaged foot and leg was propped up on a brown plastic ottoman, and she had bandages on her face and arms. She started to get up, but Enzio hurried to stop her, and I rushed to her other side.

"Please, don't get up," I said, kneeling by her chair. "We've only come to talk for a few minutes."

She stared at me and reached out with a bandaged hand to touch my face. "Mama mia, it is Alessia, reincarnated from sixty years ago," she exclaimed in Italian.

I answered in Italian. "I'm her granddaughter. You met my mother last night. Margaret and Jack Alexander are my parents. I'm Allison Allan, and this is my husband, Bart."

My gallant husband took the unbandaged hand of this tiny little lady and raised it to his lips. Her eyes grew wide and sparkled as a smile broke across her lined face.

"Oh, he is a good one. You will keep him and take care that no one steals him away? Yes?"

I laughed and translated for Bart, just in case he hadn't caught all of it. "Yes," I assured her in Italian. "I will definitely keep him."

A frown crossed her face. "I couldn't go to the market today, so I have nothing to offer you except coffee." She turned to her son. "Will you prepare the coffee, please?" She stopped and sounded dismayed. "If you can find the coffee pot."

"Oh, thank you so much, but we don't drink coffee," I hurried to assure her. "We barely finished lunch, and we don't need anything."

"You may not need it," Enzio said quietly in English, "but it will be an insult to you if she cannot serve you something. I will see what I can find."

I remembered the Italian pastries we'd purchased when we bought our umbrellas and held out my bag to Bart. "Why don't you go in the kitchen, or what's left of it, and help Enzio with some refreshment. Those should make everybody happy."

The men left, and as I turned to ask Maria about last night, a knock came at the door. I stood quickly and went to answer it so Maria wouldn't try. Three little old ladies, bruised and bandaged, stood on the doorstep.

"Come, come," Maria said, waving her good arm at them.

They filed in, nodding at me, seeming ill at ease until I introduced myself in their native tongue. When Maria told them I was the granddaughter of Mama Karillides, that broke the ice completely. As they settled themselves into the love seat and sofa, I asked the first question.

"Maria, why does everyone call my grandmother 'Mama Karillides'? Why don't they call her by her given name, Alessia?"

Maria laughed. "Because when we were hiding the wounded and taking care of them until they could be smuggled across the lines to the hospital, the soldiers called her their 'little Greek mother.' She fussed over them and tended them and bossed them around like their mamas, so she became Mama Karillides to them. It became the password to get in or out of our area."

I wanted to learn whatever they had to tell as quickly as possible, so I immediately plunged into the interrogation. "Tell me what happened last night. What do you remember? Did you see the people who threw the bomb?"

They all chattered at once. I held up my hands. "Maria, this is your home. You begin."

Maria closed her eyes, then in a dramatic gesture, opened them wide and flung out her arm. "They threw the door open like this, took one look in the kitchen, and tossed the bomb on the floor. If they had done it right, they would have killed us all. Instead, they only got poor Luisa."

"They killed Luisa?" I asked.

Everyone nodded.

"What did they do wrong? You all look pretty damaged to me." I wasn't quite sure how to phrase that. I didn't want to take away from the wounds they'd sustained, which were considerable for women of their advanced age, but neither did I want to give any success to the bombers if these little ladies weren't going to acknowledge their success.

Maria explained. "If they had thrown it at us, it would probably have landed on the table, and we would all have been killed. They tossed it on the floor away from us, and it rolled into the corner. We may be old, but we're not stupid. When we saw their shaved heads and Nazi armbands, we hit the floor."

The thought of these octogenarians diving for the floor astounded me. I wanted to laugh at the image their description conjured up. "You all hit the floor? You saw them, knew what was happening, and fell to the floor?"

Estella, one of the more stout of the group rubbed her bandaged elbow. "I think my bruises were worse than the shrapnel wounds. I just tipped my chair over and stayed in it. The chair took most of the damage—except for my whole left side, which is black and blue from hitting Maria's tile floor."

They all nodded. Apparently their stories were similar and their actions had been the same.

"But how did you react so fast? How did you know what to do?" I asked, amazed that after all these years, they'd still have the same reflex action.

Tiny Tia answered, the smallest of the group, probably a scant four feet tall and maybe all of ninety pounds. "When you spent so many years fearing the sound of planes overhead or bombs dropping around you or gunfire shattering your windows, you drop to the floor and find something to cover you. Your country was only in the war four years. We were at war for twice that."

I nodded. She was right. And the only drop and rolls I'd ever had to endure had been training to become an agent with Interpol and during some of our more dangerous escapades since that time.

"You called my parents here yesterday to tell them something." I looked from face to face, searching their faded but alert eyes. "What was it?"

Chapter 31

Maria spoke first, apparently the spokesperson for them. "We'd heard the stories of Kesselring's *acquisitions,*" she spit out the word, "and how he'd hidden our churches' treasures and had stripped the fine museums and beautiful homes of all valuables and had taken them for himself. Then to pacify his greedy generals, he tore apart Empress Elizabeth's topaz necklace and marked a clue on each stone so only by putting them all together would the treasure be located."

I nodded. His greed and theft were common knowledge—far more real to these little ladies who'd lived under his brutal heel than his brilliant execution of war battles.

Maria continued, "He hid it somewhere close to Florence. That much of the story we know to be true. Some say he used an old salt mine and had soldiers dig it out and enlarge it to hold everything he'd stolen."

This also gelled with the story we'd been told. I saw Bart leaning against the doorframe, just out of sight of Maria, listening. How much he understood of the Italian they spoke, I didn't know. Some, for sure.

"After the war, we were busy rebuilding our lives, raising our children, trying to make a living. We just wanted to forget the horrors we'd seen and experienced. Then we began talking, and someone mentioned they had a topaz they'd acquired from a wounded German officer as he lay dying. Then another came forth, and another. We discovered in the former underground organization alone, we had about a dozen of these stones. So we brought them together and tried to decipher the code. We failed."

Disappointment filled Maria's face, and she absently rubbed at her bandaged arm.

Tia spoke up. "It wasn't until a few years ago we tried again. So many were dying and taking the secrets with them. We knew we had to discover the treasure before we were all gone, or it might never be found."

Carmen, bright orange hair and lipstick proclaiming her attempt to push back the years, offered her portion of the story. "My husband had been an engineer and knew many of the old mines in the area, so he and our sons scoured the countryside using survey maps he'd found. They explored each salt mine and cave they could locate, but they found nothing."

"Maybe it's in another direction from Florence, instead of here," I suggested.

Estella shook her head. "No, we're sure it's somewhere within twenty miles of where we're sitting right now. It's here. We know it's here."

"Why? What makes you so sure if you haven't found anything?" I asked, puzzled about her absolute insistence that the treasure lay close by.

"Because Kesselring came out here more often than he ever went anywhere else when he was in Florence," Estella said. "And he spent a lot of time in Florence. He loved the city. He loved art, and Florence is the center of art and has been for centuries. It was the birthplace of the Renaissance."

"Okay, so he came here often. What did he come for?" I asked, hoping they had logical reasons they were so certain about, not just emotional and circumstantial ones.

Tia answered. "To bring more paintings, more statues, more jewels. When he came, he stopped at the bakery in the next village. He loved their bread and pastries, and he always stopped to buy whatever they had. When they ran out of flour, which was quite difficult to obtain, he delivered it so on his next trip he'd have their baked goods."

"And how do you know he brought more stolen items to his cache?" I asked.

"Because the children would run and look in his car and see what was sitting beside the driver and what was piled in the backseat next to him," Estella said. "My son described some unusual silver candle-sticks I know came from a church in Florence. Another time he described a painting that had hung in the museum. I'd seen it there with my own eyes."

"So if we assume the mine's actually somewhere near here, why can't it be found?" I asked. "Where else did Kesselring go after he left the bakery? Didn't anyone ever follow him?"

Maria all but snorted in response to my question. "Follow him? You joke, right? No, you're not joking. You have no experience with SS tactics, with Nazi torture. If you valued your life, or those of your family, you turned your back when he drove through the countryside and pretended you didn't see him."

I nodded. "So what else did you want to tell my parents last night when they came? Did you have a new idea? Some new information you've found? Something someone remembered from long ago?" There must be something besides a rehash of all the old ideas, but could I, would I, ask the right questions to find it?

They just sat, staring at the floor or at each other, everywhere but at me. "Okay, let's play twenty questions." Not that they would prob-ably understand that term, but the idea would get across in any language. "How long would Kesselring stay when he came? If he arrived at the bakery at noon, when did he come back through the village?"

Carmen answered. "Usually several hours. Sometimes after dark."

"And what was the shortest amount of time you remember him being here?"

Tia's nervous laugh broke the silence that followed my question. "I was riding my bicycle to the neighbor's a couple of hours after he'd gone by when his big black car unexpectedly came speeding down the road toward me. I had to ride off the road so it didn't hit me. I tumbled into the ravine and nearly ruined my bike. It took my father a long time to repair it because parts to replace the broken ones were so hard to find."

"So you're saying, if he was in a hurry and went right to the mine, unloaded his stolen goods, then drove right back again, the mine must be within one hour of here." I gazed around the room at the faces filled with so much character and so many years' experience and hardship. They all nodded, Carmen more enthusiastically than the rest.

I pressed on with my questions. "So I'm sure you've explored every inch of the road between here and approximately an hour's drive. What did you find?"

"Nothing."

They whirled to see Enzio standing in the damaged doorway beside Bart. "I've personally been over every inch of that countryside. There isn't a cave I haven't explored. There isn't a road or field or hillside I haven't traveled searching for something that could be the hiding place. It's just not here." He came into the room with a tray containing cups of coffee and a plate heaping with the pastries I'd bought earlier today.

Today? It seemed eons ago. For me, he'd brought a glass of water. Bart held his glass in his hand, along with a chocolate-covered confection that looked really good to me right now.

"Thank you, Enzio. Will you and Bart join us? Maybe I'm not going in the right direction with this, because I'm certainly not learning anything."

"And you won't, either, because there is nothing to learn. I think these are old wives' tales, ridiculous stories of a treasure to end all treasure hunts. It's simply not there. I've searched. I've asked the questions. I've followed the trails. They lead nowhere."

"Then why does it keep surfacing? Why does the story keep getting revived? And why is Cell Seven convinced it's real?" I watched each of the women, knowing they had heard and told the story endlessly for more than fifty years. "Tell me why you know it's true when all the evidence says otherwise?"

Each of them sipped their coffee and kept their eyes on their cup. No one looked up at me.

"Luisa gave her life in that meeting you called last night. Every one of you could have died, as well, or been much more badly hurt than you were. If you know something, or if Cell Seven and those rotten punks who tossed that bomb at you even *think* you know something, they'll be back to torture it out of you. Or your family. If you know anything at all that will help us find it, you must tell me."

Still no response, but the tension in the room increased. Or was it my frustration level rising?

I tried a new tactic. "Ladies, have you seen the explosions on TV caused by Cell Seven? Have you seen the damage they've done already?"

A couple nodded their heads faintly.

"Think about the damage those bombs caused. With a smaller one than any of those used so far, they could wipe this beautiful little village right off the map. With every soul in it. There wouldn't be so much as a chicken left." I let that sink in for minute.

"Now, you all know something. I think you're afraid to tell me because somehow you think it will reflect badly on you." I paused. "Or on your family. On your children and your children's children. You don't want them hurt, so you want me to discover this information on my own, so you don't have to make any confession."

Bingo. Now we were getting somewhere. I glanced at Bart. He nodded and winked. He'd observed the difference in their countenances.

"Okay, ladies. Either you tell me how you know this treasure is real and how you know it's here in your area, or I'm going back to Florence to see how my mother is doing. Then I'm going to finish the tour and gather up the rest of the coded jewels and return to California, where I hope Mama and Papa Karillides are waiting for me. Then Bart and I are going to have a baby. And you're going to have to contend with these terrorists on your own." I watched them and waited until each one raised her head and looked me in the eye.

"What do you say?" I waited. The silence became unbearable. Then I said slowly, deliberately, "Tell me why you know it's true. Tell me why you're so sure it exists. You want it found. Help me find it. Help me get to it before the terrorists do, because if they get there first, heaven help us all."

Tiny little Tia drew herself up in her chair, took a deep breath, and stared at the others, as if seeking their permission to confess their sins. Apparently she saw what she looked for in their faces.

"We know the treasure exists because we've seen some of it."

Chapter 32

I was dumbfounded. "Where?"

Estella wrung her hands. "The candlesticks my son saw in his car."

I nodded. "The ornate ones you knew from a church in Florence?"

"They were in a little shop just outside the city where tourists stop all the time. I needed some money for my grandson's birthday present, so I took a piece of my mother's jewelry to sell there." She hung her head as if she was ashamed she'd sold her mother's jewelry. Or was she ashamed for her friends to know she needed money?

"And you're sure they were the same candlesticks he saw in Kesselring's car?" I pressed. She hadn't seen them in the car herself, had only recognized them from a child's description. That would never hold up in court.

"Oh, yes, I'm sure. You see, they have little angels, cherubs actually, all the way up the stem. Then three little cherubim hold the candles in place. There are four arms, all having three little cherubs holding their hands up to form the candleholders. He remembered them because he was with me in the church in Florence, and we talked about how little angels bring light to the world. When he described it from Kesselring's car, that's the first thing he said. 'Mama, he took the candles from the church!' He had remembered them."

Now that was testimony that might hold up in court! "That's all the artifacts you've seen that you knew were taken by Kesselring?" I asked, hope rising within me, along with excitement I needed to suppress for the moment.

Carmen offered the next bit of hope. "Did you see the painting on TV this week? The one they just found at that art auction? The one that hadn't been seen since before the war?"

"Cezanne's masterpiece at Christie's?" I asked, holding my breath and feeling my heart beating faster. *Stay calm.*

She nodded. "The one with the yellow flowers and the skull? The TV said it was valuable because his other skull had a book and candlestick and pomegranate or apple, something red. But this one just had the bright yellow flowers and the blob of a white skull. You can imagine how a painting of a skull would be memorable to children. My daughter was with Estelle's son that day and they talked about it for a long time. Then unexpectedly, there is it on TV. She called me so excited and said, 'Did you see it? Did you see the picture? That's what Tony and I saw that day in the German general's car!'"

More evidence that would probably stand up in court. I gazed around the room. "Anything else, ladies?"

Maria looked at Enzio, then back at her hands, then up at me. She wanted so much to reveal something, but I waited to see if she'd come out with it herself without prodding and prying on my part. Enzio, however, took it out of my hands.

"Mama, what do you know?"

She closed her eyes, leaned her head back on her chair, and sighed. "I didn't want to tell you, Enzio, because I might not get to watch the little ones again, but you remember when you and Sophie took your son and his wife to Naples for the weekend and I kept their twins?"

Enzio nodded. And waited. "And what happened, Mama?" He appeared to be gripping the cushion to keep from jumping up and yelling at her to go on with the story.

"They wanted to ride on their bikes, so I told them to only go to the bridge at the end of the lane and come back again." She finally looked at Enzio. "I told them to stay away from the water, not to get off their bikes, and just to ride on the road. It's only a couple of miles, you know, so if they were obedient, they wouldn't get hurt."

Everyone in the room leaned forward, holding their breath, waiting for the rest of the story.

"Little Thomas saw something shiny on the side of the hill, so he convinced Timothy to go exploring with him. They left their bikes off the road, climbed up the hill, and found the pretty piece of white rock which had caught their eye when the sun reflected off of it." Maria paused. "It was a piece of salt. A huge piece of salt, nearly the size of a brick. And it hadn't been there before."

"Why do you say it hadn't been there before?" Enzio asked. "How long since you had been there, Mama?"

Maria drew herself up straight and stared Enzio in the eye. "I walk to the bridge nearly every day when the weather is nice. Stell comes with me sometimes, don't you?" She turned to Estella for confirmation of her story.

"Yes, she stops for me two or three times a week, and we walk to the bridge and back. There's no traffic to speak of, so we don't worry about speeders running down two old ladies with their canes." She smiled.

Slowly it was coming together, everyone relaxing a bit, each adding to the tale. *Line upon line, precept by precept, here a little, there a little.* I just didn't know if I could stand the suspense if this went on much longer and came so little at a time!

"But what if the sun was just in the right place the day the twins were there?" Enzio insisted. "You can't know every single rock on the hillside. Maybe you weren't there when the sun was in that particular spot. Maybe . . ."

"Maybe the rain the week before would have dissolved it if it had been there earlier. And maybe Timothy wouldn't have fallen in the hole and sprained his ankle when they went exploring for it if it had been there when their dad took them to the creek fishing the day he dropped them off."

"Hole? What hole?" Enzio yelled and scrambled to his feet, unable to control himself any longer. We all nearly jumped from our chairs at his outburst.

"Sit down, son, and contain yourself," Maria crooned like a mother to her two year old. "I'm getting to that point." She rubbed one of the bandages on her hand and glanced up at Enzio.

"Timothy fell into a hole. The ground just crumbled under him, and he disappeared. Thomas called to him, and Timothy answered, but Thomas couldn't get his brother out, so he came racing home to me for help. I took my clothesline down and walked with him back to the hole. I didn't think to take a flashlight to see what was there. I should have. I tied a loop in the clothesline and lowered it to Timothy. He put one foot in the loop, held on to the line, and Thomas and I pulled him out. That was not easy for an old lady and a ten-year-old boy."

"What was in the hole, Maria?" I asked, voicing the one question everyone in the room wanted answered.

"Timothy said he saw lots of boxes. He couldn't read what was written on them, though, because it wasn't Italian and it wasn't English." Marie looked at me, then at Bart with pride in her voice. "My great-grandchildren are studying English. Mine was never very good."

"So? Go on, Mama," Enzio urged. "Did you find out what was in there? Did you tell anyone?"

Tia spoke up. "She told me. Then we told Estella and Carmen, and then we decided to call the old leader of the Freedom Fighters. But we were too late. He'd just died. The day before." She shrugged in a wouldn't-you-know-it gesture. "But when we saw all the business on the TV about explosions and terrorists wanting the treasure, we were afraid to say anything to anybody."

"How did you know to call Mom and Dad?" I asked.

"I guess that's where I come in," Enzio said, settling back onto the floor cushion he'd occupied before his outburst. "When Jack and Margaret Alexander came to Florence to work on these explosions, I remembered she knew Margaret's mother, Mama Karillides. So I told her they were here."

"That's when I arranged to have them come out here to meet us, to tell them about the hole and the boxes," Maria said, obviously relieved the story had finally been told. Not to mention, now that it had been, an opportunity to learn what the boxes contained.

I turned to Bart. He shook his head. "You can stay here with these delightful ladies and get better acquainted. I'll go with Enzio, and we'll see what's there."

"You won't know where to look unless I come to show you," Maria objected.

Enzio jumped to his feet. "Mama, it's pouring rain outside. Just tell me about where it is, and we'll go find it."

"I have an idea," I volunteered. "Why don't Maria and I ride with you so she can point out the location of the hole. You'll make a quick assessment and see what you need to go down and explore, or if it's feasible in the rain. Then you can bring us back here, get what you need and return to the hole. Estella, Carmen, and Tia will wait right here for us so we can get acquainted while you two men play in the mud."

Enzio nodded quickly, apparently aware his mother's insistence on going would cause a delay. The four of us hurried to the car under umbrellas, but by the time we reached the bridge at the end of the lane, the downpour had tapered off to mere sprinkles. Maria pointed to a spot about fifty yards off the road and halfway up the side of a hill that was about one hundred twenty feet high.

Bart and Enzio hopped out of the car and, splashing through puddles, disappeared in the brush and trees, which covered most of the hillside. They emerged above the trees in an area that looked like a recent rockslide.

"Maria, has that rocky area always been like that, or did it happen recently?" I asked.

"It just happened. We had lots of rain a couple of weeks ago, more than we've had for a long time, and I guess the ground just got so wet it couldn't hold the weight of those rocks. They tumbled down one night with an awful roar. This side of the mountain sort of slid right down from the top, filling up the little valley that used to be there."

"So you had lots of rain, then the rockslide, then how soon after did you keep Thomas and Timothy?" I asked. *Here a little . . .*

Maria thought for a minute. "I guess it was just a couple of days, because the creek was still rushing with all the rainwater, and that was why I didn't want them to go to the bridge. But they promised they wouldn't go near the water, so I let them ride. They'd been cooped up in the house and needed to use up some of their energy."

"Has Enzio seen this rockslide?"

"No, and I guess I forgot to tell him about it. He's been so busy . . ."

"And you were afraid to tell him because the boys might have been hurt while in your care." *And there a little . . .*

Maria's eyes averted from mine. She turned to watch Bart and Enzio clamber up the slippery rocks, and I watched with her, both of us holding our breath. They pulled out flashlights and knelt in the rocks, taking an exceedingly long time, it seemed to me, just examining a hole.

If it hadn't begun raining again, I'd have jumped out to see what they were looking at. About the time I couldn't sit still another minute, they descended the hill, skirting the rocks and making their way through the heavy growth of trees and bushes. They smelled like a couple of wet dogs when they got in the car.

Enzio turned to his mother as soon as he climbed behind the wheel. "Mama, you didn't tell me about the landslide. When did that happen?"

"Right after the big rains."

"So what did you see?" I asked, anxious to know if we had actually stumbled across Kesselring's stash of treasure.

Bart said over his shoulder, "The boys were right. There are stacks of boxes, and the writing is German, but that's all we could tell. There's water on the floor in the hole, but we have no way of knowing how deep it may be. We'll have to go down to find out."

"Sounds like so much fun, especially in the rain, and it's getting dark." I hoped Bart caught my facetious tone. "Are you going right back?"

Enzio had already started the car, and as he turned the lights on, they illuminated up the lane about fifty feet. The road consisted of hard-packed dirt and some gravel to the little stone bridge, then beyond the bridge, it narrowed to two trails the width of tires, apparently kept from the encroachment of vegetation by car traffic.

That puzzled me. "Is this what you call the end of the lane, Maria? Right here at the bridge?"

Maria nodded. "This is as far as we ever go."

Thus, the end of the lane, as far as she was concerned.

"But somebody goes beyond the bridge, and apparently often enough to keep the weeds from growing into the road. Where does the road lead, and who drives up there?"

"The road wanders around a couple of hills to an old farmhouse," Enzio offered, turning the car and heading back to the house.

"Who lives there?" Bart asked. He glanced at me with an expression that said he was definitely on my wavelength.

"Nobody." Maria shrugged. "It's been deserted for a long time, ever since Mrs. Catarcia died."

"Don't forget about that new family, Mama," Enzio reminded her. "They bought the place about ten years ago, didn't do much for a couple of years, then started pouring a lot of money into it to make it livable after all those years sitting empty. They use it now mostly for a summer home."

"Who are they? Do you know their names?" Bart asked.

"Mmm. I'll think of it in a minute." Enzio pulled into the little curved driveway in front of the house close to the front door so Maria wouldn't get wet.

I couldn't wait to pursue the line of questioning I felt would lead to something productive. Bart and Enzio disappeared into a little building behind the house, and in a few minutes, I heard the car start again.

"Is it the treasure?" Carmen asked, jumping up when we arrived.

Estella, Tia, and Carmen all spoke at once. Maria settled herself in her chair with a warm, dry shawl about her shoulders and glanced around the room at her friends. "They said boxes with German writing were stacked in the cave, but they didn't go down. They came back to get ropes to go see what's in the boxes."

"That's all?" Estella asked, sounding so disappointed I expected her to cry.

"For the minute, but they'll be back with more information quite soon," I said, trying to sound confident while wondering about the stability of the rocks above the cave and if they would slide some more with all this rain. "But I have some questions for you. Who knows the name of the family who lives in the old farmhouse beyond the end of the lane? And who can tell me the history of that house?"

"I can tell you the history of it," Tia said. "It belonged to the Catarcia family for years. The first owner had money, built a wonderful big house on the hill, and planted vineyards, orchards, and beautiful gardens. The man knew the soil, and it produced for him. He made a lot of money, had a lot of children, and was killed in the war."

"Then it isn't just a little farmhouse? It's more of an estate?" I asked, trying to picture in my mind what lay at the end of that little lane.

"Yes, it's big, but it is the house which goes with the farm, so it is a farmhouse," Maria explained.

I laughed. "Thank you. Now tell me what happened to the family after the war, after Mr. Catarcia died."

Estella sat on the edge of her chair. "I can tell you about Rosa Catarcia. She hobnobbed with the soldiers after her husband died."

"But Mr. Catarcia did that *before* he was killed," Carmen said. "The Germans were always going up to their farmhouse, and they were invited to the parties and concerts the soldiers had in town."

"Did Mr. Catarcia know Field Marshall Kesselring?" I asked as a little shiver of excitement rushed though me.

"Oh my, no," Maria said flatly. "The soldiers the Catarcias associated with were not in Kesselring's league. They were just soldiers. He was an officer. A high-up officer. An important man."

"Did the Catarcias join in village activities? Did they come to church or the market?" I asked, knowing the answer before they gave it.

"Oh, no," came Estella's emphatic reply. "They were too good for the likes of us. We didn't have lots of land, and we struggled to make a living from the little bit we had. They had lots of money and nice clothes and a nice car, even when the rest of us didn't know if we were going to have enough flour for tomorrow's bread."

"It sounds like they were collaborating with the Germans," I observed.

The little ladies just looked at each other. Apparently, they agreed, but they weren't going to say it out loud.

"So after Mr. Catarcia died, his wife kept on friendly terms with the soldiers. Then what?"

"After the war, the kids grew up and married and moved away, and she lived there alone until she died. Up there on her hill, in her big farmhouse, all alone. And would she come down and talk to us?" Carmen shook her head. "She was still too good for us, so she died up there all alone and no one knew for months."

"Didn't her children come and visit her?" I asked, thinking how lonely she must have been and wondering what on earth kept her up there by herself. "Where did she get her food? Didn't she ever come to the market?"

"No need," Maria explained. "If you have a cow and some chickens, a pig or two, and a garden, what more do you need?"

"Flour, sugar, salt, staples you don't usually produce yourself," I said. "Where did she get those?"

This appeared to be a totally new thought to the ladies. "She must have ridden her horse over the hill to Mangia," Maria said. "You're right. She never came here, but she had to go somewhere."

"Rode her horse? She didn't have a car?"

"If she did, and it still worked, there isn't a road from the farm-house down the mountain to Mangia," Maria said. "That's why those big trucks had to come through our village and on our little lane. They nearly crushed the bridge. They even had to build some supports under it."

"Big trucks carrying what?" This had become a terribly complicated tale, taking far longer to extract than I'd expected.

"After the new people bought the farmhouse, they had to nearly rebuild it, so all those building supplies had to be hauled up on the big trucks." Maria explained it slowly and carefully so I would be sure to understand. I wondered if her patience grew thin with all my questions.

"Tell me about the new people in the farmhouse." I studied the four little ladies and wondered how they spent their days and how they'd survived the ravages of war and where their children were now, and their husbands. And what escapades could they tell from their days with the underground?

"They have lots of money," Tia said.

"How do you know?" I asked.

"Because when they drive through the village, they are in expensive cars and wear beautiful clothes." She bobbed her head once as if punctuating her reasoning.

"How often do they come?"

Carmen answered. "In the summer, they have lots of company, so there's a lot of traffic on the lane. In the winter, I think only one person lives up there, and there aren't many visitors."

"But the ones who come are extremely health-minded," Maria said. "They hike all over the hills and bicycle up and down the lane."

"The family or the guests?" I asked.

"Oh, everyone," Estella said. "They all wear backpacks and hiking boots and have walking sticks, and some days, they are out on these hills all day long. And lately they've been riding those three-wheeled motorcycles that make so much noise."

"Do you ever talk to them?" I asked, hoping, praying I would ask the right questions to extricate this complicated story from them.

"There's one friendly woman who stops and talks to me when she's here," Maria said. "She always asks for a drink of my delicious water and wants me to tell her the village news. She says she grew up in a village like this and misses it so much."

"Did she tell you her name?" I asked, feeling in my bones we were getting close to whatever secret lay hidden in the minds and memories of the four women in this room with me.

Maria thought for a minute. "You know, I'm not sure she ever told me her name. But she is such a beautiful lady. And so gracious. She brings me something each time she comes, a little jar of cream for my hands, some fancy cookies from the city, some special little treat."

"What does she look like, Maria?" Why did I suddenly have this tingling sensation that traveled all the way from my fingertips to my toes?

Chapter 33

"She has long black hair, reminds you of the gypsy girls you used to see in the movies. Big dark eyes and creamy white skin, so she looks like she'd never been out in the sun, but there she is, traipsing around the hillsides with the rest of them."

My stomach did a flip-flop. Was it possible? "Maria, has she ever talked about singing or entertaining?"

"Mmm, no, but I know she can sing, because sometimes I've heard her in the hills before she arrives to visit me."

"Was she short or tall, skinny or fat?" I tried to sound casual, to hide the excitement that built higher with each response they gave.

"Not fat, for sure. She has the kind of figure men go crazy over. And she likes to show it off. Her hiking clothes must have been tailor-made for her."

Tia laughed. "Or sewn on her."

Gabriella's face and figure filled my mind. Did she actually come here searching for the treasure? Is that what the "hikers" were doing all over these hills?

"Maria, how often does this woman come?"

Maria glanced at her friends. "What do you think? Once a month in the winter and a lot more in the summer?"

Carmen laughed. "Her memory fails her," she said, pointing to Maria. "I think she stays at the house at least a month each summer, probably more, and she's been coming most weekends for a couple of years now."

I scanned the faces of each of these ladies to see if they concurred with Carmen. Tia and Estella nodded.

"She comes a lot," Tia said. "I think she is related to the Catarcias." That comment stirred up interest in the group.

"Why do you think that, Tia?" I asked the tiny little lady with animated eyes and hands.

"Because she knows so much about the family. She knows how the house used to be before they rebuilt it. She told me about a pretty little well by the house and wondered if I knew what kind of vine grew over it. I told her I had only been there after Mrs. Catarcia died when everything had been neglected, and nothing was pretty anymore."

"You're right," Estella agreed. "She did know a lot about the farm-house. She asked me if I knew what color the roses on the wallpaper in the living room had been, pink or rose."

"Did you know?" I asked.

"I told her we were never invited up to the house and had only seen it long after Mrs. Catarcia died, when it was deserted. We all went up together to see what our children had described for years, but most of the windows and doors were boarded up, so we could only peek through the cracks, so I couldn't tell her anything about it."

"None of you ever saw it when it was newly built? When the Catarcias lived in it?"

They all shook their heads.

"Then how do you know about the vineyards and orchards and gardens and how beautiful it was and how well it produced?" Apparently I still wasn't asking the right questions. I didn't seem to be getting straight answers.

"Because they hired our children to go up and work at harvest time. Their children were away at fancy schools, so they needed workers. Our children worked up there in the daytime and then came home at night to help with our harvest."

"Did Enzio work there?" I asked Maria.

"Oh, yes. Each year from the time he turned eight, he would pick the grapes and scramble up the trees to pick the fruit. He was a good worker."

"Did he ever meet the Catarcia children? Maybe he knew this woman friend of yours as a child."

Maria frowned. "You'll have to ask him when he comes back. I don't remember."

"Do any of you remember the children? How many there were? Their ages? Names?"

"I'm not really sure," Estella said slowly. "It seems there were many children peering out the windows or crowded in the backseat when they came down the mountain in that big car. Many little faces."

"How old would you say they were?" I needed a time line to see if Gabriella could actually belong to that family. Except Gabriella was supposed to be French, not Italian.

"When the war started, the oldest boy joined the army. Then there was a girl, a few years younger, and a boy. Oh, I'm not sure." Carmen's memory faltered, and she shook her head.

"If the oldest boy joined the army, he must have been about eighteen in 1939 when war broke out in Europe. That would make him about twenty-four when the war ended in 1945." The math didn't work out. "Does that sound right? That would make him a lot older than his siblings, who you remembered as being young."

Maria thought for a minute. "Maybe the little ones were Rosa Catarcia's grandchildren."

Before we worked through the puzzle, the car drove up, and Bart and Enzio burst into the house.

"They're empty. All those boxes are empty," Bart exclaimed.

"Empty?" I asked, hardly believing him. "Every single one?"

"Every single one," Enzio repeated, stripping off his dripping coat and spraying water drops everywhere.

"Do you know what they held?" I asked.

"A lot of them still contained packing material," Bart replied. "Remember the old shredded straw they used to pack stuff in? Also, bunches of newspapers dated in the forties were crumpled in the boxes, apparently used to wrap the stuff."

"How did they get down there? Did it look like this was Kesselring's stash?" I'd forgotten to speak Italian while speaking to Bart, so Enzio translated for his mother and her friends.

Bart shrugged out of his wet jacket and leaned against the damaged door casing. "We don't know how they got there. There weren't enough boxes to account for even a portion of the things Kesselring confiscated. There weren't enough painting containers, either. Only half a dozen. If this had been Kesselring's, it would have been an extremely small part of it."

"But it *might* have been part of it?" I pressed, wanting it to be so.

"It might have been. Or somebody else's. You know how many they found after the war, and this could be a newly discovered one when the rockslide uncovered the opening."

I whirled around to the four little ladies hanging on Enzio's every word. "Has any of the family or their guests been here since the rockslide? Have they been hiking in the hills up near there?"

All four frowned, put on their thinking faces, and sat quietly for a minute.

"Let me ask you this," I said, thinking of a way to rephrase the question. "Have there been any cars up this road since the big rain?"

Tia nodded her head slowly. "Yes, the family came to the house sometime after the rain."

"Just once? Did anyone else come? Any guests or other traffic?"

Tia turned to Estella. "When did we see that blue van? Before or after the rains?"

Estella thought for a minute. "I think it was after. Yes. Maria, remember when we walked to the bridge and saw where the tracks had nearly run off into the creek. I said they must have been going too fast, and you said, no, it looked like they had pulled off the road and stopped at the bridge to see how high the water had risen before they crossed."

And suddenly it came together for everyone at the same time. Maria gasped. "They weren't looking at the water. They were loading treasures from those boxes into that van and taking them away."

"But think before you leap to that conclusion," I cautioned, although we were all thinking the same thing. "Was anyone out hiking after the rains and before that van came? Someone had to *find* the hole before they brought a van to carry anything out of it."

Carmen's hand went to her throat, and her brown eyes opened wide. "Maria's friend was in the car with the family. She waved at me as I crossed the road to have tea with Estella. I watched as they drove down the lane, wondering if the bridge had held out okay with all that water rushing under it. Their brake lights came on, but they didn't stop. I didn't think any more about it."

"If she came," Maria said with certainty, "she hiked. She never came without taking long walks. She told me that was why she visited so often. She loved walking here. She loved the challenge of climbing these hills. She always felt refreshed when she returned home."

"Did she say where home was?" I asked.

"Somewhere on the east coast, on the Adriatic," Marie said, "but I'm not sure just where. She always laughed when I asked about her, and she said she lived a dull, boring existence and knew life was much better here, where people really understood how to live instead of just exist."

Bart's eyebrows went up in an unasked question.

"I'll fill you in later. We'd better call Dad immediately."

"Yes, we need to tell him what we found—but didn't find—and while you report what you've uncovered, I'll just eavesdrop so you only have to repeat the story once."

Enzio led us to the veranda, where I called Dad on the satellite compact phone and put it on telecom so we could all hear and talk. Bart and Enzio told their part of the story, and I filled in with what I'd wheedled out of the ladies one question at a time.

"And here's the biggest speculation of all, Dad. It wouldn't surprise me if Gabriella Cardin is involved up to her fake eyelashes. It's too much of a coincidence the rockslide happened just days before the long-lost painting appeared at Christie's. Not to mention, they found newspapers from the 1940s stuffed in boxes with German written on them."

"You're right, bunny. And Maria's description fits Gabriella to a tee. But we're going to have to move fast if this is part of the treasure. We've got to locate the rest of it before anyone else does. You'll need to visit the farmhouse and make another trip into the cave. That might prove to be just an antechamber. If you could find the main room, we might beat everyone else to the jackpot."

"How are they coming on the code, Dad? Any progress that might lead us to it from Kesselring's own description?"

"Actually, I feel they're about to have a breakthrough any minute. If we had a couple more of the topaz, they might break the code tonight."

"That close?" I marveled, but knowing as I spoke that "close" didn't necessarily equate to immediate success. "Close" could easily take another week—or more.

Dad started giving orders. "Enzio, take Bart and Allison back to the cave and let Allison examine the walls. She seems to have a knack for finding hidden openings. Then will you go up to the farmhouse and see what you can find?"

"Sure," Enzio said. "You're thinking this might be Cell Seven country?"

"Exactly," Dad said. "You might even stumble onto their head-quarters, or at least another meeting place, so be careful."

"Jack," Bart said, "You don't want your daughter down in that cave with all this rain. That's what caused the slide in the first place, and we don't know how stable the hillside is."

Dad didn't answer immediately. I envisioned him looking at Mom, probably still in bed across the room, and weighing the consequences of Cell Seven, or any other group, getting their hands on this billion-dollar treasure before we did.

I took the decision out of his hands. "I'm on my way, Dad. We'll let you know what we find, if anything." I disconnected and stared at Bart. "If there was anyone else here to do this, you know I'd stay out of the rain. But remember what Mordecai told Esther? 'Who knoweth whether thou art come for such as a time as this?' And Neal A. Maxwell's idea of celestial orbits? Maybe I was brought to this place at this time to do just this very thing."

Before Bart unloaded his doubt and displeasure at the wisdom of Dad's suggestion or began questioning my speculative reasoning, I darted back into the living room, grabbed my jacket and purse, and told the ladies to keep talking.

"Remember all you can about the farmhouse and the Catarcia family and everyone who comes through this village and when. Write it down so you can give me the paper when we get back, because we'll be returning to Florence when we're finished at the cave."

Enzio held the door open, and I hurried out with Bart on my heels. "What kind of rock is the cave formed from?" I asked as Bart and I settled in the backseat.

"Probably limestone," Enzio said, starting the car and pulling out onto the little lane. After my conversation with Maria and her friends, I saw the narrow road through different eyes. It wasn't a sleepy village lane with sparse traffic, but apparently a busy thoroughfare for questionable activities.

Bart didn't try to dissuade me from going into the hole with him, but he was not happy about it, and his stony silence informed me that I'd better be extremely careful every step of the way. He grabbed the rope he and Enzio had used the first time they were here. After getting out my penlight, I returned my purse to the backseat of the car. I wouldn't need it in the hole. We waved good-bye to Enzio, who promised he'd return in forty-five minutes to pick us up. As dusk had already begun to settle, in another forty-five minutes, it would be fully dark, especially with this storm over us.

Bart led the way through the trees to the rockslide, much of the new trail a slippery muddy mess. Packed down grasses and weeds in other places attested to the fact that there had been a fair amount of foot traffic here recently, far more than just Bart and Enzio.

I eyed the rocks on the hillside above us and said a silent prayer that they would stay exactly where they were until after we'd accomplished our mission. Bart tied one end of the rope to a nearby tree and made a loop in the other end. I slipped my foot into the loop, and he lowered me into the dark hole. I would much have preferred a large, bright torch instead of a small penlight, but any light was better than none at all, which is what little Timothy had when he fell into the hole.

Bart slid down the rope behind me and flashed his light on the empty boxes, neatly stacked in rows, four high, two deep, and ten wide along one side of the cave.

"You checked all of these, and they're empty? Every one?" I asked, flashing my little light around while Bart trained his bigger one on the boxes.

"Every single one."

"Why would they restack the boxes after they'd emptied them?"

"Neatniks, maybe."

"Strange."

I shined my meager light around the rest of the narrow cave. Bare rock walls. Bart's light enhanced mine, but the small room didn't give up its secrets easily. I stared up at the hole, getting my bearings.

"This is the mountain side of the cave in front of us." I turned left. "And this is the creek side." I faced the opposite direction. "This is the road side, and that's the village side with the boxes." With an idea of what lay in each direction, I started examining the walls.

"This part's natural," Bart said, pointing to the mountain side, "granite, but these others are carved from limestone with pickaxes."

"So if you were going to make this an anteroom to a larger chamber, would you suppose that chamber is inside the mountain? And they carved out this portion to store things in while they were being moved into the larger chamber?"

"You're assuming this is actually Kesselring's mine. It may not be," Bart said, playing his light over the nearly smooth surface of the rock in front of us. No pick marks, no striations on the wall, just a hunk of granite about ten feet tall and less than ten feet wide.

I went over every inch of it with my fingers and my flashlight, feeling for indentations which might trigger a hidden door, but there were no seams in this rock, no manmade markings of any kind.

Rain pounded on the rocks above as the deluge increased, and substantial water now poured over the edge of the hole. Thunder rattled the mountain above us. This wasn't a good place to be. I glanced at Bart. His dark scowl resembled the black clouds dumping all that rain.

"We'd better get out of here, princess. I don't like the sounds from up there, and I don't like the water flooding in so fast."

"Let's just check these other walls quickly, then we'll go. I don't want to stay down here a minute longer than I absolutely have to either."

I started on the creek side wall and examined each pick mark, each indentation, poking my fingers into crevasses until they were so tender and sore, I feared they'd start bleeding. Bart trained his light on the wall, giving me additional light as I fingered and probed every mark on the limestone walls.

"Three down, one to go. If you'll move the boxes, I'll start in this corner."

Bart pushed the boxes out of the way and shined his light to augment mine as I ran my hands over the walls. The water level had risen in the cave to above my knees, and the small river flowing into the hole had become a waterfall. Empty boxes floated across the cave.

Bart's patience ended. "Now, Allison. We're out of here. You can finish this wall another time."

"Wait! I think I've found something. Give me your light." Bart exchanged lights with me, and I followed a jagged line up from the water level to about six feet above the cave floor, then across about three feet, and down to the water again.

"I found it! This has to be the entrance to the larger chamber!"

But just as I whirled to Bart in excitement, a loud clap of thunder shook the whole mountain like an earthquake, and water gushed over the edge of the hole into the cave.

Chapter 34

"Quick, grab the rope and climb up out of here before this place fills with water or the whole mountain slides down on top of us."

Bart grabbed my hand and pulled me to the rope now hidden in the cascading water. He fished it out, sputtering and choking, and forced it in my hands. I tried to grasp it to pull myself up. The waterfall surging over me was obstacle enough, but my fingers were raw and cut from the rocks. I couldn't hold on.

I stumbled back from the force of the water and held out my hands. "I can't grasp the rope with my cut fingers. You'll have to climb out and pull me up."

Bart didn't hesitate. He plunged into the midst of the waterfall and climbed the rope, slipping backward a couple of times before he finally pulled himself out of the hole. With water now waist-high in the cave and rising fast, I struggled to slip the loop over my foot. I tugged on the rope to signal I'd finally succeeded, and Bart, hand over hand, pulled me up through the torrent of water gushing into the opening until I sprawled on the rocky ground awash with muddy water.

While I scrambled to my feet, Bart untied the rope and coiled it on the run as we raced back to the lane. No Enzio. I checked my watch. It had been over forty-five minutes already, and he hadn't returned. I glanced at Bart.

He shook his head. "Not good. I wonder if he ran into trouble or if he just found something that needed further investigation." Then he stared at me. "You need to get out of those wet clothes."

I laughed. "You want me to take them off right here?" Then I remembered Cell Seven and Gabriella. "You're worried about me being in wet clothes when Enzio might have just walked into the lion's den?"

"Actually, this is Enzio's home turf, and he's an experienced agent. He wouldn't just walk into a trap."

"I hope not. In the meantime, I'm not keen on standing out in this pouring rain. Should we walk back to Maria's house?"

Bart wiped my cheek with his hand. "You're a muddy mess. It wouldn't hurt to just stand here and let the rain clean you off."

"Thanks, I think I'd rather have a hot shower!" I reached up to wipe some mud from Bart's nose and only succeeding in smearing it across his face.

He put his arms around me and pulled me close. "Is that a little better? Are you warmer?"

"I would be, if you weren't so wet." Then I remembered the door in the wall. "I can't believe we found that door and had to leave it before we found the opening."

"We wouldn't have wanted to open it anyway, princess. If that is the treasure chamber, and if it's really a salt mine, there's a very real possibility it's been dry for the last sixty plus years. We wouldn't want all that water pouring into the chamber and ruining the art and artifacts which might still be in perfect condition."

"True." I was totally miserable standing unprotected in this driving rain. "I wonder if there's space under the bridge where we'd be sheltered? Just in case Enzio doesn't come soon."

"Let's go see," Bart said, heading for the bridge. "I hate to start walking back and have him stop and look for us in the cave and think we've drowned."

Hanging onto branches, we lowered ourselves down the steep bank, then clung to bushes as we followed the creek. It appeared to be several feet higher than normal, since bushes along the banks were partially submerged in the rushing water.

I didn't have much hope at this point that we'd find any shelter at all, and we'd have to climb back up the muddy, slippery bank and wait in the pelting rain. But Bart ducked under the high arch of the rock bridge, and we found ourselves four feet above the water level on a grassy ledge.

"One of Maria's friends said that when they were carting all the building materials up to the big farmhouse to restore it, they had to stop and fortify the bridge because the trucks' loads were so heavy. I wonder if they rebuilt the whole thing or what kind of fortifying they did."

Bart shined his light on the underside of the bridge. "This doesn't look like anything's been done to it. How long ago was that supposed to have happened?"

I laughed. "That's a good question. Getting anything out of those four was like trying to take back a piece of candy from a child. They just didn't want to give it up or didn't understand what they really knew, so I had to pry it out of them, one little sliver of information at a time. If I'd had another couple of hours with them, we might put together quite a story. But I think they said it was about ten years ago."

"Mmm, that could be. Lichen grows pretty fast under these conditions."

"It's interesting how perception colors your thinking and impressions. Maria first said the farmhouse remained empty and no one lived there. Then under questioning, she said, well, somebody came there occasionally. Then it came out someone actually did live there, and they had lots of guests. But in Maria's mind, if she didn't see them coming and going daily or even weekly, no one must live there because they weren't going to the market every day."

"You're serious?" Bart laughed.

"Oh, yes. She'd been talking about the end of the lane, but when I came here with you and Enzio, I saw that the road continued past the bridge. But because Maria and her neighbors never went beyond the bridge, that became the end of the lane in her mind."

"Guess that's the reason eyewitnesses all tell different stories. Their observation is colored by their perception." Bart idly flashed his light over the underside of the bridge, then followed a seam in the rock up over our heads and back behind us. "I wonder if that rock-slide shook things up and cracked the bridge." We turned around to examine the bridge as he shined his flashlight on the blocks of stone we'd been leaning against.

"Look at this," he said, following the line with the light.

Definitely a crack in the mortar, but not jagged like a normal separation would produce. It appeared to have been sliced with something sharp. The edges were clean and straight. We exchanged glances, and I pulled out my little penlight to examine it more closely.

We followed the crack all the way to the ground, then retraced it back up to where there had been another of the same kind of line at a right angle. That ended about three feet from the beginning, then dipped at a right angle toward the ground.

"I think, Sherlock, you just found a door of some sort."

"Then, by all means, Watson, find the opening."

Examining this was more difficult and painful than the cave. My fingers were now so sore I'd have a hard time eating or brushing my teeth or doing anything that required nimbleness. But we examined the stone wall, inch by inch, touching every unnatural-looking indentation, every chisel mark. We came up empty-handed, and I was getting chilled all the way through. The thrill of the hunt lessened with each passing minute.

"You examine the underside of the bridge. I'm going to play in the mud some more." I turned my penlight to the grass hugging the bridge, pulling it gently away from the stones. I didn't want to pull it out by the roots in case someone else knew about the door, if it was a door. It needed to appear as undisturbed as we could leave it.

I'd examined the stones hidden by the grass about halfway across the three feet, to nearly the center of the door, when my light illuminated a pebble embedded in the mortar. I pushed it in the center. Nothing happened. I tried twisting it. Still nothing. It didn't budge.

I left it and kept working my way inch by inch across the stones until I came to another pebble similar to the first one in size and appearance. I pushed and pulled and tried to twist it. Nothing. Then in a few more inches, I found a third pebble, like the other two.

"Bart, push on that pebble when I push these two, and let's see if it does anything."

At first I didn't think anything happened, then I realized the crack had become more pronounced. Bart grinned, put his feet up to the rocks, and exerted just a little pressure. The door gave a little. He pushed harder. It moved measurably.

"Ready for this?" he asked as he prepared to give it a real shove.

"I'm not sure. But go for it. We might luck out and find a roaring fire and nice clean sheets waiting for us."

"You have a great imagination." He gave a little kick, and the stones slowly swung away with a grinding, grating sound that made my teeth itch.

"Doesn't sound like this is a modern innovation to the bridge." I shuddered at the sound. "You'd think it had been here for hundreds of years."

"Maybe it has. With all the intrigues in the Middle Ages and the power brokering in the Renaissance, this might have been built at the time of the Medicis. Maybe a hideout from whoever the bad guys were at the time."

"Or a hideout from the good guys," I suggested, flashing my light into the dark interior, which reeked of dust and decay. "This certainly isn't a salt mine."

"I'll go see what it is. You stay here and wait for Enzio, and then you both come and find me. I don't want him going back without us. That would send those little ladies into a tizzy, not to mention what it might do to your folks if he called them to find out where we were."

I started to object, then thought of Mom. She didn't need to be worried about me while trying to recover from her injuries. "Okay, but don't fall into any holes or set off any booby traps. I want you back in one piece."

Bart leaned over and kissed me. "I promise I'll be a regular Indiana Jones and escape unscathed."

"That doesn't reassure me much. He nearly gets killed each time he steps outside his door."

"But he survives," Bart said as he disappeared into the hole in the bridge. I watched his light play on the walls as he made his way farther into the small tunnel. My six-foot-plus husband could barely stand up straight with the low ceiling so close to his head. The passage didn't appear to be more than three or four feet wide.

I glanced at my watch. Past five o'clock. Enzio had been gone over an hour instead of the forty-five minutes he promised. We had to meet our group at seven o'clock or miss our ride to Pisa. We'd need to head back immediately if we were going to connect with the tour in Florence.

The storm increased in intensity, and the low black clouds and heavy rain made it feel like night already. I shivered with the cold and hugged myself to get warm. *Hurry up, Enzio. Where are you? I'd love to be in front of your car heater right now.*

Thunder rolled across the hills, and lightning flashes reflected in the rushing waters of the creek. Each flash was followed by a crack of thunder that came immediately on the heels of the lightning. *Closer and closer,* I thought.

The next one must have hit the mountain beside us. A tingle of electricity shot from my shoes to my head, and the hair on the back of my neck and my arms stood up. Then the mountain exploded. Rocks tumbled down the slide path, covering the area where the opening to the cave had been seconds before. I remembered my prayer and murmured a fervent thank you.

The ground trembled as huge boulders cascaded down the mountain, bounding across the lane and into the field beyond. What did that do to the passageway Bart was exploring right now? What would it do to the bridge? I didn't know whether to stay put or get out from under the bridge before it crumbled around me.

Suddenly more rumbling shook the earth. Another rockslide? An earthquake? The tunnel collapsing on Bart? *Protect him, Father, please!*

Chapter 35

I poised at the edge of the bridge farthest from the cascading rocks, ready to leave my shelter from the storm if it disintegrated. Away from the center of the bridge, the echoes lessened and the vibrations abated. The noise I heard wasn't an earthquake but all-terrain vehicles roaring up to the bridge and revving their engines.

"The road's blocked. We can't get through," a male voice called over the noise of the vehicles.

"Where do we go from here?" a second voice shouted.

"Unless he made it down the hill and across the bridge before the rockslide, he's still on our side of the creek. Let's go back and search for him. He must not leave here alive."

Gabriella! I'd recognize that sultry voice anywhere. The engines roared again and the bridge shook as they turned around and peeled back up the lane. Enzio must have been seen poking around the farmhouse, but he'd apparently gotten away. With or without his car? If they found his car, they'd find my purse. Not good.

Time to call in the Marines. I dug the compact communicator out of my soggy pocket and hoped, prayed, that it still worked. Otherwise, it would be a long, wet walk back to Maria's to call David.

My prayers were answered. *Thank you, Father for being mindful of my needs.* I heard David's most welcome voice on the other end of the line.

"Thank heaven, you're there. Dad, if we're really lucky, or blessed as the case may be, our search may be at an end as soon as the next thirty minutes, but we need some help up here. You don't happen to have access to a helicopter, do you?"

"Is that how fast you need us there?"

"This minute wouldn't be too soon. Do you know where Enzio's mother lives?"

"If I don't have the address, I can get it in about thirty seconds. How long did it take you to get there?"

"From the time we left you until we pulled into the village, under an hour, but you'll have rush hour traffic to contend with, I think."

"We'll be there in an hour," Dad assured me, coming on the line. "Are you at Enzio's mother's home?"

"No, come straight through the village to the bridge. The road's blocked at the bridge by the landslide. An incredible storm's passing over us, and it caused another rockslide. We stumbled across an opening under the bridge, and that's where I am now, waiting for Enzio while Bart explores the passageway."

"Is Enzio still at the farmhouse?" Dad asked. I heard him giving directions as we talked, getting people mobilized, I hoped.

"Apparently. I heard Gabriella say they had to go back and find him, as he couldn't leave there alive. I'm assuming it's Enzio they were talking about. He knows the terrain up there, but if you can communicate with him, you'd better."

"So you were right. Gabriella is there. Okay, bunny, we're on our way. Do you need anything else?" Dad asked.

"Clean, dry clothes, a hot shower, and how's Mom?"

"Awake and complaining because she can't come with us, so I have to assume she's getting better."

"Good. Tell her stay in bed, snug, warm, and dry, and I'll see her in a few hours. Hope to see you in much less time than that."

"Be careful, bunny. I'll look for you under the bridge."

"Or in the passage under the bridge. Bye, Dad."

The knowledge that assistance should arrive soon added greatly to my feeling of well-being. I wasn't any less cold or wet, but the fear that settled over me during the storm, then permeated my being when I heard Gabriella's voice, dissipated somewhat.

Now, should I sit tight or find Bart? Nothing need keep me here since Enzio had problems of his own and, I hoped, would assume Bart and I had taken care of ourselves. Therefore, I decided to join my husband.

I crawled back under the bridge and squeezed through the opening into the tunnel. Another couple of months, and I might not be able to perform these gymnastics as my baby grew bigger.

Should I close the door so it wasn't a gaping hole that anyone might spot immediately? I'd hate to have Gabriella find it and come waltzing down seeking the treasure. I didn't even have my gun with me. *Every time I leave my purse behind, I regret it,* I thought in frustration. I compromised and left it just slightly ajar.

My penlight barely penetrated the passage a foot beyond where I walked. Boyd K. Packer's promise flitted through my mind, that if we'd take one step out of the light into the darkness with faith, the Lord would guide our footsteps. I realized he alluded to comfort zones, but I relied on that promise now, since I'd totally lost my comfort zone.

The passageway had been carved out of limestone, much like the cave we'd just escaped, although the lower portion appeared more natural and smooth. It may have begun as a natural waterway and been enlarged by whoever carved the upper part of the passage. It sloped downward, descending so steeply at places there were stairs to check the descent.

The dryness of the tunnel surprised me. No puddles, no seeping walls, and no sign of water in the passage at all, a great comfort with all the water raging above me. Now if the creek didn't rise four feet while we had the door opened under the bridge, it should stay just this dry. I nearly turned around and went back to close the door all the way. But what if I couldn't find the way to open it again? Right now, I just needed to find Bart.

The tunnel continued descending, making a couple of turns to the right, then back to the left. I tried to keep the perspective of just where in relation to the cave this might be, but after a couple more turns, my sense of direction deserted me. I might be halfway back to Maria's for all I knew.

Many of the salt mines used to hide valuable artifacts during the war still had the original mini-railroad tracks and used the railroad cars to transport items deep into the mines. This apparently had never had such a thing. I tried to imagine someone carrying huge statues through here. It required a real stretch of the imagination.

Therefore there had to be another, more accessible, entrance, even more so than the one in the cave.

Where was Bart? I should have run into him by now, should have found something besides this miles-long tunnel. There had been no niches cut in the sides, no offshoots or branches in any direction, so I knew I hadn't missed him.

Finally, I heard sounds in the darkness in the passage ahead. "Bart?" I called softly. *That was silly,* I thought. *Who else would be here besides my husband?*

"Bart?" I called a little louder.

"Princess, here."

I saw a small light in the tunnel flashing back and forth, shined my light on the floor to avoid missteps, and hurried toward that welcome beacon and the comforting sound of my husband's voice.

"Oh, am I glad to see you," I said, throwing my arms around him. "I thought this tunnel would never end."

"It just did." Bart flashed his light on the wall behind him—a solid chunk of rock with a smooth surface. "I've spent a long time going over every inch of this and can't find a single place which could be a hidden door. This seems to be the same rock wall we found in the cave. I think we're several stories below that on the same hunk of rock. You look. You might find something."

"Did you try the walls on either side of it? If they hit a dead end at this piece of granite or marble, they'd have to go somewhere else. You check that side, and I'll do this one."

I started in the rounded corner and reached as high as I could. My fingertips just brushed the rough limestone ceiling of the tunnel. This would be a long, painful process for my already raw fingers.

"I thought you were going to wait for Enzio. Did he come?" Bart asked as he busied himself at the wall behind me.

"Actually, your friend Gabriella showed up with a couple of men on ATVs at the bridge. I think they were searching for Enzio. Their comment was, 'He can't leave here alive,' so I assumed they'd spotted him, but he had escaped. By the way, there was another rockslide, and the road's now closed at the bridge. When I heard Gabriella, I called Dad and told him we needed help out here. They're on their way."

"Good girl. Your intuition regarding Gabi was right on," Bart said over his shoulder. "I wonder how she ties in here."

"I've been thinking about that. Maria and her friends seem to think the Catarcias, the family who owned the farmhouse, didn't have anything to do with Kesselring. They insisted that the family only associated with the common soldiers, not the officers or higher-ups, as Maria called Kesselring. But just supposing he came up here to the village, then followed the road to the farmhouse—that certainly isn't a stretch. It would have been one of the nicest homes in the area, to hear the ladies tell it. If the Catarcias were hobnobbing with the Germans, they would have been quite thrilled, I would imagine, to entertain such an illustrious guest as a famous field marshal."

I stopped to examine a little seam in the rock but decided it was a natural crack, although it did run from the floor to the ceiling.

Bart glanced around at my silence. "Find something?"

"No. I thought for a minute I did, though."

"Continue with your line of thinking, princess. I'm anxious to know where it's leading."

"Now I'm going out a limb. The ladies insisted there were a lot of children in the Catarcias' car when they came down from the farmhouse, but they also said Catarcia's oldest son joined the military at the outbreak of the war. Unless Rosa Catarcia continued to have babies after her son was grown, I wondered if those small children might have been her grandchildren."

"Go on," Bart urged when I paused to concentrate on another interesting but unproductive mark on the wall.

"Then, and here's where I really get on thin ice, Maria and her friends said Gabriella seemed to know a lot about the farmhouse the way it had been during the war, as though she had been there as a child. I've been doing the math in my head, and I'm thinking Gabi is probably just short of fifty. Right?"

"Mmm." Bart thought about it. "Somewhere in that neighborhood."

"There's a possibility she did visit here as a child." I stopped. This crack paralleled the other. "Will you bring your light over here, please? I'm not sure what I'm seeing."

Bart's brighter beam illuminated the jagged crack, which extended from the floor to the ceiling.

"Now shine it on this one." I pointed to the long, natural-looking crack with uneven edges about four feet from the first. "What do you think, Sherlock?" I crawled on my hands and knees to examine the floor at the foot of the wall.

Bart focused his light at the curve where ceiling and wall met. He ran his fingers along the area barely above his head, scant inches above his eye level. "I think we may have another opening, Watson. Can you find the doorknob?"

I laughed. "I wish it were that easy. You look on that side, and I'll look on this side."

While Bart scoured the walls with his fingers and light, he made one observation I had already thought of but hadn't yet pursued through all the possible solutions. "The only problem I see with your scenario of Gabriella is she's French and the war was going on—so how did she get to Italy? And when?"

"And if she and Emile were raised in France and stayed there, instead of crossing borders at any time, that really throws cold water on my theory."

"Of course, there was travel during the war," Bart said slowly, "though limited, and the underground provided safe passage a lot of the time, smuggling people from one place to another if they had to go, so I guess anything's possible."

"Did Emile ever say anything to you about his childhood and where he and Gabriella were raised?"

Bart thought for a minute. "Not that I remember, but I've tried to wipe that whole portion of my life totally from my mind. It's too painful. So if he did tell me, I may have just forgotten."

I stopped and listened. "Do you hear something?" Bart stopped moving and faced the passageway. Faint sounds floated through the tunnel toward us.

I shined my light on my watch. "It can't be Dad," I whispered. "It's too soon."

"Then you'd better find the doorknob in a hurry, or we're sitting ducks at the end of the galley."

Chapter 36

We shielded our lights from the tunnel as much as possible to still illuminate each indentation in the rock wall in front of us. I'd been over every bit of rock on my side at least three feet out from the crack and had found absolutely nothing.

Animated voices were now discernible and were approaching way too fast.

"They'll know we're here, because I left the door open," I whispered. "They're probably running to find out who's in their tunnel."

Now on my hands and knees, scrutinizing the floor while Bart examined the area above the door, I touched an indentation, which moved slightly under my finger. But nothing happened to the wall. It stayed as solid and immoveable as ever, even when I pushed with all my strength.

"I'm feeling something up here, but it's not doing anything," Bart said. "I thought I'd found it."

"Let's hope you have. They sound like they're at that last corner before they'll be able to see us and our lights. I may have found the other part. Push on yours now." I pushed mine at the same time, and the wall moved slightly. "Push again," I whispered.

Again, it moved slightly. Bart leaned against it, and the slab of rock gave way a little more. I shined my light in the dark crack and illuminated stairs leading down.

"If I push with you, we might get it open enough to squeeze through. Then we'll still have to close it before they get here. Ready?" Together, we pushed, and the door moved slightly to the right, leaving me just enough of a crack to squeeze through. *Squeeze* being the operative word. If Alexandra had been conceived one month earlier than she was, I'd have never made it!

Bart managed to contort his way through, and we pushed the door shut from the back. Then without waiting to see if those approaching knew how to enter wherever we were, we hurried down the stairs. I kept my little light on my feet to make sure there was one next step, while Bart played his light over the area.

"Wherever we are, it's big," I whispered. "Listen to the echo."

"Stop a minute and look up." Bart put his hand on my shoulder and stopped beside me. His light illuminated the chamber, reflecting off white walls that sparkled when the light hit them. "It's a salt mine. Princess, I think we may have just stumbled onto something important."

But we didn't have time to congratulate ourselves. Those in the passage knew how to get into this chamber. I could hear their voices more clearly, even though I hadn't heard the door move. That fact encouraged me. Maybe they hadn't heard us open and shut it. They'd been talking, which might have masked the little bit of noise we'd made.

Bart ran ahead, shining his light around to find a hiding place, and I followed in his footsteps, hoping our sloshing shoes weren't making too much noise—or leaving tracks.

"Here, duck behind these boxes while we discover who comes to the mines." Bart pulled me in behind him, and we'd barely hidden ourselves when electric lights flooded the chamber, revealing a huge warehouse full of goods.

Bart pointed to the German lettering on the containers we crouched behind. "Icon, Church of St. Maria, Florence, April 1944." I surveyed the other boxes and containers of varying sizes and types. All were neatly labeled with artifact, location, and date. That would certainly make it easier returning these to their rightful owners—if we lived to do so.

I hardly dared move in the cavernous chamber that amplified and echoed each sound. It worked to our disadvantage if we were noisy, but it may also have favored us, as they were making so much noise, they wouldn't hear our little sounds, as long as we kept them absolutely minimal.

The voices weren't familiar, but they spoke impeccable Italian.

"You believe your sister may have found this place?" one deep, cultured voice asked.

"Who else could have found it? She's been coming here for years, searching for the mine. However, I can't believe she would be so stupid as to leave the door open."

"Is it possible she discovered only the opening under the bridge and could not access this chamber?"

"Good point, Victor. Since it takes two to open the chamber, even if she found the door, she wouldn't have been able to open it if she came alone. I tend to believe she would be alone. She is far too avaricious to have a partner."

"What will you take today?" Victor asked.

"We'll have to choose carefully. Nothing of too great a value. Nothing to cause more shock waves through the art world. Let's see, how about this Manet? He's not as popular as Monet, but from the right collector, this should bring enough to finance one more significant activity. If the fools follow my counsel and adhere to the plans I made, we'll have the world in our hands quite soon."

"They are young and eager for blood and success," Victor said. "Youth do not see the whole picture. They live for today, for what they can see and feel at the moment, not for tomorrow and what might be, which seems far away to them."

"Most of them will not see tomorrow if they continue to make mistakes." There was silence for a moment. I wanted to peek and see what they were doing. Then the first voice resumed speaking. "I think this is all we will take. We mustn't be greedy."

I heard them climbing the stairs. I ached to peek and see who they were, though by their conversation, I could guess. Then Victor erased all doubt.

"Your father's death was timely indeed. He couldn't have been more cooperative in leaving this life at such an important point in time, just as the organization was complete and plans were all in place."

"Victor, you are so naïve, but innocence has its reward, I suppose, in peaceful sleep at night."

They left the chamber and turned out the lights, plunging us back into darkness. Neither of us moved for at least a full minute, and I don't think I even breathed until Bart stood.

"That had to have been Kesselring's great-grandson and his manservant," I whispered. "Did you get the feeling from the conversation that Gabriella may have been his sister?"

"Not possible," Bart whispered back. "Emile said he and Gabriella were the only children his parents had. When they died and Emile was killed in Tibet, that left Gabriella an orphan."

"You're probably right. I've tried too hard to tie her to this place. I guess I just wanted her to be guilty."

Bart flipped on his light and smiled. "She's guilty enough of other things. She doesn't have to be in on everything."

"I know. Still . . ." I let the sentence drop. How did I explain the certainty I felt that Gabriella had a connection in some way to that farmhouse? I'd almost worked it out in my mind, but not quite. That Cell Seven and Gabriella were closely connected, I had no doubt. And it now appeared we had another luminary with ties to Cell Seven and possibly the farmhouse.

"You did get the impression he's connected with Cell Seven, didn't you?" I asked, following Bart and his light down the wide aisle in the chamber. The corridor seemed to go on forever with boxes piled high on either side, all neatly labeled in German by the same precise hand.

"Circumstantial evidence. Hearsay. But, yes, I'll bet a year's salary he's actually the mastermind behind the whole thing. Sounds like his subordinates are wildcards though. That must be a frustration to someone who's meticulously planned something, to have people do their own thing instead of following orders."

"Do you think we can safely leave this place now and meet Dad and whomever he's bringing with him?"

Bart finally reached the end of the chamber. He turned and draped his arm around my shoulder. "We can, if you can get us out of here then back through the opening in the bridge, which I'm sure Mr. Kesselring IV carefully shut behind him."

I groaned. "I don't know if my fingers will ever heal. I truly hope the 'out' is much easier to find than the 'in.'"

Fortunately, it was. Especially after Bart turned on the bright lights, which enabled us to see. We closed the door on the salt mine treasure house and headed back up the tunnel, finding it much harder ascending, of course, than descending had been.

"Do you realize we've just left behind one of the greatest collections of art and artifacts, if not *the* greatest ever assembled in one place, and we didn't see one bit of it?"

Bart laughed. "You're right, princess. I didn't even think of it that way."

"I know what you were thinking."

"I'll bet you don't."

"I'll bet the entire time we were in that chamber, you were picturing the last scene from Indiana Jones where the warehouseman wheeled the boxed Ark of the Covenant into the zillion rows of other treasures stored by the government."

"How did you know?" Bart asked in surprise.

I was gasping for breath after our long, hard climb up the steep stairs and slanted corridor. "Because I know you." We stopped for a minute so I could catch my breath, then continued to the door at the bridge.

"Okay, princess. Work your magic." Bart shined the light on the stone wall, and I searched for the three pebbles at the bottom of the door. He pressed two as I pressed the third, but this time we held them until the door swung open all the way. "That was easy," he said, switching off his light.

"At this point, it had to be," I whispered. "My fingers wouldn't have lasted one more big search."

Bart poked his head carefully through the opening. Night had fallen. Total darkness enveloped the world. I shielded my watch and shined my little light on it. After six o'clock. Anastasia should arrive any time if they weren't already in the area.

We climbed through the opening, tumbling onto the wet grass under the bridge, then we pressed the three pebbles, again holding them until the door had swung completely back in place. Much easier than the first time. Apparently we'd released the pebbles too soon when we tried to open it.

"Okay, Captain Marvel. What now? Do we wait here for Dad and troops to arrive or head for the farmhouse and see what's going on up there?"

"You're too impatient," a voice spoke from the darkness. "You need to stay put so you can easily be found."

"Dad! You scared me to death."

"So what did you find in the hole in the bridge?" he asked, joining us in the cramped space between the bridge and the water, which had risen considerably since we took shelter.

"Bingo!" I said happily.

"You're not kidding me, are you, bunny?" Dad asked, his voice full of hope and yet containing a tinge of doubt at the same time.

"She's not kidding," Bart assured him. "It appears, at first glance, to be all there, except what Kesselring's great-grandson has been taking out, and, of course, what the other sons may have dipped into in the last sixty years."

"Okay, you miracle workers. Let's get up to the farmhouse and see what Enzio has wrapped up for us."

"Is he okay?" I asked, knowing Gabriella would have ended his turn on earth if she'd found him.

"He called us while we were en route and told us how to get up there. He left his car about halfway and went the rest of the way on foot. If we get his signal by the time we find the car, we can take it to the farmhouse. Otherwise, we have about a two-mile walk ahead of us. Think you can make it, bunny, or do you want to walk the two miles back to Enzio's mother's house?"

"And miss out on the exciting conclusion to this improbable adventure? Not on your life. Let's go. The sooner we get Gabriella and friends in custody, the sooner I get a hot shower and clean clothes." Then I remembered I didn't have any clothes—they were all on the bus that would be leaving for Pisa within the hour. I groaned.

Bart must have guessed what I was thinking. "That's okay, princess. We'll just go buy you some more. Before we even get back to Florence," he added.

Right, I thought. *And where would we find anything open by that time of night?* But I dropped the subject and trooped after Dad up the steep bank with some help from behind by my husband, and we headed on a fast clip toward the hill to Catarcias' mysterious farm-house.

Else materialized out of the rain and darkness and joined us. "Did you find it?" she whispered.

"Yes."

She squeezed my hand, and we continued in silence until David slipped out of the trees.

Same question. Same answer, but it buoyed me up each time I gave it. David vanished whence he'd come, and a few minutes later, Dominic emerged like a ghost out of the darkness. When he heard the answer, he disappeared again.

At the foot of the second hill, weariness overwhelmed me. I didn't want to hold up the group, but my legs were leaden. I felt like I'd been on a treadmill for hours.

"Okay, princess?" Bart asked quietly, sensing my lagging steps.

"Just tired legs. I'll get my second wind in a minute. Why don't you press on, and I'll catch up?"

"We should be near Enzio's car," Else whispered. "He said it was in the trees between the two hills. Hang on." I heard her quiet murmur next to me as she asked who knew the location of the car. They were wired. I wished I had my communications gear, essential for coordinating a plan with the split-second timing this would probably require. Most climaxes to these adventures did. I felt naked without it out here in the middle of an operation and knew Bart must feel the same.

"Dom said it should be a few hundred yards farther, then into the trees to the right." Else delivered the message, then disappeared into the darkness.

Enzio lied when he said he left it between the two hills. More like halfway up the second hill. My feet were quickly developing serious blisters from soaking wet shoes. Wet chinos chafed my legs, and I didn't think I'd ever been more miserable. Even the thought of continuing with the group another half mile up the torturous climb became insufferable. Suddenly Else took my hand and drew me off the road toward the car.

"Get out of the rain for a few minutes, Alli. I want you to stay right here. If you come up in the middle of something, and we don't know where you are, you could get hurt. Promise me you'll wait for us here."

She disappeared before I voiced my objections at being taken out of the action. But again, it might be a tremendous relief to rest just for a minute. I opened the front door, expecting car lights to illuminate the night and reveal my location to everyone in the area, but Enzio must have turned them off so they didn't betray him. He'd left the front windows down, so, of course, the seats were soaking wet. I left that door ajar so I wouldn't make any noise closing it and quietly opened the back door. Those windows were up, the seats dry, and my purse lay right where I'd left it.

I unzipped my purse, felt for the padded journal in the dark, extracted my gun, and leaned back in the seat. Oh, how good it felt to be off my feet. The only thing that would feel better right now would be to ease my tired back. I stuffed my purse in the corner to use as a pillow and slid my tired, aching body down in the seat, silently thanking Enzio for not having bucket seats in his car.

Mentally, I tracked their progress up the hill and imagined what would be happening as they surrounded the farmhouse. Would Gabriella still be there, or had she fled over the back of the mountain on the little ATV she'd ridden earlier? Did any of them remain at the farmhouse? If they hadn't found Enzio, would they expect he'd bring in reinforcements, and had they all escaped before Anastasia even arrived?

Then another question popped up and nearly brought me upright in the seat. With the road blocked, had Kesselring IV climbed over the rockslide, or had he been at the farmhouse, come down from the hill, and returned? If he and Gabriella were brother and sister . . .

No, that didn't seem possible. So exactly whom *had* he referred to when he talked about his sister? Somewhere in the back of my mind, I felt sure I knew the answer and just needed to think about it long enough and hard enough, and it would emerge from that mass of data I'd stored there. But would I be too late?

Then my mind returned to the farmhouse that Anastasia should be approaching right now. Who remained in that farmhouse on the hill? Was a trap set there, just waiting for Anastasia to walk into it?

Chapter 37

I'd become so tense that I ached all over. I willed my body to relax, felt the tension finally slip from my shoulders, and breathed deeply, thinking of a hot shower and fresh, clean sheets. Worrying didn't help anything. If anyone could handle whatever waited at the top of the hill, it would be Anastasia. They were, after all, the best in the world. Dad, himself, kept assuring me of that.

They'd tie up all the loose ends tonight, put the leadership of Cell Seven out of business, then Bart and I would rejoin the tour tomorrow in Pisa. We could continue to pick up the topaz stones from Empress Elizabeth's necklace, simply to put the historic necklace back together, and I'd have the opportunity to climb the Leaning Tower of Pisa, finally open again after more than ten years of refitting to prevent it from tipping over.

I imagined the tour of the Sistine Chapel in Vatican City and pictured throwing a coin into Trevi Fountain in Rome, which would ensure our return to the Eternal City, and then on to Pompeii and Sorrento. Romantic Sorrento. Maybe even a side trip to the Isle of Capri and the Blue Grotto.

I'd enjoy finishing this tour without the threat of someone taking potshots at us all the time. We'd complete the tour in Positano and Amalfi, and I might even talk Bart into leaving the group and staying for a week, just to enjoy the beauty of that part of Italy. And to relax. This hadn't been an especially relaxing vacation. *But then,* I chided myself, *it hadn't really been a vacation.* We were pretend tourists. How nice it would be for a change to have a real holiday.

The dream of a sparkling turquoise Mediterranean paradise vanished abruptly as gunshots shattered the quiet night. My heart pounded with fear. My families—my husband and father and my Anastasia family—were up there. *Please protect them,* I prayed. Even through my exhaustion, it was all I could do to remain where I'd been told to stay. I wanted to be there, helping, seeing what was happening. Making sure they were okay. How could I possibly stay here, hearing volley after volley of gunshots and shouts echoing down the hill?

As I made the decision to leave Enzio's car, to disobey Else's directive and find out what transpired at the farmhouse, I heard crackling in the undergrowth. Someone came down the hill on the run, not even attempting to be quiet. I gripped my gun and lay perfectly still, hoping they'd run by the car and not see it. Was it possible it might be Enzio returning to his car, or had someone escaped the net Anastasia planned to throw around the farmhouse?

Seconds later, the footsteps approached the car, someone jerked the door open, leaned in, and felt the ignition for the keys. They jingled. That person slid behind the wheel, breathing hard, and started the car.

Dash lights illuminated the driver, creating a silhouette I recognized instantly. Gabriella Cardin.

She whipped the car through the brush and back onto the road, then hit the accelerator and nearly slid off the muddy lane into the trees. I held on, carefully, quietly sitting up in the backseat, remaining hidden behind the headrest so she wouldn't see me in the rearview mirror.

I braced my feet against the side of the car and the middle hump so she couldn't tip me over by swerving. Slowly, silently, I brought the gun up and jammed it against her neck at the same time I grabbed a handful of her long, thick black hair and yanked her head back hard against the headrest.

"Stop the car, Gabriella."

I knew she wouldn't give up without a fight. She swerved hard to the left and then back to the right. I jerked harder on her hair, using it to stabilize me while I kept the gun pressed into her neck.

"Stop the car," I commanded.

"Allison?" She laughed, a cold, hysterical sound. "Allison Alexander Allan." She spit on the front window. "I'd rather die in a flaming wreck and take you with me, you and that precious baby of yours, than spend one minute in prison. That will serve your husband right. No one has ever ignored me except Bart."

As she jammed onto the accelerator and careened wildly down the narrow muddy lane, I jerked her hair so hard my hand ached. She had no intention of stopping unless I shot her. Where would this wild ride take us?

My mind raced. If we made it to the bridge, the road was blocked, filled with boulders. Of course. She'd ram into those boulders at full speed, which probably would take us out in a flaming crash, just as she said.

Not if I can help it.

I leaned forward and asked quietly in her ear, "Gabi, did you ever find the treasure?"

"What treasure?" I had her head pulled back so far, she could hardly see the road, but it didn't slow her one bit.

"Kesselring's stash that he hid in the salt mine during the war."

"I know it's here. I'll find it."

"I already found it."

Her foot came off the accelerator momentarily. "You lie!"

"We stumbled across it today. It's all there, a whole chamber in the salt mine, piled high with boxes. The contents are written on the boxes, the date he took them, and the places where he acquired them."

Her foot jammed again on the gas pedal, and the car leapt ahead. "I don't believe you."

"Well, it's all there except what your brother took out." That was a stab in the dark. I had no proof of any relationship, just a deep feeling there had to be some connection. "He was there today, you know, when we were in the mine. He and Victor took a painting by Manet to sell to finance the next terrorist activity he's planned."

"My brother is dead. You're making all this up," she shouted, her voice tinged with fear and pain. Fear I might be telling the truth. Pain because I was yanking her hair out by the roots.

"You know I'm not. Take your foot off the accelerator, or I'll shoot you."

Her frantic laughter came high and hysterical. "You can't shoot me. You don't have it in you. And you're going to die with me because you can't kill me."

We approached the bottom of the hill, nearing the bridge. I had to act now.

"I don't have to kill you to shoot you. Stop the car."

She answered by jamming the accelerator even harder to the floor.

"Never underestimate a mother whose child is in danger, Gabriella. It can be a fatal mistake." I removed the gun from her neck, pointed it at her foot, which was illuminated by one tiny light glowing from the dash above, and pulled the trigger.

She screamed in pain when the bullet hit her foot, and probably from the gunshot right next to her ear. Unfortunately, I'd waited too long, and the car had too much momentum coming off the hill. Even with her foot off the gas, there wasn't enough road left for the car to slow down, much less stop before it hit the bridge and the rocks.

In the seconds before impact, I tried to remember what was on the sides of the road before the bridge. Trees and bushes. Then water. I let go of Gabriella's hair and reached over her to twist the steering wheel, heading the car for the growth lining the creek on the right side of the road. Then I slumped back into the seat and braced for impact. And prayed. *Please, please don't let anything happen to my baby.*

Mistake. I should have also asked that nothing happen to me. I had both knees braced against Gabriella's seat and my arms against the seat back to keep me from hitting it on impact. When we slammed into the bushes, the car ploughed right through them and into the water. Gabriella hit the steering wheel with a sickening thud, and I slid into the back of her seat going about forty miles an hour. I felt my left arm snap. Both knees too?

I didn't have time to think any further than that. Icy water filled the front seat through the open windows and the entire front half of the car quickly submerged in the raging creek. I tried to open my door with my right hand, but the water pressed against it with such force that it wouldn't budge. I slid across the seat and tried that door, but it wouldn't open, either.

Water now gurgled into the backseat, rising higher and higher above the seat backs. I had one chance of getting out—over the seat and through the open passenger window.

I took a deep breath and pressed against the roof of the car. Black water swirled over me as I felt my way over the seats, to the door, and through the window. I came up gasping for air. I made it!

Suddenly the front end of the car shifted with the current and turned into the creek, slamming me against a tree. *So close,* I thought, *so close to safety. And then . . .*

A light flashed in my eyes, and I heard my name. "Alli, give me your hand."

I raised my good arm toward the voice and felt someone grasp my hand, but my legs were wedged tightly between the car and the tree.

"I'm pinned," I cried. "I can't move."

Someone splashed into the water beside me, and I felt the car shift slightly, then a little more. Between the pull from the bank and the push from behind, I fell forward in the brush, released from the icy trap. I lay there, too cold, too exhausted, to move.

A deafening roar filled the night. Bright lights lit up the darkness, and Bart suddenly knelt beside me, pushing my wet hair from my face.

"Princess, are you okay? Can you get up?" Only the fear in his voice made me move. I reached up and touched his face with my hand.

"I feel like I've crushed every bone in my body, especially my left arm. I'm just afraid to move to find out."

Tender hands moved down my right arm, then my left. "Oh, that hurts."

"There's one broken," Bart said, his voice choked with emotion.

Someone else probed my legs, small gentle hands, woman's hands. "I think your legs are okay, Allison," Mai Li said, her expert fingers continuing the examination up my back and across my shoulders. "Now let's turn you over and see the rest of you."

Oz came dripping out of the water and dropped beside me. "You sure know how to make an entrance, Alli."

"That was an exit, Oz," Bart said. "Her final fling as an agent in the field."

I didn't bother to comment.

"I think you can sit up, Allison," Mai Li said. "Do it slowly."

"That was you in the water that moved the car," I said, staring at the dripping man next to me. "Thanks, Oz. I thought I was home free when I swam through that window. Oh! Gabriella's still in the car!"

"She's feeling no pain," Oz said quietly. "I went into the car to see if there was anyone else there. She must have hit that steering wheel with a lot of force. She had no pulse."

"No seatbelt. We hit those small trees and bushes on the edge of the creek going at least forty miles an hour. Fortunately, I was in the backseat; unfortunately, I had no seatbelt either, but I heard her hit that steering wheel, or it hit her."

"What were you doing in that car with Gabriella?" Oz asked, pulling himself to his feet.

"Resting. Staying out of the rain and the cold. And staying out of danger." The irony was not lost on any of us.

With Bart on one side and Oz on the other, they helped me to my feet. Surprisingly, my legs held me up. Bart enfolded me in his arms and hugged me so tight, I thought he'd break my ribs.

"How's Alexandra?" he asked quietly.

"Since she was already swimming, except in warm water, I imagine she's in much better shape than I am. By the way, I do have a broken arm."

His arms flew away, and I nearly fell to the ground. He caught me halfway down and gently picked me up in his arms. "I don't know what to do with you."

"Just love me," I said, snuggling against him.

Noise again shattered the night. Else arrived on one of the ATVs from the farmhouse. She jumped off and rushed to us. "Are you okay?" she cried.

"I will be, as soon as I have a hot shower and find an aspirin for the pain in my arm. That noise is dreadful. Is there possibly anything louder than that little monster you rode in on?"

Something much louder drowned out Else's answer. A helicopter settled on the lane, pelting us with rain and wet leaves, which became flying missiles, stinging and sticking when they hit.

"I don't know which is worse, the disease or the cure," Else said, wondering if the helicopter was worth the momentary grief it caused.

"The disease," Bart replied, heading toward the copter with me cradled in his arms. The door slid open, and he handed me to a soldier from the Italian military. "The only casualty on our side," Bart said. "This is precious cargo, so take good care of her. She has a broken arm."

"You talk like I'm totally out of it and can't speak for myself," I objected. "I'm not a casualty. More like walking wounded."

"And she can be quite obstinate," Bart added, "so no matter what she says, she must go to the hospital, have her arm set, and a complete check-up. Drop your men at the farmhouse on the hill, take Mrs. Allan to the hospital, then come back for the prisoners."

"You're not going with me?" I asked, not wanting to face a foreign hospital alone.

"I'll call Rachel and have her meet you at the hospital. She won't have to slave over the codes anymore," Else said, "thanks to your uncanny ability to stumble across treasure."

"Serendipity." I laughed. "We were simply seeking shelter from the rain."

"I'll come to the hospital as soon as we've finished here," Bart said, blowing a kiss.

"I won't be there. I'll be checked into the most exclusive hotel in Florence in the honeymoon suite. Rachel will have to tell you where it is. I'll have her take me there as soon as I'm through at the hospital, which won't take long, I promise you. I'm tired of being muddy and wet all the way through—and freezing, in case I haven't mentioned it before."

The soldier slid the door shut, and the helicopter lifted off, was airborne only briefly, and then sat down at the farmhouse. Dad waited at the door, and the minute it opened, he jumped inside, squatting in front of me while the soldiers streamed out.

"Bunny, how are you? What happened down there? They said you were in a car that crashed into the creek."

I reached out to touch him with my good hand. "I'm fine, but Gabriella's dead. She'd have walked away from the crash too, if she'd been buckled in. But she said she rather die than go to prison, so she got her wish. What did you find up here?"

"A rat's nest. Apparently this was the planning center. The cave we found earlier with all the maps seemed to be the staging center."

"Was Kesselring IV up here? Did you get him and Victor?"

"Got them both, as well as a sister and various members of Cell Seven."

"A sister? But Gabriella escaped the farmhouse."

Chapter 38

Dad laughed. "We'd be here all night if we answered all your questions. Right now you're on your way to the hospital. Else told me Rachel will meet you there. Your mother was on the line instantly. I'm afraid she'll be there too. Go get patched up, then we'll meet to debrief. I think you have a lot of puzzle pieces we need to put the rest of this picture together."

He jumped from the chopper and signaled lift off to the pilot. In ten deafening minutes, we landed somewhere in the city, where an ambulance waited, and I suddenly became a VIP—a very important patient. I'd yearned for fresh, clean white sheets, and found them on the gurney on which I settled painfully to be transported to the hospital.

Rachel's gamine face welcomed me when the ambulance doors opened, and she held my hand, literally and figuratively, through the entire process of admission, setting my arm, and the exam everyone insisted I have to make sure the baby hadn't suffered trauma. I felt sure there had been none, but Rachel said Mom only agreed to stay in bed if Rachel guaranteed I'd have a thorough examination. She'd told Rachel, "That baby is too precious to take any chances just because Allison has a personal aversion to hospitals."

That Mom didn't come indicated how seriously she'd been injured, and how far from recovery she remained. Otherwise, my intrepid mother would have been at my side to fuss over me. Fussing I didn't need. A shower I did.

But I didn't get it in the most exclusive hotel in Florence. Rachel drove me back to Anastasia's headquarters—in the building owned by the old Freedom Fighter. I couldn't complain about our accommodations, although I would have preferred a separate building for more privacy.

We were given an elegant suite of huge rooms, decorated in "regal Renaissance," which even had a canopied bed much like Mom's.

After my newly casted arm had been completely wrapped in foil from the restaurant downstairs, the only waterproof material anyone could put their fingers on at the moment, I luxuriated in an extravagantly long, hot shower and delighted in being clean and warm for the first time in hours.

When I emerged from the bathroom at least thirty minutes later, Rachel had found—where at this time of night, I had no idea—a flannel nightgown, slippers, and robe. She'd also sent word with Henry, the computer geek, to the bus to tell Jim and Carol we would not be making the trip to Pisa with them, but we would either meet them the next morning at the hotel or just have someone retrieve our luggage.

Clean, warm, and comfortably attired in the latest fashion flannel, I padded along the hall and descended one flight of stairs to the floor where Mom waited to see me. Henry and Steven nodded as I hurried to Mom's side. She patted the place next to her, and I gratefully sank against the pile of pillows she plumped for me.

"Oh, Alli, how are you? Is the baby okay? What happened?" Mom fussed and straightened blankets until I held her busy, nervous, bandaged hand in mine and assured her we were both just fine.

"I'm okay. Alexandra survived, no problems, and it's a long, complicated story. I think Dad's expecting to return for a debriefing soon, so how about if we talk about genealogy for a few minutes." I turned to the three at the computers.

"Can you come up with a family history of the Kesselring family and all the intermarrying with General Burkhardt's children and their families? I need to see, in black and white, where all these people tie in. I know you'd discovered some of it. I hope you've found some more, some of those daughters who disappeared."

"We did locate a couple of the children," Rachel said. "I'll see what we can give you."

She and Henry put their heads together and got busy on the computers. Steven rose from his computer and came quietly to the bed where I lay beside Mom.

"I understand you located the salt mine where Kesselring hid the art and treasures he'd stolen."

I nodded. "Bart and I stumbled across it."

He stared down at his smart Italian shoes. "I owe you an apology." His eyes finally met mine. "I thought it was," he hesitated, searching for the right word, "ridiculous to bring you into this. A pregnant woman, fighting terrorists? What could you do, besides get in everyone's way?" He folded his arms awkwardly across his chest. "I guess I was wrong."

"Apology accepted, Steven." I held out my hand, and he shook it. "I've learned you can't judge a person by first impressions, appearances, or the number of degrees behind their name." I pointed to my head and my heart. "It's what's in here that counts. Common sense and compassion. Now, as soon as we have this all wrapped up, I want to hear what you know about the Amber Room. I'm sure you're an expert on it. But first we have to get the topaz out of the way."

The printer in the room came to life, and in minutes, I had much of the family lineage of both Kesselring and Burkhardt spread out on the bed. Talk about complicated.

"Bingo!" I squealed in delight. "This is the connection!" I followed General Burkhardt's line with my finger. "Here is the son who married Jane Kesselring. Here's their daughter, Cora, and under that, the two American-educated boys. But look at this! General Burkhardt had a daughter, Rosa, two years younger than Jane's husband. Rosa married Vittorio Catarcia, a widower, with two children. They're the ones who built the farmhouse on the hill above the village were Enzio lived."

"And the significance of Rosa Catarcia is . . ." Mom asked, not understanding my excitement at a name she'd never heard.

"You'll understand when we finally get all of the story out, but here," I pointed to the genealogy as I explained, "is the son of Vittorio Catarcia, who went to war when it broke out. He has a sister, both stepchildren of Rosa. I couldn't figure out why there were older children and younger children, like two families. Now here's the part that's going to blow Bart away."

I pointed to the chart Rachel and Henry had prepared. "The stepdaughter of Rosa Catarcia married a Frenchman. They had two children, who she named Emile and Gabriella." I leaned back on the pillow, filled with satisfaction. "I knew Gabriella had a connection to that farmhouse. It belonged to her grandfather, Vittorio Catarcia."

Then I was thunderstruck. "But that means Gabriella wasn't the sister of Kesselring IV." I grabbed the papers again. There it was in black and white. "There's the sister. Why haven't we heard about her? You'd think the great-granddaughter of Field Marshall Kesselring would rate as much publicity as his son and grandsons."

"Not if she dissociated herself from the family because of her radical persuasions," Rachel said. "She's high on the leadership roster of Cell Seven. The rest of the family kept an extremely low profile with their political ideology, but she was vocal. She always used her married name, and most of her fellow terrorists didn't even know of her relationship to the Kesselrings."

"Thus, Kesselring IV sent his sister to do his dirty work," I concluded, remembering the conversation Bart and I overheard in the salt mine.

At that moment, Anastasia arrived en masse. The debriefing commenced immediately, after Bart made sure I was okay.

Steven counted heads, noted everyone was there, and in a panic-stricken voice asked, "Who's guarding the art and artifacts, all those billions of dollars worth of treasure?"

"The Italian government," Dad said, settling into the chair next to Mom.

"You're not even going to examine it. You're through with it?" Steven stammered, apparently not understanding Dad's statement.

"We found it for them, kept it out of the hands of the terrorists—now it's up to them to take care of it," Dad explained. "It belongs to them, the Catholic church, and the Italian people."

Steven slumped back into his chair at the computer, a crushed and disappointed man. Actually, a crushed and disappointed art and history aficionado.

"Dad, can you arrange to have Steven help catalog all those boxes? He might be the perfect liaison between Interpol and the Italian government in making sure this all gets back into the right hands."

"Good idea, bunny. I'll take care of that first thing in the morning."

Steven shot me a grateful look, much different than his countenance and attitude earlier in the day.

"The Golden Rule?" Bart whispered with a knowing smile. I nodded.

Dad walked us through the capture of those at the farmhouse on the hill. Kesselring IV and Victor were in custody, and they would never again see the light of day after their part in planning the bombings carried out by Cell Seven was uncovered.

"Explain to me what happened with those explosions. Why all the misses?" I asked. "Nothing irreplaceable was destroyed, though they announced the intended destruction of each of those sites."

"Kesselring couldn't stand to destroy anything that valuable. He actually planned the explosions to be near misses, close enough to frighten everybody but far enough to prevent destruction," Else said. "We found his original plans. Not one target was designed to damage anything of historical or architectural value. People, on the other hand, were expendable. Those he didn't care about."

"Well, thank heaven he had some value system at least!" I exclaimed. "Warped though it may be. And what about his sister?"

"The Italian government will not have to worry about the expense of her trial or housing her in prison. When we told them to throw down their weapons and come out with their hands up, she came out shooting," Dom said. "She was the first to fall."

"So the farmhouse is empty again?" I asked.

"Not for a while," Dad said. "It will be occupied by Interpol until they get all that paperwork sorted out and finish making arrests. We hope that by the time they're finished, Cell Seven will just be a bad memory."

"Rachel and Henry traced the genealogy of the Kesselring and Burkhardt families and solved some of our major questions." I glanced at Bart. "Are you ready for this?"

"Let's have it." He grinned. "I can see you're just dying to tell us."

I spread out the family history papers on the bed again and traced all the lines with my finger, as I'd done earlier. "So Gabriella and Emile were the grandchildren of Vittorio Catarcia and the stepgrandchildren of Rosa Catarcia. They'd been to the farmhouse many times. That's how she remembered it."

I smiled smugly at Bart. "I just knew she had some connection to that farmhouse." Then I turned to Dad. "This part is supposition until you prove it, but I'm sure you can. When Gabriella came back here as an adult, she bought the place. I think you'll find when you check the land records, she's the owner of all that property. She'd probably heard about Kesselring's treasure as a child, and when she returned, she connected with the great-grandson and probably his sister. With the billions of dollars in treasure as motivation, her allegiance changed from Interpol and fighting the bad guys to Cell Seven and being one of them."

"Any other questions?" Dad asked.

"I have one more," I said.

"If you have only one, I'll buy dinner for everyone here." Dominic laughed.

I wrinkled my nose at him. "How did Oz and Mai Li just happen to be at the creek just as I needed them?"

"We left them to guard the treasure. We couldn't leave it unguarded once you'd located it," Dad said.

"And we ended up saving a greater treasure than Kesselring's." Oz laughed.

"Hear, hear!" Bart agreed.

"Thanks for being on the spot. We may have to name our son after you," I glanced at Bart, "if we ever have one. And thank you, Mai Li."

"If no one has any more questions at the moment, because I'm sure we haven't tied it all up nice and neat yet, we'll adjourn until morning when we're dry and rested." That was Dad's signal to dismiss everyone from the room.

I was more than happy to head for my own bed. Bart administered my prescribed pain pills, sat on the edge of the red velvet canopied bed to make sure I was comfortable, and then headed for the door.

"Hey, where are you going? Aren't you coming to bed?"

He grinned. "I'll be right back."

He returned in five minutes with a waiter and a cart full of trays. "You missed dinner, so I thought you might enjoy an intimate candlelight feast in bed. I ordered it on our way up."

The waiter spread out the banquet and discreetly withdrew, leaving us with more food than we'd eat in a week.

"Did you think we'd eat this all tonight?" I asked in amazement. "You must be starving to have ordered all this food."

"Who said we have to eat it all tonight?" Bart laughed. "Maybe we'll lock the door and stay here, just the two of us, for a week."

"Mmm, I think I'd like that."

A knock at the door startled me. I looked at Bart. He groaned and opened the door. Else came first, then Dom, Lionel, Sky, and David and Oz, and Mai Li brought up the rear, each holding a pillow which they threw on the floor by the bed.

"This was so good of you to order dinner for us, Bart." Lion smiled, with a wink at me. "We knew Alli would have lots of questions that would keep her awake, so we thought we'd better come and answer them for her so she'd sleep well tonight."

I laughed. "You're so considerate! You just want to hear all the village gossip I had to pry out of those little ladies in order to come up with my theories."

"So tell us, belleza, the whole story, from start to finish," Dom said, reaching for a piece of focaccia and cheese.

Feeling much like Scheherazade, I launched into the story of all that transpired that afternoon. As I gazed into each of those dear, familiar faces, I felt again, even more powerfully, that this was my family—the brothers and sisters and cousins I'd never had. It felt good to be surrounded by people who loved me.

Tomorrow I'd wheedle Bart into finishing the tour to pick up the rest of the topaz so the necklace could be reassembled. And then after the tour, I thought I wouldn't mind staying at home, working in the Control Center for a while.

Just for a little while. Just until Alexandra was born.

Epilogue

April, Six Months Later

The blue Pacific Ocean spread out before us as Grandmother Karillides and I drove down from the estate on the hill toward Santa Barbara. Orange California poppies and blue lupine spread across the hillsides, interspersed with Indian paintbrush and purple and yellow blossoms in a palette of colors.

"It is beautiful, Allison, but I miss my home. Your ocean is wild and fierce, not like my quiet cove on the turquoise Mediterranean."

"I know, Grandmother. And this time next week, you'll be home again. But I'm so glad you were able to come and be with us when Alexandra was born and get to know your great-granddaughter before you return to the other side of the world."

"She's precious, Allison. And I've never seen such a doting father. Your Bart is a jewel, but you will have to be careful, or he will spoil her till you won't be able to live with her."

I laughed. "That's true, but as you've noticed in the six months you've been here, he isn't home enough to make the damage irreparable, and the times he is home will be memorable for her. Hopefully, she won't have a fatherless childhood like I did, since Bart will never have the situation Dad did, in being forced to pretend he was dead all those years."

"That was unfortunate, dear, but sometimes a few must make great sacrifices to ensure the safety and quality of life for many." She sat quietly looking out the window for a minute, then added, "I'm relieved you're going to be working in the Control Center now. I worried so much about you when you were out getting shot at and nearly drowned, and all those horrible things that have happened since you joined Anastasia. It's bad enough your mother has to play those dangerous games. I never thought you should be doing that too."

"Bart's convinced he can keep me out of danger if I'm at home on the estate." I laughed. "He doesn't see the danger in the wildfires we get, in the earthquakes that rattle our windows, and in the torrential rains that wash houses down the hillsides. His danger always takes the form of some power-hungry bad guy with a greedy agenda and total disregard for human life. I keep reminding him that I could get hurt just as badly falling down the stairs or being hit by a car when I get on the highway."

"That's true, dear, but the odds of being seriously injured or killed are probably increased slightly when someone is trying to kill you."

I laughed at Grandmother's understated observation. Of course, Bart cited that as his reason to keep me occupied answering agents' queries and filling their needs from the safety of the Control Center.

Alexandra slept peacefully in her carseat in the back of the big, new SUV Bart had given me for Christmas. It felt like I was driving a tank instead of a car since I was used to my little convertible, but it certainly had more room for groceries.

Grandmother turned frequently to check on the baby, but Alexandra didn't stir the entire trip to town. When I put her in her stroller, she opened her beautiful blue eyes, yawned, then snuggled down and closed them again. Maybe she'd sleep through our early morning excursion to the grocery store.

I filled the basket with the week's provisions while Grandmother pushed Alexandra in the stroller down the empty aisle beside me. I loved coming to the grocery store early in the morning before everyone got up and ventured out to do their shopping. Since Grandmother rose early as well, we'd made it a habit during their visit to enjoy these morning jaunts into town, just the two of us. Until Alexandra joined us. Now we were a trio.

We'd stopped at the end of one aisle to choose some cookies for Papa Karillides, when I heard a frantic gasp from the checkstand not fifteen feet away. I peered around the corner and saw two men with nylon stockings pulled over their heads and guns pointed at the two checkers on duty.

"Shut up. If you make a sound, I'll shoot," the nearest one said. "Give me all the money in your cash drawer. And make it fast."

I turned back to Grandmother and whispered for her to take Alexandra in her stroller to the back of the store. "Go lock yourself in the restroom and don't come out until I knock on the door."

Giving her a little shove in that direction, I pulled my cell phone from my pocket and dialed 911 to report a holdup in progress, then peeked again to see if they were nearly through. They were near one door and sure to leave from that same exit. I raced back up the aisle to the break in the center, darted behind the frozen food cases, and made it to the far end of the store and the other exit unseen.

I realized I didn't have a plan, I just knew I couldn't let them escape. This had to be the same two thieves who'd been hitting grocery stores, convenience markets, and even jewelry stores all along the coast. They always took a hostage. They always escaped. Sometimes the hostages lived. Sometimes they didn't.

I knew the two checkers being held, terrified, at gunpoint. I spoke to them at least twice weekly, knew about their families, knew they were both mothers with children in school. I couldn't let either one of them be taken hostage.

I waved the remote at my car as I raced across the parking lot, unlocking it as I ran. I jumped in, started it, and then wondered what I'd do when they came out. *Help me, Father, if I have to do something before the police get here. Help me know what to do and how to do it.*

Then I remembered the new padded journal I now carried under the seat, which contained my hidden gun. Bart had insisted, after all these robberies, that I not leave the house without it. Bless him and his paranoia about my safety!

I got the gun, rolled down the window, and eased the car ahead until I had a straight shot through my open window at the door. Then I buckled my seatbelt, waited, and prayed. Suddenly the door burst open. The taller of the two men had his arm around Bonnie, a petite redhead with three teenagers, using her as a shield. The other had one hand filled with bags and his gun in the other.

No police sirens. No sign of anyone else in the parking lot. I took careful aim, sent another prayer speeding to heaven, and pulled the trigger. Bonnie screamed, the man staggered and fell, slamming her to the ground with him. She rolled clear, then jumped and ran back into the store.

I jammed my foot on the gas pedal, screeching toward the escaping man. He turned and fired at me, but the bullet shattered my headlight, not my windshield. He jumped in his car, which they'd apparently left running, because it leapt forward immediately. He spun the wheel, intending to escape across the parking lot and onto the ramp to Highway 101.

Not if I can help it, I thought.

Just then a garbage truck pulled into the parking lot in the lane the man headed for. The thief hadn't anticipated his exit being blocked. He turned the car to jump the curb, but I reached him as he came abreast of the garbage truck and rammed my new SUV broadside into his car, sandwiching it between my front end and the truck. He couldn't get out.

Police sirens filled the air and police cars surrounded us. I jumped out, waved at Chief Martinez, and told him I'd be back to explain everything as soon as I rescued my baby and my grandmother from the restroom.

He just shook his head, got in my car, and backed it away from the smashed car while other officers took the angry thief into custody.

Pushing the stroller with a happily cooing baby in it, I brought my shaken grandmother out to my smashed car, which we would not be driving home. Chief Martinez opened the door of the nearest squad car and helped Grandmother inside, then I handed Alexandra in for her to hold.

Chief Martinez shook his finger in my face. "Allison Allan. Whatever were you thinking? You could have been seriously hurt, even killed. You just can't take things into your own hands, even if you are," he dropped his voice, "Interpol."

"I'm sorry, Chief. I just couldn't stand the thought of them taking Bonnie. She has three teenage sons who might easily have been motherless if I'd let them get away."

"I'm sure I don't have to say another word. Your husband will have enough to say about this when he finds out."

"Ohh, do we have to tell him?" I asked, knowing there was no way in the world I'd keep him from finding out I'd been involved in the capture of these two thieves, even if he happened to be on the far side of the earth at the moment.

"I'll send you home in this squad car. I don't think I can keep your involvement out of the press, since they've arrived on the scene already." He pointed to the news van just turning into the parking lot. "You'll have to call me with your statement or come down to the station later."

I dived for the backseat of the police car, pulling the silk scarf from around my neck as I shut the door. I tied it over my head, leaving it loose around my face so it was hidden from view.

Chief Martinez waved the officer off, and we pulled away from the scene before the media piled out for the story.

It would all come out eventually, the media would blow it out of proportion, Bart would despair of ever keeping me out of harm's way, and I was sure I'd continue to stumble across trouble in one form or another for the rest of my life. It just had a way of finding me.

But wasn't that what life was all about? Tests and trials and challenges—and opportunities to do something positive and make a difference in the world—wherever and whenever our path crossed with someone else in our celestial orbit.

Lynn Gardner is an avid storyteller who does careful research to back up the high-adventure romantic thrillers that have made her a popular writer in the LDS market.

Lynn was born and raised in Idaho, attended Rigby and Blackfoot High Schools, married her high school sweetheart, Glenn Gardner, and enjoyed her husband's Air Force career that spanned 25 years and gave her the opportunity to travel all across the United States. She used this experience to teach her children American history and to instill in them a love of this blessed country and the freedoms Americans enjoy.

Lynn and Glenn make their home in Quartz Hill, California. Among her favorite things to do, Lynn lists beachcombing, writing, family history, and spoiling her grandchildren.

Lynn enjoys corresponding with her readers, who can write to her in care of Covenant Communications, P.O. Box 416, American Fork, UT 84003-0416, or e-mail her via Covenant at info@covenant-lds.com.